HOW TO TAME A DISSOLUTE PRINCE

ROYALS AND RENEGADES

BOOK TWO

SCARLETT SCOTT

HEA

Happily Ever After Books

How to Tame a Dissolute Prince

Royals and Renegades Book 2

For more information, contact author Scarlett Scott.

https://scarlettscottauthor.com/

CHAPTER 1

The appallingly sad, terribly disheartening, utterly disappointing truth was that no one needed Prince Ferdinando of the House of Tayrnes. Not the people of the Kingdom of Varros. Not his beloved, if stern, older brother, King Maximilian. Not his sister-in-law, the delightful Queen Tansy, who'd brought Maxim to heel. Not his baby nephew Caspian Ferdinando, even if the lad had been, quite rightly, named after Nando himself.

Not even the half dozen or so enchanting denizens of the Varrosian court who eagerly warmed his bed at the slightest hint of an invitation.

Not a single damned soul.

He'd accustomed himself to being little more than a gilded ornament. The necessary heir, should something ill befall his brother. The ne'er-do-well. The irresponsible rake whom no one trusted with any duty or knowledge of import.

And that was why he was in London.

Specifically, why he was idling away his time at a Mayfair address where he'd been recently told, in no uncertain terms, that he wasn't welcome by the most infuriatingly aloof female of his acquaintance.

Why he was waiting in a drawing room teeming with hothouse flowers as he awaited his next crushing setdown. Just when Nando was beginning to despair that the fierce-eyed Miss Eleanora Brett would deny him the pleasure of smiting his soul with her searing insults, she arrived.

As usual, she was wearing a white muslin frock that did nothing to accentuate her generous curves and ripe breasts and a hideous cap over her lustrous hair. But she didn't fool him with a modest fichu tucked into her bodice. His experienced eye knew the body of a goddess when he saw one, regardless of how hideously she enrobed herself in virtue.

Nando sketched a bow for her benefit. "Miss Brett, how delightful. I began to fear you'd never arrive."

She curtsied because she had to, but she bore the tenacious expression of a dog protecting her territory, telling him she wasn't pleased by his presence. Briefly, he wondered if she'd bite him. And then he thought about how much he might enjoy her sharp little teeth. She could bite his shoulder when he made her come.

In that moment, Nando couldn't think of anything he'd like better.

"Your Royal Highness," Miss Brett clipped, as if his very title were an epithet.

And damn it if that didn't make his cock twitch to attention. He adored the disapproving tone she used in his presence. If Miss Brett had any notion of how much her frostiness affected him, no doubt she'd box his ears. That was another quality he enjoyed about her. Miss Eleanora Brett didn't give a fig if he was a prince. She didn't suffer nonsense or fools.

"My dear Miss Brett, your gown is quite becoming this afternoon," he lied smoothly.

"I would thank you, were your observation not only impertinent but patently false as well," she returned, her voice cool and unamused. "Your presence here is decidedly unwelcome. I've begged Your Royal Highness to cease paying singular attention to Princess Emmaline and Princess Annalise."

Nando strolled nearer to Miss Brett, unable to help himself, stopping by a nearby vase to trail his forefinger along the decadently soft petals of a rose. "I wouldn't quite say you begged me, Miss Brett. Indeed, the mere thought of you playing the supplicant is more delightful than I can possibly convey. Though my memory may sometimes be faulty, I assure you that I wouldn't have forgotten such a stirring exchange."

His intentionally sensual inference was met with a stern tightening of Miss Brett's lovely lips. "Your familiarity is unwarranted, Your Royal Highness."

Nando continued idly tracing the unfurling petals of the blossom, noting the way her gaze slipped to watch his progress. "Pray accept my apologies, Miss Brett. It wasn't my intention to cause you distress."

Not distress, perhaps, but irritation? Decidedly so. There was something thoroughly rousing about Miss Eleanora Brett's pique. He couldn't seem to have enough of her tart rejoinders and frigid glares. Her censure only made him want her more. She was the answer for the ennui that had been plaguing him these last few months. Nothing that had once held his interest had appeased him any longer.

Until he'd crossed paths with the princesses and their ferocious chaperone.

From the moment he'd set eyes on the golden-haired, blue-eyed spinster, he'd wanted her more than he could recall ever wanting another woman. Her allure wasn't just her beauty—a dainty nose, a mouth that would have looked more at home on a courtesan than a prim chaperone, high cheekbones, finely arched brows, and a stubborn chin. It was something indefinable that was unique to her. He'd known and bedded any number of women who were exquisite. But none of them moved him in the way she did.

She sniffed, tilting her head and regarding him in a way that made him feel as if he were a recalcitrant lad being reprimanded. "I make it a habit of never accepting apologies that are either forced or insincere. And as I'm persuaded you *did* wish to cause me distress, I'm afraid I can't accept yours, Your Royal Highness. If you wanted to express true contrition, you would cease your flagrant campaign of ruining the princesses' delicate reputations."

His cock was stiffer than a fire poker after her delightful upbraid. If only Miss Brett knew that the more she chastised him, the more he longed to bend her over the nearest piece of furniture and fuck her witless.

Nando bit back a smile, giving the rose another slow caress as he directed his best bedroom stare on the stern chaperone. "Miss Brett, I'm cut to the quick."

The object of his desire remained staunchly unmoved. "Pray, do not insult my intelligence by feigning remorse."

This time, he couldn't suppress his smile. God, she was so delicious when riled.

"I'd never insult your intelligence," he said smoothly, "nor would I dream of feigning remorse, considering that I'm proudly incapable of feeling that finer emotion."

Her eyes narrowed, her lashes long and fine and the color of sunlight streaming through a window into a darkened room. "Why have you graced the household with your presence, Your Royal Highness?"

It would seem she'd grown weary of verbal fencing.

Pity. He loved it when she snapped and crackled, all that fire seething beneath her icy exterior sizzling to life.

He gave the bud one last, lingering caress. "Is the reason not apparent, Miss Brett? It's because I longed for your delightful company."

Her nostrils flared in new evidence of her ire. "Your mere presence alone is enough to cause undue gossip for the princesses."

"The princesses create all manner of gossip without my aid," he drawled, thinking of the shock they'd caused in polite London society when they'd attended a ball wearing trousers.

Although ladies could don such a garment in their native land of Boritania, women wearing trousers were decidedly *outré* in England. To say nothing of the wild twins flirting their way through the ranks of the *ton*. Their behavior and the ensuing swirl of social doom it had provoked were the reason Miss Brett's prestigious services had been obtained.

But Miss Brett remained undeterred, staying at a polite distance as if she feared the stain proximity to him would cause her own character. "Nevertheless, the marked interest you pay to Princess Emmaline and Princess Annalise is unacceptable. It is a risk that is unnecessary for the both of them. If you hold them in regard at all, you will leave them to traverse polite society without your interference."

Her words should have stung. Perhaps they did, a bit. But Miss Brett was growing increasingly annoyed with him, and Nando was perverse enough to enjoy the knowledge. She was mistaken on one fact. Persuading her to let him bed her was the only true campaign he was waging. He couldn't be certain if her own modesty precluded her from deducing where his interest truly lay, or if she was simply so woefully inept at reading blatant carnal interest because of her own lack of experience. The reason didn't matter. He would correct her misconception the only way he knew how—seduction.

Slowly, Nando sauntered toward her, pleased by the subtle way her eyes widened at his approach. He stopped near enough to touch her. The drawing room was cavernous by London town house standards. He'd taken his time approaching her, but the potent lure of Miss Brett, vexed and stern and nettled, was just too much for him to resist a moment longer.

"I would modestly suggest your assessment is not entirely accurate," he said.

"I doubt there is even a modicum of modesty in any action you take, Your Royal Highness," she huffed.

As it happened, she wasn't incorrect. Nando wasn't modest. He didn't need to be. He was handsome, and he knew it. He was an excellent lover, and he wielded that skill often. Or at least, he had until the thorough distraction of the delectable Miss Brett. He had a big cock, he was a prince, he possessed ample wealth in his own right, he was sought after. Women—with the notable exception of the one before him—adored him. Some men did, too, and although he'd never been physically attracted to his own sex, he couldn't find fault with those men for their excellent taste.

"Perhaps," he allowed with a shrug that suggested it didn't matter either way. "You needn't insist on ceremony with me, Miss Brett. Please, call me Nando. All my friends and lovers do."

Color crept over her cheekbones. "I'm neither your friend nor your lover, Prince Ferdinando. Such untoward familiarity would be most imprudent of me."

She was flustered. He wondered if it was his attempt at coercing her into calling him by his given name or if it was his reference to lovers that did it.

"You could be," he invited.

"No, I most assuredly could not," she snapped, more color flooding her cheeks.

"Why not, Miss Brett?"

Irritation sparkled in her eyes. "Do not attempt to cozen me by playing your flirtatious games, Your Royal Highness. I know quite well that a man like you has no interest in a woman such as myself."

How wrong she was. Astoundingly so. He would show her with great pleasure. First, however, she needed to be more amenable to his advances, and Nando was thrilled by the notion of a challenge—a woman who wouldn't fall directly into his bed.

"I would never attempt to cozen you or play games with you, my dear," he said easily. "I like you far too much for that."

He liked her quite a lot, actually.

More than he could recall liking anyone, with the notable exception of his sister-in-law. The only difference was that his fondness for Tansy was entirely platonic and sisterly in nature. What he felt for Miss Brett, however?

The difference between night and day.

"If you think flattery will further your cause, you're wrong," Miss Brett told him. "But I suppose it doesn't matter. If you've come to pay a call upon the princesses, I'm afraid you're doomed to disappointment. They've left with their sister, Princess Anastasia, on an outing."

Excellent. That meant he'd have Miss Brett all to himself for an indeterminate span of time. Nando tried to hide his glee.

"I suppose I've no choice other than to await their return. You may keep me company, Miss Brett. But perhaps you ought to ring for something. I'd dearly love some whisky, although I'll settle for tea."

Whisky was a favorite vice of Nando's. One he knew quite well no respectable lady would offer him, even if the household possessed any of that spirit in its stores.

"I'll not be taking tea with you, Your Royal Highness," she denied crisply. "It would be unseemly."

"Denying a royal prince is the most unseemly act by far," he countered, not above using his title to press his advantage. "I'm sure Princess Anastasia would be displeased if she were to learn I was turned away like a common beggar from the streets."

It was wrong of him to use her desire to maintain her position in the household against her. But Nando had done many things that were wrong in his admittedly debauched life. Indeed, he had no intention of ceasing. Because seducing the virginal spinster chaperone of Princesses Emmaline and Annalise St. George, a woman who had been tasked with taming their wild ways and making them into proper London ladies, was decidedly as wrong as he could be.

He ought to save his seductions for the obliging harlots of England's finest brothels. Or for grasping widows and discontented wives. But the appeal of those women didn't compare to the potent allure of Miss Brett. He couldn't explain it. Nor did he want to examine the reasons.

It simply *was*.

And he wouldn't stop until he had her where he wanted her most.

Under him.

Or atop him.

On her knees for him.

Everywhere. Yes, that was where he wanted her. Everywhere and anywhere he could have her, as often as possible, until his needs were eventually sated and he could carry on. Because Miss Eleanora Brett was like a poison in his blood. One he would enjoy finding the antidote for.

She still hadn't made her decision. Miss Brett was nibbling on her lower lip, an action he suspected she only allowed herself when thoroughly caught in the throes of a dilemma. She was so poised and polished at all times, as if emotion were beneath her. Seeing her torn caused a guilty little rivulet of pleasure to run through him.

"Well, my dear," he prompted, feeling like the fox who'd found his way into the henhouse and was about to have a feast. "What is your answer? Will you ring for tea, or will you risk bringing the wrath of your employer down upon you?"

Her chin went up, her expression turning carefully serene. "Of course I shall ring for tea, Your Royal Highness. Forgive me for my hesitation. As you so astutely pointed out, it would be remiss of me to turn you away without proper acknowledgment."

Nando grinned. "How delightful you are, Miss Brett. I knew you wouldn't disappoint me."

He didn't miss the way she clenched her jaw as she went for the bell pull.

CHAPTER 2

*P*rince Ferdinando of Varros was the bane of Eleanora's existence.

The gossips simply called him The Adonis. And with good reason. His head of golden curls and sea-blue eyes set off the perfection of the rest of his countenance. A chiseled jaw, sinful mouth, straight nose, and high cheekbones combined to an effect that was nothing short of a merciless assault on any woman who dared to look upon him. Even the most virtuous of women.

And to her eternal shame, Eleanora was not exempt, try though she did to steel herself against the effect he had on her. Particularly when he set his mind to flirtation, which he had been doing from the moment she'd crossed the threshold of the drawing room. He'd neatly trapped her into joining him for tea, when she was more than aware that every second spent in his presence was a danger to her ability to resist the brutal force of his seductive charm.

"Tell me about yourself, Miss Brett," he invited smoothly now that she had poured tea for them both.

He'd watched her with an unnerving silence and an

intensity that had caused her hands to tremble ever so slightly, which only served to further heighten her irritation with the man.

"I am a simple woman, Your Royal Highness," she said, careful to keep her tone and expression tranquil. "Perhaps you might prefer to tell me about your native land of Varros."

She knew from experience and previous reluctant conversations with the prince that he took every opportunity to exploit weakness. He possessed an innate ability to mesmerize even the most stoic of opponents, and while Eleanora prided herself on her own steadfastness, she couldn't deny that she found herself helplessly in this man's thrall. Not that she could do anything about it. Inviting ruin and destroying the fragile life she'd carved out for herself would never be worth the fleeting moments of pleasure a rake like the prince could give her. She'd learned that painful lesson from watching her mother. A lesson she had vowed she would never forget.

"Nothing about you strikes me as simple," the prince countered. "Indeed, if I were asked to describe you, I would say you are a complex woman indeed, with hidden layers of mystery beneath your composed façade."

Eleanora's shoulders stiffened. He was alarmingly near to the truth. But there was no way Prince Ferdinando could suspect the secrets that threatened to undo her, should they ever become known.

She forced a smile. "I assure you, there is neither mystery, nor layers. There is only what you see before you."

"Hmm," he said, the sound noncommittal. "Although I do admire what I see before me, I remain persuaded there is far more you're simply unwilling to divulge. But never mind that. I'm a patient man, and I enjoy nothing so much as a challenge."

The smile he gave her made that unwanted sensation

pulse to life low in her belly. But she swiftly banished it. Nothing could come of such a foolish desire. He was a prince and an unabashed seducer of every woman with whom he crossed paths.

"Your fortitude is to be commended, Your Royal Highness," she said mildly, refusing to give in. "I tell all my charges that patience is a virtue that is almost unparalleled. However, there is no challenge for you where I am concerned. Surely a mere chaperone is beneath your notice."

He regarded her warmly. "Ever since we were introduced, I haven't noticed anyone else."

Unwanted heat suffused her. But she would not succumb. Rakes always wielded their words like weapons, carefully honed to disarm their opponent and seal their victory. Still, part of her couldn't help but revel in those words, in the notion that a beautiful man like the prince should have taken note of her at all, let alone that she had been such sufficient cause for distraction that he hadn't noticed anyone else.

It's a carefully crafted lie, she told herself. *He'll say anything to get what he wants.*

And what he wanted was every woman he could have. Apparently—and shockingly—Eleanora included. When he had begun making a nuisance of himself by appearing at every social event the princesses attended and paying regular calls upon them despite her pleas to the contrary, Princess Anastasia had warned Eleanora that the prince was a dangerous libertine. She'd seen the evidence well enough herself.

"I fear your flattery is wasted upon me, Your Royal Highness," she said calmly. "You would be better served to save it for those who welcome it. Undoubtedly, there is a host of such fortunate ladies."

With that, she took a sip of her tea.

"My, you've a sharp tongue." He grinned, seemingly

enjoying their repartee. "I dare say I've never received as many stinging setdowns in the course of one afternoon."

She almost told him he should take tea with her more often because she would be happy to pay him even more insults, but Eleanora tamped down the urge, knowing it unwise. The wily prince would likely take the slight as an invitation. And she had no intention of taking tea with His Royal Highness again.

Ever.

No, the sooner he was gone, the sooner she could breathe easily again. Her stays seemed suddenly unaccountably tight. She had to get rid of him.

"Forgive me, Your Royal Highness," she said politely. "I didn't mean to deliver any setdowns, merely to establish my insusceptibility to flummery."

"Flummery?" His brow furrowed, a look of befuddlement stealing over his handsome features. "I don't recognize the word, I'm afraid."

Save for the faint hint of an accent, the prince's command of the English language was so precise, his wit so rapier-sharp, that Eleanora had forgotten that his native tongue was Varossian.

"Nonsensical flattery," she elaborated.

"How kind of you to tutor me, Miss Brett." He paused to smile again, his silken tone falling over her like a caress. "I wonder how else you might offer me further edification."

The velvety hint of suggestion in his words sent a frisson down her spine. He made it sound as if she had granted him a sinful favor instead of explaining the definition to an ordinary word.

He made it sound wicked and...*intimate*.

And that was when it occurred to her that she wasn't simply taking the place of the princesses in their absence. Rather, she was who he had wanted to see all along. How had she missed it? Over the past few weeks, the evidence had been there, as obvious as the nose on her face. And yet Eleanora, who prided herself on her intellect, had failed to realize that Prince Ferdinando had settled upon *her*, rather in the fashion of a hunter choosing a stag from a herd before him.

The prince wanted to seduce her.

How astonishing to find herself the sole recipient of this gorgeous prince's rakish intent. He'd set a trap, and she had fallen neatly into it. Worse, now here she sat, alone with him. Utterly at his gorgeous mercy. Oh, there were servants about. But none of them would save her from the certain ruin she'd face if the prince attempted to seduce her in truth.

She straightened in her seat, resuming the icy tones she had greeted him with upon his initial arrival. "I am sure there are no areas in which you need any edification at all, Your Royal Highness."

He raised his tea but hesitated before partaking. "I'm not as certain, Miss Brett. You'll find me an eager pupil."

Heat rose to her cheeks. His insinuations were hovering on the edge of being scandalous.

Something had to be done. With all haste.

Eleanora reached for her dish of tea and instead of gracefully retrieving her beverage, she upended it. Hot liquid spilled over the table and pooled on the carpet.

She shot to her feet. "Oh, how clumsy of me. I'll have to ring for a maid to clean up the mess I've made."

And the maid would prove a suitable enough chaperone for the two of them, thereby thwarting the prince's plan.

But Prince Ferdinando stood as well. "No need to bother one of the domestics. I'll mop up the tea. I'd hate for our conversation to come to such an abrupt halt. I've been enjoying myself immensely."

She had no doubt he had, the rogue.

"That's hardly necessary, Your Royal Highness," she countered.

The notion of a prince performing the task that more properly belonged to a servant was ludicrous. But aside from that, she was hoping for a respite. She needed a shield between herself and Prince Ferdinando, who was deceptively excellent at getting what he desired.

In this case, her virtue.

And that wasn't happening.

She'd sooner toss him out the drawing room window. Eleanora had worked too hard for far too many years to surrender everything she had built for a few stolen moments of illicit passion with a rake. Even if he was a prince and more decadently handsome than any man she'd ever met.

"Nonsense," he said breezily. "I don't mind. Indeed, why trouble a maid when the matter is rectified easily enough?"

Before she could offer further protest, he took up a napkin and began cleaning the spilled tea with calm, efficient motions. When he bent to sop the mess from the Aubusson, Eleanora couldn't help but to notice the way his trousers molded to his well-muscled thighs. New warmth unfurled within her, and she forced herself to look away.

"Is something amiss?" he asked with a knowing tone to his voice.

Her gaze snapped back to find him studying her with unabashed masculine interest. He had seen her ogling him, and he wasn't going to allow her the pretense that she hadn't been.

"I was merely thinking that the trousers in Varros are uncommon," she said waspishly.

Why did he have to be here? Where were the princesses? Why, of all the men in London, had she managed to attract the attention of the one most perilous to her ability to resist him?

"Uncommon in what way, Miss Brett?"

Oh, she loathed the way he made her name sound like a caress. But part of her—the wickedest part she'd done her utmost to vanquish—liked it too.

"They appear to be poorly constructed," she lied. "Certainly, the quality seems inferior to what I'm accustomed to seeing here in London. Perhaps your tailors would be well served to pay a call to us here."

His lips twitched as if he found her amusing. "I'll be sure to invite every tailor in Varros I know to London. But then, that would rather create a conundrum, would it not, if all the tailors of Varros suddenly rushed to England's shores? The poor gentlemen in my homeland would suffer a shocking dearth of trousers. Only think of it. All the ladies in the streets would be swooning when they came upon men dressed in nothing more than their drawers."

He was mocking her. And yet doing so with such casual amusement, his eyes sparkling with infectious mischief, his lips curved into a smile that invited her to join in his levity.

She wouldn't do it.

"One would assume they would still retain their existing garments," she argued, keeping her tone mild and unaffected.

Which was difficult indeed when Prince Ferdinando was on bended knee, mopping up her spilled tea and grinning at her as if they were sharing a private jest. Because when the prince turned the full brunt of his charm upon her, he smoldered. And Eleanora felt like dry kindling that was about to catch flame.

The prince rose to his towering height, having completed his task, and placed the soiled napkin discreetly on the table. "You have an excellent point, Miss Brett. However, I can only further reckon that if the tailors were to descend upon London, they would be every bit as enthralled by its charms as I am. They'd never return. Eventually, the poor chaps in

Varros would be wandering about in ragged trousers or no trousers at all."

The intimation in his words wasn't lost on her. *Every bit as enthralled by its charms.* His gaze never left hers as he spoke. And it remained now, burning into her with a searing intensity that challenged her to throw caution to the wind and allow him to have his wicked way with her.

"What a dreadful scandal," she said, trying her utmost to tamp down the visions his words evoked.

Not the myriad, anonymous gentlemen of Varros wandering about sans trousers but, rather, Prince Ferdinando. His legs were strong and long—the lean legs of a well-versed horseman. And the rest of his form was equally spare and honed. She wondered if he engaged in some manner of physical exertion or if he had simply been blessed with uncommon good looks and the chiseled body of a Greek god.

It didn't matter.

Eleanora banished the curiosity, knowing it would lead her nowhere good.

"Quite." Prince Ferdinando had the audacity to wink. "But one would imagine the ladies might enjoy such a show."

Warmth crept up her spine, making her nape tingle. "I doubt they would, Your Royal Highness."

"Indeed," he said smoothly, "perhaps not all ladies are as discerning in their knowledge of the construction of trousers as you are, Miss Brett. They might be pleased to see their menfolk clothed in the inferior quality of Varros trousers rather than none."

Why were they discussing trousers or a lack thereof?

Her ears went hot. It was scandalous. It was wrong. It was positively perilous.

Drat. The fault was hers. She had been foolish enough to

insult his garments as a poor means of distracting him from the manner in which she'd eyed his thighs.

She had to escape. To swallow her pride and retreat from his presence.

"Of course, I'm certain you're right, Your Royal Highness," she managed to say. "But if you would excuse me, I am afraid that I must take my leave as there are a number of matters requiring my attention. You're welcome to remain and enjoy your tea as you await the return of the princesses."

She dipped into a curtsy and then rushed from the drawing room as if Cerberus were at her heels.

CHAPTER 3

❦

*N*ando had never liked bees.

Which was why, when the buzzing sound followed by the intense sting in his upper arm hit him on the Mayfair street as he approached his waiting carriage, he was so damned infuriated. It was also why he didn't understand the hot rush traveling down his arm. Or the sight of his coat sliced open to his flesh as he glanced down to find the offending insect and deliver it to its rewards.

Dimly, it occurred to him that he'd heard a resounding bang just before the infernal bee had struck him with its pestilential vengeance. Something that, now that he thought upon it, had been rather reminiscent of a flintlock firing.

"Your Royal Highness?"

The voice of his guard, Bruno, permeated Nando's bewildered musings. There was something warm and wet on his arm, something stinging and fiery too. Bruno looked distressed. Nothing made sense, Nando's mind whirling with countless thoughts that were unrelated. What social engagements had he agreed upon for the evening? He was desperately in need of a whisky. What time of day was it? Why was his vision turning black around the edges?

Something was terribly wrong with him.

Damn it all, had Miss Brett laced his tea with poison? He wouldn't put it past the cunning minx.

Nando's head continued to swim. Blood. That was the wetness. Red and dripping from his left hand.

"Your Royal Highness, you've been shot," Bruno told him in their native language, his voice curt and clipped. "We need to get you to safety."

Shot?

He swayed.

Ye gods, shot.

So that was what this was.

It hadn't been a bee after all. Fancy that.

A great commotion swirled around him suddenly. A sea of faces. Shouts. People were pouring from town houses. Horses were neighing. Bruno shielded him with his body.

"Take me home," he ordered his guard, thinking that if he had to die, he may as well do so from the comfort of his own bed.

No sense going to Hades right here in the street like a stray mongrel.

"We need a doctor, Your Royal Highness," Bruno said. "You're losing too much blood."

"Eh, I've plenty of it." He attempted to reassure his faithful guard, but his lips felt numb, and so did his tongue. "Some to spare."

Nando wasn't certain what he'd said, if anything. His vision was growing increasingly blurred and dark, as if he were watching the world become smaller and smaller until there was nothing left but a pinprick of light to call him back to the living.

He wasn't sure he wanted to go there.

His knees weren't sustaining him any longer. Drowsily, he looked down.

More blood.

So much of it.

A puddle in the street. Marring the boots he favored.

"Damn it," he slurred to Bruno, "this is my favorite pair of boots."

"Come, Your Royal Highness," Bruno said sternly, his face as tense and taut as Nando had ever seen it. "You mustn't stay on the street. It isn't safe here."

Nando wanted to argue, but his mind felt as if it were fashioned of porridge.

"Someone shot me," he announced as if it were a new development.

"Yes, Your Royal Highness." Bruno was shepherding him back up the walk as others swarmed around them.

Faceless, nameless servants. Where had they all come from?

Had the delicious Miss Brett shot him?

He didn't think she possessed the capability, let alone a requisite firearm.

"I think I'd like a glass of shiskwy, Bruno," Nando added. No, that didn't sound right.

"Of course, Your Royal Highness," Bruno said, guiding him to the front door of the town house he'd so recently vacated.

"Whisky," he tried again, pleased that his muddled brain had been able to elucidate.

"You'll be needing more than whisky," Bruno grumbled.

Nando was helped into the town house, where the butler greeted him with appalled alarm. More shouts ensued, and Nando dripped his life source all over the marble entryway.

Suddenly, Miss Brett was there. She looked like an angel with the sunlight catching in her ethereally gold locks. She fluttered toward him, a worried butterfly.

"Your Royal Highness, you've been wounded," she exclaimed.

"It's a mere scratch," he reassured her gallantly and then listed to the right like a ship about to go down at sea.

"Send for Dr. Crisfield at once," Miss Brett demanded sternly before taking Nando's uninjured arm and cleaving to his side as if it were where she belonged.

Ah, bliss. She was warm and soft and she smelled like a blooming flower garden in summer, and he wanted her to wrap him in her arms and never let him go. He'd happily get shot every day if it meant this sort of reception from her.

"Can you manage to take the stairs, Your Royal Highness?" she asked fretfully.

"If I say no, will you offer to carry me?" he asked, stumbling into her.

This damned loss of blood was causing him to feel faint. But he also thought he might be in love with the woman.

"Get me a cloth to press to his wound," Miss Brett ordered, taking command in a way not even Bruno could. "He's losing too much blood."

Domestics scattered to do her bidding. Nando swayed again, and Bruno wrapped a burly arm around him, keeping him from falling to his face. A cloth was presented, and Miss Brett pressed it to his wound.

Pain lanced him as he hissed in a breath. "Ye gods, that hurts."

"I'm sorry, but you can't afford to keep bleeding this way," she said.

Bruno muttered something about saints in their native language. Nando didn't quite catch it all. But he was moving with the help of Miss Brett and his guard, floating toward the staircase and then taking the steps in halting progression. Bleeding on his host's carpets. It couldn't be helped. He'd happily pay the princess and her husband, the wealthy commoner Archer Tierney, to have them replaced.

If he didn't die, that was.

He didn't think he was going to die.

At least, he hoped he wouldn't. He wanted to feel Miss Brett's lips beneath his at least once before he met his demise.

"I'm afraid there's no chance of that," Miss Brett told him frostily.

Well, hell. Had he voiced his desire to kiss her aloud? It must be all the cotton filling his head. And the pain from his wounded arm. And that damned blood that continued to flow. More now, soaking the cloth she pressed to his wound. Coloring her dainty, pale fingers. He looked at it and felt dizzied.

"Your Royal Highness, keep moving," she commanded him sternly. Then, in a softer tone he couldn't resist, added, "Please."

He'd do anything she asked of him. That was his stupefied thought as he stumbled his way up the stairs, bleeding everywhere and leaning on Miss Brett and Bruno for aid. Everything unfolded in a flurry as they reached the top of the stairs. A strapping footman appeared, replacing Miss Brett, and Nando was hauled into a bedchamber.

"Miss Brett," he called, needing her.

Her presence calmed him. He had to have her at his side. To the devil with this footman. He struggled with the lad, extricating his arm, roaring with exasperation and pain.

"I'm here, Your Royal Highness." Her voice wrapped around him, soothing him.

"I need to see you," he muttered.

What he didn't need was a damned footman in her place.

Their procession stumbled to a bed.

Excellent, because that was where he wanted to be with Miss Brett most. Except she wasn't joining him there, because the bloody footman and Bruno were in the way. Also, his boots. And the rest of his clothes.

"Miss Brett, I need you," he rasped, the world going sideways as he was tipped into the bed in none-too-gentle fashion.

Or perhaps he fell. He couldn't be certain. Everything was growing dim and faint at the edges.

Thankfully, he didn't land on his wounded arm. He huffed out another bark of pain at the jostling.

"Be careful with him, gentlemen," Miss Brett was chiding.

She was still here. Thank Deus. It seemed to him that he couldn't draw another breath without her. Everything was painful and jumbled. She was the sole source of comfort; not even Bruno's familiar presence at his side held sufficient weight.

With his uninjured hand, he reached for her.

"Don't leave me," he begged.

She took his bloodstained hand in hers, lacing their fingers together.

"I'm here, Your Royal Highness," she said, before looking to Bruno. "A fresh cloth, please. He's bleeding through this one."

She was still holding something to his wound, staving off the flow of blood, he realized. Miss Brett had more fortitude than he'd even supposed, and he found himself absurdly proud of that realization.

"Nando," he told her, his eyelids growing heavier by the moment. "I insist."

His eyes slipped closed. He heard her voice as if from afar.

"Stay with me."

But there was an inviting pull of darkness clawing at him, growing ever more difficult to resist. He wanted to stay with Miss Brett as she had asked. But he also wanted to go. He was weary. Tired.

So very tired.

He fell into the blackness to the soft sound of her voice, the searing pain in his arm, and the comforting sensation of her hand in his.

~

"Do you think His Royal Highness will survive?" Princess Emmaline asked, her countenance stricken, her voice subdued.

Hours had passed since the mayhem of the afternoon, when Prince Ferdinando had been wounded. The princesses had long since returned from their shopping expedition to find the house in an uproar. After changing into fresh garments, Eleanora had joined Princess Emmaline, Princess Annalise, and their older sister Princess Anastasia in the drawing room at the latter's behest.

Like almost every other female in his vicinity, Princess Emmaline had been easily charmed by Prince Ferdinando. She was smitten with him, Eleanora suspected. Princess Annalise was no different. They were both easy prey for a man so potently seductive, his every smile crafted to woo, his voice like sin, his charm as easy as it was undeniable, the words that left his tongue pure flirtation, a blatant invitation to be wicked.

As wild and wayward as the Boritanian royals were, they were kindhearted girls, every bit as lovely on the inside as they were on the outside. Eleanora didn't doubt the veracity of their concern for the prince.

Nor did she question the precariousness of his current circumstances.

He'd been shot, and he'd lost a great deal of blood.

An alarming amount.

Dr. Crisfield was a preeminent physician, and he had arrived posthaste. His work had been calm and efficient. Eleanora could find no fault with the care His Royal Highness had received. But although the bullet had narrowly avoided shattering bone, Prince Ferdinando was not by any means assured of a swift convalescence.

He'd been so pale and still when she had finally forced herself to leave his side, her garments stained red, her heart heavy with worry. Her experience in the sickroom, coupled with her proximity, had rendered her an easy option for assisting Dr. Crisfield when he had arrived. The prince's guard had poured enough laudanum down his throat to render him complacent for the serious nature of the surgery that had followed. Eleanora had remained for the grueling procedure, hating when the prince stirred and moaned, knowing how dangerous the days awaiting him would prove.

"We will pray that he does," she answered the princess firmly now, trying to keep the worry from her voice, lest the princesses fret more.

Because she wasn't certain what would become of the handsome, scandalous rogue who had been flirting with her so easily a mere half hour before he'd been laid low by a bullet. There had been so much spilled blood.

His pleading voice came back to her along with the sharp spear of guilt. *Don't leave me.*

She'd had to leave him. She hadn't had a choice. She had her position to consider, and the return of the princesses had meant she'd needed to go. Besides, it hadn't been proper. She was an unwed lady, and it was unseemly for her to remain in a bedchamber with the prince.

"We've been praying since we heard the news," Princess Annalise said worriedly.

"We all have," Eleanora agreed, feeling faint with concern and fear.

"Who do you think would have dared to attempt to assassinate a prince here in London?" Princess Emmaline asked, her fingers twisting in her pale muslin skirts.

At least she wore a gown today, Eleanora thought absently. The trousers the princesses had insisted upon wearing about society—including at balls—had left the ladies of the *ton* whispering behind their fans in shocked horror.

"A great many people would dare," said Princess Anastasia now, her tone grim. "There is danger everywhere, Emmaline dearest, and you'd do well to never forget it."

"I thought it was safe here in London," Princess Annalise said, moving to a window in the drawing room and peering out of it cautiously from the side, as if she feared the villain who had dared to shoot Prince Ferdinando yet lurked in the street below.

"It is as safe for you here as it is anywhere," Princess Anastasia answered firmly. "And we have my husband to protect us. I assure you, there is no one more adept at facing and defeating enemies than he is."

In a decision that had shocked society, Princess Anastasia had cried off on her arranged marriage to King Maximilian of Varros, a marriage that would have solidified an alliance between their troubled lands. Instead, she had married a commoner, Archer Tierney. Mr. Tierney was wealthy and had powerful connections, but he would never be a king. Theirs was a love match. Mr. Tierney and Princess Anastasia had settled into a life together in London, and they were the darlings of Society.

The princesses, however, had spent the last ten years beneath the tyrannical rule of their uncle. They desperately needed polish to be turned into diamonds of the first water. That was where Eleanora had come in.

"Thank heavens for Mr. Tierney," Princess Emmaline said, still plucking fitfully at her gown.

It was another habit Eleanora would have to try to persuade the princess to control. She committed the reminder to her unwritten list of tasks for the month.

"Mr. Tierney has been a godsend," Princess Anastasia agreed with a small, private smile that Eleanora recognized.

She tamped down the pang of envy at the princess's obvious contentment and the love she had for her husband, because Eleanora had long ago accepted that her life would never be what she had once longed for it to be. Her secrets were too great. And at eight-and-twenty, she was a spinster firmly on the shelf. No man would wed her now.

It was for the best.

"You are so fortunate to have found him, Stasia," Princess Emmaline agreed, speaking to her sister familiarly.

The family, though royal, was refreshingly honest and caring, quite without the artifice Eleanora had come to expect from the quality or those aspiring to join its ranks. She admired the St. George family, and she admired Mr. Tierney as well.

Still, she couldn't help but to feel like an interloper in this cozy scene of sisterly intimacy.

"Perhaps I should leave Your Royal Highnesses," she interrupted gently. "I had planned on some further lessons, but given the nature of the day, it may be more prudent to wait."

"I couldn't possibly think of learning dance steps when Prince Nando is so gravely ill," Princess Annalise said.

Good, because neither could Eleanora. But she couldn't

say that, of course. Nor should she even be thinking it. She couldn't afford to care about a man like him. Or any man, for that matter. But most especially not a scoundrel prince who was too handsome by far and who had all the women of London at his feet.

"Naturally not, Your Royal Highness," Eleanora agreed. "It's not my intent to cause further harm."

"Miss Brett, perhaps I might have a word with you in the hall?" Princess Anastasia requested politely.

She was a striking brunette with icy blue eyes and a commanding presence, and together with the sinfully handsome Mr. Tierney, they made a lovely couple. Eleanora was accustomed to mingling with the cream of society, but she still found herself in awe of the regal Princess Anastasia, despite the princess's agreeable nature.

"Whatever you wish, Your Royal Highness," Eleanora concurred, not wanting to cause any additional upheaval.

It wasn't her place. Her place was to be on the periphery. To play her role and never interfere. To be, in short, invisible. Unless it was required for her to appear and accede to the wishes of her employers.

Only Prince Ferdinando had seen her. Seen her in a way that had made a restless yearning burn deep inside her. In a way she couldn't afford to indulge in.

Ever.

She offered each of the princesses a humble curtsy and followed in Princess Anastasia's wake as she departed the drawing room. In the hall, Princess Anastasia made certain to close the doors so that her younger sisters wouldn't be able to eavesdrop on their conversation before turning to Eleanora.

"Thank you for your efforts on Prince Nando's behalf," Princess Anastasia said, her face fraught with worry.

It was as if a mask had slipped and the calm, poised

façade she had presented to her sisters shattered. The previously composed princess appeared starkly worried.

"You needn't thank me, Your Royal Highness," Eleanora said. "It was my honor to assist the household in tending to the prince."

A scratching sound at the door suggested that the princesses weren't above eavesdropping after all.

With a raised brow, the princess inclined her head toward the hall. "Walk with me, Miss Brett?"

"Of course." Eleanora moved to keep pace with the princess, following her down the hall and away from curious, listening ears. "How may I be of service to you?"

"Oh, my dear Miss Brett, it is too kind of you to ask," Princess Anastasia said, reaching for her arm and giving it an affectionate squeeze that defied the bonds of their relationship. She sighed heavily before continuing. "You know that Prince Nando is beloved to me, even for all his faults and despite my determination to see him stay far from my sisters, do you not?"

Eleanora nodded. "Yes, Your Royal Highness."

"His brother, King Maximilian, is married to my dearest friend, my former lady-in-waiting, Queen Tansy. I promised her that I would see to Nando as best as I could whilst he was here in London." The princess paused, her lower lip quivering. "And now, he has been gravely wounded. I fear she'll never forgive me. Nor will I forgive myself if anything…if he were to…"

Her words trailed away, as if she couldn't bring herself to give voice to the real possibility that Prince Ferdinando would die from his injuries.

"I am so sorry, Your Royal Highness," Eleanora hastened to say, feeling at a loss as to how she might proceed in such delicate circumstances. "If there is any way I can be of assistance, please know I'm here in every capacity you require."

"I was hoping you would say that," Princess Anastasia said as they approached the grand staircase. "Because—and pray tell me if I am overstepping, Miss Brett—Prince Nando is in a great deal of pain. He's been calling for you ever since you left his chamber earlier after you assisted with Dr. Crisfield."

"It was most inappropriate of me to be so bold," Eleanora said, terrified that she was about to lose her position for daring to enter an unwed man's chamber and aid a doctor. She had seen the prince without his shirt. In a bed. And whilst she had been preoccupied by his state and the sight of so much blood, she couldn't deny that it had been most scandalous of her to be present. Under any other circumstances, it would have been beyond the pale. Indeed, perhaps the princess felt it was.

"It was perfect, Miss Brett," the princess shocked her by saying. "Just as you are. I am heartened, as I know my dear friend the queen would be, that you were there to aid Nando in his time of need. And I am selfishly hoping you might be willing to do so again."

Eleanora was hardly perfect. Far from it, in fact. If the princess had any notion of just how far, she'd likely be shocked. They were on the staircase, slowly ascending, leaving the younger princesses behind in the drawing room. The house was wreathed in funereal silence, even the domestics traveling with a more pronounced, ominous hush than before.

"I'm afraid I don't understand what you're asking of me, Your Royal Highness," Eleanora said earnestly. "But whatever it is that you wish, rest assured that I'll be more than happy to do it."

"Nando is restless," Princess Anastasia said, frowning. "He's in quite a state. I've seen him myself, and he was thrashing and carrying on in such a fashion that I can't do anything but fear for his welfare. If indeed he doesn't contract an infection or worse after the injury he suffered today…"

"How may I help?" Eleanora asked, fearing she already knew the answer to that question.

"He has been calling for you, Miss Brett, and insists no other will suffice," Princess Anastasia said, her countenance a mixture of worry and regret. "He says he won't rest peacefully unless you're at his side, and I very much fear he will do himself greater injury if he doesn't stay calm. Perhaps you might spare him a few minutes to put him at ease. His man Bruno will be in attendance, of course. You have nothing to fear where your reputation is concerned."

Either Prince Ferdinando was delirious with fever and laudanum, or he was being his scoundrel self once more.

It didn't matter. Eleanora would deal with him. She needed this lucrative post. Needed the unrivaled éclat she could receive from aiding royal princesses.

She didn't hesitate in her response.

"If it is what pleases Your Royal Highness, I would be honored," Eleanora lied.

"Oh, Miss Brett." The princess blinked furiously, her long, dark lashes doing nothing to stay the flow of tears threatening to spill. A few trailed down her cheeks. "I'm indebted to you, truly."

"Nonsense," Eleanora said with false brightness. "I am indebted to *you*, Your Royal Highness. With your blessing, I'll pay a quick call upon the prince's sickroom."

"Thank you, my dear. You're an angel," Princess Anastasia said.

Eleanora stifled a guilty flush, but she held her tongue and followed the princess back to the rooms where Prince Ferdinando had been taken.

Just in time to hear His Royal Highness shouting that he must see Miss Brett or he wouldn't have another drop of bloody laudanum, followed by a crash.

Oh dear heavens. Eleanora stiffened her spine, preparing to enter.

It sounded as if sitting with Prince Ferdinando was going to be a greater challenge than she'd feared.

CHAPTER 4

*N*ando was reasonably certain that Bruno had
poured an inhuman amount of laudanum down
his throat. Partially because he felt like he was floating on a
cloud made of shimmering mountain mist and partly
because the wound in his arm was only producing a small
ache. He felt hale enough to climb a tree, for God's sake.
Surely that couldn't be right after he'd been shot. Could it?

He would worry about that pernicious question later. For
now, he had more pressing concerns to fret over. Namely,
one. She was a golden-haired spinster who had disappeared
from his side in his time of need, and he didn't like her
absence one damned bit.

As the hours had worn into the evening and the sun had
faded from the sky, he had decided that if he was going to
die, he wanted to do so with Miss Eleanora Brett at his side.
No one else would do.

"Your Royal Highness," Bruno was saying in a coaxing
voice. "You need more laudanum to calm you so that you
don't tear your stitches."

Bruno was playing nursemaid. Nando didn't want Bruno. He wanted Miss Brett.

"Go to the devil," he growled, picking up the nearest object and using his uninjured arm to hurl it across the room.

The tumbler crashed into the wall with a satisfying smash, sending shards flying to the floor.

"Your Royal Highness," his loyal guard chided. "That wasn't necessary."

"It was necessary," he argued, quite irritable at having been repeatedly thwarted and denied his requests. "I'll have you sent to the dungeon in Varros for your insolence."

That was an empty threat, of course. But he wanted Bruno to understand that the man had damned well overstepped. He was Prince Ferdinando of Varros, curse it. He *always* got what he wanted.

And if there was any moment when he most assuredly should have everything and anything he wished for, it was now, when he was perhaps lying on his deathbed. And what he wanted was decidedly not more laudanum.

It was *her*.

"Of course it was," Bruno agreed submissively. "Forgive me, Your Royal Highness. I'll attend to the broken glass as soon as you take your laudanum."

The cloud Nando was inhabiting became a thundercloud. "I don't want any bloody laudanum. Give me Miss Brett, or give me nothing."

He'd rather raised his voice by the end of his booming demand, and it sounded to his mind every bit like a brutal summer storm cracking across the landscape. Bruno looked alarmed.

As well he ought to.

"I'm afraid Miss Brett is otherwise occupied, Your Royal Highness," Bruno said. "Now just a small amount of laudanum. Dr. Crisfield said it was important that you stay as still as possible, and I—"

"No, no, no," Nando roared, interrupting. "I don't give a damn what the doctor said. I don't want more of that poison. I want Miss Brett. She is essential to my recovery. Bring her to me at once."

Surely there was something else within reach that he might throw. Nando looked around wildly and saw a book. He seized it and drew it into his cloud, thinking it weightless and airy. Existing in a cloud wasn't particularly vexing. But he would like it far more if Miss Brett were here. Not Bruno. Bruno could lie down in a busy thoroughfare for all he was concerned at the moment.

"Get out of my cloud," he added, tossing the book toward one of Bruno's two heads.

Two heads?

What the devil?

The book sailed over both of his guard's heads and hit the wall just as the door opened.

And there on the threshold, thank the angels in heaven, was Miss Brett. Her countenance was pinched and distraught. She looked as pleased as a woman marching to the gallows. Dare he hope it was worry for him that rendered her so grim? Either way, there was more than sufficient room in his cloud for her.

His arm was beginning to pain him, damn it all. His skin felt too tight, and a persistent ache was throbbing to life. Who'd had the gall to shoot him?

"Eleanora," he greeted the woman whose presence he'd been demanding for what felt like the last century.

It must have been the last few hours, at least. A lifetime. Fifteen minutes? Who cared? He had her where he wanted her now.

She glided into the room like a spring breeze, cooling and

self-assured. Was she floating? God. He couldn't see her feet. The ceiling and floor were swirling, and in between, there was her loveliness. He never wanted to look upon anyone else for as long as he lived.

"Miss Brett," she corrected.

Of course she did.

"I'm in pain," he told her, which wasn't a lie.

Her lush lips thinned, her eyes straying to the bandage on his upper arm. "I'm so sorry to hear that, Your Royal Highness."

"Come and sit by my side," he invited. "Only you can assuage my agony."

"I'm certain that isn't true, Your Royal Highness."

He raised an imperious brow. "Are you daring to suggest I'm wrong?"

She shared a glance with Bruno that Nando didn't like. Why was she looking at his guard when she ought to be looking at him? Bruno wasn't the one who'd lost his lifeblood all over the street.

"His Royal Highness should take more laudanum," Bruno told Miss Brett quietly.

As if Nando weren't present in the room.

He may have been inhabiting a cloud, but his ears worked perfectly well.

"Bruno, you are happily relieved of your duties," he told his unwanted guard. "Get out."

"Your Royal Highness—"

"Out," he interrupted, not wishing to hear anything else. "I'll see you sent to the gallows for disobeying me."

Bruno paled, as if he considered the threat a legitimate one. Good. Let him think it was. Nando wanted Miss Brett alone, and he wanted her alone with him.

Right bloody *now*.

"Leave the laudanum with me, if you please," Miss Brett

told his guard, taking command in typical Miss Brett fashion. "I'll see to His Royal Highness for a spell."

Bruno looked dubious. Nando was suddenly possessed by the notion that Miss Brett could lead an army into battle without so much as faltering.

"Listen to Miss Brett," Nando commanded Bruno in a tone that brooked no argument.

"As Your Royal Highness wishes," Bruno acceded with a bow, his reluctance obvious.

Finally. Progress.

Nando watched as Bruno took his leave, the door closing at his back, before turning his attention to Miss Brett.

Eleanora.

"Come," he beckoned, crooking a finger.

The throbbing in his arm was enough to make his eyes water. He ignored it. Nothing mattered as much as her nearness. He wanted her to sit by him. He wanted her to join him in his cloud. He wanted to drink her in like fine wine. He wanted…

He didn't even know what he wanted.

At the moment, his cock was sadly uninterested in making itself useful. He ought not to have been so enamored with her. He couldn't bed her at present. And yet, he somehow desired her despite his infirmity.

She approached his bedside, more glorious than any woman had a right to be. It wasn't ordinary beauty that Miss Eleanora Brett possessed. It was something so much rarer, something innate and uniquely hers. He couldn't elucidate what it was, the laudanum and pain rendering him much less capable of eloquence.

"I prayed for an angel to save me, and at last, here you are," he told her dramatically.

"Your Royal Highness, I cannot fathom why you would wish for me to attend you."

"Sit," he ordered her.

She seated herself primly on the chair, arranging the fall of her skirts as if it were of the utmost interest to her. Looking anywhere but at him.

"You ought to try to rest, Your Royal Highness," she told her lap.

Blast it, he finally had her where he wanted her, and she was denying him the full force of her gaze.

"I'm up here," he told her wryly. "And please, call me Nando. Given the rather intimate nature of our current tête-à-tête, it only seems right."

At last, she looked at him. "Your Royal Highness."

"Nando."

"I cannot call you by your given name."

"Of course you can. Try it."

She huffed a sigh. "If you take your laudanum, I shall."

And this was why he had welcomed her into his cloud. She was every bit as diabolical as he was. How excellent. It pleased him greatly.

"Ah, a bribe. That is surprisingly cunning of you, my dear. I like it."

Miss Brett frowned. "I was thinking of it more as a compromise."

He twirled a finger. "Call it whatever you like. Very well, I'll have the laudanum if you call me Nando."

"Only when we are alone."

He grinned wolfishly. "Wonderful, for I intend us to be alone often."

And naked. But he refrained from adding that rather salient bit.

Her nostrils flared. He thought she might chastise him. Actually, he hoped she would. There was something about her frosty rebukes that made him want to kiss her. And more.

Pity he was wounded. There wasn't much he could accomplish with his arm as it was.

"I expect this will be the last time we'll be alone," she countered with her impeccable poise.

"And I expect you're wrong, my darling Eleanora, but you may think that if you like." Because he was a prince, and he always got what he wanted.

He shifted in the bed, trying to find a more comfortable position, and pain shot through him, making his gut clench. Damn it, perhaps the laudanum he'd consumed earlier at Bruno's behest was losing its efficacy.

She must have taken note of his contorting face because she sprang to her feet, hovering like a fretful little bird.

"Are you in pain, Your Royal Highness?"

Her scent washed over him, familiar and decadent. He wanted that scent on his pillow. On his skin. It was a testament to his desire for her that he could even entertain such thoughts now, after losing a good deal of blood, his wound paining him dreadfully.

"I thought we agreed you'd call me Nando," he gritted from between clenched teeth.

"Your laudanum first." She flitted away, returning with the medicine in hand.

It was just as well that he take it. His cloud was dissipating, and the agony was returning. Besides, he wanted to hear his name on her lush lips. He was beginning to feel weak again, and he needed the distraction.

"Fair enough." He accepted a measure of the bitter liquid and forced himself to swallow it down.

Laudanum was bloody terrible. He hated it.

"My name," he gritted when she hesitated, lingering near to his bedside.

The instinct to draw his uninjured arm around her and

haul her onto the mattress beside him was strong. He resisted, clinging to what little compunction he possessed.

"Nando," she said, her voice so faint he thought he must have imagined it at first.

But she'd said it.

His name.

"That wasn't so difficult, was it?" he asked, wincing as another sharp stab of pain radiated from his wound.

"You should get some rest, Your Royal Highness," she said gently.

"Damn it, you're to call me Nando. I drank your poison."

She gave him a small smile. "You didn't specify how many times I was to say your name. Once shall suffice."

Once would never suffice when it came to this woman. He wanted to hear her saying his name again and again. He wanted her to moan his name when she came. He wanted more from her than he could even comprehend. Certainly more than he could tell her.

She'd flee like a frightened doe alerted to the hunter's approach if he did.

"That was positively Machiavellian of you," he praised her instead. "I've been soundly routed at my own game."

She was frowning again. "I've never seen a wounded man so full of vigor."

"How many wounded men have you seen?"

"Only you, Your Royal Highness."

He stared at her, his vision beginning to soften at the edges as the laudanum took hold. "It's not every day I'm nearly assassinated. I'm not certain what manner of vigor is called for on such occasions."

Eleanora shook her head at him. "How can you find levity in your present circumstances?"

"Easily enough. I didn't die, therefore I'm vastly amused.

Whoever intended to kill me had dreadful aim. The poor fellow really ought to practice more."

This time, a sound stole from her, small and sudden, before she pressed a dainty hand to her lips to stifle it.

"Too late, my dear. I already heard your amusement."

Deus. He wanted to worship this woman. He coveted all her smiles. He longed to kiss every inch of her. To pleasure her as she deserved. To melt her ice. *Everything.* He wanted her complete and utter surrender. She was more intoxicating than the finest spirits, and he wanted to drown himself in her potent allure.

"I shouldn't have found humor in the situation. Forgive me, Your Royal Highness."

"I insist you do penance by sitting with me," he said, doing his best impression of his imperious brother.

She eyed the chair she had so recently vacated as if it were a peril she couldn't bear to face. "Why do you wish for my presence?"

"Because you soothe me," he said easily. "And because I like you, Miss Brett. I want you here, and so here you are."

"You were being a petulant child, Your Royal Highness," she told him.

"My dear Eleanora, have you met me? I *am* a petulant child."

Her lips twitched as if she wanted to smile but refused to allow further amusement to crack her grim shell.

"You aren't even making an effort to defend yourself."

"Why should I? You aren't wrong. But you see, I'm too complacent to change my ways."

She sat at last, her reluctance obvious. "Someone ought to shake that complacency."

"I wouldn't be averse to your trying. Perhaps you might administer corporal punishment. Wait until my wound heals, however, if you please. I have no wish to lose any more blood today."

"You're the most peculiar man I've ever met," she grumbled. "I'll not be administering any punishment to you, corporal or otherwise."

"Oh, but I think I might enjoy it if you did. I'm a wicked man, and I ought to be punished." His tongue felt fat now, the laudanum fully taking hold, his head floating, the pain in his upper arm blessedly diminished.

He should rest as the eminently wise Eleanora had advised him. He'd been shot, for God's sake. But he didn't want to close his eyes and surrender to the abyss. He wanted to stay awake, talking with her. Looking at her. She pleased him greatly. Everything about her, from her stiff spine to her lush mouth.

A flush had stolen over her cheekbones at the insinuation in his words.

"Your Royal Highness, I'll ascribe your unseemly suggestion to the laudanum. It must have addled your wits and loosened your tongue."

She folded her hands primly in her lap.

"Admit it, I charm you," he said, because he couldn't seem to help himself.

Weariness was drawing over him, but he would fight it. He wanted to spend the night basking in her husky voice.

"I find you as charming as a rash," she told him curtly.

"A compliment if I've ever heard one," he said, unperturbed.

Because she didn't fool him. He *did* charm her. She wanted to be insusceptible to him; that much was apparent. But beneath her cool façade, Miss Eleanora Brett could be tempted. His intuition in such matters never failed him.

And Nando intended to use that weakness in his favor.

CHAPTER 5

*E*leanora woke with a start to inky darkness.

At once, she was aware that something was amiss. She was seated upright instead of lying comfortably in the bed she'd been provided, and her surroundings were unfamiliar. Where was she?

Realization hit her like a bolt of lightning.

Somehow, she must have fallen asleep in the chair at the prince's bedside. A host of unanswered questions flitted through her sleep-fogged mind. Had no one thought to wake her? To check on his condition?

The candle that had been lit had long since sputtered out, leaving them cloaked in the shadows of night. The remnants of a banked fire smoldered in the grate across the room, serving for a pitiful source of illumination.

Her gaze instantly went to the still form of the prince. He had fallen into the depths of slumber from the laudanum she'd persuaded him to take. And she had remained at his side for a moment, thinking that she would rest until a servant arrived to take her place. It must have been the upheaval and shock of the day that had rendered her so exhausted that she'd fallen asleep.

Concern for him instantly sliced through her.

How was he?

She had no wish to disturb his rest, and yet she needed to know. As quietly as she could manage, Eleanora rose and hovered over his bedside, gently laying a hand over his brow to detect whether he had a fever.

His skin didn't feel hot. But she couldn't account for the jolt that shot through her at touching him. It felt forbidden. *Dangerous.* It felt impossibly, erroneously right. As if he were hers to touch and tenderly care for. But that was as foolish as it was impossible. The Prince of Varros belonged to no woman.

She snatched her hand away, telling herself she needed to collect her wits and flee this room at once. Because her reputation was all she possessed, and it was without reproach. She needed to preserve it at all costs. She had neither lineage nor wealth to rely upon. Not even youth, for she was approaching her thirtieth year. She had only herself and the lone skill to which she steadfastly clung—that of churning out marriageable ladies, even though Eleanora herself would never be a bride.

She turned to take her leave.

"Don't go."

The low rasp was so unexpected that she paused and spun to face him in the darkness. But there was also a note of underlying pain in his voice that made her linger when every other part of her knew she ought to flee.

"Your Royal Highness," she said, finding her voice. "Is something amiss?"

"Yes. You're intending to leave my side when I have need of you."

His voice had gained strength and yet it remained

strained. It occurred to Eleanora that he must have mistaken her for a servant in the darkness.

"I'm not a nursemaid, Your Royal Highness," she explained gently. "I can fetch someone else to attend you if you like. Your bodyguard, perhaps? Or a footman?"

"I only want you, Eleanora."

Something inside her seized. So, he did realize she was the one at his side. He hadn't mistaken her for a maid after all. And he wanted her to remain. Ruthlessly, she tamped down the unwanted feeling.

"I'm afraid that I have stayed longer than I should have already. Is there something you require? I'll see that a servant is sent to you."

Tending to him was private. Intimate. Dangerously scandalous. She couldn't remain. That she had stayed this long was a testament to her own recklessness, and it wouldn't be repeated.

"No one else," he insisted stubbornly.

"Your Royal Highness—" she began, only to be interrupted by his surprised grunt of pain.

She rushed to his side instinctively. "What happened? What is paining you?"

She didn't have sufficient illumination to see his expression. The absence of candlelight frustrated her, but there was no hope for it at the moment. She leaned nearer, peering through the shadows.

"My arm. I dare say I shall only survive with your tender care."

There was no mistaking the flirtatious tone that had crept into his voice. The utter scoundrel. It was also a definitive indication that it was time for her to go. He was confounding.

"I'm afraid I know precious little about tending to

wounds," she told him tartly. "The hour is late, Your Royal Highness. I must go, but rest assured, I'll be certain to send one of the servants to your aid."

"I do wish you'd call me Nando again," he said with a sigh.

And yet she lingered, quite against her better judgment. "We've already established that it is improper for me to be so familiar with you."

Strangely, she found herself yearning to be familiar, however. Clearly, spending so much time in this jaded rake's cunning presence was rendering her mad.

"Just once more before I die, please?" he asked as if she hadn't spoken.

"You sound well enough to me," she pointed out.

"Ah, but the agony of my wound, you see. It feels as if someone has thrust a hot poker through my flesh. I'm burning from the inside out. The wound is festering, I have no doubt of it."

"Surely it's not. You didn't feel feverish to me just now."

"Feel my brow again, my darling Eleanora," he urged, his voice suddenly sounding thready and weak. "I fear I am."

She caught her lower lip between her teeth, finding herself in a fine predicament.

"I'll fetch you more laudanum," she suggested. "It will help you to remain calm and rest."

"I don't want more laudanum. Give me your hand."

She had already moved nearer to the bed, quite stupidly drawn to the man despite all reason. She knew better than to grant Prince Ferdinando such proximity. She knew just what manner of persuasion rakes were capable of. She'd witnessed it on many occasions.

And yet, she was doing as he'd demanded. Allowing him to bring her hand to his brow. His flesh didn't feel any hotter to the touch than it had before. But her body's reaction was the same. A stunning sense of awareness fell over her, so potent that it made her belly tense. As if he sensed her susceptibility, his fingers tightened over hers. He gently caressed her hand.

It was the most sensual touch she'd ever received, and yet it was so light. So unassuming. On her hand, no less. Not some other portion of her person that would be far more daring and damning. Her breath had caught in her lungs. She struggled to find words.

"Do you see, Eleanora?" he asked, voice low and silken when she failed to speak. "I'm on fire. I have been from the moment I first saw you."

That same fire he spoke of rushed through her.

She tugged her hand away at once. "You haven't a fever at all, Your Royal Highness. I must bid you good evening."

Eleanora turned to go.

"Please."

One word, and it stopped her as if it were a physical restraint. Because it radiated with raw emotion. Real emotion, she thought. Not his practiced flattery and seductive persuasion. Genuine emotion.

Fear with a hint of pain, tinged with something else.

Longing.

It was as if the mask he wore for the world had suddenly shattered and fallen away. Instead of playing the role of experienced seducer and devil-may-care rake, he was showing her the man hiding beneath the façade. A man of vulnerability.

And she found herself, despite every reason she should retreat at once, remaining. Relenting. Feeling things for this wicked prince she had no right to feel.

"Perhaps for a few minutes more," she allowed, feeling her way through the darkness to her chair.

"Do you think you might light a candle before you sit?" he asked with a boyish hope that further unsettled her. "I'd prefer to see your lovely countenance thoroughly illuminated."

She tamped down any yearning that his comment about her loveliness caused. She knew it was empty flattery anyway. Eleanora was more than aware of what she looked like, and she was no beauty. Not as her mother had been. But then, Mama had possessed a truly rare and original beauty, a vivacity that had shone from within and had attracted men to her the way a Siren lured sailors into rocky shoals.

Working her way through the shadows, she found a spill and lit it in the remnants of the dwindling fire before lighting the candles on a candelabra whose form she'd taken note of in the murkiness. She carried it to the table near his bedside, trying not to look at the way the golden light lovingly highlighted the elegant planes of his handsome face. He was a beautiful man. Even in his present state, looking exhausted, the bandage around his upper arm, he was the most breathtaking gentleman she'd ever beheld. A dangerous man, to be sure, and not just because of his undeniable looks, but because of a host of other reasons as well.

Not least of all the way he made her pulse flutter.

Averting her gaze, Eleanora resumed her seat at his side, taking care to primly smooth her skirts and gather her wits.

"Thank you."

His silken voice and gratitude had her gaze lifting to meet his against her better judgment. He was watching her intently, but his expression had changed. His jaw was clenched, and as he shifted in the bed, he made another grunt of pain.

"Allow me to fetch some laudanum for you, Your Royal Highness," she said hastily, thinking it would be better if she were occupied with a task and if he soon returned to the depths of slumber where he belonged so that she might make her escape.

If the princess and Mr. Tierney were to discover she'd been lingering here alone with Prince Ferdinando all night long, she had no notion of what they would say. It was entirely possible she might be dismissed, despite it having been the princess's idea for her to attend him earlier. If Eleanora had learned anything from her time beneath the thumb of the quality, it was that they were mercurial creatures.

"I've already told you that I don't want the damned poison," he grumbled.

But Eleanora ignored him. Rising from her chair and going to the tray where the laudanum was kept, she poured him a measure.

"It will help with the pain," she told him, returning to his bedside with the medicine and offering it.

He winced but quickly replaced the expression with a devilish smile. "Will you come closer, my dear? I fear I'm too weak to partake on my own. Sit here."

With his uninjured arm, he patted the area to his right.

The bed.

No, she would not—dared not—sit on the bed with him. Even in his weakened, wounded state, it would be ruinous.

Eleanora shook her head. "It wouldn't be proper."

"Do I look like I'm concerned with propriety, Eleanora?"

She wished he would cease calling her by her given name. The familiarity sent a frisson down her spine whenever he called her Eleanora in that deep, mellifluous voice of his.

She swallowed. "You may not be concerned with it, but I must be. As we've established, Your Royal Highness, I am dependent upon my reputation. Without it, none of the lords and ladies of the *ton* will allow me to guide their daughters."

"Yes, but none of them are about at the moment, are they?" he asked smoothly. "How would they know?"

"Of course not, but word travels quickly in circles such as these, as you must surely know. Servants gossip. Whispers carry."

She was reminding herself as much as him. But then, likely Prince Ferdinando had never needed to worry about scandal broth. He was celebrated for his reputation rather than scorned as a woman in his position would be. The unfairness of polite society was not lost upon her. She'd witnessed what it was capable of in the most brutal and exacting way. Her mother had paid the price for it. Eleanora had managed to escape relatively unscathed thus far. But she certainly hadn't managed that by lingering with libertines in their chambers.

"No one would dare gossip about you," the prince countered with a conviction he had no right to possess. "I'd never allow it."

A reluctant smile tugged at her lips, but she sternly chased it away. "That is most generous of you, Your Royal Highness. However, I don't see what control you could have over all polite society."

"I'm a prince." He patted the bed. "Sit here for a moment, won't you? The way you're hovering over me is giving me an aching head. I'm usually the tallest man in the room unless my brother is about."

His brother, the King of Varros. Eleanora had not met Prince Ferdinando's sibling, although word of his recent visit to London had left the *ton* positively abuzz. The king had been the subject of innumerable scandal sheets. But not in the way Prince Ferdinando had.

All the more reason for Eleanora to avoid sitting on the bed in dangerous proximity to him. Wounded or no, he was positively perilous to her reputation, her determination, her livelihood.

She offered him the laudanum. "I'm afraid I don't dare accept your offer, Your Royal Highness."

"Then I won't take the laudanum," he said stubbornly.

They stared at each other, at a stalemate. The prince grimaced, stirring as he sought a more comfortable position. He was suffering. Her inner urge to come to his aid surmounted all other concerns. Eleanora gingerly seated herself on the edge of the bed. Not where he had requested, but a safer distance.

Again, she extended the laudanum to him, the measure in its small tumbler. "Now will you take it?"

"You've convinced me." He accepted her offering, his fingers grazing hers as he did so. Holding her gaze, he brought the laudanum to his lips, making an expression of discontent as he swallowed the liquid down. "Bloody terrible stuff."

"It will ease the pain," she reassured him, taking the tumbler from him. "And allow you to rest. You need to regain your strength."

"On that we agree, my dear. I certainly do. Without my strength, I'll never be able to win your heart."

Once more, the mask of roguish charmer was firmly in place. She wondered what he used it to shield, beyond the pain of his injury. And then she promptly told herself it hardly mattered.

Eleanora struggled for a light tone. "How amusing you are, Your Royal Highness. I haven't a heart to win, but even if I had, I do not doubt you'd be the last person attempting to win it."

"Do you mean to say you haven't a heart at all, or that it cannot be won?" he asked, his tone curious.

"Of course I have a heart," she conceded. "However, it is

firmly out of consideration. I'm far too old for such nonsense."

"Old?" He arched a golden brow, his blue gaze sweeping over her form in a thorough way that made her flush. "You couldn't be more than five-and-twenty. Hardly ancient."

"I'm eight-and-twenty," she countered primly. "Quite on the shelf."

"Young enough to come off the shelf, certainly," he observed. "With the proper motivation, of course."

She understood the subtle suggestion in his voice all too well, along with the way he looked at her. It was the look a wicked rake bestowed upon his prey. But Eleanora had no intention of allowing herself to fall beneath this handsome prince's spell.

"I'm comfortable as I am, Your Royal Highness," she said.

"Are you, truly?" he asked shrewdly. "You don't seem to be the sort of woman content to blend in with the shadows. To help others shine like diamonds of the first water while hiding yourself in dowdy gowns and dreadful fichus and caps."

His words startled her. Disturbed her. What did he see in her that no one else had? How had she given herself away?

He was disturbingly close to the truth. Once, she hadn't been content to hide herself. But she needed to do so now, for her own survival.

"I enjoy helping others," she told him curtly. "As you can see by my unwise presence at your sickbed."

"You're here because you want to be."

His tone was knowing. And more alarming still was that he was not wrong with his assertion. She *did* want to be here. She was enjoying his company. She liked the way he flirted with her. Liked the way he made her feel. Old feelings, dangerous feelings, feelings she couldn't afford to indulge in. And yet, she remained perched on the edge of his bed, a bird prepared for flight, her wings tied by her own wayward inclinations.

"There are many other places I would rather be," she countered firmly.

His eyes dropped to her lips before rising again. "Name them."

That look had her so flustered that she had quite lost the thread of their conversation. Her heart beat rapidly, new warmth creeping through her. The way he examined her—it was not just scandalous. It was intoxicating too.

"As I thought," he said, a note of smugness entering his voice.

She blinked, realizing he had soundly routed her. Eleanora tried to summon up places she would rather be.

"A boat," she blurted.

"A boat." He rubbed the hand from his uninjured arm slowly along his jaw. "What sort of boat?"

She hadn't thought that one through.

"The sort that travels over the water."

Oh heavens, this was going poorly. He had her quite flustered, the combination of his nearness and regard, coupled with the fact that she was seated on his bed and he wasn't even wearing a shirt beneath the counterpane...

No, she mustn't think about the shocking expanse of shoulders and chest revealed to her whenever he shifted beneath the bedclothes. He was only wearing half a dressing gown. She'd done her best not to acknowledge it, but the lateness of the hour, the intimate tone of his voice... It was all swirling together into one unending sea that was steadily rising and threatening to drown her.

"Is that not, by definition, *all* boats, Eleanora?" he asked, his lips twitching.

He was finding her discomfiture amusing, the scoundrel.

"Your Royal Highness is, of course, correct," she said sweetly, forcing a smile.

"I begin to think you are finding yourself growing fond of me against your will, my dear," he said, his mouth tipping up at one corner into a half smile that stole her breath. "You're enjoying yourself. Admit it."

She was. And how hideous of him not just to realize it, but give voice to it.

"I'm merely pleased to see that you're doing so well after suffering a grievous wound and losing so much blood," she said, which was also true.

He may have been a conscienceless seducer and the most handsome man she'd ever seen, but that didn't mean she wanted any harm to befall him. She had been terribly worried for him. Was still worried, if she were honest with herself. There was still ample time and opportunity for an infection to set in.

"Your tender feelings for me are a balm to my heart," he said with a courtly air.

He was ridiculous. He made her want to smile. He made her want to take him gently in her arms. He made her want to kiss him and fall under his maddening spell and cast her future aside for just one night with him.

And she hated him for that. For the way he seemed to sense her weaknesses with such ease, toying with her, charming her, flirting with her. Leading her ever closer to ruin.

"You should get some rest now, Your Royal Highness," she said, summoning what remained of her ability to resist his potent allure as she rose. "The laudanum ought to do its work."

His eyelids appeared to be growing heavier as the medicine took effect once more.

"I wish you wouldn't go."

"I must," she forced herself to say, dipping into a curtsy.

"Eleanora?"

Her gaze tangled with his. "Yes, Your Royal Highness?"

A faint smile curved his lips as thick gold lashes swept lower over sky-blue eyes. "Thank you."

She took her leave from the room before she was further tempted to linger.

CHAPTER 6

"*H*ave you been threatened, either recently or at any time in the past?"

Nando glared at Archer Tierney, thinking that if this interrogation was to continue, he'd require either the calming presence of Eleanora or another dose of laudanum. The hour was far too early, and he'd spent the torturous night unable to sleep, his arm paining him unmercifully.

"No," he answered grudgingly.

Tierney's eyes narrowed. "No missives, no angry letters, no furious husbands?"

Damn it. His reputation apparently preceded him, even in London.

"Undoubtedly there are any number of furious husbands," he drawled, feigning boredom.

There had been that ruddy-faced earl—Levering—who had caught Nando with his adventurous countess... Vague recollections of the lady in question on her knees before him when the chamber door had opened swirled, but Nando banished them swiftly. The irate earl had challenged him to a duel, but Maxim had bribed the cuckolded husband, and the entire incident had been forgotten, if not forgiven.

"Do you have any enemies?" Tierney asked next, using a no-nonsense tone Nando couldn't help but feel was better reserved for naughty children.

And whilst Nando was unassailably naughty and had been for the entirety of his misbegotten life, he was no child.

"I reckon that depends on one's definition of the word," he said, needling the man just because he could.

Yes, Nando was reliant upon Tierney's hospitality. However, he also didn't like being questioned so soundly when he was exhausted, weak, and in pain. Even his shimmering cloud had long since faded, leaving him mired on the bed with no one, save Bruno and Tierney to attend him.

Both were a far cry from the delectable Eleanora.

He wanted her back.

He *would* have her back. Perhaps he had to throw another object to get his way. He wasn't above further destruction.

"My definition is someone who hates you enough to shoot you," Tierney said, his voice as grim as his expression. "Do you have any enemies of that sort?"

"I appreciate your efforts on my behalf, Tierney. Truly, I do. But can you not simply set a Bow Street Runner on it? I'm reasonably certain the entire affair was a dreadful mistake."

"A mistake?"

"An error," Nando elaborated, as if Tierney didn't understand.

All the better to nettle him.

"I'm aware of the meaning of the word." Tierney's tone was pointed. "I was merely baffled that you would consider being shot in the street a mistake. Bullets don't ordinarily fly through Mayfair. Moreover, you could have been killed."

Nando preferred not to think about that.

"An unpleasant thought," he said, something else occurring to him suddenly. "I do hope you haven't sent word to my brother about this little bit of nonsense."

He wasn't certain that Tierney would have the means of reaching Maxim, but his wife, Princess Anastasia, certainly would. And Nando wasn't in the mood for tongue-lashings from his stern, formidable older brother. He'd had enough of those to last a lifetime already.

Also, he didn't want Maxim to worry. His brother deserved happiness. He'd lost his first wife in brutal fashion during the war, and he was blissfully content with his new queen. Nando would be damned before he would be the one to encroach on their much-deserved idyll. Indeed, that was partially why he'd left Varros for London.

"I won't have to send word to him," Tierney was saying now. "When a royal prince is nearly assassinated in the street, the newspapers tend to report on such matters."

Assassinate is such a strong, misleading word," Nando said with a wave of his good hand. "I suffered a mere scratch. Nothing more. Only look at how hale and hearty I am."

"The bullet that grazed your arm was far more than a scratch." Tierney frowned. "You're fortunate it avoided muscle and bone. A few steps in the other direction, and your injury would have been far more grievous. Indeed, I daresay you wouldn't be lying here attempting to dismiss my inquiries."

Tierney was an intelligent man and cunning as well. Nando respected him for it, even if it was proving irritating in the moment.

"I'm doing nothing of the sort. But I confess, I'm rather weary. Do you think we might carry on this conversation later?"

Never would be preferable. But Nando kept that to himself. Archer Tierney was like a terrier with a bone.

"When would be a more appropriate time for Your Royal Highness to consider that you were nearly murdered?" Tierney asked, his voice dripping with sarcasm.

"Why are you so concerned about what happened to me?" Nando asked, curious.

It wasn't as if the two of them were friends. He'd rather had the impression that Tierney suffered his presence for the sake of Princess Anastasia. Nando hadn't minded. He wasn't certain he liked the Englishman, and he hadn't come to England to make friends. He'd come to distract himself and get lost in a sea of petticoats. And he'd managed to accomplish both objectives.

Except now, he didn't want a sea of petticoats. He only wanted one particular set. At least, until he had her. Nando had no doubt that after he assuaged the intense lust he possessed for the icy Eleanora, his voracious appetites would once more return.

"Because I need to make certain my wife isn't in danger," Tierney answered solemnly. "I would give my life for hers. When a man is shot in the street outside my town house, I'm left with no option, save finding out who committed the act and why, so that I can be assured it won't happen again. If someone is daring enough to shoot at a royal prince in daylight where anyone can see him, he's not just foolhardy and reckless, he is dangerous. I need to know who did this. It may be related to enemies of Boritania or enemies of Varros. Either way, no one will be truly safe until we find the culprit."

Blast.

Nando didn't want to think about any of that just now. He wanted to bask in Eleanora's attentions and forget the outside world existed. But Tierney wasn't wrong about what he'd just said. Someone *had* been daring and brazen enough to attempt to end him in the midst of the day on a busy

Mayfair street. He ought to make that his primary concern and not the seduction of Miss Eleanora Brett. How boring.

He sighed, relenting. This business of his would-be assassin was most disagreeable.

"I understand your concern, Tierney." Nando looked to Bruno, who was silently standing sentinel at the door, his countenance severe and unsmiling. "Have you learned anything?"

"I have some men investigating, Your Royal Highness," Bruno offered. "Thus far, the only thing they have to report is a woman who made haste in fleeing. It's possible she was frightened by the firing of the pistol and commotion, but we have yet to discover who she was so that we might make inquiries."

"Have you recently bedded any murderesses, Your Royal Highness?" Tierney asked.

Deus. Nando thought about the women he'd flirted with and seduced since his arrival in London. Was it possible that he had somehow offended one of them? Each woman had been more than satisfied. He was a generous lover, a skilled lover. He knew how to please a woman. No woman left his bed—or hers, or the carriage, or the wall, or the table, or even the garden path—unsatisfied. He made certain of it.

"When I part with my lovers, it is always on excellent terms," he said.

But was it? There had been some lovers, certainly, who had wanted far more from him than he had been willing or able to give. Still, none of his lovers had been furious with him, and none of them was the sort of woman who would try to kill him.

Were they?

"Excellent terms for you, no doubt," Tierney drawled as if reading Nando's mind. "But what about for them? Have none of your paramours been upset that you've ended your liaisons with them?"

There had been a rather furious viscountess, now that he thought upon it. She'd been a red-haired beauty with generous breasts. He couldn't recall her name. Or had she been a duchess? She had thrown a vase at his head when he'd ducked out of her bedroom just after dawn.

"Who is she?" Tierney asked before Nando could offer a response.

He narrowed his eyes at the man. "You have an alarmingly uncanny ability to know what I'm thinking before I say it."

Tierney gave him a rare grin. "Blame it on my days as a spy for the Crown. Now tell me, what is her name?"

Nando winced. "I'm afraid I can't recall."

No matter how much he tried, he couldn't summon a name to go with the lovely face. In fact, he wasn't even certain he could remember her face. Her breasts, however, had been quite memorable. If she were to show him her ample assets once again, he would recognize her instantly.

"So many conquests that you can't recall their names, Your Royal Highness?" Tierney guessed, his voice sharp with disapproval.

"Perhaps," he allowed, shame creeping over him. "I may have been inebriated at the time."

Very likely, he had been. His appetite for debauchery had known no ends since he had aimlessly drifted back to England like an autumn leaf blown from a tree. He had nowhere to belong, no one to belong to. His own kingdom didn't need him, and his protective, commanding older brother had Tansy now. With the birth of his beloved nephew, Nando was no longer even next in line to the throne. He was, effectively, utterly useless.

"I can assemble a list for Your Royal Highness to peruse," Tierney suggested. "Doing so may spark your memory."

"I find it doubtful that a woman would want me to meet my untimely demise," Nando said.

"Women are capable of treachery every bit as much as men are," Tierney countered. "Trust me on that matter."

"Fair enough." Nando sighed again. "I will do my utmost to recall her name. She may have been a countess, however. Of course, there was also that delightful evening when I was accompanied by both a marchioness and a baroness."

"The names of every titled woman in London, then," Tierney said dourly.

"I've also made the acquaintance of several lovely goddesses at a particular establishment," Nando admitted wryly.

Truly, if it was a woman who had shot him, then discovering which of his lovers was the one responsible might well prove a Sisyphean feat.

"Bloody hell," Tierney muttered.

"Bruno," Nando called out to his bodyguard. "Would you be capable of compiling a list of my recent…friends?"

Bruno nodded. "Of course, Your Royal Highness."

That was excellent. Bruno was dutiful in all tasks, and he likely knew the names of Nando's recent conquests better than he did.

"We will compare our lists and reconvene," Tierney said, rising from his chair at last. "For now, you should rest so that you can heal, Your Royal Highness."

Nando didn't want to rest. He wanted Eleanora. But he also didn't want to cause any problems for her. She was currently guided by the thoroughly wrongheaded notion that she needed her position. He would rectify that presently. As soon as he was no longer an invalid, dash it all.

"Fear not," he told his reluctant host. "I'll be gone soon enough. I'm already feeling stronger."

Of course, he had no intention of healing too quickly. He was enjoying the proximity to Miss Brett far too much.

Tierney raised a brow. "I'm pleased to hear it, Your Royal Highness. You are welcome to take all the time you need."

The invitation sounded almost as if it had been torn from his reluctant host.

Nando grinned. "That sounded rather pained."

"It was. To be perfectly blunt, you're trouble, Your Royal Highness. However, I'll do anything my lovely wife asks of me, and she has asked that I keep you here until you're well enough to leave for the sake of her friend, the queen."

Nando hadn't been wrong about his suspicions, then. Archer Tierney didn't like him. Hardly a disappointing discovery. Nando didn't particularly like the other man either. Tierney was far too perceptive and clever.

"I'm indebted to Her Royal Highness," Nando said smoothly.

Which only made Tierney pin him with a glare. "If you attempt to seduce my wife, there will be another attempt on your life. However, I'm a far better marksman. I wouldn't miss."

Nando chuckled. "Have no fear, Tierney. Your wife is perfectly safe from me."

It was another member of the man's household that he wanted. And Nando fully intended to have her.

Soon.

∾

ELEANORA RETURNED from a trip to the modiste with her charges utterly exhausted. Her feet ached. Her back ached. And her head ached. The twins were a whirlwind of garrulousness. Princess Emmaline had insisted upon wearing trousers for the excursion, which she had done despite

Eleanora's firm opposition. The shocked stares and horrified whispers they had endured had made her wither inside. But outwardly, she had maintained her serene poise, quite as if she weren't accompanying a hoyden who refused to take propriety into account when she dressed.

She handed off her wrap, gloves, and hat to a diligent servant and waited as her charges did the same.

At least Annalise had worn a lovely sprigged-muslin gown, Eleanora thought as she watched the less rebellious of the twins removing her bonnet. To their credit, the attending servants didn't even bat an eyelash at Princess Emmaline's trousers. The latter was likely down to the princess wearing them with alarming regularity for the entire time Eleanora had been in residence.

She had a great deal of work ahead of her if she wanted to polish the tarnished reputations of the princesses. They were wayward, they were loud, and they were rebellious. All of which was to be understood, given the repressive nature of their upbringing.

Their father had gone mad, leaving their depraved tyrant of an uncle to usurp the throne. He'd had the former queen put to death, and the young princesses had come of age under their uncle's harsh rule. At last freed of the despot, they were now like caged birds who had suddenly been allowed to roam the world beyond the gilded bars that had been keeping them.

Eleanora couldn't blame them for the unabashed joy they found at their new liberty. However, she hadn't been hired to allow them to run roughshod over polite society and its many rules. Rather, she had been hired specifically so that she might persuade the princesses to conform to propriety. To do what the *ton* expected of them. To dress properly, to eschew scandal, to speak and dance and even walk with elegant grace.

It was the same role she'd taken on many times before, and quite the opposite of the one she had once played, what seemed a lifetime ago now. Eleanora had always found a sense of accomplishment in her duties. Strange that today, every minute of the passing hours had felt hollow and meaningless. She refused to believe it had anything to do with the handsome, wounded prince she had attended well into the darkest depths of the evening the night before.

"Pray tell me that is the end of our lessons for today, Miss Brett," Princess Emmaline said as Eleanora began shepherding her charges from the entryway.

If only.

"I'm afraid we must also attend to your dancing," she answered with a serene smile she didn't feel.

It was her obligation to pretend as if she delighted in every moment of her duties. Even if she didn't.

The princess wrinkled her nose, quite as if she'd scented something dreadful. "Dancing?"

"Surely not more dancing today," Princess Annalise added in a more polite manner. "Perhaps it might wait for tomorrow. My sister and I are both sufficiently taxed from our outing to the modiste."

Eleanora knew the feeling. However, there was an important ball growing ever nearer, and Princess Anastasia had been firm on the need to teach her sisters the steps so held dear by the fashionable set in London. Apparently, their uncle had not seen fit to allow their dancing master to teach them anything other than traditional Boritanian steps. The result had been disastrous. At least, according to Princess Anastasia. The princesses had learned the waltz and a handful of dances here in London, but their movements were far from refined, assured, and elegant.

"I'm sure you are quite tired," Eleanora allowed softly. "However, the ball honoring your family is but a few weeks away. You will wish to be as prepared as possible, will you not?"

"You mean to say that *our sister* would have us as prepared as possible," Emmaline countered as they moved to the music room, where there was sufficient space for Eleanora to play the pianoforte and the princesses to master their steps. "Staying in London is hardly what either of us wishes to do. Learning the steps seems a moot point when we'll be returning to our home in Boritania soon enough. Is that not right, Annalise?"

Princess Annalise looked torn as she considered her response. "Perhaps we might remain, at least until the Season's end."

Emmaline made a dismissive sound. "Pfft. You only wish to remain for the Season because of the Duke of Lockhart."

The Duke of Lockhart? Alarm settled over Eleanora, for the duke's reputation was as black as Prince Ferdinando's.

She cast a concerned, searching glance in Princess Annalise's direction. "I have yet to see the Duke of Lockhart at a proper social event this Season. Have the two of you been introduced?"

There was a flash of something in the princess's eyes, there and gone before Eleanora could decipher what it was. "Of course not. My sister is being silly."

Eleanora studied the princess, wondering if it was possible that the twin she'd believed least likely to cause trouble was secretly the most capable of causing it. Because the Duke of Lockhart was most certainly not a suitable match. The rumors swirling around him were nothing short of shocking.

"You would do best to keep your distance from the duke, Your Royal Highness," Eleanora cautioned sternly, worry for her charge taking root. "He is a dangerous man."

"He doesn't look dangerous," Princess Annalise said,

doing nothing to ameliorate the fears growing within Eleanora.

An innocent like the princess would be no match for a depraved man like the Duke of Lockhart.

"The most dangerous ones never do. Pray trust my judgment on the matter, Your Royal Highness," she urged.

"Your judgment is always impeccable, Miss Brett," Princess Annalise said with an innocent smile.

No, her judgment was dreadful, which was why she had spent half the evening before in the presence of one of the most notorious libertines alive, Eleanora thought grimly. But in this instance, she was not wrong about Lockhart, and Princess Annalise would do well to stay far, far from the man. He would devour a naïve girl like her without compunction, debauch her, and then leave her. The man had no soul, and his depravity knew no bounds.

"Thank you, Your Royal Highness," she managed, hoping that the princess was not merely saying what she believed Eleanora wanted to hear and that she was truly taking her warnings to heart.

Princess Annalise's future depended on it. But not just hers—Eleanora's did as well. She needed to leave each circumstance with an irreproachable record of success. Anything less would jeopardize what she had worked so diligently to build these last few years.

"Miss Brett?"

The voice of her employer, Princess Anastasia, intruded upon Eleanora's thoughts. She looked over her shoulder to find the princess hastening down the hall in their wake. Her expression was one of pinched consternation, and for a moment, Eleanora's stomach felt as if it were upended. Had she done something to displease the princess? Or worse, had someone discovered she had inadvertently fallen asleep in Prince Ferdinando's chamber last night?

"Your Royal Highness," she greeted demurely, dipping into a curtsy in deference, hoping she only exuded calm poise and none of the guilty fear plaguing her.

"Might I have a word with you?" Princess Anastasia asked.

"Of course." Eleanora presumed the request meant that they ought to leave the earshot of the younger twin princesses. "Where would you prefer to have it, Your Royal Highness?"

"The drawing room shall do nicely. Annalise and Emmaline, why do you not retire to your rooms?" Princess Anastasia requested, giving her sisters a pointed look.

"But we were going to practice our dancing," Princess Annalise objected, pouting.

"You may practice that later," Princess Anastasia said. "Now, run along, the two of you. There are some matters that I must attend with Miss Brett."

"In private?" Princess Emmaline asked with a knowing grin. "If you're going to be speaking about us, it is only fair that we remain."

The princess's stubborn nature once more emerged. Eleanora wasn't surprised.

"What I have to speak with Miss Brett about doesn't concern either of you," Princess Anastasia countered firmly, doing nothing to ameliorate the concern and dread tightening Eleanora's belly.

"Then whatever can it be about?" Princess Annalise wondered aloud.

Princess Emmaline smirked. "Likely about Nando."

Nando.

Eleanora didn't miss the familiarity implied in the princess's use of the prince's given name. And not just his full given name, but the shorter version he preferred. The very name he had so recently been requesting Eleanora call him by. The sharp pang of jealousy tearing through her in that moment was unwanted and foolish, but it was beyond her control.

"How is he faring today?" Princess Annalise wanted to know.

"Fortunately, the prince is recuperating well," Princess Anastasia said. "But I've had quite enough questioning for now, if you please. I wish to speak with Miss Brett. *Alone.*"

Princess Emmaline harrumphed. "You're not our mother, Stasia, no matter how much you like to act as if you are."

"I could never replace her," Princess Anastasia said sadly, softly. "But it's my duty as your older sister to watch over you. Our mother would have wanted that."

Princess Emmaline's countenance instantly crumpled. "I'm sorry for mentioning her. I shouldn't have done so."

"I wish we remembered her better than we do," Princess Annalise added, her tone wistful.

Their older sister's eyes shone with unshed tears, her smile bittersweet as she clearly struggled to suppress her emotions. Eleanora felt as if she were intruding upon a private family moment. She would have excused herself had not Princess Anastasia requested an audience with her. As it was, she held her tongue, stepping away to a discreet distance, allowing the sisters the opportunity to bond over their grief. Her heart broke for the three of them.

Eleanora knew how difficult and painful it was to lose one's mother. Mama's death had left a gaping hole in her life that would never be fully healed, although time and distance had done their best to blunt the anguish.

Princess Anastasia sniffed, still battling for control over her composure. "Please, sisters. Allow me a few moments of privacy with Miss Brett now."

At last, the younger princesses took their leave, subdued.

Eleanora followed her employer to the drawing room,

waiting patiently as Princess Anastasia secured the door and ventured to the seating area.

"Please sit, Miss Brett," she invited.

Eleanora did so, her mind churning. Would this be the moment that all her hopes would be ground into a thousand tiny, jagged shards? Was she about to descend headlong into ruin, just as her mother before her had done?

Princess Anastasia occupied a Grecian couch, turning to Eleanora with a heavy sigh. "We've received an offer for Annalise's hand today."

That wasn't what Eleanora had been expecting.

Her spine straightened, and she was instantly both relieved and on her guard. "Oh, Your Royal Highness? I hadn't realized the princess possessed any suitors so keen upon coming up to scratch just yet."

"Nor had I." The princess paused, wincing. "The suitor in question is the Duke of Lockhart."

The revelation made Eleanora certain that something indeed was afoot between Princess Annalise and the duke. But she was keenly aware that such a circumstance could only reflect upon her poorly.

"Are you acquainted with His Grace?" she asked gingerly.

Princess Anastasia's expression turned pinched. "Naturally not. However, his reputation is notorious enough that even someone relatively new to the *ton* such as myself is more than aware of it. I cannot fathom allowing my precious sister to make such a match. I was hoping you might offer some insight."

Eleanora well understood the princess's dilemma.

She nodded. "Although Lockhart is a duke, his reputation is quite dire. In your circumstances, Your Royal Highness, I, too, would be hesitant to encourage Princess Annalise to make such a misalliance."

"As I thought. There are rumors swirling about Lockhart…" Princess Anastasia's words trailed away.

Eleanora was more than aware of the rumors. Lockhart's duchess had died under mysterious circumstances. Gossips suggested the duke was responsible and that she had been murdered. A shiver went down her spine at the notion.

"I have heard the rumors as well. If there is any grain of truth to them, then by marrying the Duke of Lockhart, Princess Annalise would be in grave danger," she said grimly.

The princess sighed heavily. "And after what my sisters have so recently escaped in Boritania under our uncle's spurious rule, I would never again place either of them in harm. Thank you for your wise counsel, Miss Brett. I can always count on your excellent knowledge of the *ton*. Your advice is indispensable. I don't know what I would do without you."

Eleanora smiled, pleased to know the princess considered her such a vital part of the household. Her circumstances were always tenuous at best, but Princess Anastasia and Mr. Tierney were the kindest employers she had yet known. They listened to her opinions, treated her with the utmost respect, and best of all, Mr. Tierney was madly in love with his wife. Eleanora didn't have to contend with wandering eyes or hands, and it was a welcome relief. Indeed, she felt, for the first time in as long as she could recall, comfortable.

Which was why she was also fearful that at any moment this idyll might end. Experience suggested it would.

"You need not thank me, Your Royal Highness," she said modestly. "I am merely performing the duty you have hired me for. It is my honor to attend Princess Emmaline and Princess Annalise and to act as a guide in whatever capacity I may offer."

"I do wish you might call me Stasia," the princess said wistfully.

It was not the first time the princess had made such a request. But Eleanora was keenly aware of the vast disparity in their social standings. And she had come to understand that it was of the utmost importance that she refrain from becoming too friendly with her employers. The invisible division between them must remain.

"You honor me, Your Royal Highness, but I dare not," she demurred, trying to keep her voice gentle.

"Of course not. You are a paragon of virtue, Miss Brett." Princess Anastasia chuckled, standing. "Quite unlike myself. I applaud you for it. And now, I suppose I must let you retire to your chamber for a spot of rest after your shopping expedition with my sisters."

Eleanora rose as well, relieved by the princess's understanding.

She offered a curtsy. "Thank you, Your Royal Highness."

But as Eleanora took her leave of the drawing room and ascended the stairs, it wasn't her own chamber she found herself visiting. Her feet, quite of their own accord, took her to another's.

CHAPTER 7

*N*ando was beginning to despair that he had truly died the day he'd been wounded, and that, given his sinful nature and depraved past, he'd been consigned to his fate—a hell consisting of lying in bed like an invalid, presided over by a scowling Bruno and the occasional maidservant who delivered him trays of broth and gruel.

It was, in a word, mind-numbingly horrid.

No, he reckoned that was two words.

Anyway, he was weary unto death of looking at Bruno and the maid, who rather resembled a mouse in both her countenance and her bearing and refused to meet his eye when she delivered the slop he was meant to eat.

He had been lying abed long enough.

Grimly, Nando threw back the bedclothes with his uninjured arm and swung his legs to the side. He was wearing a dressing gown—not for his sake, but for that of the mousy maid—and nothing else. But he didn't give a damn. Nude was his preferred state, and he didn't care if the damned maid arrived with the next tray of swill and the sight of his bare feet and calves made her swoon. He was getting out of this cursed bed.

Now.

Bruno, as predicted, hastened to his side, his expression one of stark worry. "Your Royal Highness, you must rest. What are you doing?"

"What does it look like I'm doing?" he grumbled, feeling rather like a raging bull who had been made to remain still and silent in a barn. "I'm standing up."

"But your wound."

"I need to take a piss," he snapped. "Would you like to hold my prick whilst I do it?"

Bruno paled. "O-of course not, Your Royal Highness. That is, unless Your Royal Highness would prefer me to do so?"

"Deus," Nando grumbled. "No. Get out of my way and leave me in peace to do what I must."

Bruno, looking crestfallen, nodded. "It is my fault you were wounded, Your Royal Highness. If I had but been more vigilant, none of this would have happened."

He took pity on the mammoth man, who looked as impossibly out of place in this gilded and overwrought chamber as Nando felt. "The fault lies in whoever shot me, Bruno. But I still wish to be alone. Go to the kitchens while you wait and see if you can procure me something other than the vile broth that little mouse has been delivering to me, won't you?"

Bruno nodded, tugged at his forelock in a show of respect, and bowed before hastily taking his leave of the chamber.

Nando knew a moment of guilt for his vulgarity and animosity. But it quickly faded when he was reminded of how his bodyguard had conspired with Tierney to keep him trapped here under the guise of healing. The sole reason he had allowed himself to linger after it had become apparent that he wouldn't die after all—much to the dismay of the bastard who'd shot him, no doubt—was because he wanted to see more of Eleanora. But his delectable spinster hadn't appeared since she had slipped from his room in the midst of the night. And he was rather cross with her for staying away. Cross with anyone responsible for keeping her from him.

That included bloody Bruno.

His wound ached and burned and throbbed as he made his way to the screen and the awaiting chamber pot across the room. Thus far, he had been making use of the bowl by his bed whenever he had a moment's privacy. But he was tired of remaining abed. He'd been shot in the arm, damn it, not in one of his legs. He was alive, and the wound had yet to fester. If he wasn't going to be graced with the privilege of Eleanora Brett's company, then there was no reason for him to remain here at Tierney's town house.

Nando relieved himself and completed some hasty ablutions, thinking it a mercy that he'd been shot in the opposite arm of his dominant hand. Otherwise, he might well have required Bruno's aid in holding his cock. And how lowering that would have been.

He had just finished carefully blotting his face with a cloth single-handedly when the door to his room opened and closed beyond the privacy screen.

"Damn it, Bruno," he growled. "I thought I told you to be gone. Why have you already returned?"

"Why are you out of bed?"

The crisp, feminine demand that reached him decidedly did not belong to Bruno. And Nando would recognize it anywhere. He dropped the cloth and stepped around the privacy screen, warmth already sweeping over him.

"Eleanora," he greeted, offering her as elegant of a bow as he could muster, given the state of his wounded arm.

As it was, the action left him grimacing as agony tore through him when he tested his stitches. He hoped she would be polite enough not to comment upon it.

"You are in pain," she said, instantly dashing his misplaced optimism, her lips tightening into a thin line of disapproval. "What are you doing out of bed so soon, Your Royal Highness?"

Had he expected anything less than her taking him to task?

If he had, he ought to be ashamed of himself. But her cold tone and stiff shoulders had his cock waking up for the first time since his wounding, and that pleased him greatly—he hadn't lost his voracious appetite for the fairer sex. Not, of course, that the confirmation pleased him as greatly as the sight of her in his chamber did. For nothing could compare.

She was *here*.

And she was lovely.

And he wanted her more than ever.

Best of all, she hadn't come because he'd demanded it of her. Rather, she must have ventured to him of her own free will.

Like a seasoned general watching his enemy's flank disintegrate before him, Nando seized the advantage, charging.

"Perhaps you might be willing to tuck me back in," he suggested smoothly.

Pink washed over her cheekbones, and he didn't miss the way her gaze dropped, taking in his dishabille. "Your Royal Highness, you are utterly without compunction."

He grinned. "I'm without anything that keeps me from what I want most."

She stared at him, for once apparently having been left speechless. Nando might have reveled in the brief victory, but a sudden, brilliant idea had occurred to him. A means of keeping Eleanora close even after he left this town house.

She still hovered hesitantly at the door, as if she would flee at the slightest provocation. He couldn't have that.

Nando moved toward her slowly, trying to make his actions appear nonchalant rather than calculated. In truth, he was a hunter stalking his prey, each footfall on the rich Aubusson bringing him nearer to his quarry.

"I should take my leave," she muttered, almost to herself.

And yet, she didn't move.

"Nonsense," he countered softly. "You should remain precisely where you are. I'm pleased you've come to me, my dear."

"I merely wished to inquire after your recuperation," she said, fingers twisting in the fall of her muslin skirts at her sides in an obvious show of her inner turmoil. "Where is Mr. Dimitrius?"

Mr. Dimitrius. For a moment, Nando didn't know who the deuce she was speaking of, until he realized Bruno's surname was Dimitrius.

"I sent him to the kitchens to fetch me something reasonable to eat," he explained, skirting a table as he approached her. "I've been given nothing more than bone broth and gruel. I feel like a prisoner."

She pursed her lips. "Surely Her Royal Highness and Mr. Tierney have instructed the servants to follow the directions of the physician who attended you."

"Perhaps," he allowed, stopping almost an arm's length from her, near enough to catch the faintest hint of her scent. "But I have no wish to starve to death. If I'm to heal, I require sustenance."

And you, preferably riding me.

But he didn't say that aloud. He had no wish for Miss Brett to run screaming into the hall.

Her eyes narrowed, almost as if she had heard the wicked, unspoken addition. "Nonetheless, I am certain you should be resting and eating what the doctor has ordered for you. You are a dreadful patient, Your Royal Highness."

"I truly am dreadful, Eleanora. You're not mistaken. However, I'm famished. Starving. My appetite requires sating."

Yes, he was villain enough to be speaking of two different appetites at once. But he was also cunning enough to know that she could find no fault in the information he had just imparted.

The color on her cheeks deepened, but the rigidness from her posture didn't relent. "How kind, then, of Mr. Dimitrius to fetch you sustenance. I'm pleased to see you are healing well, Your Royal Highness. I bid you good evening."

Did she truly think he would allow her to leave him so quickly? Nando would have been amused had he not been so determined to keep her precisely where she was.

He strode nearer, reaching her in time to lay a flattened palm on the door above her head using his uninjured arm. "Don't go with such haste."

She spun about, eyes wide and startled, her back pressed to the door. "Your Royal Highness!"

He had shocked her. He didn't care.

"I'd like to make you an offer," Nando said smoothly, disregarding her surprise.

He was determined to implement the notion that had seized him in its relentless grip.

Her golden lashes fluttered over her icy eyes for a moment, the sole indication that his words had an effect on her sangfroid.

"I won't be your mistress, Your Royal Highness," she said coolly.

Ah, yes. For all the games she played with him, his Eleanora knew what he wanted from her. It was elemental.

Something deeper and larger than the both of them. Inevitable, too.

But Nando smiled, ignoring the searing pain in his wounded arm, which paled in comparison to the thwarted lust boiling in his blood. "Eleanora, you wound me. I have a proper circumstance in mind for you. Not something scandalous."

He couldn't be certain if it was their proximity—his body almost aligned to hers—or that he had been on his feet for longer than he had since being shot that was dizzying him. But he decided he didn't give a damn.

"What manner of circumstance could you possibly have to offer me, Your Royal Highness?" she asked, her tone skeptical.

"You can teach me how to dance and be proper."

A blatant lie. No doubt they both knew it. But Nando was hoping she might fool herself into accepting the temptation he offered.

Her chin tipped up. "You already know how to dance quite elegantly, and as for the latter, I harbor a strong suspicion that it is an unattainable feat."

She wasn't wrong. Nando had no intention of being proper. Especially not in her presence.

He removed his palm from the door and waved his hand. "Something else, then. What is Tierney paying you? I'll offer you triple the sum."

"Your Royal Highness, even if I were inclined to accept your offer, which I most assuredly am not, leaving my current employer in the midst of my duties would reflect poorly upon me. My charges require my further aid, and I would never abandon them to take on a dubious role in your household."

Well, that was rather a bruising and crushing refusal. But Nando didn't expect anything less from her. A renewed determination to make her his roared forth within him. He would simply have to find the means of flouting her stern opposition to himself.

"I never said that you needed to abandon your present post," he told her mildly. "You may complete your duties first. I have it on good authority that Tierney is a gentleman one shouldn't cross, and having already been shot once, I have no desire to suffer a second such wounding."

This was only partially true, and he promptly banished the minuscule shards of conscience that attempted to ruin his plans.

"I hardly think Mr. Tierney would do you violence, Your Royal Highness. But while I thank you for the generous proposal, my answer must be a firm and resounding no."

Damn her resolve.

He wanted to kiss it right out of her. But he was no neophyte to seduction. He knew that he had to proceed at her pace. Which was to say with excruciating torpor.

"Why must it be?" he asked. "I'm a wealthy man. Hideously so. You might find yourself set up comfortably for the rest of your life after accepting my offer."

Particularly after he managed to secure what he wanted from her. Nando was a generous man in all things. In his estimation, pleasure and wealth were best enjoyed with others. He had no reservations about dispersing both. He wanted to shower Eleanora in jewels and pleasure her until she was mindless.

He wanted her naked in his bed and covered in diamonds and rubies and sapphires.

Best not to reveal that part of his plans to her just yet, however.

"I don't require your largesse, Your Royal Highness."

"Of course you don't require it. But what one requires

and what one *wants* are two entirely different birds, are they not?"

He didn't miss the flare of awareness in her eyes. She was no naïve innocent, even if she wasn't a seasoned woman of experience as he had oft preferred in his women. She knew what he was implying quite well. And despite herself, she was tempted.

Watching Eleanora Brett fall would be the most potent aphrodisiac of his admittedly dissolute life. Of that, Nando had no doubt.

But she wasn't there yet.

He watched as she summoned her icy reserve as if it were a suit of armor she could don and prepare for battle. Her shoulders straightened. Her lips firmed into a thin, grim line. Her spine stiffened with renewed resistance.

"I concern myself with what I require. Frivolous cares are for those with the liberty of basking in them."

It was a pointed little barb. But it bounced off Nando. She could insult him all she liked. He was still going to woo her and win her. And bed her. As many times as he could until the poison of desiring Miss Eleanora Brett was out of his blood.

Nando was reasonably certain his attempt at a smile resembled a grimace more than anything else.

"But only think, my dear," he said smoothly, "of how enjoyable it would be to bask in wants rather than needs. I can assure you that it is most rewarding."

Her wintry determination showed no signs of melting. The challenge was almost as rewarding as his inevitable victory would be. She was utterly intoxicating. He wanted to kiss and lick every inch of her delectable body.

"I would prefer not to think of such things since I cannot accept your offer. Now, if you please, Your Royal Highness, I must attend to the duties awaiting me. I shouldn't have come here at all, and I most definitely shouldn't linger. Pray excuse me?"

"What duties can be more important than the well-being of a prince?" he asked, shamelessly invoking his royal heritage and not moving from his position, keeping her pinned between himself and the door.

In truth, he had never felt like much of a prince. His brother, Maxim, had shouldered all the burdens and responsibilities of their kingdom. It had been Maxim who had fought in the Varros Great War to reclaim the throne. Maxim who bore the weight of duty with regal grace and responsibility. Nando, meanwhile, had been left to his own devices.

Protected. Spoiled. Debauched.

"Your welfare is of the utmost concern to this household, as evidenced by my presence at your sickbed when you requested it. However, I fear I've already spent far too much time alone with you. My reputation is paramount, and now that you're obviously healing nicely enough to be on your feet, I cannot help but to think further lingering here in your chamber would prove disastrous."

Ah, now she was wanting to abandon him altogether? He must have pierced her armor more fully than he'd believed.

"It can hardly prove disastrous when I'm an invalid," he said, although aside from the pain in his arm, he felt perfectly hale.

He was possessed of a hearty disposition. His wound was already healing. He would survive despite the intentions of the bastard who had dared to lay him low that day. There remained, of course, the unpleasant business of finding out precisely who it was who had shot him and why. But Tierney was a man of many talents, and he had eyes and ears everywhere in London. Nando had great faith in the man's ability. And in his present state, all he wanted was to further his cause where Eleanora was concerned.

"You are looking rather well for an invalid," she observed shrewdly, tearing him from his whirling thoughts as her gaze traveled up and down his dressing-gown-clad form.

He grinned. "My dear Eleanora, I'm so pleased to know you've been inspecting my person."

The flush on her cheeks deepened.

God, she was adorable.

And eminently fuckable. Oh, how he would enjoy debauching her.

"I was hardly inspecting your...your person," she stammered, as if she could scarcely bring herself to mention his body in any fashion.

Her hesitation and stumbling over her words were so unlike the stern, unflappable woman he'd come to know that it left Nando with no doubt that she wasn't as unmoved by him as she pretended. In fact, he would wager it was quite the opposite.

"You weren't?" He pretended to frown and reached for the fastening on his robe as if he intended to whisk it away. "Perhaps we ought to rectify that matter."

"No." Eyes wide, she laid her hand over his with haste. "We will do nothing of the sort. This is positively scandalous. I must go."

But her fingers had tightened on his hand rather than releasing him, and the air was suddenly filled with undeniable, potent awareness.

"Stay," he said simply.

Her lips parted, their lush fullness on display along with her hesitation. She wanted to linger here with him, despite all her protests to the contrary. He could see it plainly in her countenance, feel it in her touch.

"Please," Nando added when she continued to look torn between what she ought to do and what she longed to do. "Must I beg you, Eleanora?"

"I've told you not to be so familiar," she said, her voice husky and distinctly lacking the reproach she likely had wished to instill in it.

"And I've promptly ignored you, just as you want me to," he said. "You like hearing me say your given name."

"I'll admit no such thing."

But still, she had yet to pull away from him.

"You needn't make the concession. I can tell well enough from your reaction every time I call you by it."

She stiffened and withdrew her hand quickly, as if she'd inadvertently burned herself. "As I said, I must return to my duties."

"Must you, or are you merely afraid that if you linger, you won't be able to resist me?" he couldn't help taunting.

"There is nothing to resist," she denied.

But he didn't miss the breathless quality of her voice.

"Isn't there?"

The scent of her, clean and womanly—soap with a hint of roses—wound itself around him. Her lips were parted. Blue eyes wide and no longer cold, but sizzling with the same fire he felt in his veins.

"Your Royal H—"

He ended her protest with his lips. Partially because he didn't want to hear her call him *Your Royal Highness* one more bloody time, and partly because he couldn't exist another second on this earth without knowing what Eleanora Brett's mouth felt like beneath his.

Heaven.

Exquisite.

Perfection.

That was what her mouth felt like. Like the last mouth he wanted to kiss. The force of his reaction to her was astonishing. Nando had never felt anything so overwhelming. Her lips were silken and soft, hot and lush and giving. She tasted

85

like tea and innocence, and he wanted more. Had to have more.

He could never have enough.

Nando cupped her cheek with his right hand, gently angling her face so that he could deepen the kiss. With a soft, almost breathy sound of surrender that he felt in his ballocks, Eleanora opened for him. He gave her his tongue.

Her arms wound around his neck, and she pressed herself against him fully. Her diminutive height kept her from coming into contact with his wounded arm, sparing him from pain. But he would have kissed her anyway. No kiss he'd ever known in his life compared to this one, Eleanora Brett coming so deliciously undone for him.

He swept his hand from her jaw to her nape, cupping her head and keeping her from colliding with the door at her back as he kissed her deeper. Harder. Her tongue answered his, tentatively at first and then with greater confidence.

Deus, it was heady, the feeling of her in his arms, her completely yielding to him.

And just as quickly as it had begun, it was over. Interrupted by three sound raps on the chamber door. She flew away from him like a startled bird, darting to the side, staring at Nando with a dazed expression, her lips swollen from his kisses. A thundering bolt of possession jolted through him.

He wanted to see her thus again.

Soon.

"Your Royal Highness?"

But Bruno's untimely return and his unwanted voice from the hall, hesitant after Nando's somewhat ungracious treatment of him earlier, shattered the possibilities of the moment.

"What is it, Bruno?" he demanded harshly, raking his hand through his hair.

Of all the times for his bodyguard to return.

If he'd been but half a minute longer, Nando could have pressed his advantage. He'd have had Eleanora eating out of his hand.

"I was able to procure some sustenance from the kitchens, Your Royal Highness."

Fuck.

"I'm no longer hungry," he tried, hoping Bruno would go to the devil and leave him alone with Eleanora.

The only sustenance he wanted was more of the woman before him, whose breathing was erratic and whose eyes were wide. He was reasonably certain he could spend the rest of his life on nothing more than her kisses alone for succor.

"Come to me later," he told her lowly. "We've not finished this discussion."

Her nostrils flared as she inhaled sharply at his boldness. "No."

Damnation.

Thwarted.

"Perhaps Your Royal Highness will change your mind when you see what I've managed to obtain," Bruno suggested, the latch on the door lifting as his bodyguard decided to let himself into the room.

Bruno faltered as he spied Eleanora, whose countenance couldn't have been more horrified if she'd just been invited to her own funeral.

The bodyguard attempted a bow, no easy feat given the laden tray he bore. "Miss Brett."

She dipped into an elegant curtsy. "Mr. Dimitrius, good evening. I was just taking my leave." She ventured a fleeting glance in Nando's direction and another curtsy. "Your Royal Highness."

And then she fled his chamber, leaving Nando alone again, save for Bruno and a tray of pilfered food he no longer wanted to eat.

CHAPTER 8

"*B*ut trousers are so much more comfortable to wear than gowns and petticoats. No doubt, it's why the gentlemen here in London insist upon keeping them for themselves."

Princess Emmaline accompanied her pronouncement with a pout and a stomp of her dainty foot.

Eleanora suppressed a sigh as she took in the sight her charge presented in the drawing room—billowing trousers and an accompanying jacket fashioned of silk, belted at her waist. There was no denying the quality and cut of her outerwear. But it was wholly unseemly. And yet another reminder that just when Eleanora thought she had made some progress with the princesses, one of them insisted upon either wearing inappropriate garments or sneaking away to find time alone with scandalous dukes.

Or both.

She forced a commiserating smile to her lips. "You are undoubtedly correct, Princess Emmaline. However, given that we have no control over polite standards, I'm afraid we haven't any choice other than to surrender to the *ton*'s notion of what a lady ought to wear."

"I've already worn trousers to a ball," Princess Emmaline pointed out.

Yes, much to Eleanora's abject horror, the princesses had both attended a ball wearing trousers before their older sister had hired her.

"Your doing so resulted in a flurry of scandal," Eleanora reminded her sternly.

"And also in Miss Brett being hired to give us town silver," Princess Annalise added, addressing her sister.

"Town *bronze*," Eleanora corrected gently.

"Why would it not be gold?" Princess Emmaline asked, her brow furrowed. "Gold is worth more than bronze and silver, is it not? If we are to be trained like little dogs until we are above reproach, then one would truly think it ought to be called *town gold*, at the very least."

Eleanora winced at the princess's reference to being trained like little dogs, which was hardly what she hoped for her charges and yet undoubtedly what it must feel like to them. Particularly after the repression they had faced in their own kingdom. To finally be enjoying liberties long denied them, only to have to be molded into the precise image of womanly virtue the *ton* expected must have been a shock to their sensibilities.

She smiled tightly, hoping her expression was encouraging rather than severe. "Her Royal Highness doesn't wish for me to train you, but to *guide* you. To ease your presence in the oft-dizzying social whirl."

Princess Annalise blinked. "To keep us from further horrifying the lords and ladies of London, you mean to say, Miss Brett."

It was the first time any of her charges had directly discussed her role, and Eleanora could privately admit that the conversation was causing her rather a lot of discomfiture. Mostly because she knew the depths of irony involved in someone like herself now guiding noble ladies through polite society. If anyone who had procured her sought-after services had the slightest knowledge of her past, they would dismiss her without a moment's hesitation.

Her past work and successes, combined with her faultless reputation, wouldn't be sufficient to atone. Nothing and no one would save her from a terrifying end of penury and obscurity. She would simply cease to exist to all who had once heartily embraced her. And without the significant coin she was able to command from the wealthiest nobles and cits in London for her services, she would be cast to the streets. Forced to sell the last thing of value she possessed—herself.

Thrusting that terrifying thought aside, Eleanora hastened to reassure Princess Annalise. "Your Royal Highness, neither of you could horrify anyone. I am merely present to act as a guide. Think of me as the grease in the pan —a facilitator, rather than the lovely dish which is brought to the table and laid before all the guests."

"I wouldn't wish to think of you as grease, Miss Brett," Emmaline said, frowning. "How dreadful. You're far too lovely to be something so common and unappealing."

"It was a figure of speech, my dear," she said gently, inwardly tamping down any hint of her former vanity that made her want to preen at the young royal's words.

She *was* common, and there was no changing that. And for the last few years, she had done everything she could to make herself as unappealing as possible. Particularly after she'd been forced to introduce her knee to the Earl of Walcot's nether region when the roué had ventured to her private chamber late one evening. Her resultant dismissal had been both expected and infuriating. She had been fortunate he hadn't pressed his unwanted attentions. Some women in service, she knew, were not so lucky.

"A figure of speech?" Princess Annalise asked, her expression perplexed. "Who is that?"

The princesses' mastery of the English language sometimes made it easy for Eleanora to forget that it wasn't their native tongue. Here was the second reminder in less than one quarter hour.

"Not a person, Your Royal Highness," she advised softly. "Rather, the phrase means that one is using words in a different sense than the expected. I don't mean to compare myself to grease, not truly. I only meant to say that you should think of me as someone present in your life to aid you. Not to keep you from horrifying anyone."

Although, in truth, that was part of it. However, Eleanora hadn't been able to earn her bread over the last few years by telling anyone the truth. She certainly had no intention of beginning now.

"I see." Princess Annalise regarded her gravely. "But I do not think I like these speech figures of yours, Miss Brett."

Eleanora was accustomed to choosing her battles, which was why she didn't bother to correct the princess a second time. "The English language is remarkably peculiar, Your Royal Highness. I shan't argue about that. Now, then. I do believe we have thoroughly exhausted the subject, and I've been most remiss in today's lesson. Shall we continue?"

"Only if I can remain in my trousers," Princess Emmaline said, her expression mulish.

"Whilst you are in Her Royal Highness's household, and as she sees fit, you may dress however your heart desires," she said smoothly.

"Not at balls, however?" the princess wanted to know.

Good heavens, Eleanora was beginning to develop a headache.

"Not at balls," she confirmed. "The gowns we have commissioned will suit quite elegantly for such a purpose."

"It is a wonder anyone chooses to live here," Princess Emmaline sniffed. "All this dreadful rain, a dearth of sun and warmth, and women cannot even wear trousers."

"Undoubtedly you will grow accustomed to it when you are here long enough," Eleanora said with a hopeful tone. "I promise you that, aside from our peculiar notions of dress, it is a reasonably civilized society."

That was a lie, of course. Polite society was neither reasonable nor civilized, but no need to frighten the princesses. They had already endured enough heartache in their homeland. They were yet young and naïve, and their royal bloodlines suggested they would never need to learn the truth.

"Peculiar notions of dress?"

The smooth, silken voice coming from behind Eleanora was as unexpected as it was familiar. And her body's unwanted reaction to it was the same. Heat curled through her, lingering low in her belly.

Prince Ferdinando.

Eleanora whirled about to face him, forgetting herself for a moment as she was faced with the portrait of beautiful elegance he presented. Golden hair swept from his high forehead and worn in perfect curls, his cheekbones sharper than blades, his bright-blue eyes searing her to her soul as he gazed upon her as if she were the sole occupant of the room.

"My dear Miss Brett, whatever nonsense are you instilling in my dear cousins?" he drawled, strolling deeper into the drawing room as if he had been invited to join them.

He decidedly had not.

His nearness and audacity jolted her from her stupor. She dipped into a curtsy.

"Your Royal Highness," she greeted. "I thought you were still confined to your sickroom."

"Mercifully, I've escaped." The smile he sent her way melted something deep inside her.

She ignored it, summoning all the inner ice that dwelled in the darkest corners of her ragged heart.

"Her Royal Highness Princess Emmaline and Her Royal Highness Princess Annalise are no relations of yours," she pointed out coolly, irritated with him for appearing when she had spent the last few days happily avoiding him.

And pretending he—and his sinful, smoldering, wondrous kisses—hadn't occupied her every waking thought since she had foolishly allowed herself to be alone with him that last time. He'd been dangerous then. She'd seen it. No longer on his sickbed, pale and wan from loss of blood, mind befuddled by the laudanum. Rather, he'd been sharp and clear. Beautiful and masculine and painfully compelling. The air between them had fairly crackled with fire. She should have run at the first opportunity. Yet, she'd remained, knowing what would happen.

Wanting it, to her everlasting shame.

But she couldn't say any of that aloud. So instead, she had chosen to comment upon the prince's ridiculous claim that he was a cousin to the princesses.

"We may as well be," he said easily, offering a gallant bow. "Their sister was practically married to my brother. We were very nearly almost siblings by marriage."

"And how does that make you their cousin, Your Royal Highness?" she asked despite herself.

He straightened to his full, maddening, handsome height. "I'll admit I am woefully inept at understanding familial ties, particularly in the English language. However, the princesses *are* family to me."

"Nando," Emmaline greeted, closing the distance between

them with such exuberance that she nearly bounced as she floated to the prince. "Stasia refused to allow me to come to you. How is your wound?"

"Healing quite nicely," he announced, his gaze traveling over the princess's head and melding with Eleanora's. "I owe an eternal debt of gratitude for the angels at my side during my convalescence here."

There was an underlying, pointed aspect to his tone, and Eleanora knew he was referencing her absence from his sickbed these past few days. She had missed him—she wouldn't lie to herself, even if she had to lie to everyone else. But she also knew all too well what would have happened if she had gone to him again after those breath-stealing and mind-numbing kisses.

She would have returned to his chamber again and again until she had finally surrendered to what the prince wanted —namely, her in his bed. But Eleanora knew how damning such a choice would be. She could resist him. She *had* resisted him.

And he had been irritated by it. Good. Let him be. Perhaps if his vanity were sufficiently damaged, he would decide to pursue someone else.

"Angels at your side," Princess Emmaline repeated, casting a sly glance in Eleanora's direction. "Never say Miss Brett was attending you."

"I wasn't," she hastened to say, hoping the look she sent the wicked prince was suitably hard and discouraging.

"Of course she was," he said, dashing her hopes as he continued to smile knowingly in her direction. "And pray, do not let the humble Miss Brett dissuade you that her loving ministrations were anything other than miraculous."

She nearly swallowed her tongue.

Loving ministrations. Why, she ought to box his ears, the scoundrel!

Eleanora's gaze frantically swept the chamber for a weapon she might take up and use against him, just to keep him from speaking. There was a poker by the fireplace. An accommodating vase filled with hothouse flowers. An ormolu clock on the mantel. She didn't want to murder him, however. Merely stun him.

"What are you looking for, Miss Brett?" he asked.

She clenched her jaw and forced a smile that felt more like a grimace. "Something I misplaced."

It was yet another lie in a seemingly endless string of so many.

For this one, she felt no guilt. He had brought it upon himself with his ceaseless flirting and innuendos and his casual grace and his gorgeous blue eyes and sinful lips and those kisses that had seared her to her soul.

"Your pleasant disposition is perhaps what you've lost?" he asked innocently.

Princess Emmaline chortled. Princess Annalise gasped, the sweet child.

Eleanora forced her expression to remain at ease, quite as if Prince Ferdinando weren't the most irksome, handsome, frustrating man she'd ever met.

And she had crossed paths with rather a lot of handsome, maddening men. The prince before her was simply incomparable.

"Is there something you require, Your Royal Highness?" she asked through clenched teeth.

"Life as an invalid has lost its luster," he said. "I grew weary of hiding in my room."

"If you are well enough to emerge, then should you not also be well enough to return to your own residence?" Eleanora was careful to keep her tone polite.

"You are not wrong in your assumption, Miss Brett," he answered smoothly. "However, I am to remain as a guest here for an indeterminate span of time. Mr. Tierney is convinced I'm safer here than at the opulent town house I bought for a small fortune. Thus, here I remain, a slightly willing prisoner."

Her heart sank to the soles of her slippers.

The look he gave her was laden with smoldering sensual intent. It would be impossible to reach any conclusion other than that the prince fully intended to seduce her during his stay here. Why, she could not begin to fathom. She was a woman nearing the age of thirty. She dressed simply and with the allure of an elderly maiden aunt. Her gowns were unbecoming sacks, and she regularly hid her natural curves and golden hair beneath drapery, fichus, and caps. A man such as him—rich, handsome, royal—could have his choice of any woman in not just London, but all the world. His singular pursuit of her made not one whit of sense.

"Whilst I am a guest beneath Mr. Tierney and Princess Anastasia's roof," Prince Ferdinando continued smoothly, still holding Eleanora's gaze, "I may as well be of use. Do you not think so?"

Heat flared up her throat, suffusing her cheeks. The gall of the man, to speak with such blatant carnal insinuation before her charges. How *dare* he? Years ago, in what seemed another life, when she had been a different woman entirely, she would have slapped his cheek for his audacity, prince or no. Some of the wealthiest, most powerful men in the world had filled her mother's sitting room and salon. She had flirted with them, spoken with them, charmed them. She'd had them eating from the palm of her hand with intrepid ease.

But now, she was Miss Eleanora Brett, and her mother was gone. So too, all her mother's amassed wealth. Fleeting, just like her life had been. And Eleanora had no choice other than to play the role in which she found herself—no better than a servant.

"Of course you must do as you wish, Your Royal Highness," Eleanora told him. "I have no doubt that you have never done anything less."

"Ah, but there you would be wrong, my dear Miss Brett, and regretfully so," he countered. "However, in this instance, it would please me greatly to remain here with my cousins and aid them in obtaining their…town silver, is it?"

She might have laughed were the circumstances any less dire. As it was, she was in peril of wilting like a flower in a drought beneath the prince's knowing gaze. All she could think about was the way his sinful mouth had felt angling over hers. The way his tongue had slid sinuously against hers. The way he had tasted.

The way he'd made her feel.

Wrong, all of it. So desperately, dangerously wrong.

"Town bronze," she forced herself to correct in the same gentle tone she had used for Princess Annalise. "The phrase is *town bronze*, Your Royal Highness."

"Just so." A smile toyed with the corners of his lips.

And that was when Eleanora realized he was teasing her. But not just that, he had been standing at the threshold for far longer than she had realized. Watching her. Listening.

Renewed heat crept up her throat, making her ears sting. And to her utter shame, the peaks of her breasts went hard and tingling. An ache throbbed to life between her thighs. Despite her every intention to remain impervious, and in direct opposition to all reason, she wanted this man.

Wanted him more desperately than she had ever wanted another.

But she could not have him.

"Well, then," she managed crisply, straightening the skirt of her gown and smoothing imaginary wrinkles from the voluminous muslin. "Your dedication is most respectable. However, their royal highnesses and I were just about to begin our dancing lessons. Given your unfortunate state, I cannot help but think you would be incapable of rendering us any manner of aid. We do thank you, Your Royal Highness."

"Nonsense!" Princess Emmaline interrupted. "Cousin Nando would be an excellent judge of our form. Would you not? Surely all your...*experience* in the Varros court would make you a perfect connoisseur."

Eleanora stared at the princess, aghast at the patently obvious insinuation in her words. And truly, a naïve young girl such as herself should have no notion of what manner of experience the prince possessed from his days at court. No doubt it was lewd and lascivious and beyond depraved. A shiver went down Eleanora's spine that she told herself was pure disgust.

"Princess Emmaline," she began in a scolding tone.

"You are correct, of course, cousin," Prince Ferdinando said easily, grinning as if the princess's pointed words hadn't affected him one whit.

And perhaps they hadn't. Men of his ilk ordinarily reveled in their dubious reputations and endless conquests. She knew his sort all too well. Wealthy, silver-tongued rogues had ruined her mother's life more times than one. They'd professed their love, taken her mother under their protection, and broken her heart. They'd given her priceless jewels that turned out to be paste. They'd been faithless and cruel. Eleanora should know better. Better than anyone in the prince's gilded sphere, certainly.

She might have objected over his incorrect claim to a familial relation again, but she knew there was no point in it, so Eleanora kept quiet, not wishing to draw attention to herself any more than she already had.

"I shall seat myself and observe," he added, sauntering toward a nearby Grecian couch. "Forgive me my lack of manners, ladies, but if I remain standing any longer, I may swoon. On account of the blood I've lost, you understand?"

"Of course," Princess Emmaline and Princess Annalise chirped in unison.

The rogue. He hadn't lost enough blood to keep him from kissing her. But she couldn't say that. Nor should she think of it. She needed to tamp down the memory. Banish the dangerous yearning he'd brought to life within her. Forget it ever had happened.

Impossible.

She brushed that witless thought aside.

"You needn't observe," she gritted through clenched teeth, trying not to watch as he folded his body into the couch with leonine grace and failing.

He crossed his long legs and settled into the cushions like an indolent king.

"My cousins wish me to do so," he told her with a beautiful smile that emphasized his neat, even teeth. "Do you not, cousins?"

"Yes," Princess Annalise said dutifully.

"Oh yes. Of course we do, cousin," said Princess Emmaline like the hoyden she was. "Nando simply must stay, Miss Brett."

"You see, my dear Miss Brett?" Prince Ferdinando's smile turned smug. "I'm a fortunate man indeed, to be surrounded by such tenderhearted ladies. Carry on, I pray you. Forget I'm even here."

As if such a feat were possible. Eleanora would be as likely to ignore an elephant bounding across the chamber, intent upon trampling them all. And if she didn't take great care, the prince would indeed be trampling—her ability to resist him, her reputation, and her future all at once.

But he'd neatly trapped her, and not for the first time. She didn't dare draw the suspicion of the princesses by demanding Prince Ferdinando leave. Nor did she dare gainsay them in desiring his presence during their lessons.

So, she raised her chin, took a deep, determined breath, and proceeded as if they didn't have an audience consisting of the most maddeningly attractive man she'd ever met. One whose kisses had nearly brought her to her knees mere days before, threatening the resolve that had never once faltered in the wake of her mother's death.

"Princess Annalise," she said calmly, settling upon the more malleable of her two charges intentionally. "You join me first, if you please. We shall be turning our attention to your waltz since the dance is newest to you. Princess Emmaline, if you would be willing to play at the pianoforte?"

"Yes, Miss Brett," said the latter, dutiful for possibly the first time in Eleanora's acquaintance.

Her lack of hesitation raised Eleanora's suspicions. She watched through narrowed eyes as the princess crossed the music room and settled herself at the pianoforte as she'd requested.

"Now, then," Eleanora said, turning to her other charge, cursing her weakness for the breathlessness that had entered her voice, even as she applauded herself for successfully keeping her gaze from the prince occupying the Grecian couch.

"This is an excellent diversion," Prince Ferdinando drawled. "Far preferable to watching the walls in my chamber and listening to Bruno's dreadful attempts at providing me with amusement. Tell me, Miss Brett, do you intend to play the role of gentleman for this particular lesson?"

He was demanding her attention. She would have to look at him now, and he knew it.

With great reluctance, Eleanora glanced in the prince's direction—fleetingly, but it was sufficient to make unwanted heat rise within her. "Yes, Your Royal Highness. I am indeed playing the role of gentleman. It is a common enough practice when no gentleman dance instructor is present. You do not object, do you?"

"Not at all," he said, his tone mild. "I find myself rather intrigued by the notion of you taking command."

Her stomach performed a queer little flip. She ignored it. Ignored *him*.

Deliberately, she presented Prince Ferdinando with her back as she took up her position opposite Princess Annalise, doing her best imitation of a prospective suitor. Her posture was stiff and stern. She told herself she could play the gentleman in this waltz and then cry off their dancing lesson for the remainder of the afternoon. She could easily turn her attention to singing or poetry or something Prince Ferdinando wouldn't find so amusing a diversion.

She bowed to Princess Annalise.

"Oh no, I'm afraid that shan't do. Not at all."

Him again.

Clenching her jaw, Eleanora straightened from her bow and cast a vexed glance at Prince Ferdinando. It was unfair for him to look so perfect, even with the sleeve of his wounded arm empty, a coat draped causally over his shoulders. His long legs were spread before him, crossed at the ankles.

"What is amiss, Your Royal Highness?" she asked when he didn't elaborate on his objection.

"It is merely that a gentleman would never bow thusly," he said with deceptive innocence. "I'm afraid you've done it all wrong."

"I've done perfectly well," she countered tightly,

rethinking her earlier quest for a suitable weapon with which to brain him.

"There is *well*, and then there is *believably*, my dear Miss Brett." He shook his head sadly. "I'm afraid that if you want to enlighten my cousins, you must perform better than merely *well enough*. Cousin Annalise has to look upon you and see a dashing, handsome duke, and that bow won't suit at all."

She clasped her gown at her sides in such a tight grip that it was a miracle the muslin hadn't rent. He was playing a game with her. And before the princesses, no less. She ought not to be surprised. She'd known, almost from the moment they had met, that Prince Ferdinando was capable of anything. That he was scandalous and dangerous to all she held dear.

Fair enough. She could play his game as well as he could. Indeed, she could soundly trounce him at it.

"Perhaps Your Royal Highness might edify me on the proper sketching of a bow," she suggested with feigned sweetness, hoping he would be duly chastised and hold his wicked tongue.

He grinned at her. "You're thrusting your derriere out too far, if you must know. A gentleman would never thrust his rump out in such a feminine manner."

Heat crept over her face. He was speaking about her *bottom*. And in front of Princess Annalise and Emmaline, no less.

"It is wonderfully curved," he continued thoughtfully, "which no doubt hinders the impression as well. However, that can't be helped."

From the pianoforte, Princess Emmaline chuckled into her hand in a quite indiscreet fashion.

"Your Royal Highness, you are beyond the pale," Eleanora clipped out coldly.

But she didn't feel cold. Not at all. What she did feel was hot. Hot. *Hot.*

She was unbearably aflame, something deep within her, forbidden and wholly unnecessary, burning with an ardor she feared she would no longer be able to contain.

As if he could read her mind, his smile deepened, unrepentant and roguish. "Always, Miss Brett."

She could do this. She could carry on this lesson, this lone dance, and then somehow remove herself from this room and from Prince Ferdinando's dangerous presence. She could escape this unscathed.

She could.

She would.

She *had* to.

Grinding her molars and giving him what she was sure resembled more grimace than smile, she said, "Thank you for your suggestion. I shall endeavor to form all future bows with greater care."

"By all means," he said like a benevolent ruler seated upon a dais.

"Princess Emmaline, begin the waltz," she commanded sharply, the edge in her tone not intended for her charge but for the grinning, smoldering, beautiful prince in their midst.

The first notes filled the air, and Eleanora busied herself with helping Princess Annalise with hand placement and positioning, before turning her attention to her steps, which were still halting and foal-like.

"No, no, no," called the prince over the pianoforte. "Halt."

The music died.

Nettled beyond the limitations of her patience, Eleanora spun about to face him, forgetting her place in this household and that she addressed a royal prince.

"What in heaven's name can it be now?" she demanded curtly.

"You do not move like a man, Miss Brett," he said, shameless in his continued disruption. "How is my cousin to pretend you are a gentleman if you are moving with a woman's lithe grace?"

She wondered if his ploy was to drive her so mad with fury that she succumbed to his seduction, irritated beyond all rational thought. If so, he was certainly succeeding.

Eleanora pinned the handsome devil with a glare. "I do not find it imperative that Princess Annalise pretend I am a gentleman. The purpose of this lesson is for the princess to practice her steps and posture, not for her to imagine she is dancing with a lord."

"Nonsense." He rose to his feet with a casual ease that belied his recent sickroom stay. "If you will allow me to offer my assistance, Miss Brett, I do think that my cousin would benefit from a gentleman and lady couple dancing the waltz."

"I cannot think it wise for you to dance with Princess Annalise," she protested instantly, thinking of his dangerous reputation and her charge's wide-eyed innocence.

He could claim the princesses as his cousins all he liked, but the truth of the matter was, Prince Ferdinando was not related to the princesses in any capacity. He wasn't family. And he was a wicked rakehell, notorious for his bad behavior.

He was already striding in their direction with the assured footfalls of a man born into royalty. "And that is precisely why I'm dancing with *you*, Miss Brett."

CHAPTER 9

Nando knew he wasn't playing a fair game.

But the expression on Eleanora's face was nothing short of delectable. *Deus*, he wanted to devour her. Slowly and with infinite attention to detail. He'd start with that lush mouth of hers and then proceed down the creamy skin of her throat. He'd take great pleasure in dragging her hideous fichu away with his teeth and then move on to the bounty of her breasts.

But first, a waltz.

It didn't matter that he had only one arm that was capable of working properly thanks to the stitches and bandaging on his wound. It didn't matter that he was still in a more weakened state than he preferred and that he'd spent far too much time on his arse over the past few days.

He was damned well dancing with Miss Eleanora Brett.

Nothing, and no one, would stop him—not even the august, frowning lady herself.

Her response was as swift as it was predictable. "I am not dancing with you, Your Royal Highness."

"Of course you are." He cast an encouraging smile in

Princess Annalise's direction. "Run along and sit down, cousin. Miss Brett and I shall show you how it's properly done."

"No, we most assuredly will not!" Miss Brett denied, but the becoming color creeping up her throat to her cheeks was giving her away.

As was the way her body angled toward him, as if in unspoken invitation. She wanted to dance with him. And more.

He hadn't mistaken those heated kisses they'd shared, even if she had hidden from him ever since. And oh, he knew well why she'd retreated like a frightened little mouse running from a cat. It was because she didn't trust herself to be able to resist him.

"But you *do* wish to instruct the princesses properly, do you not?" he asked gently, keeping his voice low and intimate.

Again, he was preying upon her weaknesses. Miss Brett was a determined thing. He admired her tenacity. And he was all too aware of how she regarded her responsibility where the princesses were concerned—they were paramount.

He watched as indecision flitted over her lovely countenance, wishing he might pluck that dreadful cap from her head so that he could glory in the golden beauty of her hair. Knowing he didn't dare push her that far with an audience.

"You must know that I do," she said coolly, her nostrils flaring in that way she had, which told him she was agitated.

"Then 'tis settled." Nando offered her as gentlemanly of a bow as he could muster, given his injury.

It was still a better effort than she'd made, although he would be happy to admit that he'd enjoyed ogling her backside. If Eleanora had known the view she'd given him of her derriere as she bent over, he knew she never would have presented him with her back. But she wasn't always as diabolical as he was, and he'd sat there on the uncomfortable couch, drinking in the sight like the bounder he was.

Looking as if she'd just taken a great gulp of lemon juice, Eleanora dipped into a curtsy. He wanted to kiss her witless.

"Cousin Emmaline," he called to the princess at the pianoforte, who was ever eager to be complicit in his adventures, "please do begin."

"The princesses are not your cousins," Eleanora reminded him icily.

He scarcely contained his grin. Claiming a familial connection to them suited Nando for two reasons. One, it annoyed her. Two, it allowed for greater freedom. He enjoyed the company of the princesses. However, he had absolutely no designs on their virtue.

There was only one woman he wanted, and she was currently glowering at him with thunderstorms in her eyes.

Damn, but he adored her.

Nando grinned as Princess Emmaline obligingly began playing the music, effectively negating the need for a response from him. He stepped into Eleanora, too close for propriety or a proper waltz and not caring one whit, flattening his palm on the small of her back. Such a perfect place on a woman—one of his favorites, as it happened, for it seemed to have been uniquely carved by God himself for a man's possessive touch.

His hand on Eleanora's back was like the fit of a perfect glove, quite as if it belonged there. As if it always had. Her lips parted as he pulled her into him, her expression suggesting she felt the same sense of rightness that he did.

"I'm afraid I can't hold your hand and raise my arm up properly," he told her quietly. "You'll have to settle your hand on my shoulder instead."

Eleanora's brows snapped together, her scowl doing

things to his cock that he had no doubt she would be horri-fied—and secretly intrigued—to learn.

"How is this example any better than my own?" she demanded curtly.

As he began guiding them around the room, Nando leaned close, almost setting his lips on her ear. "Because you wanted to dance with me, my dear."

"I did not."

Her denial was predictable.

And patently false.

Nando ignored it, sweeping them in circles in the best rhythm he could manage, for Princess Emmaline was proving a remarkably abysmal hand at the pianoforte. They kept time, their feet and bodies moving in steady unison. Eleanora quite obviously cast her gaze anywhere but at him as they went. He didn't mind, however, taking advantage of the opportunity to admire her as they danced.

"I knew you were lying about dancing," she said suddenly. "When you offered me that spurious position."

"My dear, nothing about my offer was spurious unless that means wonderful. I'm afraid your vast English language occasionally leaves me perplexed. However, I never specified which dance I would require assistance in. The minuet, if you were wondering."

Yes, more nonsense.

The expression on Eleanora's face said she knew it to be so, but before she could counter him, the princess hit too many keys at once, resulting in a discordant sound that nearly had him missing a step. Fortunately, Nando was more than proficient at dancing and saved them. The chance to hold Eleanora in his arms again—albeit not as closely as he would have preferred—was too heady to be ignored. He'd happily saw off his wounded arm entirely just to waltz with her like this.

"Perhaps pianoforte lessons are in order next," he told Eleanora wryly as he whirled them again.

To his amazed delight, a vibrant burst of laughter escaped her. Small and dainty and reluctant and easily the best sound he'd heard in years, far different from the choked half chuckle she had given him the day he had insulted the aim of his assassin. He almost stumbled at the impact that lone laugh had upon him. She clapped a hand over her mouth, as if the act could somehow rescind her levity. Too late.

He, Prince Ferdinando of the House of Tayrnes on the Island of Varros, had made Miss Eleanora Brett truly *laugh*, unfettered and without an effort to squelch her mirth.

"Good heavens, I do believe Miss Brett chuckled," Princess Annalise announced from her perch on the gilded settee. "Emmaline, did you hear? Cousin Nando made Miss Brett *laugh*."

Poor Emmaline, apparently incapable of playing and speaking at the same time, stilled her hands over the keys, the music dying. Eleanora stopped dancing immediately, leaving Nando no choice but to follow suit. He refused, however, to relinquish his hold on her delightful form, and she seemed so mired in embarrassment that she failed to take note of their indecorous proximity now that the waltz had abruptly ended.

"Miss Brett laughed?" Princess Emmaline echoed, her tone shocked. "I didn't think it possible."

Nando was grinning like a fool and he knew it, but pride was rushing through his veins along with something that felt a whole lot like victory. He had made the indomitable Miss Eleanora Brett's icy façade melt. He'd made her so lose control of her sangfroid that it had fled her utterly, even if only for a fleeting moment.

He *had* her.

The kisses they'd shared in his chamber, the chuckle he'd

wrung from her, the way her body responded to his, the undeniable pull between them—it all added up to one inevitable conclusion. The woman in his arms was his. He'd won.

Oh, he might not have her in his bed this very night, but have her in his bed, he would. And she would adore every second of the pleasure he visited upon her. He'd make more than certain of that.

"Astounding," Princess Annalise was saying, as if she had just witnessed an angel descend from heaven before her.

The poor chit was going to be chewed up and swallowed whole by the *ton*. It was a miracle she hadn't been already, Nando thought grimly. But that wasn't his problem, nor was it his concern.

"It would seem I am capable of remarkable feats," he said to Eleanora, though he allowed his voice to carry to the princesses.

Eleanora's hand was still pressed to her lips, her eyes wide on his. Understanding flared in those mysterious blue depths. She knew as well as he did that he was speaking about feats that had nothing to do with dancing the waltz.

Nando smiled at her, feeling the heat simmering between them as palpably as if they stood before a roaring fire.

"I have no doubt that you are, Your Royal Highness," Eleanora said, her voice low and for him alone. "However, I've no wish to know about them. You would be wise to practice them elsewhere."

It was his turn to chuckle now. "Lie all you want, my dear. We both know the truth."

Her nostrils flared, and her spine went rigid, almost as if she were remembering herself. "I'm not lying."

Nando lowered his head and pressed his lips to her ear as he whispered, "You may tell yourself that if it makes you feel better. But your kisses said otherwise." He straightened and released her in one motion, stepping away and offering her another bow. "As you can see, cousins," he said, addressing the princesses who were watching their little drama unfold with rapt attention, "skilled waltzing has its infinite uses."

And one of them was most assuredly seducing their stern, relentless chaperone.

"Now, if you ladies will excuse me, I fear I must return to my chamber, for all this waltzing has reminded me that I yet remain an invalid."

The princesses offered him a chorus of well-wishes. Eleanora stayed notably silent. Nando was lying, of course. If anything, his waltz with her had given him new life and heightened his hunger for her.

He quit the room, flexing the hand that had so recently been pressed to the small of her back, for he swore that he could still feel the alluring heat of her searing him even as he walked away.

∾

"Your Royal Highness, you should be abed, getting your rest," Bruno fretted.

Nando was too busy pacing the floor, trying to plot a means of catching Eleanora alone, to be in bed. Besides, if he was to be abed at this juncture, with his wound healing nicely, it most assuredly wouldn't be *alone*, nor would he welcome his bodyguard hovering over him like a worried hen on her roost.

"I don't need rest." Nando stopped at the mantel, examining an ormolu clock that depicted Diana, the Roman goddess of the hunt, complete with stags and hounds on a marble base.

It was a remarkable piece with intricate attention to detail. And although he enjoyed collecting beauty—whether it be women, clocks, paintings, or sculptures—he found himself oddly disinterested in the ormolu depiction. When he looked at the huntress's serene expression, all he saw was Eleanora smiling up at him with genuine amusement that he'd been the cause of.

He needed to press his suit. As soon as he was able. This obsession with her was beginning to grow tedious. The sooner he had her to himself, the sooner he could carry on with his unapologetic debauchery.

"Forgive me for my impertinence, but you should take greater care with your person," Bruno continued. "King Maximillian will be vastly displeased if any further harm should befall you. As it is, I'll likely lose my head for failing to protect you when you were shot."

The mention of his beloved, if overbearing, older brother had Nando turning back to his bodyguard. "Calm yourself, Bruno. My brother never needs to know about any of this. I have no intention of telling him. It will only make him worry, and he's worried quite enough in his life, don't you think?"

"Of course, Your Royal Highness, but—"

"Then it's settled," Nando interrupted, not wanting to hear further arguments. What Maxim didn't know couldn't hurt him. And that was one of the reasons Nando was in London instead of at home in Varros.

"But Your Royal—"

Knock, knock, knock.

Three sound raps at the door interrupted Bruno's further fretting, which suited Nando perfectly well. The man could be as nettlesome as a fly, buzzing about his head.

"Enter," he called, hoping it was Eleanora, coming to him freely and saving him the trouble of manufacturing another reason to be with her.

He was doomed to be disappointed, however, as his illustrious hostess bustled past Bruno into his room, bearing an arm full of fresh flowers.

"For me?" Nando asked, fluttering his lashes like a coquette as he offered a gallant bow. "My dear lady, you do know how to charm."

Princess Stasia harrumphed and approached an empty vase which he'd failed to take note of previously, situated on a nearby table. "I'm hardly trying to charm you. I'm merely trying to brighten this dreadfully dark room with some cheer. Why are the window dressings pulled closed?"

He might have asked the same. "Bruno thinks it imperative that I remain unseen in the windows." He glowered at his bodyguard. "I told him it's unnecessary and that each time he departs the room, I open them once more. But he insists upon closing them when he returns."

"My husband did say that it would be best if we kept your presence here as much of a secret as possible," the princess said, taking Bruno's side.

The utter traitor.

"Your husband is an Englishman," he said dismissively, as if that explained everything.

Which, in Nando's estimation, it did.

"He's also quite adept at knowing what to do in moments of dire danger," she said, stuffing the stems of her blossoms into the vase.

"Not roses, surely?" he asked just to be peevish. "They make me sneeze."

"Then hold your breath," she suggested, grinning.

Had he thought her a friend? Had he claimed her as an honorary cousin as he had her sisters? If so, he must have been thoroughly soused at the time. Her time in England with her husband had clearly addled her mind.

"I would, but then I cannot speak," he countered mildly, rubbing his uninjured hand over his chest.

"Precisely." Her grin deepened as she placed the last of her flowers into the vase.

"I rescind every good thing I ever said about you," he told her without heat.

The princess directed her attention to Bruno, who stood as impenetrable as a boulder by the door, guarding him, Nando supposed.

"Mr. Dimitrius, would you be so kind as to go to the kitchens and fetch His Royal Highness the honey cakes I've asked Cook to prepare for him? I know how partial he is to them, and I do so want to aid in his recovery."

She wanted to speak with Nando alone, then.

Bruno cast a searching glance in his direction, and Nando nodded. What other choice had he? His hostess was about to interrogate him, and he knew it. Hell, he deserved it, even, for he fully intended to seduce a member of her household. Thoroughly, repeatedly, and utterly without compunction.

Bruno bowed and exited the room, leaving Nando and Princess Stasia truly alone.

"My sisters tell me that you waltzed with Miss Brett today." Her voice was nonchalant as she continued to arrange the hothouse flowers in the vase, quite as if they were the most intriguing assortment of color and blooms she'd ever beheld.

But he knew better than to trust her distraction and the lightness in her tone. There was an underlying question in her voice. Nando might have known that his escape from his chamber would be remarked upon. And further, that it would necessitate a visit from Stasia. Now she wanted to know what his intentions were where Eleanora was concerned. Well, to the devil with her. Did she expect him to admit it, if doing so would hinder his cause? What a silly widgeon she was.

"I was merely doing my cousinly duty," Nando said, smiling back at the princess.

She looked up at him again, frowning. "Miss Brett is not your cousin."

"I'm more than aware that the lady in question and I have no familial ties." And thank God for that. He moved away from the mantel, taking care to keep his voice light. "I've claimed your sisters as honorary members of the House of Tayrnes."

Stasia stared at him as if he'd announced his intention to wage a one-man battle against England's navy using a thimble and a teacup. "How generous of you."

"Only for the sake of their reputations," he told her, the levity fleeing him. For he did truly like the princesses, and he wanted it to be known that he had no intention of causing either of them any trouble, lest it was a concern of his hostess. "The English are dreadfully uninformed about our bloodlines and history. Tell them that I'm a distant cousin, and they'll eat it up like it's their dinner."

"That's an appallingly cynical view of the *ton*," Stasia observed, her frown heightening.

"But true," he pointed out, stopping by the vase and bending his head to sniff the blooms.

Stasia regarded him with a raised brow. "I thought roses make you sneeze."

"Achoo," he said, winking.

She made another sound of disapproval, whisking herself to the far window, where she busied herself with opening the curtains and allowing some meager London sun to pass into the room. "Are you never serious, Nando?"

Idly, he traced the unfurling blossom of a red rose as he watched the princess play the part of chambermaid. "Why should I be? I'm no longer the spare. I have neither duties nor obligation to weigh me down."

Although he said it flippantly, the truth was that Nando had rather come to resent his older brother's lack of confidence in him. When Maxim's opinion had finally altered, Nando had already been on his current course to depravity. And with Maxim's happy marriage to Tansy and their new son and heir to the throne, there was even less of a place for Nando in court than there had been previously.

"You were nearly killed," Princess Stasia reminded him, moving to the last window.

"It would seem you're not of the same opinion as my bodyguard," he observed wryly. "Unless you wish for me to be seen so that I'm no longer an unwelcome presence in your home?"

"I'm hardly hoping for your murder, Nando." Stasia sighed as she opened the final curtain. "My husband has guards posted—his best men. I have faith that no villains will be lurking in the street, hoping for a glimpse of your face. And you're looking remarkably pale. The sunlight will do you good, I think."

"Pale?" Frowning, Nando ventured to a nearby looking glass, examining his reflection.

Perhaps he was a bit wan; the golden coloring that so favored him was difficult to maintain on England's rain-and-fog-laden shores. Nonetheless, he was still in fine form.

"Now, then. Let us have a seat and you can tell me what it is you want from my sisters' chaperone."

Stasia's voice was uncomfortably knowing. He turned away from the mirror to meet her pointed stare.

Blast. The woman was certainly persistent; he would give her that.

"Who might that be?" he asked, feigning ignorance.

"Miss Brett," his hostess replied sternly. "Subterfuge ill becomes you, Nando."

"Subter what?" he asked, pretending that his English was lacking, which always proved an immensely useful ploy.

"Cease pretending you don't know what I mean. If you insist upon playing games, then it would seem *I* am the one who must speak plainly. I forbid you from seducing Miss Brett."

Her words rankled. His reaction was instant—*how dare you, madam*—but he tamped it down.

"Who said anything about seducing her?" he asked smoothly. "I mean to offer Miss Brett gainful employ in my own household—and at a much fairer rate of recompense as well."

"You?" Stasia's tone was steeped in disbelief. "Do you have a young lady in need of preparing for her debut that I'm unaware of?"

"No." But he did have need for Eleanora. Rather a great lot of need. "But I do require assistance myself in the finer art of being proper."

She had the temerity to laugh.

"Do you have any notion of how *im*proper it would be for you to employ Miss Brett for such a task?" Stasia asked, laughing some more.

He might have said it wouldn't matter how proper or improper such a circumstance would be, because he fully intended to pay Eleanora enough that she could spend the remainder of her life as she wished instead of working at the behest of others.

"Why should it be improper?" he asked instead. "It isn't as if I would ask her to be my mistress."

For the simple reason that he never kept a mistress. He had lovers. They intrigued him until they didn't, and then he moved on to others. No one had ever held him in her thrall long enough to merit such a complicated arrangement.

"I should hope not," the princess said in a chastising tone.

"Have you come for a reason other than to upbraid me?" he dared to ask wryly.

"To bring you flowers and open your curtains," she returned, without a hint of shame. "In addition to warning you that if you trifle with Miss Brett, I'll blacken your eye."

Damn it, the woman made it impossible *not* to like her. Even if she was intruding on his plans and questioning him over Eleanora. Threatening him, too.

Nando gave her a crooked grin, eyeing her dainty hands. "Something tells me your threats aren't as perilous as you would have me believe, Princess Stasia."

"She's a good woman, Nando," Stasia said, her countenance serious now, the levity having fled.

"I know." Eleanora Brett was nothing *but* good. And he wanted some of that goodness for himself. Even if only for a stolen few moments. He wanted whatever he could have.

"And you're a very bad man," his hostess added.

"I'm a bad man with good intentions," he said, pressing his hand over his heart. "This, I swear to you."

The princess narrowed her eyes. "Do you give me your word?"

He didn't hesitate. "Naturally."

Because his intentions *were* good. Just not honorable. A trifling difference. He intended to make Eleanora Brett a wealthy and satisfied woman. In Nando's opinion, that was better than good.

Stasia considered him with a searching gaze before finally nodding. "Thank you. I'm sure there are any number of ladies in the *ton* who would be more than happy for your attentions."

There were. But unfortunately, none of them was Eleanora.

It had to be her or no one.

Bruno returned with the plate of honey cakes, and

Princess Stasia took her leave, mistakenly assured that he would be leaving her hired companion alone.

But the only way he would be leaving Eleanora alone was when they parted ways after he'd slaked his need for her. And with the alarming manner that need grew by the day, it was fast becoming apparent that his need wouldn't be satisfied for some time.

CHAPTER 10

"*I* don't think it would be wise for you and the princesses to attend the ball this evening," Princess Stasia said, taking Eleanora by surprise as she entered the princess's private salon at her request.

They had been preparing to attend the formal ball honoring the House of St. George for the last fortnight. Eleanora had struggled to convince her charges that their trousers must be left at home for the first time since her arrival. But persuade them, she finally had. And now, for her successes to be so summarily lost…

She couldn't bear to finish the thought. Working with the headstrong Princess Emmaline and the naïve, but also opinionated, Princess Annalise had proven exhausting. All her frustrated attempts at refining their manners, gowns, dancing, and conversation, only to *not* attend the ball being held in their honor, would be a grievous disappointment.

"Their ball gowns are ready," Eleanora hastened to reassure her employer, praying that the reason for the princess's words wasn't displeasure with her performance of her duties. "Neither Princess Emmaline nor Princess Annalise will be wearing trousers. We've been working to perfect their steps in the waltz as well."

The princess's eyes narrowed. "I heard about your demonstration with Prince Ferdinando."

Heat instantly suffused Eleanora's face as she remembered what it had felt like, being held by him, dancing so near to his tempting heat and strong, masculine form. And then, before she could banish it completely, the thought of his kisses returned.

Swiftly, she tamped down all such forbidden yearnings. They were impossible, foolish, and improbable. If she wanted to keep a roof over her head and continue providing London's wealthiest aristocrats and merchants with her services, then she most certainly needed to forget the dance and those kisses both had ever happened.

"His Royal Highness was kind enough to offer his assistance in showing the princesses the proper steps for the dance," she offered lamely.

What a dull, cool way to describe what had happened between them. That which must *never, ever* happen again.

"How unexpectedly charitable of him," Princess Stasia said, her tone verging on mocking.

"His Royal Highness doesn't strike me as a particularly uncharitable gentleman," Eleanora found herself saying, much to her horror.

How and why had she come to that rogue's defense with such haste and ease?

"Miss Brett," the princess began, placing a hand on Eleanora's arm in entreaty. "Must I call you Miss Brett? I feel as if we are friends now, you and I. Perhaps we might dispense with formality, and I may call you Eleanora, whilst you shall call me Stasia."

It was not the first time Princess Anastasia had made the request. That Eleanora, the daughter of one of London's most notorious courtesans, should be the friend of a princess was nothing short of preposterous. And yet, the princess was looking at her with an open candor and kindness.

"I fear it would be unwise," she protested again out of duty.

"Then allow me to be the unwise one amongst us, Eleanora," Stasia said with a conspiratorial smile. "I insist."

Eleanora hadn't a choice in the matter. But she couldn't deny it—eschewing the strict protocols she had allowed for herself wouldn't be entirely hateful. Even if it did remind her of the carefree girl she'd once been.

"If you insist," she allowed at last, and not without reluctance.

"Excellent." The princess linked her arm through Eleanora's and began guiding her to the windows overlooking the town house's gardens. "I feel it's important for us to be friends, given the nature of the warning I'm pressed to give you now."

The warning?

That didn't sound promising.

"I'm afraid I don't understand, Your Royal Highness," she protested gently.

"Stasia," the princess reminded her firmly. "You simply *must* call me Stasia, for we are friends now, which also means it is imperative that I warn you about Nando."

It would seem that the entire household was familiar with the prince. Eleanora didn't want that to rankle nearly as much as it did.

"A warning about His Royal Highness? I cannot think of why."

Heavens, how she hated deception. She'd always been a dreadful liar, even if her livelihood required it.

"His reputation is terribly wicked," the princess continued. "The gossip I heard about him at court in Varros and here in London is the sort that ought never to be repeated."

"Although it ill-becomes me, I'll admit that I have heard some whispers myself, concerning the prince," she said, choosing her words with care. "I hope you do not fear I will conduct myself in any manner other than with strict adherence to propriety. I shall make certain to banish His Royal Highness from all future dance lessons during his tenure here."

The princess patted her arm gently. "You need never fear that your conduct is being called into question. Quite the opposite. Rather, it is Nando's I fear. He is notoriously unruly, and I'm afraid he has taken an interest in you."

Why, oh why, did those last few words fill Eleanora with such intense and frenzied longing?

She swallowed hard against the rush of feelings she must never indulge, regardless of the temptation. "His Royal Highness scarcely even takes note of my existence."

"He favors you." The princess's voice was as shrewd as her gaze. "I have seen the way he looks at you, Eleanora, and I well understand the allure. You are lovely, intelligent, and generous of spirit. To a man like him, a paragon such as you must make an intriguing challenge. However, I fear the danger he presents to you. He is handsome and charming, and he could likely seduce even the paper-hangings off the walls."

Eleanora bit her lip to keep a wild chuckle from escaping her. If only the princess knew the astounding accuracy of her words.

They had long since stopped before the windows, where the world beyond was gray and bleak, rain dripping steadily down the panes in fat droplets that made a rhythmic sound.

"I don't want him to hurt you," the princess added, her tone gentling. "Nando is the sort of man who acts first and considers the consequences afterward. Often, only when it is too late."

Eleanora found herself wondering at the connection between her employer and the prince. The princess had once been betrothed to Prince Ferdinando's older brother the king, after all. She had spent time in Varros at the capital, mingling in court, before she had forsaken the king and returned to England to marry for love. Was it possible that Princess Stasia and the prince had enjoyed some manner of arrangement themselves?

The notion troubled her far more than it should.

"I understand," she said quietly, choosing her words with utmost care. "You need not fear on my behalf. I am impervious to him and his rakish charms both. I do thank you for your concern."

"You needn't thank me." The princess gave her another pat, quite as if they were old friends instead of who they truly were to each other. "I like you, Eleanora. I have from the moment I first met you. You don't suffer fools, and you are determined. I would hate to see Nando callously break your heart. You deserve better than a man who is only interested in seeking his own pleasure."

Was that what the princess thought of Prince Ferdinando? Eleanora wanted to correct her, to say there was a great deal more to the man than she had ever supposed. That he possessed hidden depths that she had never imagined existed. And that pleasure did not seem to be his sole concern, even if he was clearly a man who had capitalized upon his looks and noble birth.

But she knew she could not dare come to his defense a second time in the same conversation. To do so would be beyond perilous, and particularly after she had just avowed her complete disinterest in him.

"You pay me a great honor," she said instead.

"Nonsense. I am only telling you the truth," the princess said in that pragmatic way of hers that Eleanora always ascribed to her hailing from Boritania, knowing the princess had been raised in different customs and a vastly different land than England. "Now, then. Let us speak of the reason we must cry off the ball. I am afraid that my husband has discovered there is some new danger concerning Prince Ferdinando, and that he has reason to believe we may all be at peril. He's asked that we remain here at the town house until he can be assured of our safety."

In Eleanora's experience, Mr. Tierney was a fair and intelligent man who happened to be besotted with his wife. They made a lovely pair, both hopelessly in love with each other. But Eleanora was no stranger to intrigue, thanks to her upbringing. She had harbored a strong suspicion that Mr. Tierney's business involved shadowy dealings of some sort. The implication that he was privy to information concerning Prince Ferdinando certainly suggested as much.

But it wasn't just the realization that her employer was far more than he appeared that had Eleanora's stomach twisting in knots. Nor was it the reason for the heavy weight of dread descending upon her. The looming threat of further violence befalling Prince Ferdinando was.

Because, as much as she had done her utmost to guard herself against the charming prince, Eleanora had come to care for him.

"His Royal Highness is still in danger?" she repeated, trying to keep the dismay from her voice, lest Princess Stasia discern far too much from it.

He could play the devil-may-care all he liked, but someone had tried to kill the prince. And that someone was still in London, likely lying in wait for a second chance to strike. The notion left her chilled to the bone.

"I fear so," the princess said, frowning. "I didn't wish to

worry you. Please rest assured that we are safe here. Mr. Tierney has his best men guarding the town house, and if anyone can find out who was behind the attack on Prince Ferdinando, it's my husband. I have implicit faith in his abilities."

"Of course," Eleanora hastened to say, even if she didn't feel reassured at all.

"You may have the afternoon and evening to yourself, Eleanora," the princess added, taking her by surprise.

"But surely you have other need for me, despite the ball," she protested out of habit, for she had long since come to understand what an employer desired of her and to make herself indispensable.

"My sisters are otherwise occupied. In truth, I don't think that either of them was displeased to have to forgo the ball. You're free to do as you like."

"Thank you." Eleanora didn't know what to do with the unexpected reprieve, but she would somehow make the best of it. "Perhaps I'll tend to my correspondence."

In truth, she had no one to write to. Her mother's family had long since disowned her, her mother was gone, and she had neither siblings nor friends. But she didn't reveal any of that to the princess. Instead, she quietly took her leave.

But as she set about returning to her chamber, her duties summarily suspended for the day, she couldn't seem to keep herself from the last room that should concern her. And yet, it was the *only* room she could think about, a forbidden temptation she couldn't seem to resist, regardless of the dire consequences and all her employer's stringent warnings.

Prince Ferdinando's.

～

Eleanora was back.

And sooner than he'd expected, which suited Nando just fine.

Better than fine, in fact. Because he'd just been on his way out of his bedchamber in search of Eleanora when he'd spied her in the hall. As usual, she was wearing one of her hideous gowns, this one in a shade of jonquil that did nothing for her creamy skin and golden hair. It was too large and ill-fitting in the bodice, which had yet another lace fichu tucked within it for modesty. And her locks were covered with a cap that he would generously describe as ridiculously ugly.

His cock went instantly hard anyway.

Bruno was blessedly gone—sent to fetch Nando the furred companion he'd been missing since it would seem he was to be a prisoner here at Tierney's town house for longer than previously supposed. Benvolio was likely forlorn without him.

Nando offered a courtly bow as Eleanora approached.

"Your Royal Highness." She dipped into a curtsy.

"How good of you to pay a call upon me," he said. "I was beginning to get dreadfully lonely."

A charming flush crept along her cheekbones. "It was not my aim to pay a call upon you."

He didn't believe her. Not for a moment. But he wouldn't argue the point.

"Regardless, join me before my ennui becomes too much to bear, won't you?" He retreated into the chamber, making an expansive gesture of welcome to her with his uninjured arm.

Her gaze flitted from his room to his face, then back again, her hesitation making him long to throw her over his shoulder and simply cart her over the threshold.

"I should not," she demurred. "I have a great deal of corre-spondence to attend to, and it would hardly be proper for me to be alone with you now that you are no longer confined to your sickbed."

She wasn't wrong about any of that, and his intentions were the furthest one could get from pure, but Nando wasn't going to allow that to get in the way of what he wanted. Which was Eleanora. He wanted her mouth on his, her sweet sigh of surrender. He wanted her curves pressed against him, her body giving in to temptation.

"My dear Eleanora, you cannot mean to say you would prefer to put pen to paper than spend a few moments conversing with me. I can assure you that I'm ever so much more riveting than an inkwell and an empty page."

Her indecision was written on her lovely face. She *wanted* to join him. His luscious spinster's ice was melting faster than a snowball in a desert. She found herself drawn to him, and it nettled her, but she was helpless to stop the undeniable connection between them.

He was spared from her refusal when the sound of a door opening somewhere down the hall intruded. Her eyes went wide. She didn't want anyone to see her here. Fair enough. He would bustle her into the privacy of his chamber. No one needed to know, save the two of them.

"Make haste before someone sees you," Nando said urgently, keeping his voice low.

She swiftly crossed the threshold, and he closed the door at her back.

"Excellent decision," he purred. "We wouldn't want one of the servants to see you lingering in the hall outside my room and decide that the proper Miss Brett has been seduced by the evil prince."

Her flush heightened, her countenance turning severe. "I am impervious to your wiles, Your Royal Highness. I would think that has already been made apparent."

Quite the opposite, but he would allow her to keep her false sense of comfort for the moment.

"I was making a joke," he explained, flashing her a conspiratorial smile. "Perhaps a poor one. Forgive me."

Her shrewd blue gaze bored into his, and he couldn't help but to note the stiffness in her shoulders—she looked as rigid as a marble statue. "Your apology sounds distinctly insincere. I shouldn't be here."

"And yet, here is where you are." He couldn't hide the smugness from his voice.

"Only until I can remove myself, whilst keeping my reputation firmly intact."

Her cool voice did nothing to quell his ardor.

He had her where he wanted her. And despite all her blustering, she was exactly where she wanted to be as well.

"Tell me, what were you doing in this hall, if not seeking me?" he pressed, for he knew well that her bedroom was on another floor.

"I took a wrong turn." Her chin went up in a little show of defiance he found utterly mesmerizing.

"Perhaps you took the turn you wanted to take," he suggested, reaching for her hand. She jolted when he laced his fingers through hers, but she didn't pull away. "Come and sit with me for a few moments, won't you? I've grown weary of all this isolation."

"You hardly seemed isolated when you invaded the drawing room during our dancing lessons."

Her tone was arch, but her fingers remained entwined with his. Ye gods, she was delectable. He was beginning to think he was in love.

"No need to be harsh with me, my dear. My feelings are quite tender."

"Tender feelings? You?" She gave a short laugh. "Is that

another sally, Your Royal Highness, or do you think me an imbecile?"

"I would never think you an imbecile, nor would I jest about something so serious." He stopped as they reached the seating area near the hearth, and he pressed her hand to his chest. "You see? I possess a heart just as surely as anyone else."

Awareness flared in her eyes, and she kept her hand splayed on him, the warmth of her searing him through his shirt.

"I never doubted you do," she said, sounding suspiciously breathless. "It was the noble sentiment you claimed to have that I questioned."

"You're not wrong for that," he acknowledged, his gaze dipping to her full lips. "I'm not generally known for my noble sentiments."

Particularly where she was concerned.

He couldn't wait to debauch her. Thoroughly.

Her lips parted. "You delight in your wicked reputation."

Perhaps he ought to warn her. Nando grinned.

"I delight in wickedness, full stop."

And still, she didn't move away. Nor did she rescind her hand, which remained over his thudding heart. The air between them hung heavy with sensuality. He didn't want to frighten her away, but he also wanted to take her mouth more than he wanted another breath.

In the next moment, she solved the conundrum for him by rising on her toes and suddenly pressing her lips to his.

And it was a miracle.

A revelation.

It was incendiary.

He wrapped his arms around her, not giving a damn about his wounded arm or the way the action pulled at his stitches or the pain shooting through him at the abrupt movement. He'd happily bleed for the chance to hold her.

She twined her arms around his neck, her lush lips open and hungry and demanding a response from him. There was precious little mastery in her artless kisses, and yet they were more rousing than even the most practiced seductress's. He couldn't get enough of her.

Nando kissed her with all the pent-up passion and yearning burning inside him. He held her against him, their bodies straining together, her supple breasts crushing into his chest, her soft belly cradling his rigid length, thanks to the disparity in their heights. He didn't bother to restrain himself but allowed her to feel him—*all* of him. To feel how badly he wanted her.

She made a sound low in her throat, a husky half moan, and then she was boldly taking control of the kiss, a new finesse replacing the awkward exuberance she'd initially shown. With his lower lip, he urged her to open for him, sliding his tongue into her honeyed depths when she did. She tasted sweet, so sweet. Like tea and refinement and Eleanora, and there had never, in the entirety of his years on this earth, been a finer taste or a better kiss.

Because it was *her*.

There was simply something about Eleanora Brett. He didn't know what it was. But it was consuming him. *She* was consuming him—thoughts of her chasing him through each hour of the day and every second of the night. Nando had to touch her, to learn her curves. He moved his hands, pain accompanying each caress, molding to her lower back, to her determined spine, burrowing in the soft hair at her nape and knocking her dreadful cap askew. He wanted to undress her. To worship every inch of her. To make love to her so thoroughly and please her so well that she would forget her own name, let alone propriety.

Her tongue glided against his, and he nearly lost control.

Just as abruptly as it had begun, the kiss ended as she tore her lips away with a shocked gasp, clapping a hand over her mouth, eyes wide. Desire roared through him. He hadn't released her just yet; she was still in his arms. He never wanted to let go.

"Forgive me," she said, her voice shaken and breathless, so unlike the cool, unflappable Miss Brett she oft pretended to be. "I don't know what came over me."

Nando licked his bottom lip, still tasting her. "I do. Lust. You want me, Eleanora. You may as well admit it."

He wasn't going to allow her to deny the passion so obvious and potent, burning between them with the force of a thousand suns. To do so would be a sacrilege.

"Admitting any such thing would be nothing short of absolute folly." She flattened her hands on his chest and pushed. "Please, release me."

He did as she asked, mourning the loss of contact with her, his frustration soaring to rival his need.

"What are you so afraid of?" he asked softly.

"Myself," she answered instantly.

"You needn't. I'll take care of you, Eleanora. I can promise you that."

"And I've already told you I'll not be a kept woman. I'm no man's mistress."

"Then be my lover instead."

She shook her head. "One is not different from the other, and both would cause me to lose everything."

"Or gain something far more important than playing chaperone to wealthy hoydens and teaching them how to waltz."

She stared at him, looking stricken. "It's not as wretched a fate as you suggest. There are worse situations for women such as myself."

"Oh yes, I am sure you wake each morning positively thrilled by the notion that you must don ill-fitting gowns and subject yourself to the whims of your employer," he drawled.

"I have witnessed what can become of—" she began, her voice taking on an impassioned quality he'd never heard before, but then halting, shaking her head. "Never mind. It doesn't signify."

He couldn't shake the feeling that he had just had his first glimpse of the true Eleanora Brett, the woman she kept hidden beneath her dreadful muslins and fichus and caps and her icy, proper façade. He wanted more. He wanted to know about her. He wanted her darkest secrets, every facet of her past, all that had happened to make her as she was, an enigmatic woman who never showed anyone the true Eleanora Brett.

He wanted to be the man she revealed her true self to, not just the man she gave herself to. The realization shook him; he had never felt such a deep bond with a woman as he did with her. It went beyond the physical.

Deus.

When had he ever wanted more from a woman than a tup?

"I must leave," she added, shaking him from the stranglehold his own thoughts had taken upon him.

Damn it, he couldn't lose her. Not now.

"Not yet." He drew her against him, and to his relief, she didn't stiffen or push away but came willingly, her softness pressing temptingly into his hardness. "Tell me, Eleanora. Finish what you were going to say."

Nando could see her warring with herself.

He lowered his head, nuzzling her temple, breathing in the clean, pleasant scent of her to further torment himself. "I want to know your past, your secrets, what you think about late at night when you're lying alone in your bed."

Her hands had settled on his shoulders again, her fingers gently gripping him in a hold that was as tentative as it was delicious. "You want too much from me."

He smiled, kissing her temple. "I want everything from you, sweetheart. But only when you are ready to give it to me, and not a moment sooner."

She tipped her head back, and she studied him with an intensity that was almost blistering. "That is the problem. I want to give you everything. But I know too well how this tale ends."

For a wild moment, he thought about how their tale wouldn't have to end at all. He could marry her. Make her his. Bed her witless. Watch her grow heavy with his child, again and again.

His prick thickened. He had never been so crazed with lust to consider matrimony, nor having a child. Although he was a devoted rake, he took care to prevent unwanted entanglements or, worse, diseases. Now, the notion of Eleanora Brett in his bed at home in Varros, of filling her with his seed whenever and wherever he wished, was enough to nearly make him come in his trousers.

He inhaled sharply, casting those ludicrous thoughts from his mind, knowing he could never remain constant and that she deserved faithfulness instead of a devil-may-care rake who couldn't even be trusted with the particulars of his brother's kingdom.

"You came to me today," he said instead, capitalizing on her own reckless desire, which was so strong that it surpassed her need to protect herself.

So strong that it brought her back to him, time and again.

So strong that it was inevitable.

"It was a mistake." But despite her words, she had pressed her face into his throat.

"It doesn't feel like one to me, Eleanora." He kissed her ear, caught the shell in his teeth.

What he wanted to do to her.

His injury scarcely even concerned him. A twinge here, a stab of pain there. It was nothing compared to the ability to hold her like this, to have her where she belonged.

His.

Damn it, this woman was *his*, and he knew it to his marrow. She would know it soon enough if she didn't already.

She shivered. "Your Royal—"

"Nando," he interrupted, his lips grazing her throat as he kissed his way lower. "You called me by my given name once, and the world did not end." He raked his stubble against her skin, one hand coming up to snag that inglorious fichu, pluck it away, and send it to the floor. "Try it. I've longed to hear it on your lips every second that has passed since then."

And that was no exaggeration.

"Nando."

He raised his head, tearing his lips from her silken skin requiring all his might, and fell into her eyes. That was what it felt like. Falling and yet being saved, all at once.

"Say it again," he told her hoarsely. "Please."

She hesitated, and for a moment, he feared she would deny him and retreat, like a butterfly flitting away to another flower. But then her perfect, kiss-bruised lips moved, and she obliged him.

"Nando."

And he was lost and found in that moment.

CHAPTER 11

*T*he prince's lips were on hers, hot, demanding, knowing. He kissed like an angel and a devil all at once. This was the true meaning of sin, and now she understood why a woman would surrender her pride, her reputation, her virtue, even her future, just for one stolen moment with a rake. Just to be wrapped in his arms. Just to know his silken seduction. Because it was heady and powerful. It was dangerous and wonderful. It was forbidden and wrong and yet, somehow, it felt wickedly, deliciously right.

But she didn't dare fool herself into believing that she would be so moved by any other skilled seducer. That any other rake would make her feel this way, surpassing all her carefully constructed walls. No indeed, there was something about this man that called to her on the deepest, purest level of her being.

Nando.

She shouldn't think of him in such intimate terms. She shouldn't have called him by his given name. She shouldn't have kissed him. She shouldn't have come to his chamber.

Wrong, Eleanora told herself as she returned his kisses,

this was so wrong. She was following in her mother's ill-fated footsteps. If anyone were to discover her here, she would be finished. And yet, she couldn't stop.

He kissed down her throat. "Eleanora."

Her back arched, her body beyond her control. It was as if her desire for him ruled all. She was his. Helplessly, hopelessly his.

Just for this stolen moment, she told herself as his sinful lips blazed a path over her collarbone. He kissed her as if he had all the time in the world, savoring every inch.

"You're so beautiful," he murmured, kissing his way to the curve of her shoulder.

His teeth gently nipped the skin there, through the layers of her gown and chemise, and she felt a corresponding ache deep inside her. She knew she wasn't a beauty. But she felt like one beneath his sensual spell, his worshipful touch and skillful mouth.

He made her feel as beautiful as she'd ever felt.

"I want you desperately." He kissed back to the dip at the base of her neck, bringing one of his hands up to gently cup the swell of her breast.

She inhaled sharply at the contact. He rolled his thumb over her nipple through her stays, and she thought she might perish from the wonder of it.

"Nando." His name left her in a broken pant.

He was going so slowly. She needed more. Faster. *Now.*

"Yes, love?" He rubbed his face against her throat, the prickle of his golden stubble making her intimate flesh pulse.

"Please."

She wasn't even certain what she was begging him for. Release, perhaps. She was aching and ready for him. So, this was it. This was the reckless, dangerous rush of a woman casting her future to the wind.

"Tell me." He found her ear, nibbling on the lobe, licking

the hollow behind it until she shivered. "I want your complete surrender."

He was going to make her say what she wanted. And she was going to oblige him. Because she'd come too far. There was no turning back now. What was happening between them was inevitable.

"Take me," she whispered. "Take what you want."

"What I want is to please you." Again, the rasp of his whiskers on her throat sent heat pooling between her thighs. "I want to please you so well that you forget everyone and everything."

Blessed angels.

"Then do it."

He strung a line of ravenous kisses along her jaw. "Patience, sweetheart."

"We haven't time for patience. Someone could find us here alone together."

He lifted his head, his blue gaze searing into hers. "I don't give a damn about anyone else right now. All I care about is you."

Pretty words. The practiced promise of a rake. Eleanora knew that. Or, at least, her rational mind did. The rest of her, however—her wanton, aflame body—wasn't interested in examining his motives.

All I care about is you.

No man in all her life had ever truly cared about her. They had wanted her for their various reasons, but none of them had harbored a single concern about her. And foolish though she was, she believed Nando when he said those words.

His hands were traveling over her, following the curves of her body that she took great care to hide in her shapeless, unbecoming gowns. And then tapes were coming undone, and her gown was loosening, the bodice gaping, the entire dress falling to the floor. She stood before him in her chemise, stays, and petticoat, toeing out of her slippers.

The heaviness of desire mingled with the weight of the moment. She was going to give herself to this man. To this sinful prince who had been waging a campaign of seduction against her from the moment they had met.

For the first time since she had started her new life as Eleanora Brett, she was seizing what she wanted. Making a choice that was for herself alone. She wanted the pleasure he promised. Wanted *him*.

She reached for the buttons on his shirt, wondering at how he had managed to get the garment over his head, given his injury.

"It required rather a lot of patience that I no longer have," he said, as if he had read her mind.

No doubt, he had seen the question on her face.

It hardly mattered, because in the next instant, he grabbed hold of his shirt with one hand and rent it entirely in two. She stared at the ripped halves, drinking in the sight of the golden, muscled skin beneath. He was lean and powerful and deliciously male, his chest lightly dusted with a smattering of hair that caught the light, making it glint. Her fingers itched to touch him.

He tugged the ruined shirt from his upper body using his good arm, and she spied the bandage. The reminder of the would-be assassin's bullet was sobering, stealing some of the fire from the moment.

"Your injury—" she began, only to be cut off by him.

"Can go to the devil. I'd take you if I were on my deathbed, which I am, quite thankfully, not."

She might have laughed were the circumstances not so dire and had her heart not been thudding so violently and had her entire body not been on fire. He was grinning, and he looked so deliriously appealing that all she could do was give in to the need to touch him. Her hand on his bare skin. He was hot, so hot, his skin surprisingly sleek and smooth, the crisp hairs a delightful abrasion to her wandering hand.

Oh.

She liked the way he felt. Liked the way the scent of soap clung to his skin. He must have recently bathed. Perhaps even that morning. Unbidden, an image of him fully naked at his bath flooded her mind, making her knees go weak. Before Eleanora could think further, she stepped into him, closing the distance between them, her other hand tracing lightly over the chiseled wall of his abdomen.

"Yes," he said, his voice a low growl. "I love your hands on me."

She loved her hands on him, too. And her mouth. Before she knew what she was about, she pressed her lips to his chest, just over his thudding heart, then over the prominent ridge of his clavicle. Up his neck as he had done to her, the corded muscles tensed as she boldly opened her mouth, tasting the salt of his skin.

"Eleanora, you undo me." He wrapped his uninjured arm around her waist and guided her to the bed at the opposite end of the chamber.

The rest of her garments came off in a haze of lust, his mouth traveling reverently over every new patch of skin he revealed. Until finally, there was not so much as a stitch left to cover her, and he positioned her on his bed in a sideways fashion. She found it most peculiar until he sank to his knees before her, nudging her legs apart.

She stiffened instantly, her thighs tensing, keeping herself shielded.

But then he gazed up at her, such raw, naked longing on his handsome face, his eyes hooded and his gaze darkened. "Trust me, Eleanora."

She shouldn't, and she knew it.

But somehow, she did.

He kissed each of her knees, and she softened, her body relaxing, her thighs parting. And then he dragged his mouth higher, all the way to her center. He kissed her.

There.

On her aching sex.

Eleanora nearly swooned. She wasn't entirely an innocent; one couldn't be, given the life she had lived in her earlier years and the people with whom her mother had surrounded herself. All denizens of the underworld in one form or another, whether noble lords who were indecent voluptuaries or actresses who were seasoned mistresses. Mama and her friends had talked, particularly when they had been in their cups, without regard for who was listening.

Yes, she had known such an act—shocking and sinful and intimate as it was—was possible and, more than that, enjoyable. But knowledge and experience were two entirely separate entities.

Because Nando's lips on her throbbing flesh was a revelation. And then he deepened the kiss, his tongue flicking out to tease that sensitive bundle of flesh that she sometimes toyed with alone in the dark of night, until the pressure building inside her bubbled over and pure bliss rocked through her. Recently, she had touched herself with thoughts of him in mind. But she had never imagined his beautiful face buried between her thighs. Nor had she imagined how impossibly good it would feel, the velvety heat of him laving her swollen bud, of his mouth sucking on her until her toes were curling in the air, until her bottom was rising instinctively from the bed and she was pressing herself shamelessly against him.

She felt helpless, on the edge of something incredible. His gaze found hers, relentless and scorching, and the intensity of his stare and the pleasure he was giving her were so overwhelming that with a whimper, she fell back against the bedclothes, her eyes fluttering closed.

His mouth left her. "No hiding, Eleanora. I want you to watch as I make you come."

Oh, he was wicked. She should ignore his command, and yet she braced herself on her elbows, surrendering to his whim as she had everything else this evening. She had already decided she would be his, so why not indulge both him and herself? Later, she would have nothing but the memory of these lone moments of sinful surrender to keep her warm through the lonely nights.

"Mmm," he hummed, the vibration making her bud pulse, and then he resumed his sensual torture, licking and sucking until she was writhing beneath him.

Her hips pumped in desperate rhythm, and he cupped her bottom with one hand, still favoring his wounded arm. He released her with a lusty, wet sound that should have embarrassed her and yet had the opposite effect.

"Perfection," he praised before capturing her swollen nub and sucking hard again.

It was more than she could withstand. The pleasure that had been building to a crescendo finally burst, and she threw the back of her hand over her mouth to stifle the moan she couldn't hold in. Wave after wave of pleasure washed through her, leaving her lying limp and sated, certain she would never be able to move again.

But he wasn't finished. His tongue flicked, fast and frenzied, working the flesh that still buzzed from her release back into a state of desperate need.

"More," he demanded, sucking, licking, nipping. "Come on my tongue again. I want you screaming my name."

She intended to tell him that she wouldn't be screaming at all because she was far too dignified for such a response, when he lapped at her entrance. Any hint of coherent thought vanished.

A few shallow strokes, and then his tongue sank inside her. And it was glorious, the slick glide of him penetrating her slowly, again and again. Her hips swiveled, her fingers clasping the bedclothes in a tight grip as her body twisted and tangled around him, seeking more, more, more. He gave it to her, plundering her deep. Again and again, the friction of his stubble against her highly sensitive folds taking her closer to her second pinnacle.

He made a low sound of approval, rubbing his face in her sex as he filled her with his tongue. Just when she thought she couldn't bear any more, he stroked her pearl with his thumb. Pure sensation seized her in a ruthless grip, so powerful that she couldn't hold it off even if she wanted to. She was helpless to do anything but surrender, riding out her pleasure, her heart galloping.

When the last wave swept over her, she was out of breath, collapsed in the bedclothes. Nando lifted his head for a moment, his mouth and chin glistening with her wetness, his breathing ragged, his blue eyes scorching. To her shock, he licked his lips, as if savoring the taste of her, like she was delicious and he couldn't get enough.

"You need a cloth," she protested, trying to scramble into a sitting position, embarrassed by the mess she had made of him.

He shook his head. "No cloth. I want you all over me so that when I go to sleep tonight, it's to your scent."

His words ought to have left her cheeks stinging. Instead, all she felt was more desperate longing. She took in the sight of him, so impossibly gorgeous and strong, bare-chested. Her nipples ached, her breasts were heavy and full, and every part of her felt as if she were meant to be here, in this moment, with this man.

"Once more," he told her, the tone of his voice leaving no question as to what he meant.

He intended to pleasure her *again*.

Eleanora wasn't certain if she would survive a third such climax, and yet she knew he would wring another from her with his expert hands and mouth.

"I'll swoon," she protested lightly.

He grinned. "I'll be gentle, sweetheart."

She thought she might burst. Such care, all for her. He was a more-than-proficient and generous lover. He was, she knew instinctively, the sort that her mother's friends had sighed over once upon a time. Hers until she had to return to the world she now inhabited and left this unfettered wanton she'd become behind forever. There could be no place in Eleanora Brett's life for sin. The only pleasure she could know was from her own shy fingers, nervously exploring hungry skin.

How lonely and empty the life she'd forged for herself seemed, compared to this decadent taste of freedom and iniquity. But then, Nando was joining her on the bed, helping her to position herself with her head on the pillows, as if she were to spend the night sleeping at his side. It wasn't sleeping he had in mind, however, and he made that apparent when he leveraged himself on his uninjured forearm and dipped his head, his lips latching on to the peak of her breast.

He slid the hand of his injured arm slowly up her inner thigh, until his long fingers trailed deliberately over her seam. He grazed her almost painfully sensitized bud, and she jolted beneath his touch, renewed need burning instantly to life. He sucked hard on her nipple, and her back arched from the bed, her body desperate for more of his lovemaking.

When her hips danced beneath his ministrations, his swift inhalation made her realize she had jostled his injured arm, which he had taken care to keep mostly still.

"I'm so sorry," she said on a rush. "Have I hurt you?"

He kissed the swell of her breast. "Never mind a small bit of pain. I'd die a thousand times over, and gladly, just for the chance to lick your sweet cunt and your hard nipples and make you come on me a third time."

With that, he sucked the tip of her other breast into the silken heat of his mouth and strummed over her clitoris with greater determination.

She swallowed hard at his blunt words, at the vulgarity. She was more than familiar with such plain speaking from her past, and yet Eleanora had never known until now the effect such sinful words could have upon her. The combination of his bold speech and the attention he lavished upon her breasts and sex had her already at the edge.

He caught her nipple in his teeth and tugged, eliciting a sharp pull of desire from deep in her womb—a need to be one with him, to be claimed by him. The sensual torture he spoiled her with was glorious, but her body still wanted his completely. She wanted him inside her.

Again, as if he were so attuned to her that he could sense her every want, read her mind, Nando gently grazed a fingertip over her opening. She spread her legs, beyond the point of caring about her conduct or fretting over how she would feel about her actions later. She flattened her feet on the mattress. One upward tip of her hips brought him where she wanted him, his finger invading her. It was torment. It was exquisite. She wanted more.

"Nando." She rolled her hips restlessly, seeking, endlessly seeking.

He dappled kisses between her breasts, over her shoulders, her collarbone. "Deus, I love it when you say my name. I don't think my cock has ever been this hard."

With that, he sank his finger all the way inside her, grimacing as he did so, for the action was not without pain on his behalf. Nor was it on hers—the sensation was unfamiliar, so good and yet almost beyond her body's ability to withstand.

Everything was building within her, making her senses intensely aware. Her toes curled into the smooth, cool bedclothes. Her head tipped back on the pillow. Her hands sought his body wherever they could reach, committing every stern angle and elegant plane to memory.

Later, she would think of this. Later, she would remember how wondrous it felt, Nando's finger deep inside her, his thumb stroking her bud, his lips traveling over every inch of her skin as if he could not get enough.

He took her mouth in a deep, drugging kiss as his fingers worked their magic on her, his tongue slipping inside to tease hers. Another stroke and she came undone, crying out into his kiss as she tightened on his finger, a potent surge of pleasure overtaking her. His kiss gentled as he coaxed the last ripple of her release from her. Until slowly, he withdrew, lifting his head to stare down at her with raw tenderness, his customary devil-may-care air entirely gone.

"You are the most glorious woman I've ever beheld," he murmured with such conviction that she believed him.

Words failed her. She could do nothing but cup his cheek, astounded by the rush of feelings coursing inside her. Perhaps it was the effects of what he had done to her, perhaps her wits had been thoroughly addled by desire. But she couldn't stem the tide of emotion, rising ever higher, threatening to drown her.

No, she could not, must not, did not dare to fall in love with Prince Ferdinando. And that was how she needed to think of him again. Not as a man whose body had worshiped hers, but as a powerful royal who would forever be unattainable in all the ways that counted to a woman of virtue.

Even if she was now a woman who had decidedly cast her virtue to the wind.

He turned his head and pressed a kiss to her palm. "Bruno will be returning soon. We should get you dressed."

Dressed?

Her dizzied mind whirled. Somehow, she hadn't expected that. She had anticipated that he would finish what he had begun, that he would take her fully. But the mention of his dedicated manservant had her jolting to reality with the swiftness of a dousing of cold water.

What had she done?

She was lying naked in bed with a prince. With a man who was a notorious rake. And beneath her employer's roof.

"No," he said suddenly, bussing a kiss over her brow. "Do not regret what we've shared. I'll not allow it. I can see your clever mind at work."

"This was a mistake." Eleanora disentangled herself from him, feeling suddenly cold.

She had wanted more, and now she would not have it. She had wanted his body atop hers, his cock inside her. Had wanted to give herself to him. But perhaps he had taken his fill. Perhaps the conquer was all he had been after.

Eleanora slid from the bed.

"It was *not* a mistake." He followed her, looking regal and feral at once, clad in nothing but his trousers.

Her gaze dipped for a moment to a place it ought not, the thick ridge rising in stark relief beneath the fall of his trousers. Evidence of his own unsated desire. He had wanted her, then. Still wanted her. She didn't mistake that.

Not that it mattered now.

Her hands trembled as she took up her chemise and threw it over her head to shield her body from him. "Pray do not argue with me, Your Royal Highness. I never should have

147

come here. Doing so was terribly foolish. And what I have allowed…"

Her words trailed away. What she had allowed could not be undone. She would harbor the memories forever.

"What you have allowed, you will allow again." He retrieved her stockings for her, his jaw tense. "This is just the beginning, Eleanora."

She shook her head, averting her gaze from the sight of him, so unfairly handsome, so very much everything she wanted and could never have. "This is the end of something that should never have begun."

"Damn it, do not be so stubborn. Look at me."

Eleanora couldn't bear to. With grim determination, she donned her stockings.

"Eleanora."

She finished and found her stays, discarded on the floor in the same haphazard fashion as the rest of her garments.

"*Eleanora.*"

His voice was more insistent, but she was determined to remain impervious. He had given her pleasure. Intense, wonderful pleasure. That was all. Nothing more could come of this impossible situation. She pulled on her stays and reached behind her for the laces.

"Let me." He clamped a hand on her waist and turned her.

"Your injury," she protested.

"If I could pleasure you, I can bloody well tie your laces."

Heat washed over her, her cheeks warming as thoughts of just how thoroughly he had pleasured her returned. "Thank you."

"Come to me again tomorrow," he said, his voice urgent at her ear as her stays tightened.

He knew his way around a woman's undergarments.

But of course he did. She knew his reputation all too well.

"I cannot come to you, Your Royal Highness, and you know the reason," she managed, trying to ignore how wrong it felt to refer to him formally now that she knew him so intimately.

"Call me Nando as you did when I was inside you."

When I was inside you. Yes, he had been, had he not? His finger long and deep, reaching a place she had never known existed before.

Her eyes fluttered closed. How was she to withstand him? Or, for that matter, withstand her own yearnings? Even now, she craved him.

She inhaled sharply, then exhaled, slipping out of his reach to retrieve her petticoat. "You mustn't speak of such things."

"Oh, mustn't I?" he drawled, following her like a beast stalking its prey. "Then I suppose I also shouldn't speak of how delightfully wet you were for me or how deliciously your sweet cunt gripped my finger when you came. I certainly won't speak about how I love the way you taste, how I could lick you all day long."

Her ears were on fire as well as her cheeks now. She didn't want his words to affect her, and yet how could they not? She was still wet, and the place where his finger had so recently been throbbed with remembrance. As for his tongue…

No, she wouldn't contemplate the rest.

Eleanora yanked the petticoat over her head. "Surely you have any number of ladies eagerly vying for the chance to occupy your bed. Save your vulgarity for them."

"To the devil with anyone else. They aren't the one I want. You are."

Her fingers fumbled over the buttons fastening her petticoat into place. "Flattery won't sway me."

"Then perhaps this will." In two strides, he was before her, crowding her body with his, one arm banding around her back to pull her into the wall of his bare chest.

She had time to refuse him. She knew what he was about to do as his mouth descended for hers. But she didn't want to. She wanted one more kiss. Her lips met his, clinging hungrily. The kiss was furious and frenzied, a collision of need and frustration. She wrapped her arms around his neck and held him to her for as long as she dared.

Surprisingly, he was first to break the seal of their mouths, staring down at her with a fierce expression. "You are mine, Eleanora Brett. You have been from the moment I first saw you, and nothing and no one can change that."

She licked her lips and stepped away, finding her gown. "I belong to no one. You would do best to forget me. Forget any of this ever happened."

"Impossible," he bit out.

She hauled the gown over her head and stuffed her arms into the sleeves. "Good day, Your Royal Highness."

With what she knew could scarcely pass for a curtsy, Eleanora fled from the chamber and the temptation of a prince who could never be hers.

CHAPTER 12

*S*he'd left her fichu behind.

And his raging cock, begging for release.

The latter had been Nando's own fault. He had decided, drunk on the sweet elixir of Eleanora's cunny, that he would wait to take her. That he would make their first time together about her and her pleasure instead of himself and his own selfish needs. He had intended to take himself in hand after she fled his chamber as if it were Hades.

But then Bruno had arrived with Benvolio, and his plan had dispersed like a flock of startled fowls. Because Nando could not milk his cock until he came whilst he had an audience of a gray-and-white cat who possessed a tendency to curl up on his chest whenever he was lying in bed. Thwarted, he had enjoyed a happy reunion with the feline he had rescued from the London streets and who had been his constant companion ever since. He'd spent the remainder of the evening frustrated and sullen, attempting to sleep, Benvolio's fur stuck to his cheek and making his nose ticklish.

He had risen this morning with a desperate cockstand

and no means of sating himself until later that evening. Supposing Eleanora would be persuaded to come to him again, that was. Which, given her ability to avoid him thus far today, seemed increasingly less likely. She'd been conspicuously absent at breakfast, which he had taken below instead of in his room. She and the princesses had then enjoyed luncheon an hour before the rest of the household. And now, it was approaching dinner, and he was roaming the halls like a starving wolf desperately attempting to scent his next meal.

Pathetic, really.

Nando didn't chase women. He didn't need to. They fell into his lap. But here he was, chasing shadows on the Aubusson, hoping for the slightest glimpse of Eleanora's figure enrobed in whatever hideous muslin frock she'd chosen for the day.

"Just the man I was looking for."

Damnation.

At the sound of Archer Tierney's voice behind him, Nando halted and spun about.

"Well, if it isn't my beloved jailer," he said, not without a hint of bite, for even if he was beneath the same roof as Eleanora, he was growing weary of his host's insistence upon keeping him here.

It was indeed beginning to feel just a bit like a gaol.

"Your protector is a much more apt descriptor, Highness," Tierney countered, unperturbed. "Since you appear to be in full possession of your faculties this fine evening, perhaps you will join me in my study."

He was referring, no doubt, to the laudanum Bruno had insisted upon pouring down his gullet.

"My wound is healing nicely. No need for laudanum at present." He smiled as if he didn't have a care.

In truth, laudanum might be required if he couldn't soon rid himself of the nettling urge to ease his sensual frustration. Not even the sight of a frowning Tierney and the notion of enduring another interview with the man was enough to entirely assuage his lust. It was damned disconcerting. He didn't recall ever being in such a state.

But perhaps that was because he had never previously encountered such obstacles in quelling his need. Certainly, he couldn't remember ever having wanted a woman as badly as he wanted Eleanora. She made him desperate for her.

"Excellent news," Tierney said, jolting Nando from his thoughts. "This way, if you please."

The man had the same way of commanding a room that Nando's older brother Maxim possessed, but Archer Tierney was no king. It was rather annoying.

"Is that a request or a command, Tierney?" he asked, his voice emerging harsher than he had intended.

After all, the man had extended his hospitality. And all indications from the reports Nando received from Bruno suggested that Tierney had the investigation into his attempted assassination firmly in hand. Nando himself didn't care to contemplate such troubling matters. The notion of his own mortality was disconcerting. He far preferred to distract himself with pleasure and indulge his whims rather than contemplate the finite nature of his time on terra firma.

Tierney raised a single brow, his countenance haughty enough to resemble any king's. "Mayhap it's both, Highness. Test me and see."

With that, he turned his back upon Nando and began striding away.

No one turned their backs upon the House of Tayrnes. The slight was no doubt intentional. And then there was the distinct and intentional abbreviation of his address—*Highness* instead of *Your Royal Highness*. Setting his molars on edge, Nando followed in Tierney's wake, joining him in a dark-paneled room that smelled distinctly of tobacco and smoke and looked far less regal than the rest of the town house. It was, he knew instinctively, a chamber that was Tierney's domain. No hint of a feminine hand here as was evidenced so plainly in all the other rooms with their abundance of flowers and lovely gilt-framed paintings and sumptuous furniture.

The chair upon which he sat was bloody hard.

"Whisky?" Tierney asked. "Cheroot?"

Ah, two vices he adored, along with women, of course. Finally, he was beginning to like the hardheaded bastard a bit.

"Both," he said mildly.

Tierney poured him a measure of amber liquid and presented a velvet-lined case bearing cheroots before serving himself as well. Silence reigned as they lit their cheroots and his host settled himself in his infinitely more comfortable-looking chair, thanks to the velvet cushion and back. The arms, however, were carved mahogany, a tusked wild boar represented on each.

Nando cast an acidic look in the direction of that seating instrument. "My goodness, you've had your likeness carved upon it."

Unkind of him, he knew, but he'd been walking about with a nearly perpetual cockstand all day, and he was feeling positively bilious as a result.

"A gift from my beloved wife," Tierney said smoothly. "Her Royal Highness informs me that the boar is a revered animal in her homeland." He paused, puffing thoughtfully on his cheroot. "She also told me she rather thought it resembled you."

Nando had taken a sip of his whisky and had to swallow with such haste that he nearly choked. The result was an indelicate, loud spluttering and a fine mist of Scots whisky raining on Tierney's desk.

"So sorry, old chap. I say, you aren't choking, are you?" Tierney asked with deceptive innocence and blatantly false concern.

"If you were in my homeland, I would have you jailed," Nando rasped without heat, his voice scarcely more than a croak. "I'd send you a diet of nothing but pig snouts for two weeks, and I would give you the leaves of the Iccysle plant to wipe your arse."

The Iccysle plant was native to Varros, and its deceptively inviting, lush greenery left anyone who touched it with a terrible, blistered rash.

"Fortunately, I have no notion of what the Iccy-lickle-whatnot plant is." Tierney grinned. "Else I might consider that a threat."

They locked narrowed stares for a moment. Nando gave in to temptation and took a long drag from his cheroot. It was excellent. Better than he'd expected.

He tipped his head back and exhaled a perfect ring of smoke, a trick he had learned long ago when he'd spent an indeterminate span of time at a seraglio during his more youthful and eventful travels.

"I'd never threaten you, Tierney." He grinned. "Where else would I have my supper or a roof over my head since I'm not permitted to return to my own abode?"

The truth of it was, he could return any time he liked—he wasn't being held against his will. But here he remained, bearing the insults of an English jackanapes. Sitting on a hard chair that was making his left arse cheek fall asleep. Suffering through the worst bout of unrelieved ballocks he had ever endured. His cock, now that he had allowed his mind to stray to the memory of Eleanora's cunt gripping his finger, remained half erect despite his present position and although he was occupying a room with another man whom he didn't particularly like.

"Indeed," Tierney drawled, exhaling his own cloud of smoke as he lifted his whisky in a salute. "However, I do believe you may be closer to returning to your own town house, Highness."

Highness. There it was again.

Nando sipped his whisky, telling himself to let the trivial insult go. "Oh?"

"My men and I have been making a great deal of inquiries, searching for anyone who may have been on the street the day you were shot," Tierney said, his tone businesslike once more. "We have discovered three different people who recognized a man in a greatcoat bearing down upon you that day. They all vow that it was the man who also raised a flintlock pistol and fired a shot at you before disappearing into the crowds."

This was news at last.

Nando's spine stiffened. "Who?"

Tierney exhaled a plume of smoke. "Are you familiar with the Earl of Levering?"

Nando's stomach clenched. The Earl of Levering. Damn the bastard to hell—he ought to have suspected the earl's furious hunger for vengeance hadn't been satisfied by Maxim's coin.

Nando flashed a grim smile. "I happen to be more familiar with the Countess of Levering than with the earl."

But Levering was no stranger to him after the man had caught Nando with his lusty countess. Lady Levering's carnal appetite had been astoundingly immense and perverse even by Nando's admittedly sordid standards, and although she had vowed that her husband would never know about their affair, her assurances had proved false.

Apparently, the bribe to avoid the duel hadn't been nearly as successful as Nando and Maxim had believed.

Tierney's mien was equally forbidding. "Good God, you've been bedding Lady Levering?"

Nando winced. "Our association is not a recent one. During my last trip to London, the countess and I enjoyed a brief entanglement that ended when her irate husband discovered us in an unfortunate state of dishabille."

A nice way of saying he'd been fucking the countess's mouth whilst she'd been on her knees, moaning around his cock.

The memory made Nando's gut curdle now. What the devil had he been doing, shagging his way through London without a care for whom he bedded or why or what the consequences might be? The notion of making love to anyone other than Eleanora felt suddenly foreign and as appealing as a spoiled bowl of fish soup. She was his, the only woman for him, and the knowledge was as profound as it was undeniable.

Why had he not realized it before now? Why had he ever believed that seducing her would be enough?

"Levering was furious with you?" Tierney pressed. "What did he say? Did he threaten you in any way?"

"He challenged me to a duel." Nando's right arse cheek was falling asleep now too. He squirmed on the seat. "Fortunately, we were able to avoid one."

"How?"

There was no polite way to phrase it that Nando could find. Not in English anyway.

"My brother bribed him with a massive sum," he admitted wryly. "Levering accepted the funds, and I was under the impression that the entire affair had been forgotten, if not forgiven."

"It would appear otherwise."

Nando took a sip of his whisky, needing distraction. "Indeed, it would."

157

"You have not been bedding her during this visit?" Tierney demanded.

Nando's ears went hot—he felt like a lad who had been caught with his first wench. "No. Not that it is any concern of yours where I put my prick, Tierney."

"I am conducting an investigation," Tierney said coolly. "Trust me, the last thing I wish for is to fret over the women you've been indiscriminately fucking."

Nando clenched his jaw. "You go too far, Tierney."

He inclined his head, looking decidedly unrepentant. "I am a man of plain speech, Highness."

"I do not bed every woman I meet," he felt the need to point out.

As he'd said, it was no business of Tierney's. However, the mantle of rakehell he'd always worn felt far too heavy suddenly. No longer a good fit.

Tierney shrugged. "As you say. Our primary concern is proving Levering tried to murder you. I had heard whisperings that there was an enemy of Varros and Boritania in London who perhaps wished to do you harm. However, I've discovered no evidence of that. I learned this morning that the man I suspected is, in fact, a Varrosian spy, sent by your brother to watch over you in secret."

How like Maxim to spy on him from afar. Nando was not surprised to learn that someone other than Bruno had been sent to London.

"Thank you for your efforts on my behalf," he offered grudgingly.

Tierney raised a brow. "Reserve your gratitude for my wife. I've expended these efforts on her behalf far more than yours. She considers you a trusted member of her inner circle, given your connection to the queen."

Tierney was making it more than clear that he harbored no love for Nando. Fair enough. Nando didn't particularly like the Englishman either. He couldn't begin to imagine why Princess Stasia had thrown over his brother Maxim to be this rugged, raffish rogue's wife.

"I will throw myself at her feet," he said.

Tierney's eyes narrowed. "If you venture anywhere near to my wife's feet, I'll kill you myself."

Unconcerned, Nando took a small puff of his cheroot, contemplating the information Tierney had just imparted. "Levering is an earl. I don't imagine that having him arrested for trying to murder me would prove easy."

"Nearly impossible," Tierney confirmed. "We have no proof to suggest he was responsible for shooting you, aside from the witnesses, and as a murder has not truly been committed…"

Nando wasn't familiar with the vagaries of English law, but the other man's countenance as his words trailed off suggested there was no hope at seeing the earl jailed for shooting him.

"Understood. Perhaps Levering's desire to kill me has been satisfied by my wounding," he suggested. "He's had his bit of vengeance and flesh now, along with a small fortune. One can only hope he is finally willing to move past any ill will he harbors against me for my association with his wife."

"I don't prefer to operate on hopes, Highness."

"And I don't like to be an unwilling guest at the town house of a cantankerous Englishman," he countered, feeling absurdly freed by the news. "I would prefer to return to my own home at the earliest convenience."

That would mean leaving Eleanora behind. Nando loathed the thought. Realization dawned on him suddenly with utter, perfect clarity. There was an option far preferable to abandoning Eleanora.

And that was taking her with him.

But there was only one way she would agree to accompany him, and he knew what that meant. He also found himself strangely at peace with the notion. The thought of wedding and bedding her had been a maggot in his brain from the moment he had first conceived it, refusing to let him go. The more he turned it over in his mind, the more natural and necessary it felt.

"I recommend remaining here under the watch of my own men," Tierney said, frowning, "but if you wish to go, I have no means of stopping you. All I can say is that you should take great care. Inform your bodyguard of what I've learned concerning Levering. And perhaps return to your homeland as soon as you are able to travel."

There would be no returning to Varros. At least not until he had what he wanted most.

A smile crept over Nando's lips. All he had to do was convince Eleanora to marry him.

※

"ALL MY TROUSERS?" Princess Emmaline demanded, her countenance a commingling of outrage and dread that would have been amusing were not the circumstances so dire.

Eleanora sighed, keeping her tone gentle, for she well understood the princess's fury was not directed at her. "I am afraid so, Your Royal Highness. The choice is your sister's and not mine. I am merely following her edict."

Her efforts at remaining sympathetic to the princess's plight went unappreciated.

The younger woman crossed her arms over her chest in a defensive pose, eyes flashing with defiance. "I won't do it. I won't give up my trousers. They are mine, and she cannot take them."

Eleanora resisted the urge to dig her fingers into her temples in an effort to relieve the dreadful ache in her head, which had been omnipresent throughout the day and was growing worse the longer she spent enduring Princess Emmaline's tantrum.

As it was, she'd spent the night before tossing fitfully in her narrow bed, unable to sleep for thoughts of Nando and the pleasure he had given her, tormented by longing and guilt in equal measures. And then she had returned to her duties by morning, dark circles beneath her eyes, utterly exhausted, contending with a charge who had somehow slipped from the town house without alerting the watchful eye of any of Mr. Tierney's guards and had gone riding.

Alone.

But that had not been the worst of it—oh no.

For the headstrong Princess Emmaline had also chosen to wear trousers for the occasion.

Eleanora had only made the discovery of Princess Emmaline's misadventure too late, when the princess had returned, sneaking through the halls like a thief intent upon filching the silver. Eleanora had known she needed to go to Princess Anastasia with her discovery for Princess Emmaline's own safety. It was a miracle that an unchaperoned woman in trousers hadn't been attacked or absconded with. All London was atwitter with the presence of the princesses and their outlandish ways. An enterprising criminal would have only had to take one look at the lovely woman in trousers and recognize her as one of the wealthy Boritanian princesses.

The result had been a stern admonishment for Princess Emmaline, followed by banishment to her room whilst Princess Anastasia decided how best to punish her sister for her misdeeds. Eleanora had been relieved when Princess Anastasia had reassured her that her position was not in jeopardy after the princess's antics.

And now, that punishment was finally being delivered by

Eleanora—Princess Anastasia wanted every pair of trousers her younger sister owned.

"Princess Emmaline," she tried again, keeping her voice calm by miracle only. "You must understand how deeply worried your sister is by your actions today. There is great danger for a woman alone, particularly when she is dressed as you were and when she is easily recognized as a woman of great wealth."

Princess Emmaline's chin went up. "I will own that what I did was foolish. However, I would not have had to resort to such desperate measures had she and Mr. Tierney not chosen to keep me here as if I am a prisoner. I lived in a prison in Boritania under my evil uncle's rule, and now it would seem as if I have traded one gaoler for another. Furthermore, I fail to understand what my trousers have to do with any of this. They are not hers to take. They are mine."

"As you have said, my dear." Eleanora approached the furious princess, placing a gentle hand on her arm. "Your sister loves you and only wants you to remain safe during your time in London."

"No, what she truly wants is for me to marry some English fop so that she can forget all about me and carry on with her beloved husband," Emmaline countered. "She wants to wash her hands of me."

The princess was vibrating, such was her dudgeon. It didn't bode well for Eleanora's headache or her ability to collect the trousers.

Heaven save her from sisters. Eleanora found herself thankful in that moment that she had been her mother's only child.

She gave her charge another commiserating pat. "I understand it may seem that way, but I can assure you it is not. Your sister only wants your happiness, Princess Emmaline."

"If she wants me to be happy, then she will not take my trousers! They are perfectly acceptable in Boritania and the height of fashion. I'll not be forced to adhere to the silly rules of empty-headed aristocrats."

Eleanora winced. "What you did was reckless and foolish. If you will but calm yourself, you will acknowledge that your actions require an answer from your sister. What else is she to do? What would *you* do, if you were in her position?"

"I would allow me to keep my trousers because I would understand how terribly burdensome these English gowns are." Princess Emmaline issued a shout of pure, unadulterated rage that bordered on animalistic as she stomped her foot and clasped her fists. "May all the saints preserve me."

Eleanora's head throbbed with increasing insistence. Her day had been nothing short of terrible, from the moment she had risen from her bed to now. Dinner had been no better. She had been invited to accompany the family—*sans* Princess Emmaline—for their meal. Eleanora had been astonished to find Nando in attendance, looking unfairly dashing and quite as if he had never suffered a bullet wound. His unflappable charm had been firmly in place, and he had lavished attention upon everyone at the table.

Including Eleanora.

Every time their gazes had connected, she had felt it as viscerally as a touch. Of course, she had been thinking about what had happened between them every second since she had run from his chamber in disgrace the night before.

But she had to concentrate on the furious princess before her now and the unwanted task awaiting her.

"If you will not surrender them willingly, then I shall have no choice but to search for them," she told Princess Emmaline, resigned to her fate.

"No," the princess denied quickly, eyes going wide.

Too quickly.

Eleanora's eyes narrowed as she studied her charge. "Is there something you would not wish for me to find?"

"Of course not," the princess denied with similar, suspicious haste.

Oh dear. It would seem her day was going from dreadful to completely terrible. Eleanora was well-versed in the art of wrangling headstrong and rebellious charges. She had been at this inglorious vocation for years. And she knew when someone was hiding something.

"What is it?" she asked, hoping Princess Emmaline would make the concession and spare her the task of rummaging through her belongings.

The princess said nothing, her countenance torn.

"You have my promise that if the object is of no danger to you, I will not tell your sister," she added when her charge continued to hesitate.

Princess Emmaline heaved a sigh. "Very well. It is a book, if you must know."

"What manner of book could cause such concern?"

The moment the question left her, Eleanora understood. The expression on the princess's face spoke for her.

"*The Tale of Love*," Princess Emmaline answered quietly.

The bawdy book was a compilation of lurid stories, supposedly written by one of London's greatest courtesans. Eleanora had heard her mother's friends speaking of it, and once, she had found a volume left in the drawing room after one of Mama's more raucous soirees. She had given in to curiosity and peeked.

"Ah," Eleanora said. "I understand your reticence. However, I can assure you I will keep the knowledge of the book to myself in exchange for your trousers."

The princess pinned her with a glare. "That is bribery."

She smiled serenely. "Occasionally, I am Machiavellian."

Nando had told her so. And thinking of him stirred the restless longing that had not been far since last night.

With a flounce, Princess Emmaline went to retrieve her trousers. No fewer than a dozen pairs, as it happened. Grimly, Eleanora departed from the princess's chamber, bearing all twelve of Emmaline's beloved garments. She was halfway to her room, where she would store them until she met with Princess Anastasia in the morning, when she rounded a corner and nearly collided with the very man who had been plaguing her thoughts.

Nando's hand clamped on her waist. "Steady, my dear."

His deep rumble, faintly laced with the traces of his native tongue, sent heat unfurling through her.

"Thank you." She stepped neatly from his grasp and dipped into a curtsy, trying to cling to her ever-diminishing modesty. "If you will excuse me, Your Royal Highness?"

His jarringly blue gaze slipped to the pile of folded trousers in her arms. "Why are you carrying garments about? Never tell me the princess has reduced you to a maid."

"Not at all. Her Royal Highness enlisted me in securing Princess Emmaline's trouser collection. Her defiance has led to some unfortunate…difficulties today."

And speaking of difficulties, the longer Eleanora lingered in the hall alone with him, the greater the temptation to steal away with him again. As it was, his scent had curled around her, shaving soap and a hint of smoke. His beauty was cruel. She wanted to look away just as much as she never wanted to stop drinking in the sight of him in his elegant evening wear, his snowy cravat tied in a simple knot that was a stark contrast to his golden skin.

The urge to place her lips there rose, strong and wild.

"Allow me to carry them for you," he said, reaching for the stack with his uninjured arm.

"But your wound—"

He plucked them from her grasp with ease. "Has healed sufficiently. Tell me where we are going with Emmaline's trousers."

His proximity had an alarming effect upon her. Her foolish body had come to life, her nipples going hard against her stays, the ache between her legs renewed with such insistence that she had to press her thighs together in a discreet effort to quell the desire.

"It isn't proper for you to be so familiar with Her Royal Highness or her garments," Eleanora forced herself to point out.

Nando just grinned, the effect deadly to her ability to resist his charm. "My dear Eleanora, when have I ever given you the impression that I give a damn about what is proper?"

"Never," she admitted.

His grin deepened. "Then lead the way. I do so admire watching your hips sway when you walk."

Heat crept up her throat. "Your Royal Highness."

He leaned in to her, his lips so close that they grazed her ear as he spoke. "Don't pretend to be scandalized, darling. My tongue was inside you last night."

A strangled sound fled her. She felt as if she were about to have a fit of the vapors.

"This way," she clipped, forcing herself into motion before he goaded her into doing something utterly shameful.

She stepped around his tall, elegant form and hastened down the hall, doing her utmost to keep her hips from moving in the fashion he had suggested. The nerve of the man! Had he truly ogled her from behind as she had walked? No doubt he had.

His low chuckle, far too near behind her, told her he was aware of her thoughts and her attempt to keep from giving him something to watch. She might have decided against leading him to her bedroom, but she was keenly aware of the need to keep the trousers somewhere that Princess Emmaline would not have access to them. Fortunately, she had been given a chamber that was in a tucked-away corner of the town house where they ran little risk of being seen together.

She stopped before her door and turned back to him, reaching for the trousers. "Thank you for your help, Your Royal Highness."

"My pleasure." He relinquished the trousers as she struggled to keep herself from staring at his lips and remembering what they felt like on hers.

Eleanora cleared her throat. "Good evening."

She expected him to request an invitation into her private chamber. Or to offer some manner of resistance to her curt dismissal. Instead, he reached around her to open the latch and then offered her a courtly bow.

When he straightened, he held her gaze, his expression solemn for once—notably bereft of his usual endless humor and wry charm. "Come to me tonight, Eleanora."

The low words stole her breath.

"I cannot," she managed when she at last found the capacity to speak.

"Then I shall come to you."

"No." Her denial was swift and forced. "It is impossible, Your Royal Highness, and you know it."

"There's something I want to speak with you about," he said, startling her by tucking a stray tendril of hair behind her ear. "A matter of grave import."

Her mind whirled with possibilities. Why would he wish to talk with her? Was it just a ploy to have her where he could seduce her? Did she dare risk discovery a second night by obliging him?

No, she couldn't.

"It would be a mistake for me to come to your chamber,"

she told him quietly. "I must put my duties to the princesses first."

As it was, she was on perilous ground, given Princess Emmaline's shocking defiance. No respectable household would ever again offer her a situation if she were to be found cavorting in a bachelor's room whilst she was meant to be guiding her charges on the principles of the *ton*.

"I'll be waiting for you," he said softly.

Bemused, she watched as he took his leave, striding down the hall with the purposeful walk of a man who knew his own glory all too well.

"Vain rogue," she grumbled to herself as she crossed the threshold of her modest chamber.

There was no way she was going to do something as foolish as seeking him out in his bedroom again. Not after what had happened last night.

CHAPTER 13

*E*leanora didn't even need to tap at the door. It swept open with surprising haste to reveal the man who had been taunting her every thought ever since they had parted several hours earlier. He was no longer wearing his evening finery but a loose silk banyan the color of aquamarines.

Wordlessly, he stepped back, gesturing for her to enter. With a furtive glance over each shoulder to ensure the darkened hall remained silent and empty, Eleanora slipped into his chamber. She took in the glowing sconces and candelabra, the fire burning cheerfully in the hearth. There was no sign he had made any preparations for sleep, despite the lateness of the hour.

"You were waiting for me," she observed, turning back to him against her better judgment.

The banyan brought out the vibrancy of his eyes. It was unique, embroidered with rich gold thread and the letter F on his lapel, lest she have any doubt that it was a garment his man had fetched for him from his own town house. The flicker of candlelight caught in his golden curls. He smiled, and she tried not to throw herself at his chest and kiss him until she couldn't think.

"I knew you would come."

He was more certain of her than she was of herself. But then, perhaps Nando was merely certain of the effect he had upon all women.

"How could you have known, when I only just decided a few minutes ago?" she asked, even though that wasn't quite true.

She had waged an inner battle over the decision; it was true. She had also held a lively debate with the stack of Emmaline's trousers. She had enumerated a list of all the reasons why she must stay far, far away from the Prince of Varros's bedroom. But in the end, she hadn't been able to quell the restless need to see him. To learn what it was he wanted to speak to her about.

Foolish.

Downright stupid.

But here she was, in the lion's den.

He cocked his head at her. "My dear, do you expect me to believe such rubbish? We both know you were planning to come to me tonight whether I invited you or not. I gave you too much pleasure for you to stay away."

Her chin went up. "You, sirrah, are a vainglorious popinjay."

"And you are charmed by me despite yourself." He winked. "Confess."

The knowing, intimate expression on his face made her stomach flutter as if it were inhabited by a dozen butterflies.

"I tolerate you," she countered, knowing that if she gave him any hint of her susceptibility to his rakish wiles, he would seize upon her weakness.

And summarily destroy what remained of her already flagging defenses.

But she hadn't come to him to be seduced. Had she?

Of course she hadn't.

"You more than tolerate me, my darling Eleanora." He caught her hand in his and brought it to his lips, bussing a light kiss over her knuckles with a courtly air. "You like me."

She *did* like him. She liked him far too well and against every instinct and shred of reason she possessed. Men like Prince Ferdinando didn't flatter and woo women such as herself because they intended to marry them. They did so because they wanted them in their beds.

And if Eleanora gave him her virtue, she would lose everything she had worked so diligently to build. Her entire life would be upended, whilst the prince would saunter off to charm another all-too-eager victim. She had almost given herself to him entirely last night, but she had returned this evening with restored determination. She would not allow herself to relent.

"I hate to disappoint you, Your Royal Highness, but I do not like you at all," she lied.

"Oh?" He was undeterred, brushing another kiss over the top of her hand now. "Is that so?"

She shivered. "Yes, regretfully so."

"Have you taken a chill, my dear?"

Of course he would have noted her reaction to him. His touch was like fire. He filled her with heat and desire. Made her think things she must not think. Made her long for more of what she must not want. How dangerous he was.

"I have," she fibbed again. "The air is rather cool today."

"I do believe you're deceiving me," he said smoothly, before turning her hand over to kiss her palm. "You'll have to prove that you don't like me."

"How should I prove such a thing?" she asked sharply. "I've already told you."

"And yet, your body reveals the lies you tell just as it did last night." His gaze holding hers, he traced one of the lines on her palm with his tongue.

That persistent ache between her legs throbbed. She knew she ought to yank away from him and return to the haven of her bedroom, where she could not be tempted by this sinful devil. And yet, she couldn't seem to sever the connection. She held herself impossibly still as the velvet, wet sweep of his tongue slowly turned her to flame.

He glanced up at her, his expression serious, his eyes intense. "You see, Eleanora? I can feel you tremble for me. Only think of how lovely my tongue would feel on your pearl again. And deep inside you."

She didn't want to think about that.

She couldn't *stop* thinking about it. Her body remembered it all too well, and every part of her was crying out for more.

"No." She shook her head firmly, hoping she could send those dreadful, wanton, best forgotten notions from her mind.

"Yes." He gave her a soft, almost tender smile and kissed the sensitive skin of her inner wrist, his tongue flicking over the tracery of veins there. "Give yourself to me, Eleanora. Don't you see how inevitable it is? Of course you do. It's why you've come here tonight, against all your better judgment. It's why your prim and proper ice melts for me."

She wanted him. Ached for him. She'd never known such frenzied yearning was possible.

But that didn't make it right. And it didn't render her any more able to succumb to the decadent seduction he promised.

Just one more night, her reckless body whispered. She summoned her strength, ignoring it. Because one more would turn into another, and then another, and another until he had tired of her and cast her aside as he would inevitably do. He would return to his homeland and his court and the women who adored him, and he wouldn't even remember her name. Whilst she would be heartbroken and alone, her life lying about her in ruins that no amount of effort could resurrect. She had seen it with Mama time and again. Every protector had left in the end, and there had been nothing left.

She shook her head. "I cannot, Your Royal Highness."

"Nando," he purred. "Say it."

She had said it last night. She thought of him in those same, intimate terms. And she couldn't deny she liked the way it felt on her tongue, the intimacy it implied.

Meow.

The sound was so abrupt and out of place that for a moment, Eleanora was convinced she had imagined it. But then it came again, the loud, undeniable call of a feline, followed by a trill.

She stiffened. "Is there a cat in here?"

His grin deepened until fine lines creased at the corners of his brilliant eyes, and he released his hold on her hand. "Of course there is. Why wouldn't there be one?"

She stared at him, feeling oddly bereft without his touch, and wondered if he were truly and utterly mad after all. "Why do you have a feline in your chamber?"

As if on cue, a cat leapt to the back of a chair by the hearth, balancing precariously on the stuffed edge. The little fellow must have been curled up on the seat, which wasn't visible to Eleanora from her current vantage point.

"He's not just any cat," Nando said smoothly, moving toward the cat in an unhurried gait. "He's Benvolio."

The prince made the declaration in the same manner she imagined he might make an announcement at court. As if it made complete and utter sense, and perhaps to him, it did. Her lips parted, but words were beyond her.

"Benvolio," she managed to repeat. "After the character in *Romeo and Juliet*, I presume?"

He stopped at the back of the chair and ran the backs of his fingers over the gray-and-white cat's head. "Ah, you are familiar with the tragedy, Miss Brett?"

Her mother had been an actress. Eleanora knew the lines of every role Mama had played by heart. She had helped her mother to rehearse, as a naïve child secretly in love with the sweeping emotion and the pageantry. The seedier side of her mother's life had been unknown to her then, in those innocent days when the world had seemed a much brighter, happier place.

She had learned the truth soon enough. It was a lesson she would never forget.

Eleanora forced a smile. "Quite. It seems an odd name for a cat."

"Does it? How strange. I took one look at him when we met in the streets and simply knew he was a Benvolio. Call it an instinct, if you will."

The man was getting more preposterous by the moment.

"You met him in the streets?" she asked, the invitation to sin with him momentarily supplanted by the presence of a feline he had apparently taken under his wing.

He raised an imperious golden brow. "Where else is one expected to make the acquaintance of a cat?"

"In the bedchambers of dissolute princes," Eleanora quipped before she could think better of it.

Before she could recall she was not the lively, carefree girl she'd once been but the severe, joyless woman she'd been forced to become. This was no pleasant drawing room flirtation. This was the beginning of her fall from grace if she but allowed it, cat or no.

"Tell me, my darling Eleanora, how many bedchambers of dissolute princes have you visited?" he asked, his voice silken.

"Only one," she answered tartly. "And I am not, nor shall I ever be, your darling."

"Hmm," was all he said in response, a noncommittal hum that suggested he didn't believe her denial whatsoever.

She wouldn't be distracted or goaded by him, she decided sternly.

"The cat," she reminded him. "You found him in the streets?"

"In a positively dreadful stew," the prince confirmed, still idly stroking the feline's soft-looking fur as Benvolio lovingly rubbed his face against Nando's arm. "Near a house of ill repute, if you must know, though I'm ashamed to admit it now. The little fellow was meowing quite loudly, and he had the biggest eyes I'd ever seen on a cat. I petted him and could feel each bone in his spine beneath my hand. He was clearly in need of food, and I was in wont of a companion." He flashed her a grin. "The rest is history, I reckon."

Nando had rescued a starving cat from the streets. Of course, in true rakehell fashion, it had been during a visit to a brothel. Eleanora could not quite tamp down the stinging tide of jealousy that rose inside her at the thought.

He gave the cat a few more fond caresses and then turned back toward her, giving Eleanora his full attention. "But Benvolio was not my reason for inviting you to my bedroom this evening."

"What was, then?" she dared to ask, even though part of her feared his answer.

And her own response to it.

Because she didn't even trust herself any longer. Not when it came to this maddening, alluring, dangerously seductive man.

"To tell you that I am leaving."

The heat burning inside her turned abruptly to ash, and all she felt was cold. Cold, cold dread. The ferocity of her reaction surprised her. What had she expected of him? He had summoned her to him for one last attempt at seduction before he left.

"You are leaving England?" she asked through numb lips.

He drew to a halt before her, his impossibly blue gaze searing hers. "Would you miss me if I were?"

"Do not toy with me, if you please," she bit out, horrified to discover her hands were trembling with the force of her emotion. She sank her fingers into her muslin skirts, clenching tightly so he wouldn't see. "Answer the question."

"I'm leaving this town house," he said simply. "Not England."

Relief flooded her, followed quickly by alarm. "But Princess Anastasia said Mr. Tierney feared you remained in great peril. It was the reason we avoided the ball meant to honor the princesses. You should not leave with such haste."

"It's hardly haste. I've been here for what seems an eternity. You were the only bright light in an otherwise dark and dismal stay."

His words were gratifying, but he was still leaving. And the effect his imminent departure was having upon her was just as distressing. She very much did not want him to go. It astonished her to realize that she felt the same way about the prince—he had been a bright spot in an otherwise arduous routine of drudgery.

She cared for her charges; of course she did. But that didn't mean her task wasn't a thankless one. She had spent each day in breathless anticipation of seeing him again, of crossing his path and drawing nearer to him. He was like the sun, bringing light and warmth to all in his presence, and she was the moon, a creature of darkness, doomed to dwell only in the night. To scarcely be seen and oft ignored.

"Your presence here will be missed," she said quietly, her throat thick with suppressed emotion. "But I understand your desire to return to your own home. However, can you not see the danger?"

"The danger doesn't concern me," Nando told her easily. "It never did, and now Tierney has reassured me this evening that I need no longer fret over another such attempt."

"I am relieved for you." More relieved than she could convey. More relieved than she had imagined possible.

Good heavens, it was almost as if she had begun to develop tender feelings for this man, this prince who could never be hers.

"Thank you." He reached for her, taking one of her hands from the folds of her gown and grasping it. "But that's not all I need to tell you."

Heat chased up her arm from the connection, bringing the fervor of her desire for him back to life. "I don't understand."

He brought her knuckles to his lips for a lingering kiss that was somehow every bit as intimate as his mouth on her most private flesh the night before. She felt it to her toes.

When he had finished, he raised his head, entrapping her gaze with his. "When I go, I want you to accompany me."

CHAPTER 14

*N*ando watched Eleanora intently as he awaited her response. She was dressed as sparsely and primly as she had been earlier, her golden hair beneath a cap, tucked into the same serviceable chignon she always wore, but this time nary a stray tendril having escaped to curl about her face. Perfect in her poise, as icy and glorious as ever. She gave him no hint of what she was thinking, her face as still as a mask.

He had expected more. A reaction, at least.

"You must know that I cannot." Her tone was measured, calm.

Ah, the answer he had been anticipating, a denial, a refusal. But Nando had spent the hours since his meeting with Tierney considering all the ways in which he might somehow persuade the stubborn Eleanora Brett to accompany him, and the answer, when he had fallen upon it, had been obvious. The more he thought about it, the more pleased he became.

"I want you to come with me as my betrothed," he added.

And then, the mask broke.

Her lips parted, her eyes widened, and the velvet depths of those blue orbs seemed to plumb his soul. "You make a mockery of me."

"Never."

He could understand her distrust of his proposal. He was not often a serious man. He was a voluptuary who had spent much of his life in search of pleasure as a means of distracting himself from the sorrows that haunted him. He had come of age in the shadows of war, and though his older brother had shielded and protected him, Nando had been more than aware of the danger, the blood that had been shed, the loss.

"I…I fail to understand." Her words were slow, halting.

Nando took both her hands in his, drawing her against him. "I want to marry you. From the moment I first saw you, you have haunted my dreams and all my waking hours. Come with me. Be my wife."

Her hands trembled in his, and a laugh bubbled up from her, the sound incredulous. "If this is your attempt at a sally, forgive me for finding it cruel."

He gave her hands an urgent squeeze. "This is no jest. Marry me, Eleanora."

Nando had turned the notion over in his mind, again and again. The thought of this woman being his had been more intoxicating than any opium or whisky he had ever consumed. He'd been obsessed with the prospect ever since it occurred to him. He would marry her, pleasure her beyond her ability to comprehend. Her artless sensuality the night before had proven to him that she was his match. She was responsive and eager, and he could scarcely wait to begin teaching her the art of pleasure.

"You are a prince."

He had never cared for the title less than he did now,

standing before a woman who deemed it an impediment rather than a boon.

"Regretfully, yes." He grinned. "I do hope you would have me anyway."

She shook her head. "What I meant to say is that you are a prince, and I am not just a commoner, but the daughter of an actress."

This was news—his stern Eleanora the daughter to a woman who had trod the boards. However, he didn't care.

"I am more than aware of who you are, my dear."

"No, you are not." She tugged her hands from his grip and turned to walk the length of the room, her back to him as she waged some inner battle he didn't comprehend. When at last she spun to face him, her expression was stricken. "You cannot possibly believe that a marriage between the two of us could ever happen. It would be the misalliance of the century. Princes do not marry spinster chaperones who were born on the wrong side of the blanket."

Her words took him aback.

Nando went to her, genuinely confused. "The wrong side of the blanket? I don't understand. Forgive my pitiful English."

His English was eloquent, far from pitiful, but the term was unfamiliar to him.

She squared her shoulders. "I was born a bastard. That is what it means. My surname is not Brett. All that I am, all that I have made of myself, is a lie. If any of the grand households where I have been employed knew what and who I truly am, they would have cast me into the streets rather than expose their innocent daughters to me."

Her confession astounded him. Not because he was horrified to discover her mother had been an actress who hadn't been wedded to her father. Not even because he was surprised to learn she had been deceiving everyone with the proper façade of Eleanora Brett. But rather because of what her revelation meant. Everything she had just told him could lead to her ruination, and yet she had trusted him with this information.

A rush of something foreign and potent swept over him, and he took her into his arms instinctively, ignoring the nagging pain of his wounded arm. He held her stiff form in a gentle hold that she could escape if she wished.

"Thank you."

Her brow furrowed, her expression one of pure befuddlement. "Why do you thank me?"

"For your honesty. For trusting me with your secrets." He kissed her softly, quickly, chastely—a gesture of gratitude rather than an attempt at seduction. "I don't care about your past, Eleanora. Your future is what I covet. You, in my arms, in my bed. I want you to be mine."

As the last word left him, he almost shuddered at the rightness of it, the potency. What a giddy feeling. His cock went hard again at the notion—Eleanora, *his*. He had never, in his storied career as a rakehell, had a woman who had been his alone. And that this magnificent one could be made him feel more powerful than he ever had. How he had imagined he could take her as a lover, bed her a few times, and then excise her from his blood, was a mystery to him.

"Marriage," she repeated, sounding dazed. "How shockingly bourgeois of you."

"Have I ever given you the impression that I take myself seriously?" he teased gently. "If so, I must offer my most sincere apologies."

She laughed, a true laugh. More like the giggle of a carefree young girl, the same way she had laughed when they had danced together and he had suggested Princess Emmaline needed pianoforte lessons. He felt as if he had emerged from war the victor.

"You are mad," she said.

And she was not wrong.

Nando kissed her again, needing that laughter on his lips. Her response was to wind her arms around his neck and sink her fingers into his hair. She clung to him as if he were a tree she intended to climb. And her mouth opened without any coaxing from him, her tongue darting hot and wet against his. He moaned, wanting her more than ever, his prick raging with need as he cupped her arse and pressed her more fully against him.

He kissed her and kissed her, until they were both breathless. His wound was paining him, but he didn't care. He was intent upon the woman in his arms.

When at last he lifted his head, her mouth was dark and swollen from his kisses, her eyes slumberous with desire. And he knew he had won her at last.

"What say you, Eleanora? Will you marry this mad prince?"

She was silent for a heartbeat. "Yes."

∽

ELEANORA WOKE AS WAS CUSTOMARY, alone in her narrow bed as the faint strains of dawn began to paint the London sky with color. For a moment, she lay there, silent and still, convinced that the recollections of the night before flooding her mind had been nothing more than the fanciful imaginings of her dreams.

But no.

As the traces of slumber fled and she rose in her nightgown to stir the embers in her hearth to warm the cool morning air, she realized it had been real. Nando had asked her to marry him. And she had agreed, after which he had kissed her soundly and then bundled her off to her room.

She had been too confused by the unexpected develop-ments of the evening to offer much protest. They'd walked silently, hand in hand, through the darkened halls, and he had left her with another kiss before urging her to get some rest. She had somehow expected more, his continued expert attempts at seduction. But he had disappeared into the shad-ows, and she had been left to undress in a state of shock.

What had she agreed to?

Had he been truly serious?

He hadn't felt feverish. He hadn't seemed delirious. He hadn't smelled at all of spirits, so he had not been in his cups. He had appeared perfectly rational even as he had made her an utterly *irrational* proposal.

Eleanora prodded the coals and then straightened, her mind still whirling. Marriage. She had never thought it a possibility for herself. And certainly not with a prince. For so many years, she had banished all thoughts of husband and family from her mind. Longing for that which was impos-sible had only made her circumstances more dire.

With shaking hands, she set about donning her stockings and chemise. How was it possible that the life she had yearned for had somehow fallen into her lap, given to her by a silver-tongued rakehell prince? What manner of husband would he make—or, for that matter, father? If she were fortunate enough to have children, would he love them?

Her own father had been present only occasionally during her youngest years. Her memories of him were faded like a dyed cloth left too long in the sun. He had been an important man, Mama had warned, and they mustn't ask for too much of his time. Their few visits had been dour and unsmiling. The man who had sired her had observed her as if she were a strange new insect that had appeared before him and he wasn't certain whether he should squish it beneath his boot or capture it for further study.

Then one day, Mama had asked the servants to pack up their belongings and leave the elegant town house that had been their home. They had left in a hired carriage and never returned. Her mother had taken a role that returned her to the stage and a new lover, although Eleanora had not understood who the gentleman who paid calls upon her mother had been at the time. As she had grown older, she had come to understand why the gentlemen visited Mama and why they moved so frequently. No town house was ever a home for more than a year, and not all of them had been as luxurious or stately as others.

Eleanora sighed heavily, smoothing wrinkles from her chemise. How could she expect a prince to be any different from the sire she had scarcely even known? She drew on her stays, tightening them so much that they bit into her sides, but she scarcely noticed. Was she making a dreadful mistake?

And how would she tell the princesses that she was leaving them?

Where would Nando expect them to live? In Varros?

The questions that had kept her awake, plaguing her through the night, returned with a vengeance. She took up her petticoat and gown, finally finishing her toilette with a modest fichu and a cap over her hair.

Nando had shown kindness to the cat he had rescued from the mean streets of London, she reminded herself. Benvolio had certainly seemed to adore his master. Surely that was a sign that he would not be a cruel father to any children they might have one day.

Eleanora left her chamber, no more certain of her decision by the light of day than she had been the night before. She wasn't even certain when she and Nando would marry. He wanted her to go with him when he left the town house this morning, but that was a scandalous suggestion. She could not live with him until they were wed.

She didn't have to go far to find Princess Anastasia, who came upon her in the hall, wearing a look of unabashed concern. "Miss Brett, just who I was looking for."

Eleanora offered her a curtsy. "Good morning, Your Royal Highness. I hope I did not keep you waiting."

Her duties for the day did not begin for another half hour, but she was quite accustomed to the demands of aristocratic employers. Most expected their servants to be at the ready upon a whim.

"Perhaps we might have some tea in my salon," the princess suggested, neatly avoiding Eleanora's polite question.

Something in the other woman's tone and unsmiling visage told Eleanora that Princess Anastasia *knew*.

"Of course."

The princess offered her a smile that didn't reach her eyes. "We have much to speak about, haven't we? Come, Eleanora."

The air between them changed as she accompanied Princess Anastasia to the salon. Once they were comfortably ensconced within, they made polite conversation as the tea tray arrived. The princess poured, offering Eleanora a dish of tea with a wan smile.

"I do hope you know what you are doing, my dear."

Eleanora swallowed hard against a rush of emotion—dread, uncertainty, excitement, longing. "I am sure I don't."

"I wish you would have told me the truth when we talked about Nando's interest in you."

"I didn't know what the prince's interest was." Eleanora paused, frowning as she considered her words. "Indeed, I still don't know. I am at a loss as to why he would wish to bind himself to someone so socially inferior."

"You needn't be modest," Princess Anastasia said, pouring her own tea with elegant, efficient motions. "You are quite lovely despite your efforts to hide your looks. Nando is drawn to beautiful women."

Women.

She did not miss the emphasis the princess placed upon the last word, and she could not quell the sting of jealousy at the reminder that he had an endless string of lovers in his past and likely an equally unending string of more in his future. She didn't expect him to be faithful. She knew his reputation.

"I would hardly describe myself in such flattering terms, though I do thank you," she said.

The princess took a delicate sip of her tea. "And now, we are to be without you. Your loss will be felt by us all, but particularly by my sisters. You have been such a boon to them, and I am grateful for all your efforts on their behalf. You've done wonders to rein in some of their wilder Boritanian ways."

That was a polite way of describing the headstrong ladies and their penchants for scrapes.

Eleanora smiled, deciding it best to remain politic in her response. "I will miss Princess Emmaline and Princess Annalise as well."

She would not, however, mourn no longer having to contend with Princess Emmaline's affinity for trousers. Eleanora wisely kept that to herself.

"You will, of course, remain here with us as our guest until you marry," Princess Anastasia added, her tone growing stern. "Nando was insistent that you must accompany him this morning, but I refuse to allow it. He is…rather imprudent at times."

Imprudent. It was one way to describe the wickedly handsome prince who somehow wished to marry her. Certainly, no outside observer could call his decision to wed an unsuitable spinster who was his inferior in every way *wise*.

But there were other words she would use to describe him as well. Charming. He had that way about him of making it feel as if all the world were a jest presented for his benefit. He was quick to laugh, even at himself. He knew how to seduce, yes, but he was not selfish when it came to pleasure. Generous. He had given her so much without ever asking for anything in return. Kind. Witty.

Heavens, if she didn't take greater care, she would fall in love with him. And that would never do. Nando might, through some outlandish flight of fancy, choose to marry her. But he would never love her. She knew his sort of gentleman well, for she had seen them with Mama often over the years. Inconstant, their devotion at first a roaring fire that eventually subsided into cooling ash.

"I can only suppose how this must seem to you," Eleanora managed, turning her attention back to the conversation at hand. "I assure you that there was no scheming on my part to win the prince's favor."

"Oh, my dear, you need not worry in that regard," the princess reassured her. "I know your character. A more trustworthy, honest, good person I have yet to meet."

The unexpected praise made Eleanora's cheeks heat, for she had not been entirely honest and she had stolen to Nando's chamber in secret. She had not been good. The secret she had kept about her background had been necessary for her own survival, but the knowledge didn't ameliorate her guilt.

"Thank you." Her hand trembled on the dish of tea, her cup rattling. "You are far too generous in your praise, of which I am undeserving."

"You need not be modest. I have witnessed your patience and sincerity, your kindness and your gentle wit, on many occasions. I have come to like you a great deal during your time here, and that is why I wished to speak with you now in private. I am concerned for you, Eleanora dear."

"What is your concern?"

"Nando is reckless. He has spent his time in London engaged in all manner of debauchery, and now he has suddenly settled upon marriage, seemingly in the blink of an eye. Between the two of us, I am not certain he has the capacity to be the sort of husband you deserve."

Reckless. Yes, there was another fine word to describe him. Eleanora couldn't deny it. Nor could she deny that she harbored some misgivings of her own regarding Nando and their marriage.

"Do you suppose he will change his mind?" she asked, her tone sharper than she had intended, for the frantic thought had occurred to her more than once.

The princess appeared pensive, her lips flattened into a thin line. "I do not doubt that he is serious about marrying you. However, I find myself wondering what will happen after you are wed."

Eleanora managed a thin smile. "That makes two of us."

"Oh dear." Stasia's expression shifted, sympathy lining her lovely countenance. "You need not marry him, you know."

"I want to marry him," she said, shocking herself with the vehemence of her own words.

Because she realized the veracity in them. She *did* want to marry Nando. Even if she regretted it later and despite all the concerns and worries crowding her mind.

Perhaps she was every bit as reckless as he was.

CHAPTER 15

M arrying in London was damned annoying.

Marrying in London *in haste*, however, was nigh impossible.

But after what had seemed an eternity of waiting with limited patience as Nando's future bride was held captive by Stasia, it was done. Propriety, she had claimed, and he had only relented when she had mentioned the damage it would do Eleanora if he did whatever he wanted.

Nando excelled at doing what he wanted. In all things. Denying himself Eleanora for five more days—procuring a special license as a scapegrace foreign prince was unfortunately not as easy as he had hoped—had been torment, pure and simple. And now, at long last, that torment was coming to an end.

Because he had what he wanted—Eleanora, his *wife*—in his carriage.

She was wearing a gown he had never seen her in before, and for the first time, it was one that suited her lush figure instead of hiding it. Fashioned of a pale blue that made her eyes seem so much more vivid, the gown also had a daring decolletage that put her breasts on display without the hindrance of a fichu. Silk roses festooned the full skirt and bedecked the smart bonnet on her head. She was bereft of ornamentation aside from a sapphire parure he had gifted her with.

Too dear, she had claimed. But he had asked her to wear it for their wedding day, wanting to see her looking the part of a princess—*his* princess—even if she remained reluctant to assume the role. Her wrap had slid from her shoulders as the carriage swayed over a bump. Flimsy and nearly transparent, it was the most imprudent garment he had ever seen her don.

His hands itched to tear it off her, along with the beautiful gown and every other stitch of misbegotten muslin and silk and lace that was keeping him from her delectable bare skin.

"Is something amiss?" she asked him, color rising on her cheeks.

Ye gods, she was fetching when she was discomfited. But then, she was lovely, no matter the occasion. Upbraiding him icily in a dour gown. Trading barbs with him as she hid her lustrous hair beneath a hideous cap. Laughing, smiling, frowning most ferociously. Regardless of the occasion or the garments, Eleanora Brett made his cock painfully hard, and he suspected she always would.

It was almost alarming, this monstrous amount of feeling inside him where she was concerned, growing and blooming greater by the day, the hour, the minute. Why, he was far more than halfway in love with her. He truly ought to have realized it before now. What a dullard he was.

"Nando?" she pressed, making him belatedly realize that he had failed to answer her quiet question.

"Yes." He reached across the carriage and snatched her

from the squabs she occupied in one swift motion, hauling her into his lap. "You were too far away."

"Your arm," she protested, attempting to straighten herself into a more suitably demure position.

The weight of her soft, supple curves in his lap was so entrancing that for a moment, he could not speak. All he could do was hold her, this mysterious, wonderful woman he had married a mere hour ago that morning. Eleanora Harriet Merritt, as it happened. That was her true name in its entirety.

"My arm is still attached," he told her mildly, slipping a hand up to cup the fullness of one breast.

An arrow of pure need shot through him. He thought he might catch flame there on the Moroccan leather, sending the entire carriage up as well. Her stays were impeding him from the joy of her hard nipple, but he knew it was there, waiting for his mouth.

She squirmed in his lap, clearly vexed by his lack of concern for his healing wound. "What if you tear your stitches?"

He chuckled. "Darling, I am going to be engaging in far more strenuous activity than holding you in my lap as soon as we reach my town house. At present, I don't give a damn if all the stitches tear and I bleed to death on the floor, so long as I've had you first."

"You must not speak of something so horrid," she chastised, frowning at him in that way she had, that made him want to kiss her.

Her bodice gaped, giving him an indecent view down it, and he was nearly unmanned by so much pale, creamy skin and the way she continued to wriggle on his lap.

Nando lowered his head and pressed a reverent kiss to the top of her left breast. "Trust me, what is about to happen between us won't be horrid at all."

"Not *that*," she protested, sounding breathless. "Bleeding to death. It has scarcely been any time since you were wounded, and the man who shot you is still out there somewhere in London. You could be in danger. Even Mr. Tierney said so."

"I'm not concerned about him, nor should you be." Nando cupped her cheek, running the pad of his thumb along the elegant architecture of her cheekbone. How was it that every part of her could entrance him, from the bridge of her nose to the curve of her shoulder, from the shell of her ear to the hollow at the base of her throat, or the slight dimple in her stubborn chin?

"Why are you not concerned?" she pressed.

"Because he surprised me once, and he shan't surprise me a second time," he reassured her, watching his thumb travel along her jaw and down her neck to where her pulse beat fast. "And because I now have more guards at my disposal than a king."

He also hoped that, now that he had taken his shot at Nando, Levering's bloodlust had been satiated. Besides, Nando was a married man now. He expected alarm to settle over him at the reminder. But instead, all he felt was a calm, peaceful sense within, a rightness he hadn't known in…

Well, ever.

"I am not sure I find that as reassuring as you do." Eleanora was frowning at him, her gloved hands resting lightly on his chest.

"All will be well, my love." He traced slowly down the soft cord of her throat, then traced the gold and diamonds of her necklace to the large Ceylon sapphire situated in its middle. "Trust me."

She said nothing for a moment, so he settled his lips on her neck and kissed her there, hot and openmouthed, feeling as if he could devour her.

"Nando."

"Mmm," he murmured against her skin, his hand dipping lower, to slide into her bodice, between her stays and chemise and her bare breast.

Her nipple was hungry and pointed, and he could not wait to suck on it. He would have done so now, were he not persuaded that they had nearly arrived at his town house.

She gasped, arching into his touch, as responsive as he had remembered. "In the carriage? Should we not at least wait until we are inside?"

This would not do. The proper spinster in her would not be permitted to emerge.

He tugged down her bodice with one fast motion, leaving her breast bare, her stays and gown lifting it high, her nipple like an erotic offering for him alone.

"I've been made to wait for five endless days." He lowered his head and sucked on the pretty pink nipple he had revealed, gratified when she moaned and arched her back, her fingers gliding through his hair in wordless encouragement.

He suckled her, astounded at how the simple action could heighten his own need to such a shocking crescendo that he felt the slight wetness seeping from his cock and into his smalls. He was so ready for her. Would she be similarly ready?

He had to know.

Ignoring the tightness in his arm, he found the hem of her gown and slipped his hand under her skirts. He found the heart of her, soft and hot and so very wet, and teased her swollen pearl. There was his answer as her hips moved, lifting, chasing his touch, demanding more.

He released her nipple, wanting to see the sight she presented, rosy-cheeked, bonnet half off her head, her eyes stormy with desire, lips darkened from his kisses, one breast freed from her gown, her skirts gathered around her waist. Stocking-clad legs on display to the tops of her thighs where pink garters met more bare skin.

"Nando." His name was a restless moan on her lips now.

And he knew that he had pushed her beyond her proper façade. That she wanted him so badly that she would writhe in his lap, seeking more of the friction she craved to find her completion.

"You are so wet for me," he said, stroking her harder, his fingers finding the seam of her sex and parting her folds to slick her wetness up and down, all over her, swirling around and around that demanding bundle of flesh that made her jerk and pant. "So ready, aren't you?"

She didn't acknowledge his question, her ragged breaths falling from her parted lips. Of course she wouldn't admit something so vulgar, even if she loved every moment of what he was doing to her. But she didn't need to say anything at all. Her body spoke for her as she thrust her hips against him, wordlessly begging to be fucked. He would give her what she wanted soon. He would give her everything she wanted and everything she had never even dreamed possible.

"Say it," he urged. "Tell me, Eleanora mine."

"I… I can't." She tipped her head back, her bonnet hanging precariously now, and there was her glorious golden hair, still confined in its customary chignon but glinting from the sunlight streaming through the carriage windows.

He hadn't seen fit to close the Venetian blinds when they had entered, and he was glad of the lack of circumspection now, for it meant he could see her better. Admire her more fully.

He worked her pearl with his thumb and then moved his fingers lower, through that satiny, welcoming heat, needing to be inside her however he could. He found her entrance with his forefinger, probing gently. Her thighs parted in invitation he gladly accepted, sinking his finger deep. Her cunt gripped him deliciously.

He took a moment to collect himself, gathering his control. And then he returned to her nipple, sucking hard, nipping her with his teeth as he began fucking her with more deliberate intent, a second finger joining the first.

"Say my name when you come," he ordered her against the swell of her breast, needing to hear it, needing her submission.

Needing to know that this glorious, bold, beautiful, passionate woman was his in every way. In and out, he pumped, crooking his fingers, using slow, measured strokes until she was making inane sounds and grasping at his clothes, his hair, any part of him she could reach. His cravat came undone. Christ knew what happened to his hat. He didn't care. She tightened on him, her body stiffening as her release claimed her, and he was blissfully unable to breathe for a handful of seconds as her perfumed breast crushed into his face and he sucked her nipple while her eager cunny tightened on his fingers.

"Nando," she cried out, obliging him.

Her surrender was the most potent aphrodisiac in all the world.

And Prince Ferdinando of the House of Tayrnes, notorious rakehell and dedicated sybarite, promptly lost all control and came in his smalls like a virgin.

∾

Nando made an expansive gesture in the marble entryway of the handsome town house. "Your home, my dear."

Home.

That word sent unexpected feeling coursing through Eleanora. It had been ten years since the roof over her head had last been a true home. For so long, she had been living in elegant town houses belonging to London's wealthiest, flitting from one to the next, the life she had known forever gone. And now, suddenly, she was no longer a stranger invited for a temporary stay, but the mistress of the household.

"It is lovely," she told her new husband, still overwhelmed by the pleasure he had given her in the carriage and now doubly stunned by the realization that she was a married woman with a husband and a home to call her own.

Her rational mind had known, of course, the changes that were upon her. But the notion of marrying Nando and the reality of it were two disparate things.

He caught her hand in his and raised it to his lips for a reverent kiss. "You have *carte blanche* to do whatever you like with it. Anything you wish."

She was far more accustomed to simply inhabiting rooms rather than contemplating how she might change them, but his easy acceptance of her pleased Eleanora. "Thank you."

He smiled, the effect stunning as always. "You needn't thank me for your due."

Her due. What a foreign—and alluring—concept.

"Nonetheless, I am grateful to you."

He leaned nearer, his lips grazing her ear as he spoke in a soft voice not intended to carry. "It isn't your gratitude I want, darling."

Heat blossomed deep within. She knew what he wanted. And she wanted it too.

Still, she was keenly aware of the servants who were hovering nearby, awaiting introductions.

"We've an audience," she murmured.

"Alas." He straightened, his devil-may-care grin firmly in place, and proceeded to perform the formal introductions.

A whirlwind of faces and names ensued. When Nando

introduced her as Princess Eleanora of Varros, she nearly expected to turn and find someone else ready to take her place. After the formalities were observed, he accompanied her upstairs to her room.

The bedchamber adjoined with his. It appeared to have been recently opened and given a thorough cleaning. Paintings hung on the walls in an assortment of gilt frames. The bed was far larger than the narrow bed she had become accustomed to.

"If the furniture isn't to your liking, buy whatever you wish."

Nando's voice was a low, decadent rumble at her back as she circled the chamber. She turned to find him watching her intently, and a surge of desire went through her. It was their wedding day. They were alone. She knew what was meant to happen next, and she was both eager and nervous for the consummation of their union.

She summoned up a smile even as her pulse began to race. "In truth, I don't know what is to my liking. It has been quite some time since I've had reason to choose my own furnishings."

"How long?" he asked, coming nearer to her.

"Ten years."

"Too long, then. I'll take you shopping. You can buy all of London."

A chuckle fled her. "I hardly think all of London shall fit in your town house, despite its impressive size."

He grinned, stopping before her. "My town house *is* large, isn't it? Do you know what else is large, my dear?"

His tone was teasing. She knew him well enough by now to understand that he was speaking of a certain portion of his anatomy.

Nando was being so silly that she couldn't help but to

laugh, some of the tension easing from her. His lightheartedness was, as ever, infectious.

"Your feet?" she pretended to guess.

"My cock." His head dipped toward hers. "Naturally, I would be more than happy to offer proof."

"What manner of proof?" she dared to ask, enjoying their banter, their proximity, this chance to flirt with each other and no need to worry over being caught in an indelicate position alone together.

How freeing it was.

No more icy Miss Brett.

Now, she was someone else. Not the girl she'd been a lifetime ago, but certainly not the prim spinster who had grimly led her charges across the dance floors of the *ton*.

He took her hand in his and brought it to the fall of his trousers. "Will this suffice?"

Good heavens. He was indeed large. And long. And distinctly hard.

She had felt him against her before, but this was different. He molded her fingers around his length, granting her a liberty that both shocked and titillated her.

Feeling bold, she met his gaze, falling into the astounding sea-blue. "I'm not certain I am convinced just yet."

His lips twitched. "A closer inspection, then."

She explored him tentatively, growing accustomed to the feeling of him, so big, so bold, curious about how best to please him. The more she stroked him, the more her own desire heightened.

"Ye gods, Eleanora." He lowered his forehead to hers, his breath falling hotly over her lips. "I need you now."

Her pulse quickened.

"Whatever shall the servants think?"

He kissed her swiftly and then raised his head, nimble fingers undoing the retied knot of his cravat. "That I am besotted with my wife and intend to shag her silly for the rest of the day." He pulled the neckcloth free and tossed it to the floor. "And they would be correct."

Nando was *disrobing*. And whilst she had seen the glory of his bare chest before, she had never seen his entire form. Eleanora couldn't look away from the sight of the potently masculine prince undressing before her. Not just the prince, she reminded herself, but her *husband*. How was it possible? It seemed a dream from which she would wake up.

Just one week ago, she couldn't have imagined the turn her life would take. That she would go from being a spinster chaperone hired to guide unmarried ladies through polite society to being this beautiful man's wife.

She swallowed as he shrugged out of his coat and moved to the buttons on his waistcoat. "It's highly improper, surely."

He chuckled. "The best things in life always are."

How she wished she were so carefree. Perhaps she could be, in time. Her role as Miss Brett, chaperone to London's innocent misses, had become so ingrained that she wasn't even certain who she had been before. The reckless girl who had wholeheartedly embraced the gaiety of her mother's scandalous circle had long since faded into a dreary version of her former self.

"You're frowning." The buttons of his crisp, white shirt were undone at his throat now, a slice of sun-bronzed skin visible. "I can see your clever mind at work, fretting over propriety. Stop thinking at once. You are meant only to feel."

Nando held her face in his hands and kissed her again, slowly, sweetly. How easy it was to forget everything else when his lips claimed hers. She surrendered easily to his expert mouth, to his tongue, and—good heavens—even his teeth as he caught her lower lip in a gentle nip that sent a bolt of liquid heat rushing between her thighs. Despite the pleasure he had given her in the carriage, she already wanted him again.

Oh yes, he had her feeling. Feeling far, far too much.

His lips left hers to nuzzle her ear. "This moment is all I've been longing for."

It occurred to her suddenly that he was a practiced seducer and she was woefully inexpert. The tip of his tongue traced the whorl of her ear, eliciting a shiver from her.

"What if it proves a disappointment?"

"Not a chance." He kissed her throat, her jaw, found his way back to her lips and kissed her until she was breathless again.

His mouth on hers was sufficient distraction. All worry over what the servants might think of her or whether she would prove a woefully inadequate lover to a skilled rake fled. Nando's fingers sank into the careful precision of her chignon, sending pins raining to the floor. Her hair fell heavy down her back, and then he moved on to the tapes of her gown, unfastening them.

He broke the kiss to pull the garment over her head, his movements knowing and sure. With a flick of his wrist, he sent the gown sailing halfway across the chamber. Eleanora, still unaccustomed to her new husband's lavish wealth, winced at the brutish treatment.

"Thinking again," Nando said, kissing the tip of her nose as he looked down at her with mock severity. "I forbid it. Besides, I'll buy you a hundred more gowns just like that one if you like."

"I would never wear that many gowns in my lifetime," she protested as he found the buttons on her petticoat and slipped them from their moorings.

"Suit yourself, my dear, for I have a suspicion I will prefer you naked." He grinned, then whisked the petticoat away with as much speed and ease as he had the gown.

His words were wicked. Again, she ought to have been scandalized. But he was her husband. They were wed. And there was no fear of being discovered, of losing her livelihood, of her reputation being dashed to bits.

This newfound freedom felt dangerous.

When he moved to her stays, she decided that it was time to return the favor. She reached for his shirt, plucking it from his trousers and then pulling it over his head, taking care not to cause injury to his wounded arm, which was healing well by now. Still, the skin was dark and puckered where it had been sewn back together, an unsettling reminder of just how close he had come to death.

"I suppose I'll be hideously scarred forever now," he said absently, taking note of the direction of her gaze.

"Not hideously. You wear your scar as a mark of honor and strength, a reminder of what you have withstood to be where you are." Without hesitation, she pressed her lips to the healing flesh, kissing him there. "I find it quite heroic, actually."

Her words pleased him. Nando's grin deepened. "You do?"

"Of course I do. How can I not?"

"No one has ever called me heroic before." He cupped her cheek, gazing at her with renewed tenderness. "Though they have called me many things."

There was something in his voice and gaze, a neediness that she had never seen before. It startled her to realize that this silver-tongued rake longed for praise. Certainly, he must have received a great many compliments concerning his looks and his prowess in the bedchamber, but he wanted to hear it from her. A strange new warmth crept into her breast at the notion.

"Then I am happy to be the first," she said. "There is far more to you than the devil-may-care you show to the world."

And she couldn't help but to feel she was glimpsing Nando—the real Nando, not just the rakehell prince with the self-deprecating grin and the flirtatious air. That revelation was gratifying on a deeply intimate level.

He kissed her by way of response, hungry and demanding. More garments were removed. Stays, stockings, and trousers dropped to the Aubusson, until they stood in only chemise and smalls, and then with sure hands and well-placed caresses, those were gone as well. The difference between his body and hers intrigued her. His legs were long and lean, stippled with golden hair. His cock protruded, thick and erect, ruddy and ready and a thing of unique beauty.

She thought of how he had lavished pleasure upon her most intimate places before they had wed, using his mouth on her, and suddenly, she wanted that too. Wanted to worship every inch of him that was exposed to her, to taste him on her tongue. She knew enough to understand he would find it pleasurable for her to do so.

Without thought, Eleanora dropped to her knees before him.

"What are you doing, love?" Nando asked, his voice thick with need.

"Pleasuring you." She reached for him tentatively, wrapping her fingers around his shaft, wondering at how much more delightful it was to touch him thus, no barrier of cloth keeping her from him.

"Eleanora."

Her name was a strangled plea from above.

She glanced up to find him looking down at her, his jaw rigid and tensed, his eyes smoldering. "Am I doing it wrong?"

As she asked the question, she gave him a firm stroke, reveling in the way he felt, hard and yet smooth, his skin hot, his length growing stiffer as she worked him.

He groaned. "Ye gods, no. You're doing it too *right*. But damn it, I'll not have you on your knees before me this first time."

"I want to." She continued her ministrations, noting a bead of moisture seeping from the slit in the tip of his cock. Curiosity seized her, and she leaned forward, catching the drop on her tongue.

"Fuck, Eleanora."

The word was vulgar. Crude. She'd heard it before, of course, but it had never particularly moved her either way. But there was something about the way he said it now, his voice laden with desire, tinged with a hint of desperation, that made her feel powerful and sensual. Spurred by his reaction, she flicked her tongue over him again, circling the head.

"You'll unman me a second time."

She kissed the glistening tip, looking up at him again. "A second time?"

His nod was grim. Jerky. "The first was in the carriage. You felt so delicious on my fingers that I couldn't restrain myself. You make me lose control."

His admission filled her with fire. "Good."

She wanted him to lose control. Wanted him to lose himself in his need for her.

Holding his gaze, she opened her mouth over him, engulfing the bulbous end of his hard length, ridiculously roused by the way his expression went slack, desire darkening his eyes. She thought about how he had suckled the small bud hidden in the folds of her sex, of the conversations she had heard from her mother's laughing companions from another room, when they had all believed she had been abed and was no longer listening. And she knew what she had to do.

Eleanora sucked hard, drawing him deeper into her mouth, angling her head, breathing through her nose. He pumped his hips, sending himself to the back of her throat, and still, there was so much of him.

"This isn't what I intended," he rasped, but his fingers were sifting through her hair, and he was not making any attempt to withdraw from her.

She grasped his lean hips, holding him to her, and followed her instincts.

∼

THE SIGHT before Nando was the single most erotic scene he had ever beheld. Eleanora was on her knees before him, naked, taking his cock between her lush pink lips. It was wrong, so wrong, but Deus, he liked her this way, loved watching his prick, glistening with her saliva, disappear into her sweet mouth. And when the tip of him reached her throat, it was almost more than he could withstand. He had to close his eyes against a stinging rush of need. His sac was heavy and full, and he thought he might shoot down her throat at any second.

But he was greedy. He didn't want her to stop. Not yet. He opened his eyes again, wanting to watch.

He was far more experienced, a rake. He was meant to be the one seducing. But he didn't fool himself now. The only one performing a seduction was Eleanora. His wife. Yes, she was *his*. His at last.

The reminder made him harder. He caught a handful of her hair and fed her his cock with slow, short thrusts. And she took him. Eagerly, with inexpert abandon that somehow more delicious than the most knowing of mouths. He didn't want to come yet. He wanted to come inside her. To mark her as his in that most elemental of ways, to consummate their marriage as he had been longing to do.

She rocked back on her heels, lavishing attention on the

sensitive head of his cock. Then she licked along the underside, grasping him in a firm hold that had him clenching his jaw so hard to delay his release that a muscle began twitching near his eye. He had never been so caught up in need. All he could think was Eleanora. All he could see was her, so lovely and perfect on her knees, her breasts full and tipped with hard nipples he couldn't wait to suck. And the scent of her, musky and flowery—soap and woman and the perfume of her desire—surrounded him.

He should have married this woman the moment he had first met her. She was going to kill him with her innocent abandon. He had always suspected she had a sensual nature beneath her prim ice, but she was a revelation. A revelation on her knees before him, sucking his cock deep. She took his cock so well, moaning softly, as if she was every bit as moved as he was.

Was her cunny wet again? Did sucking him make her want him more? He had to know. His cock reached the back of her throat again, and she swallowed, and he thought his head was about to explode along with the rest of him.

He couldn't bear another second of this sensual torment. There would be plenty of time for him to come inside her mouth. This was but the first day of their marriage. She sucked and stroked, and it required all the restraint he possessed to keep from shooting his spend on her clever tongue. Yes, he would paint her with it one day soon. Spurt after spurt on her breasts.

Damn, that was too much. He would never last now.

"Enough," he gasped, breathless, heart pounding.

Gently, he withdrew from her mouth, his cock aching, his seed leaking from the tip. He caught her hands in his and drew her to her feet. Her face was flushed, her eyes heavy-lidded with desire.

"You didn't like it?" she asked, sounding hurt.

"Dear God." He chuckled, drawing her against him. "I liked it too much. If you want to swallow me, you can do it some other time. I want to be inside you now."

Her lips glistened. He couldn't resist the urge to kiss her, tasting the faintest traces of salt and himself on her tongue. His cock strained between them, prodding her belly. She kissed him eagerly, her tongue lashing his.

Caught up in her, their mouths still fused, Nando guided her to the bed. He broke the kiss long enough to help her climb into the high bed and took a moment to admire her. Fucking hell, every part of her was perfection. Lush hips, curved waist, rounded breasts, and hungry nipples. Her hair was a cloud of golden silk on the pillows, her short legs pressed together in maidenly modesty he found helplessly charming. He joined her on the bed, a ravenous beast he would have to rein in somehow, lest he hurt her.

Nando caressed her thigh, the smooth softness of her skin a luxury he never wanted to live without. "Open for me, love. Let me see you."

She knew what he wanted. Wordlessly, she spread her legs apart, revealing the pink folds of her sex, gleaming with dew. He couldn't resist lowering himself there, cupping her bottom in his hands, and lifting her to his mouth so that he could feast. He licked into her entrance, lapping her up, all that sweet cream making him wild. She rolled her hips, seeking more, and the soft, breathy sounds she made had his cock harder than ever.

He'd wanted her to come, but if he didn't soon get inside her, he would lose control. Realizing his endurance was stretched past its limits, he moved up the bed until they were perfectly aligned, her hips cradling his, her bountiful breasts cushioning his chest.

Yes, yes, yes.

His body sang with the knowledge he was home, where

he was meant to be. This was what he wanted. What he craved. It had been far too long since he had last made love, but he didn't fool himself into believing that was the reason for his intense ardor. No, that was all Eleanora.

He kissed her, his fingers dipping between them to tease her wet, swollen flesh. "You're so ready for me aren't you, love?"

She moaned in agreement, her arms winding around his neck and holding him tight, as if she feared he would leave. Not a bloody chance in Hades of that.

He toyed with her pearl, circling it. "Sucking my cock made you wet."

And that pleased him.

Eleanora arched her back. "I like having you in my mouth."

Hell and damnation.

He almost came from her words alone. He kissed her jaw, her shoulder, the curve of her breast. "I like watching you take my cock. Next time, I'll spend in your mouth. Would you like that?"

The insistence of her hips and the soft sounds of need she made, along with a new rush of wetness on her sex, said that she would. Why had no one told him it would be this good, bedding his wife? Having a woman who was his alone? His to please, his to fuck.

"You would, wouldn't you?"

"Yes," she hissed, growing restless beneath him.

"Naughty minx."

What a joy she was. He stroked her pearl harder, faster, giving her what she wanted until she stiffened beneath him, crying out. Bringing her to her release was his new favorite pastime. He wondered if he could convince her to start every morning by sitting on his face. He would happily devour her for breakfast.

Nando waited until the last of her tremors had subsided, and when she was pliant and sated beneath him, he knew he couldn't last a second longer. Possessive pleasure shot through him as he gripped his shaft and notched himself against her. He rubbed his cock in her slick dew, up and down her swollen folds. The sound of her wetness was almost obscene in the hushed stillness of the chamber. He'd never heard anything better.

Until finally, he could take no more of the torture he inflicted on them both and pressed his slippery cock to her entrance. He had never taken a virgin before, and he wasn't certain what to expect. This would be a first for them both. Leveraging himself on his forearm, he ignored the insistent pain in his arm as he guided himself into her. A shallow thrust of his hips, and he was encased in her snug heat, and he lowered his head to take her lips in a passionate, claiming kiss.

Mine, roared the beast within him. *This woman is mine.*

He couldn't keep himself from pumping into her again. He was deeper, and she was hotter, tighter. Sweet Deus, the pleasure was enough to kill him, and he had only just begun. He lifted his head, the control he exerted over his rampaging body nothing short of miraculous.

"How does it feel, sweetheart?"

Her eyes were luminous, and he had never seen her more beautiful than this, under him, her body surrendering to his, passion making her cheeks flushed a becoming pink, her hair wild around her heart-shaped face. She was completely undone, wearing nothing but the glinting sapphires and diamonds at her throat and ears.

"Perfect," she murmured, her kiss-darkened lips remaining parted for her ragged breaths.

"I don't want to cause you any discomfort or pain," he added. "Tell me if you wish for me to stop, and I will."

She cupped his face, her touch almost reverent, looking at him with a countenance filled with tenderness, raw and profound. "Don't stop."

A growl of satisfaction was torn from him as he flexed his hips, harder this time, not stopping until he was fully inside her, her slick heat having swallowed the entire length of his cock. He remained still for a moment, overcome by the sensation of being fully seated within her, their hips pressed together, her cunt gripping him like a manacle. His heart galloped, his cock ached. It was the closest to heaven, no doubt, that a sinner like him would ever manage to find himself.

"Pain?" he gritted.

"None." She caressed over his shoulders now, her fingers taking care to avoid his wound, then to his back. "It is different and new. I feel so full of you."

"Because you are full of me." He pumped his hips. "My cock is deep inside you."

"Oh," she breathed, awe in her voice. "Oh, that feels wonderful."

He couldn't agree more. Except perhaps he would argue that it felt better than wonderful, planted within her like this, their bodies pressed together, becoming one. He had never felt the true intimacy of a joining before. It had been pleasure, pure and simple. But being with Eleanora felt starkly different. Different in a way that alarmed him for its potency and newness.

He moved before he could allow any more maudlin sentiment to overtake him, consigning himself headlong to the lust pounding through his veins. He moved in and out of her, his thrusts slow and measured at first, allowing her to adjust to the strange invasion. He knew he was large and that she was untried; he had no wish to hurt her. And so, he kept himself on a tight rein, pacing himself, dropping kisses on her lips, her breasts, her throat.

Her hips began dancing beneath his, increasingly demanding. He sucked her nipple, and she moaned, arching her back. So, he sucked harder, tonguing the peak as he slid into her again and again. He had never been so lost. He was mindless; he was hers.

This English beauty fashioned of ice had turned to flame, and he wanted to burn in the glorious fire of her sensual awakening. Her nails raked down his back. She cried out his name. He kissed her throat, her shoulder, her ear. Thrust harder and faster, his sac tightening and aching until he knew that he would not last much longer.

Finally, Nando raised himself so he could drink in the sight of his thick cock gliding through her pink folds. He reached for the bud peeking from her sex, strumming over her as he had learned she liked, wanting her to come again as he watched himself fuck her. She rewarded him with a new rush of wetness sluicing down his cock.

"Come for me, my love," he urged, barely capable of forming words. "Come on my cock. I want your dew all over me."

More pressure, faster, his fingers flying over her as he continued thrusting deep. The view was almost more than he could bear. But he continued, riding her and pleasuring her until she tightened on him with such sudden strength that she nearly squeezed him from her cunny. He took her hip in hand, holding her to him, and rutted into her slippery warmth.

The pulse of her release was still all around his cock as he lost control, sinking deep and emptying himself inside her. As he flooded her with his seed, the truth struck him with the undeniable jolt of a lightning bolt through the sky.

He had fallen in love with his wife.

CHAPTER 16

"*A*nother biscuit?"

Eleanora shook her head. "I couldn't eat a thing."

Nando grinned wickedly. "You need your strength. Have one more, my dear."

She was reclining on a mountain of pillows in his bed, wearing one of his silk banyans and not another stitch, and she had never felt more contented. They had spent the entirety of the day alternately making love and sleeping, moving between bedrooms and beds, avoiding the outside world. Nando hadn't wanted to dress to go down to dinner, and she hadn't argued, enjoying the familiarity and ease they could have in his bedroom together. They were barefoot, sated, and relaxed.

"You have already fed me far more than I am accustomed to eating."

He took a bite of the biscuit he had offered her, chewing thoughtfully. "Did that bastard Tierney not feed you properly? I'll have to give him a sound thrashing."

Dressed in a banyan as well, his golden curls ruffled,

lounging on his side across his bed, he looked like an invitation to depravity. Although his tone was mild, she had no wish for Nando to find trouble with Mr. Tierney.

"He was an excellent employer," she hastened to defend. "No thrashing, if you please. Besides, I hardly think you are in a condition to thrash anyone."

She cast a pointed look in the direction of his injured arm. He had proven himself more than capable of making love to her—thrice over—despite the pain it must have caused him. However, Nando was her responsibility now. She felt astonishingly...*wifely* where he was concerned.

"I am in excellent condition, as you can surely attest." He gave her a heated look that made her belly tighten.

Little wonder he was a legendary rake. He had reduced her to nothing more than a witless, boneless puddle of desire over and over again. Just when she thought that her body was not capable of experiencing more pleasure, a caress or a kiss or a sinful lick from Nando, and she discovered how wrong she was.

"I simply wish it to remain so." She reached for her nearby glass of wine, retrieving it from a bedside table, feeling unapologetically sinful as she did so.

She had never in her life lolled about in a bed, eating and drinking and wearing scarcely any clothes. Less than one day of being married to Nando, and he had thoroughly debauched her. She didn't regret it, and she hoped she never would. Unbidden, the warnings Princess Stasia had left her with returned, but Eleanora tamped them firmly down.

"Be careful, my dear, or all the concern you show for me will make me think you've grown fond of me," he teased, before taking another bite of the biscuit, somehow managing to make the act sensual.

Although he was being his usual, lighthearted, devil-may-care self, and she knew she must not take his words to heart, something in Eleanora's chest tightened painfully. She was desperately fond of him. It was impossible not to be so. Nando simply possessed a magnetic, captivating presence which was every bit as much to do with his easy charm and wry humor as it was to do with his undeniable good looks. If her feelings for him were so strong after less than a day of marriage, what would they be like in the days, weeks, and months to come?

The years?

He was a rake with an unabashed appetite for all things carnal. Would he grow weary of her? What would happen when he did? And why had these alarming questions not felt so potent and real to her until now?

She took a sip of her wine to calm her whirling thoughts and distract herself from the uncertainty of the life awaiting her as his wife.

"Of course I am fond of you," she said simply, gratified at the composure she showed. "If I did not like you, I wouldn't have married you."

Not a hint of a quaver in her voice.

He arched a golden brow, stretching with leonine grace, as if he hadn't a care in the world. "Not even to remove yourself from your previous circumstances?"

"My circumstances were not so dire," she said, although that wasn't entirely true.

Her position in Mr. Tierney and Princess Stasia's household had been the best she'd had yet. Other situations had not been so egalitarian, nor so understanding. And it had certainly been a relief to have a master of the house who hadn't attempted to foist his attentions upon her.

"But you must admit that marrying a prince surely has a certain allure," Nando continued.

"Marrying you had a great deal of allure for me," she

conceded quietly. "Else I would not have agreed to such a preposterous suggestion."

His lips twitched with mirth. "Surely not preposterous."

"Of course it was. Me, a woman far past her prime, of no social standing, save what I was able to glean for myself as little better than a servant, the illegitimate daughter of a man who abandoned her and a mother who was an actress and a kept woman. And you, the handsome, dashing prince."

His amusement fled. "I don't like the way you speak of yourself."

She shrugged. "It is the truth. It is also the way the world will see us, even if they never discover the truth of my parentage."

"Well, they can all go to Beelzebub for all I care. I do what I like when it pleases me, and that extends to marrying whom I wish."

"Will your brother not be displeased with you for making such a misalliance?" she asked, the thought occurring to her for the first time.

"It is no concern of Maxim's whom I marry either."

Her husband's words were not quite the reassurance she might have hoped for.

"Have you sent word to him?"

"Not yet." Nando offered her a bowl of hothouse berries. "Have some more, darling. You've scarcely eaten a thing."

She relented, taking a strawberry. "You spoil me."

He winked. "My motives are impure."

Eleanora couldn't suppress the laugh that escaped her at his unrepentant pronouncement. "I'm not sure your motives have ever been pure to begin with."

He chuckled, the sound low and mellifluous. "I can assure you they have not. Tell me, how is it you know me so well already, having only been my wife for the span of mere hours?"

His teasing query sobered her as she swallowed the sweet, juicy bite of berry she had taken. "I scarcely know you at all. You're quite mysterious."

"Mysterious? That is not a word I've ever heard used in conjunction with myself before."

"Perhaps that's because everyone else accepts the face you present to them. You are Prince Nando, who takes nothing seriously, especially not himself. But beneath the charm and flirting and seducing, there is the true you, the one you hide from everyone."

He stared at her intently, as if he were considering her words with great deliberation. For a moment, she feared he would brush her observations aside and feign ignorance. Or worse, that she had angered him.

But at last, he spoke, lifting his shoulder in an elegant shrug. "What do you wish to know?"

The answer to that was easy. Everything—that was what she wanted to know. She wanted to learn all she could about this enigmatic man she had married. She wanted to discover what had made him into the man he was. But she would begin with one question, for she didn't know how far she could push him, how much he would reveal.

"What was young Prince Ferdinando like?" she asked, choosing an innocuous starting point.

He raised a brow. "Are you daring to suggest I am now elderly and decrepit?"

His tone was still teasing and light. She wondered if he would simply jest his way out of a serious conversation. Or seduce her until she forgot what she had asked and was too distracted by the pleasure he gave her to insist upon answers.

"You *are* older than I am," she pointed out, keeping her voice similarly pitched—teasing, carefree.

"By three years," he countered swiftly. "I would venture to say we are of an age, my dear."

"Three years is rather a lot of time."

"My brother is the ancient one," Nando said smoothly. "He has ten years more than I do. If anyone is elderly and decrepit, it is Maxim."

He spoke of his brother the king with undeniable fondness, and she was gratified that he hadn't sought to sidestep the topic yet again. "You are close to him."

"I love him." Nando paused, smiling wistfully. "For many years, we were all we had on this earth. The Varros Great War had taken almost everyone from us. But now he has a wife and a son. He no longer has need of me, if indeed he ever did. Most, including his privy council, would suggest he didn't. And they would probably not be wrong."

There was a hint of hurt lacing his voice as he finished. Eleanora did not miss it.

"Is that the reason you came to London? Did his privy council send you away?"

"Maxim would never listen to them if it came to banishing me. He loves me far too much, though he is loath to admit it."

"You came to London of your own volition, then?" The realization surprised her.

She had supposed that the king had sent his brother to London.

He nodded. "When my nephew, Prince Caspian Ferdinando, was born, I knew that Maxim had finally found the happiness he deserved. I was superfluous. I decided to roam."

His use of the prince's full name took her by surprise. "He is named after you, the young prince?"

Nando's chest puffed with pride. "Of course. I suggested Ferdo, but Maxim and his queen decided against it."

Eleanora bit her lip to stifle her chuckle. "Ferdo is a rather...interesting suggestion."

"Now you sound like my brother," Nando groused,

looking sullen. "He told me it was a terrible name. I'm still quite vexed about it. But in the end, Caspian is an honorable choice, after our father."

More delicate threads of his past were being revealed, little by little.

"Were you close to your father?"

Stark sadness flashed across his expressive countenance before he hid it. "I scarcely knew him. I was a lad of ten when he was killed in the Varros Great War. Much of my life, he was in battle, leading his army, fighting for what should have rightfully been his." He paused, biting his lower lip as if to collect his composure before continuing. "He never had the opportunity to ascend the throne. I was kept hidden safely away, cosseted and soft, scarcely knowing a hint of the death my brother and father and the loyalists to the House of Tayrnes faced daily. It was only when my father died that I began to realize what being at war truly meant."

Her heart ached for the young man he had been, hidden away, barely having the chance to know his father, losing him at such a young age.

She placed her hand on his, wanting to give him comfort. "I am sorry for what you endured."

"You needn't be sorry for me." His smile was bitter now. "As I said, I was coddled. I've never had to kill a man, nor have I ever shed blood. Until recently, that is."

"That doesn't make the loss of your father any less," she said with feeling. "I lost my father as well, but not to death. Rather, it was his own callousness. I was a bastard, and he scarcely cared for my existence at all. I met him only on a few occasions, and when he had tired of my mother, he evicted us from the home he had settled my mother in, and our life changed. She had to return to the stage, and although she did her best to keep the truth of our situation from me, I understood that something had happened. Our house was not as large, not as tidy, our furniture not as elegant. We had only two servants instead of the maids, butler, cook, and housekeeper to which I had grown accustomed. Later, I realized the bevy of servants and fine home and furnishings had been for his benefit, not ours. And when my mother had no longer been of use to him, he had cast us away as if we were rubbish."

Realizing she had been talking about herself, and revealing far more than she had intended, Eleanora stopped her tale of woe.

"As I said," she added, intensely aware of his stare upon her, studying, searching, seeing, "it was naught compared to what you faced in the Great War."

"To the devil with what I faced. Your father was a heartless scoundrel. Tell me his name. I'd like to challenge him to a duel in your honor. I'd never more happily shoot a fellow at dawn."

He was grim, his jaw tense and hard, and the harshness in his voice melted something inside her. He was outraged on her behalf. But that was not the way the world worked for women like her mother, for women like Eleanora. No one was outraged for them.

"I don't know his name," she admitted. "I couldn't tell you if I wanted."

And she most assuredly didn't want her husband to challenge the man who had sired her to a duel. Although she did appreciate the sentiment behind Nando's declaration. It was almost as if he was being protective of her. Championing her.

"I'll set Tierney and his men on it," Nando said, determined. "I'll find out his name and make him pay for what he did to you and your mother."

"No," she said swiftly. "Thank you, but no. Mr. Tierney

has enough to concern him, particularly since he still has men making certain to keep you safe."

"I don't need them."

The worry for him that had never been far returned, a bud unfurling into a full blossom. And it was the perfect moment to say what she had been thinking since well before they had wed.

"Perhaps we should return to Varros, where you will be safer in the court with your brother's men to surround you."

"Like a mongrel with his tail between his legs?" Nando curled his lip. "Never. I do not flee from my enemies. Ferdinando of the House of Tayrnes is no coward. I face my enemies like a man. I will not run. I would rather die first."

"But the danger to you—"

"The danger to me is nothing," he interrupted. "I have already told you, Eleanora. This is my concern and not yours. I'll not speak another word on the matter."

The sharpness in his voice cut her as surely as a blade. After learning so much about him, she couldn't help but to feel his hasty denial was the verbal equivalent of a slamming door. And she was left on the other side of it, helpless and alone. The sensual abandon that had held her in its spell dissipated.

"As you wish it, Your Royal Highness." She rose from the bed, shaking out the banyan he had given her to wear, which was rather voluminous, given her size compared to his.

If he did not want her to pry in his affairs, then she would treat him with the formality she knew he despised.

"Eleanora."

She moved across the chamber, intent upon finding one of her new dressing gowns and donning that instead.

"I've angered you."

She said nothing. His voice was near. Eleanora turned back to find him hovering over her, his expression pained.

"Forgive me, please. It wasn't my intention to speak so crossly. It is merely that I don't wish to have such a serious discussion on a day that is meant to be nothing but happy."

He was a man well accustomed to having his own way in all things. A prince, for heaven's sake. Worry settled over her yet again. How would they make this marriage work? Would he eventually grow bored or tired of her? What would she do when his attentions inevitably strayed? She couldn't bear to think of it. She ought to have known how far she was out of her depths with him. Only a fool would have agreed to this union.

"I forgive you, and you are right, of course. We should leave such a heavy conversation for another day," she relented, forcing a smile.

He took her hands in his. "You are thinking again. I have not distracted you sufficiently. I don't like to see you frowning so."

Perhaps his plan was to distract her, to seduce her. To wash away her concerns.

I want you to be mine, he had told her when he had asked her to marry him. And at the time, she had been warmed by the possession in his voice, by the notion that Nando should want her with such ferocity. Now, she began to wonder whether he had simply wanted to marry her because it had been the only way he would be able to bed her as often as he liked.

He kissed her swiftly, chasing the lingering worries for now. Nando was the sun banishing the clouds, shining bright and hot. She wrapped her arms around his lean waist and held him tightly, hoping her worries were for naught.

Either way, she was going to have to make certain she kept a firm distance between them. She couldn't afford to risk her heart with a man who would never give her his own.

~

NANDO WOKE up at dawn to Benvolio purring on his pillow and an empty place beside him where Eleanora should have been.

Also, to the glaring realization that he had been an arse the night before.

He had dismissed her concern—not because it was unwarranted, but because it was an unpleasant subject. One he didn't want to think about on their wedding day, a day that was to have solely been devoted to making her come as many times and in as many ways as he possibly could. The thought did nothing to assuage the morning cockstand he was currently sporting.

"Benvolio, go sleep somewhere that doesn't involve my head, won't you?" he grumbled to the cat through the murky shadows.

Once again, there was errant fur tickling his cheek.

And, in typical feline fashion, Benvolio refused to move. Because as far as the cat was concerned, *he* was the master of the house.

Eleanora had slept in her chamber last night. It ought not to bother him, the distance between them. He had never slept with any of his lovers unless he had been thoroughly sotted. Such intimacy was the sort that he avoided at all costs, even if he had no qualms about burying his face between a woman's thighs.

Emotion, sentiment, a sense of familiarity too uncomfortable for him to allow—these were what he had managed to avoid for one-and-thirty years of carousing and wenching his way through life. Clinging women bored him. Women who told him they loved him—and there had been many—made him itchy.

Now, he was the one who had fallen in love. What an astounding turn of circumstances.

Benvolio stretched and yawned, leaving one of his paws draped indolently over Nando's nose.

"Damn you, feline," he muttered, gently removing the paw before sitting up. "You're fortunate I've grown inordinately fond of you, else I would relegate you to the kitchens."

Benvolio yawned, looking distinctly unconcerned.

As well he might. They both knew that Nando couldn't live without the little beggar. Saving Benvolio from the street had been one of the best things Nando had ever done.

That and making Eleanora his wife.

At the renewed thought of her, Nando hastily donned a banyan, leaving Benvolio to further slumber on his bed without him. He knocked gently at the door adjoining his chamber to Eleanora's, not wishing to wake her if she was still sleeping.

"Come," she called softly.

A pleasant surprise—she was awake.

He didn't waste any time in opening the door and entering her room, finding her completely dressed and ready to begin her day. She wore an elegant gown of pale pink that was quite unlike her customary, ill-fitting dresses—perhaps it had been a gift from Princess Stasia. Her golden hair had been swept into a coil at her nape, a few curls free to frame her face. And Deus, she was lovely, even if he mourned the lack of skin on display.

He smiled, so taken with her that he could scarcely bear it. "Good morning, my dear. You are looking unspeakably gorgeous."

An understatement. She was looking like a goddess. Like a woman he couldn't wait to strip naked and pleasure until she was mindless. She was looking like the only woman he ever wanted for the rest of his life.

Eleanora dipped into a perfect curtsy. "Good morning to you as well. You needn't flatter me, you know. We are already wed."

"And you needn't curtsy to me in private," he countered, unable to resist going to her and taking her in his arms. "But I was hardly flattering you. I was simply telling you the truth."

She settled against his chest with a rightness that couldn't be denied. "I know I am quite plain. Not at all the sort of beauties to which you are doubtlessly accustomed."

He had known many women who were, objectively speaking, quite beautiful. But he had never known a woman who affected him the way she did. Every part of her was a revelation.

"You are not at all plain," he countered firmly, kissing the bridge of her nose. "I refuse to hear such nonsense from you again."

She smelled like the bath they had taken together the night before, like a lush summer garden thanks to the Winters soap. It was intoxicating. *She* was intoxicating. His cock pulsed.

"The truth is not nonsense."

"It is when it's not the truth," he countered effortlessly, wondering if he could persuade her to never leave this room.

They stared at each other, and then he couldn't refrain from kissing her. His mouth took hers, and she kissed him back with gratifying urgency. He was awash in her, her scent, her taste.

He lifted his head reluctantly. "You've taken your tea already."

"I'm accustomed to taking my tea when the servants take theirs."

The reminder of the way she had been made to earn her

bread irked him—he wished he had met her before she had embarked on her career as Miss Brett.

"I'll feed Tierney's ballocks to my pet alligator," he vowed fervently. "You never should have been relegated to taking tea with servants below stairs."

He regretted referring to the other man's anatomy in such vulgar fashion at once, but he needn't have worried over her missish sensibilities.

Her brow furrowed. "You have a pet alligator?"

Perhaps she didn't know what the word ballocks meant.

"No." He kissed the furrow on her forehead, smoothing it with his lips. "But I will find one just for that purpose."

Eleanora giggled, and the sound was girlish and filled with light, and he wished he could somehow capture it so that he could hear it, again and again, and know that he was the source of that lighthearted mirth.

"You are positively outlandish." There was no heat to her words.

This was what Nando wanted, this easiness between them. No weighty concerns of the outside world to intrude. It was just the two of them in a bedroom, lost in each other.

He grinned. "I like to make myself memorable."

Another chuckle escaped her, merriment dancing in her blue eyes. "You are indeed memorable. No one could ever say otherwise."

"I shall consider that a compliment of the finest order, my dear." He grew serious, searching her gaze. "But you are a princess now, Eleanora. You needn't wake at dawn with the chambermaids and the footmen. Sleep until noon if it suits you."

"I expect it will take some time for me to grow accustomed to this new life I lead." Her tone turned wistful.

"You are not regretting your decision to marry this mad

prince already, are you?" he was quick to ask, not accustomed to feeling so lacking in confidence when it came to the women in his life.

Ordinarily, they lost their hearts to him. They chased him. They wanted him. Instead, he had been the one to lose his heart to Eleanora. The one to chase, the one to want. More than that, however, he understood that a great change had happened for her yesterday. She had gone from Miss Brett to Princess Eleanora, from being little better than a household domestic to being the mistress of a town house in her own right. The adjustment would perhaps be even more difficult when they returned to Varros, for she didn't speak the language and he kept his apartments in the palace.

There, she would be revered, just as she deserved.

She shook her head. "Of course not. Are you regretting marrying a woman so far beneath you?"

He kissed her to banish any doubt she might have, not stopping until she was pliant in his arms, her tongue mating with his. When he lifted his head, they were both breathless. "Does that feel like regret to you?"

She pressed her fingers to her lips, her eyes wide. "No."

"Good." He kissed those fingers, for they were in his way, then nibbled at the tip of one. "I would also like to remind you that there is only one way in which you are beneath me, and that is when we are in bed."

"*Nando.*"

Her scandalized voice left him feeling ridiculously pleased. "Of course, you might also be atop me. I do have so much to show you, wife."

A light, becoming flush swept over her cheeks. "Atop you?"

He couldn't quell his smile. "Oh yes. Shall I demonstrate now?"

Mischief sparkled in her eyes. "Indeed, I think you must."

And if Nando hadn't already been hopelessly, helplessly in love with her, he would have certainly fallen then.

CHAPTER 17

Guarding her heart against her husband grew more difficult by the day.

"Where are we going?" she asked Nando as their carriage rattled through the streets of London.

"If I tell you, then it won't be a surprise, will it?"

"Why does it need to be a surprise?"

He grinned. "Because when you are excited, you wriggle your bottom about, and I find it utterly adorable. Also, I happen to be extraordinarily fond of your bottom, whether it is wriggling or not."

"I do not wriggle."

Did she? Certainly, she had never taken note of doing so, nor had anyone ever told her she did. But then, she hadn't had cause for excitement in years. Just a handful of days as Nando's wife, and she'd already experienced it more times than she had in the last decade. She shifted on her seat nervously at the thought, for she knew all too well that contentedness in her life was always followed by disaster. First, it had been her childhood when she and Mama had lived in that grand house, only to be thrown to the streets when her father had tired of her mother. Then, there had been the comfort afforded by the protectors who had followed, always coming to an abrupt halt.

Until there had been the last protector, and Mama had grown desperately ill—too ill to act, too ill to entertain her wealthy benefactor. In just a few short, terrible weeks, Mama had no longer been on her sickbed, and Eleanora had stood at her grave, alone in the world with scarcely anything but the clothes she could carry and the little money her mother had left her.

"Is something amiss?"

Nando, ever too perceptive, brought Eleanora back to the present with his question.

She blinked and smiled at him, thinking he looked unfairly well-rested and handsome for a man who had been up half the night making love to her. "Nothing is wrong. Why do you ask?"

"Your countenance is rather expressive, my dear."

No one had ever told her so before Nando. But then, she wasn't certain anyone had ever looked at her—truly looked at her—the way he did.

"Quite." She inhaled deeply, attempting to dispel old, painful memories. "I was thinking of my mother, if you must know."

Eleanora hoped he might accept her answer and change the subject, for speaking of her mother's death was not something she liked to do. It still, even after so many years, brought her to tears.

"Ah." There was a wealth of meaning in his tone as he took her hand, cradling it in both of his on his lap. "Do you want to tell me?"

Equally perceptive of him to give her the opportunity to speak of it or avoid the most painful remnants of her past.

And she was startled to realize that she *did* want to tell

him. That she had been keeping the secrets of her past for so long and with such protective ferocity that sharing the truth with him would be a burden finally lifted from her shoulders.

She allowed him to keep her hand, studying him for a moment as the carriage rocked them in rhythmic motion, admiring the way the sunlight filtering through the Venetian blinds caught in his golden curls. How angelic he looked. No one gazing upon him now would ever suppose him capable of such sinful, wicked pleasures of the flesh.

"I was thinking about how all the times in my life where Mama and I were happy, we were quickly dealt a bad turn of Fortune's fickle wheel," she said softly. "It started with the man who was my father. Mama had been a famed actress when they had met, one of the most sought-after thespians in all England. He fell in love with her almost at once, she said, but he was a wealthy and powerful man, and taking an actress to wife would have proven too much of a scandal for his family to bear. So, he gave her a fine town house to use and installed her there as his mistress."

Eleanora paused, thinking of those charmed years, when she had yet to realize her true place in life and how tentative it was. Then, she had been a spoiled girl, for Mama's protector had spent a fortune on her, and Mama had diverted a great deal of that fortune to Eleanora. Nothing but the finest dresses, a polite governess to teach her everything a genteel lady should know, dolls, and whatever trinkets she had wished.

"If he loved her, he should have married her, whatever the cost to his reputation," Nando said with great feeling. "The man was a coldhearted coward, as evidenced by the manner in which he later so callously abandoned the both of you."

She squeezed Nando's hand in appreciation. "When he gave her the congé, it tore our world apart. I believe with all my heart that she thought he would keep her forever. That the three of us would be something like a family, even if he did have another wife and other children, who were legitimate, at home."

Her mother had been disconsolate for months afterward, scarcely able to force herself to resume acting. Only the need for a roof over their heads and food in their bellies had done so.

"Are you certain you don't know the bastard's name?" Nando asked, his voice taut, his jaw tensed.

He was angry on her behalf, and the realization touched her.

She shook her head. "My mother never told me, not even on her deathbed. I am grateful, in a way, because I wouldn't have wished to know him. If I had, I would have run the risk of recognizing him in society, and my emotions may have been too much to control."

"The reserved Miss Brett?" Nando brought her hand to his lips for a reverent kiss on first her knuckles, then her inner wrist. "I doubt she could have been so lacking in circumspection."

"I think I've proven my lack of circumspection by now," she said wryly, thinking of how easily and thoroughly she had succumbed to her own wanton nature.

"No, my dear. You've just proven yourself deliciously susceptible to corruption." He winked, bringing her hand back to his lap. "And I am devious enough to capitalize upon that weakness."

There was something beneath his lighthearted quip that sank its claws into her heart. He excelled in self-deprecation, forever painting himself as the villain. And yet, for Eleanora, Nando had very much been the hero.

She swallowed hard against a sudden rush of emotion and forced her mind back to the original thread of her story.

"The day that the man who sired me ended his arrangement with my mother, Mama and I had been shopping on Bond Street. We returned with a carriage laden with all manner of things, including a beautiful new doll made of porcelain for me, along with a miniature house for her to live in. When we had to leave our happy home, the doll and her house were some of the first to be sold off, along with Mama's jewels. Many of the gifts he had given her, we were to discover, were worthless paste, and the sum he had settled upon her had been a pittance too small to provide for a woman and child alone in the world for long."

Her heart ached anew as she thought of how much her mother had endured, how hard she had worked to ensure that Eleanora would continue to enjoy the sort of life she had once lived in that glorious town house, providing her with an education and fine dresses. Even if it had meant, as Eleanora had only realized far too late, sacrificing herself.

"How old were you?" Nando asked softly, stroking her palm with his thumb.

"A girl of seven."

He ground out something guttural and utterly foreign in his native tongue. It was the first time she had ever heard him speak it, and the abrupt switch startled her, for she hadn't expected it.

"What did you say?" she asked. "I'm afraid I don't understand Varrosian."

"And it's fortunate you don't." He was grim. "I said something that doesn't bear repeating. I'm sorry, Eleanora. Sorry for you and for your mother."

She managed a tremulous smile for his benefit, grateful for him, for his understanding, for this weight lifted from her. For everything.

"Thank you."

He shifted on the squabs suddenly, peering out the

carriage window to the street, then rapped on the roof. "Stop," he called out loudly enough for his coachman to hear. "Stop right here, if you please."

The conveyance swerved and nearly sent Eleanora careening to the floor before coming to an abrupt halt.

"Is this where you are taking me?" she asked, confused.

"No." He kissed her hand again. "Stay right here, my dear. There is something I need to fetch. I'll be back."

"But—"

He silenced her protest with a swift, hard kiss before withdrawing and giving her a smile. A genuine one. Not his ne'er-do-well grin. But a true smile that reached his eyes.

"No protesting, if you please. I'll be but a few moments."

He kissed her again, and then he threw open the door to the brougham and leapt to the street, leaving her alone.

◇

NANDO STEPPED up into the carriage less than five minutes after he had left it to peruse the wares at Bellingham and Co. In his arm was a porcelain doll. He fretted over the impromptu gift, hoping Eleanora would like it.

She wasn't the seven-year-old girl whose doll had been sold, after all.

She was all woman now.

But his gift was for the woman she'd become and for the girl she had once been.

He settled on the squab at her side, offering her the doll. "Here you are, my dear. Not the one you lost, but an acceptable enough replacement, I hope."

She reached for the doll he had spied in the window of the shop along with toy soldiers and other games—a clever ruse by the shop owner. Every child passing on the street would beg his or her parents to go inside.

"A doll," Eleanora said, her voice strained.

He couldn't tell if she was pleased with him or outraged.

"One you'll not have to sell. I know it is foolish, buying a toy for a woman grown, but I couldn't resist—"

She halted the nervous flow of his words with her lips, her turn now to silence his protests instead. Openmouthed and heady, her kiss told him more than words could. He slid an arm around her waist, drawing her tightly to his side.

Eleanora broke away from the kiss first, cradling his cheek with one hand, her eyes sparkling. "Thank you."

As he watched, a tear gathered on her lashes and then spilled down her cheek. He caught it with his lips.

"I cannot change the past, nor can I undo the wrongs which have been done. But I can damned well do my best to give you everything you deserve from now on."

What she deserved was so much more than objects. It was more than mere money could afford. It was love. He could give her that in full measure, but he wasn't ready to say the words yet. The depth of emotion he felt for this woman terrified and humbled him all at once.

"You are too good to me, Nando."

"No," he said firmly, turning his head to press a kiss to her palm. "I am not good enough for you."

She frowned. "Why do you say that?"

"Because it's true. I'm a rake. You were an innocent. I've always taken what I wanted, and everything you wanted was taken from you. I don't deserve you, Eleanora, but I'm a selfish and greedy man, and I intend to keep you anyway."

Before he could offer any further maudlin sentiment, he rapped on the roof of the carriage, signaling for the coachman to continue to their intended destination. Emotion was welling up inside him, rising like a tide, but he felt woefully clumsy and incapable of articulating. Being with a woman had never been about feelings for Nando. It had always been about raw, animalistic need. With Eleanora, it was so much more, a vast and uncharted landscape.

He knew how to fuck, but he had never needed to know how to love. He could only hope that, in time, he could learn. That he could become the man and husband who was worthy of her.

"You are a prince," she reminded him as the carriage rocked into motion, "and I am far from noble."

"The circumstances of our birth don't define us," he countered.

"But we live in a world that decrees it does."

"Then perhaps we can change that world."

"How optimistic you are. What if the world refuses to be changed?"

"Then we will tell the world to go to the devil and do whatever pleases us anyway." He grinned. "That is what I've been doing my whole life. I highly recommend it."

His lightheartedness won a laugh from her. "You truly are incorrigible, do you know that?"

"I pride myself upon it."

They stared at each other, grinning like fools, as if they were the only two people in all existence, sitting in the charmed haven of their carriage, the sun shining in the window, the day crackling with possibility. How he loved her. He had never imagined such depth of feeling possible.

Before he could say anything more, the carriage came to a halt outside the bookseller he had directed his coachman to visit.

"Here we are, my dear," he said lightly, telling himself to wait. That there would be time aplenty for sentiment later.

She peered out the window, giving an excited wriggle despite her claims that she did nothing of the sort.

"A bookshop!" The delight was evident in her voice, in the radiance of her smile.

"I thought that perhaps you might like to fill the library with some books of your own choosing."

The library of his town house had been lined with shelves of books from its previous inhabitants. A great deal of Latin treatises, from what he had seen.

"How thoughtful of you," she said, smiling at him in a way that made his cock rise to prominence against the fall of his trousers.

An unfortunate state, because there was nothing he could do about it at the moment.

"As you know, I have ulterior motives for almost everything," he teased.

The look she gave him turned sultry. "I suppose you will want me to thank you for your generosity."

Ye gods. Eleanora was going to be the death of him. He was never going to be able to get out of this carriage.

"I accept gratitude in all forms," he managed tightly, trying to think about anything other than her implied invitation.

He had been bedding her for days, and she was still a fire in his blood. He wanted to fuck her a thousand different ways. To empty himself inside her again and again until there was nothing left of him.

Damn it, this vein of thoughts was not helping his current predicament.

Eleanora licked her lips, her gaze dipping for just one sizzling second to his lap before rising again. "You appear as if you are presently in need of…gratitude."

The minx.

He choked out a laugh. "How diabolical of you to notice."

She smiled. "I've learned how to be diabolical from one of the best."

She was using his own tricks against him. And he found it

rousing as hell. She never ceased to surprise him, his Eleanora.

The door to the carriage opened, letting in a burst of cool air that did nothing to quell his raging cockstand. He forced himself to look at the doll perched on her lap and think about young Eleanora in tears when she had been forced to sell her precious toy, and finally, the beast within him subsided.

He handed her down from the carriage and followed in her wake, before offering her his arm and escorting her into the shop. Within, the place smelled of books and leather and musty paper. Not entirely pleasant.

But Eleanora inhaled deeply, her expression rapt. "Books."

He had chosen their destination well, it would seem. "Get as many as pleases you, my dear."

She walked down one of the narrow aisles, Nando trailing her once more. "I can't recall how long it has been since I've had books of my own." She traced a finger over the spines with a worshipful air. "When Mama died, I was forced to sell nearly everything I had."

The thought of her, alone in the world, selling her books and clothes, being forced to forge her own way, had him clenching his jaw. "Buy the whole damned shop."

She chuckled. "I suspect we wouldn't have room for that many books. But perhaps just a few…"

By the time she had finished selecting the books that appealed most to her, Nando and the footman who had accompanied them each bore a precarious stack of tomes.

"I do believe this is an excellent start," she said, smiling with anticipation as she eyed Nando and the footman.

And Nando decided that he couldn't agree more, but it wasn't books or the library he was thinking about.

CHAPTER 18

"*H*ave you finished arranging your spoils?"

Nando's amused drawl had Eleanora whirling about to find him standing at the threshold to the library, booted feet crossed at the ankles, hip leaning against the doorjamb. He was handsome and informal in his shirt-sleeves, waistcoat, and trousers. Her heart gave a pang at the sight of him, and so did the rest of her.

She suppressed the impulsive urge to race across the Aubusson like an impish girl and throw herself into his arms and held up the book in her hand instead. "One more to go, but I believe I will take this one to my room for reading. How was your session with Mr. Winter?"

The famed prizefighter, Mr. Gavin Winter, was the proprietor of Winter's Boxing Academy. Nando had declared himself sufficiently healed and in need of resuming his customary daily exercise with Mr. Winter.

Either that, he had told her, mischief dancing in his eyes, *or I will have to continue shagging you senseless every afternoon.*

Eleanora hadn't considered that to be a problem, but she was also keenly aware that she and her husband could not spend every waking hour together and that, for their marriage to thrive, they would need to develop something of a routine. She had sent him off earlier that day with the concern that he might not yet be healed properly, which he had reassured her was misplaced.

"Terrible." He straightened before sauntering into the room. "I reckon I'm not as healed as I would have liked to imagine. Winter trounced me quite soundly."

Eleanora started forward, meeting him halfway, her gaze inspecting his person for any hint of blood. "Are you injured?"

He held a hand over his heart in dramatic fashion. "Indeed, my pride is irreversibly destroyed."

Relief washed over her. "Are you saying I was right about it being too soon to resume your sessions with Mr. Winter?"

"You were right, my dear." He took her free hand and raised it to his lips for a lingering kiss. "I should have known better than to doubt you."

A wicked flare of heat sparked to life deep within her at the brush of his mouth over her bare skin. Good heavens, all he had to do was be near her, and she was aflame for him.

Their marriage, thus far, had been almost too wondrous to be real. The part of her that had seen every period of happiness in her life supplanted by struggle had her on edge, fearing that it wouldn't last. That a handsome, rakehell prince would never be contented with the plain, spinster daughter of an actress for long.

But she was foolish enough to enjoy their marital bliss whilst it lasted.

And that meant seizing every opportunity to be with him that she could.

"I think you owe me penance," she suggested.

His countenance instantly changed, his disarming grin and nonchalant air fading, replaced by stark, sensual hunger.

"What manner of penance? If it involves me on my knees for you, I would be more than happy to oblige."

She was shamelessly wet between her legs already. If he put his mouth on her, she would combust.

"Here in the library?" she asked, her voice husky with desire.

Thus far, their lovemaking had been relegated to their bedchambers, aside from that lone instance in the carriage after they had first wed.

He took the tip of her finger in his mouth and sucked, bathing her in wetness and heat, ending with a small nip. "Why not?"

"Anyone could come upon us."

"The door is closed."

She glanced over his shoulder. So it was.

"It is the midst of the day," she offered.

He took the book from her other hand and gently set it upon a nearby table. "I could lick you each second of every day and still never have enough of you."

His claim stole a laugh from her even as her nipples tightened. "Your tongue might grow weary of such an endless pursuit."

"Excellent point, my dear. Perhaps I would have to supplement with my cock. You wouldn't mind, would you?"

The ache between her thighs intensified, sharp and sweet.

"I'm sure I could be persuaded not to mind at all," she managed breathlessly.

"Good. Now come with me. I want to see how much you've missed me." He caught her hands in his, guiding her to a table on the opposite end of the library.

She went willingly, trusting him implicitly. "How will you tell?" she asked, though she was confident she knew.

"Sit on this table, and I'll show you."

The table was elegant and high, its legs tapered and narrow. She eyed it with misgiving. "What if it breaks?"

"It won't." He took her waist in a firm grip, lifting her with ease and settling her atop the piece of furniture.

They were suddenly at the same height, nose to nose.

He stepped into her, her legs parting naturally for him, and rubbed the bridge of his nose along hers in a tender gesture that made something inside her come loose. How was it possible to want him so much, with such marrow-deep need? Her response to him terrified her, because she knew that with each passing day, he only drew her further beneath his spell. And that inevitably, there would come the day that he would grow weary of her. She knew the ways of the world.

But Eleanora wouldn't think of that now, for it would only spoil a moment she intended to savor. She inhaled his scent, shaving soap and man, and took his lips in a fierce kiss, showing him how he undid her without words. He groaned, his fingertips digging with delicious pressure into her hips, his tongue plundering her mouth.

She needed to be closer to him. Needed his skin on hers. Needed more than a kiss. And she couldn't wait. She moved her hand from his shoulder, finding the fall of his trousers, and cupped his length. He was thick and hard, as ready for her as she was for him. How she ached for him, sex pulsing with a restless desire that could only be soothed in one way.

She needed him inside her.

Eleanora abandoned his cock to find the buttons she sought, undoing them. The slit in the front of his smalls was easily breached, and then she had him in her hand, hot and smooth and tempting. She gave him a firm stroke the way she had learned he liked, gratified when he made another low sound of surrender, his hips pumping in time with her hand's movement.

Nando raised his head, staring down at her with sea-blue eyes that were drenched with desire. "Not yet, love. I want to bury my face in your cunny first."

As much as she loved his tongue on her, she was already beyond the point of patience.

She continued to work his cock unmercifully, keeping him in a tight grasp, swirling her thumb over the bulbous crown. Moisture seeped from him, slicking her hand in a sign that he wanted her every bit as much as she wanted him.

"I need you inside me," she told him without preamble.

"Deus," he muttered. "Are you ready?"

As he asked the question—ever concerned for her pleasure, as he always was—he caught her gown and underpinnings, hauling them up to her thighs. Air kissed her legs through the thin barrier of her silk stockings. He parted her slick folds to tease her pearl.

She held his gaze, still milking his cock, and licked the fullness of her lower lip. "Do you think I am?"

"You're soaked." He made the observation with reverence and awe and unabashed lust, continuing to rub her sensitive nub just as she liked.

"It's your fault. You make me into a wanton."

"I've debauched you, haven't I?" He glided his finger through her wetness to her entrance, dipping it inside.

"Oh yes." She slid forward on the table, drawing him into her, mindless in her pursuit of everything he would give her.

She had never known such wondrous sensations existed, that lovemaking was far more complex than her simplistic understanding of what happened between a woman and a man. But Nando had opened her eyes to a world of possibilities. Wicked, sensual possibilities, and for the first time in her life, she was able to revel in her own body and desires. He made her feel powerful, beautiful, and wanted.

She stroked him faster, already on the edge of an orgasm.

His finger sank all the way inside her, and she gasped, tightening her hold on his steely length. It was good, so good.

"So wet and hot," he praised, adding a second finger, driving in and out of her. "You're such a good girl, primed for my cock. What can I do but give you what you want?"

His thumb rubbed over her pearl in tight circles, fingers thrusting. And when he buried his face in her throat, pressing hot, openmouthed kisses to her skin, she lost all grip on her fragile control. She came, the force of her peak making her body bow toward him, her hips pounding mercilessly against his probing fingers. His cock was pinned between them as wave after wave swept over her.

She sagged backward, struggling for her breath as the fury of her spend waned, and tugged his cock to where she wanted him most. His fingers slid away, and then they were wrapped around hers, slippery and covered in her dew. As one, they guided him to her entrance.

But just when she was ready for him to plunge inside her, his hand fell away and he tore his lips from her neck. The same hand that had pleasured her rose, slick and glistening, to cup her nape. His fingers tangled in her hair, tugging her head back with enough firmness to dance on the line between pleasure and pain. He was beautiful in his need, his eyes smoldering into hers.

"Put me inside you," he said.

And somehow the command made her hotter, wetter. She drew him to her opening, the thick head of his cock making her inhale swiftly.

"Go on, love," he prodded softly.

She urged him closer, his cock partially inside her, the same, by-now-familiar stretching of her body to accommodate him making heat glide through her veins. He felt impossibly wonderful, filling her, claiming her. She grasped his hip with her free hand, roughly pulling him so that his cock surged into her some more. And then she wriggled on the desk, bringing her bottom to the edge of the table so that she could welcome him completely, wrapping her legs around his waist in shameless invitation.

"Yes," he hissed, kissing her everywhere—lips, cheek, chin, ear, throat. Again and again, his mouth a hot benediction falling over her flesh. "Yes, sweetheart. Take my cock. Take what I give you."

She rocked against him, and he sank into her to the hilt, his cock lodged where it belonged, deep inside her. They stayed thus for a moment, bodies entwined, connected, as close as two people could be.

And then he straightened, dragging her skirts away with one hand and using the other to brace himself against the table. His head was bent, gaze intent upon the place where they were joined as he slid almost completely from her and then back inside her again.

"You're so perfect. I love the way your cunt feels, wrapped around me, so snug, so hot, so wet."

More praise. She lost all restraint, her channel tightening on his, wetness gushing from her in an abundance that would have been embarrassing had his reaction been any different.

"Oh fuck. You're so... I can't... My love..."

He said something more, but it was in his native tongue, and Eleanora couldn't understand the words. He sounded as if he were in ecstasy and pain all at once, and she knew the feeling, because she was coming on him, and he began to plow into her with more fervent thrusts, slamming deep and then withdrawing, only to slide inside her again. The table tilted, balancing on two legs and then thumping to all four, then back to two.

She reached for any surface to keep from tumbling backward, coming on him as he drove into her wildly, as if it were the first time and the last time they would ever make love. Her hand snagged in smooth cloth, and she clutched it, another peak hitting her as he surged forward, his cock buried so deeply in her that sensation made black stars speckle her vision. A mindless yank, and the curtains came tumbling down around them.

Later, she would concern herself with how she would explain the mess they had made to the servants. Now, she was too consumed in Nando. Now, she was wanton and wicked, her breasts heavy and full, nipples abrading her stays with every thrust she matched him for, her hips dancing from the table as it wavered and crashed about.

He thrust in and out of her wetness, groaning, praising her.

"You look so beautiful." He sank deep, then withdrew. "Such a good girl, coming all over my cock again and again. I'm drowning in you."

"Yes," she whimpered, matching his movements, hands splayed on the table, hips mindlessly working, bringing him into her over and over, her entire body sensitized beyond all control. "Fuck me, Nando. Fill me with your seed. I need it. I need *you*. Please."

A confession of sorts. Perhaps she would regret it later. But her mind was not functioning as it ought, drenched as it was in filthy, debauched pleasure. She was more desperate than she had ever been, drawn to the height of something bigger than she was. Something bigger than the both of them.

He tugged at her hair, pulling her head back, holding her gaze. "Say it again."

She had said so much. Her wits scrambled, trying to recall the words that had only just left her lips. How was she to think with his big cock filling her?

"I…" He sank into her quickly, deeply. "Oh."

He withdrew, the glide of his thick erection something close to pure bliss. "Say it."

"Fuck me."

He slammed into her, the table shuddering beneath them.

"Not that." He found her mouth with his, kissing her harshly, deliciously, his tongue mating with hers before he lifted his head again. "Tell me to come inside you. To fill you with my seed. Tell me you need me."

"Come inside me," she begged without hesitation, wanting to do anything to please him, to please them both. "I need you. Fill me up with your seed. Make me with child."

She didn't know where the last request came from. In all the years she had been working so steadfastly as a paid companion, she had never dreamed of children of her own. It had been elusive, something that would never be hers. And she hadn't thought about children with Nando either. But the words left her, coming from some place of validity, from some part of her she hadn't ever acknowledged.

The effect upon him was instant.

He hastened his pace, his strokes deep, hard, and fast. Not hurried but frenzied as he sank his cock into her again and again. Until, with a choked sound, he buried himself inside her and stiffened, his spend spurting into her, hot and wet and so delicious that she trembled, pressing her breasts shamelessly into his chest, her mouth seeking his. They kissed as the last spurt of his seed left him, warmth blossoming inside her like a summer bloom.

Nando collapsed against her, still nestled deep, and she wrapped her arms around him, holding him close, never wanting him to part from her. Even as she knew that one day, he inevitably would. Because there was one lesson Mama had taught her that Eleanora had never forgotten—men always left.

245

~

HE LOVED FUCKING.

Ye gods, did he *love* fucking.

However, Nando had discovered there was something he loved more than fucking. Several things, actually. One of them was his wife. Another of them was having said wife on his lap, as he did now, in his arms, with Benvolio curled on her. The cat sleepily purred as she rubbed the soft white patch of fur under his chin where he loved to be petted most. They had been spending their evenings thus for the last few nights.

Just after dinner, they would retire to the salon that she had yet to decorate and make her own, the hearth cheerily crackling, Benvolio twining about their ankles in an attempt to kill them, as Nando teasingly claimed. They would settle upon the same obliging Grecian couch and talk.

Yes, *talking*—to his wife. That was another thing Nando loved more than fucking. Getting to know her was a joy he had not previously imagined existed. Certainly, he had never shared such jarring intimacy with another woman. Marriage had taught him that there was far more to a relationship between a man and a woman than merely the carnal aspect. And although his appetite for his beautiful wife did remain ravenous, he couldn't deny that quiet moments such as these, Eleanora snuggled in his lap, were every bit as glorious as making love to her was.

"Tell me about Varros," she said softly, her husky voice a welcome intrusion on his thoughts. "What is it like there?"

He thought of his homeland, the small island kingdom where he had spent most of his life, and a pang went through him. "It is beautiful. Summers are warm and filled with sunshine and blue skies. We've beaches of white sand where wild horses roam."

"Do you not miss your home?"

He did and he didn't. The truth of it was, he had been unsettled when he had left for England. Seeking something. He hadn't known what until Eleanora had swirled into his life wearing a fichu and a frown.

He sifted his fingers through her unbound hair, mesmerized by the way the candlelight brought the burnished strands to life. "I do in some ways, I suppose."

"How long do you intend to remain in England?"

"I hadn't really thought about it," he admitted. "I bought this town house on a whim, but staying here certainly has its merits."

She glanced at him over her shoulder, her gaze searching. "Are you saying you never intend to go back to Varros?"

"I don't know. My life there was…different."

Incomplete, he wanted to say. Each day the same as the next, an endless blur of fucking and fêtes and the unceasing pursuit of pleasure that could never truly be obtained. Because pleasure like this—Eleanora in his arms, the night quiet and still around them, save for Benvolio's contented purrs and the crackling of a warm fire—couldn't be found in a stranger's bed.

"But surely you would want to return to your homeland," she pressed.

He didn't want to go back to his old circle, no. Not to the courtiers who would welcome him with open arms. Nor to the lovers he had left behind. He wanted a new life, a new purpose. He wanted what he had with Eleanora, this charmed existence they had been building together, this stunning idyll. And part of him was terrified that if they returned, and if she were to discover all the sordid secrets of his past, she would no longer want him.

"There is much for me here," he explained, stroking her jaw, then tracing an absent fingertip around her lips.

"What of your brother, the king? Your baby nephew and your sister-in-law? Have you no wish to see them again?"

Of course he did. He loved Maxim and his brother's burgeoning family. But Nando wasn't sure how to explain himself to Eleanora without revealing his true motive for not wanting to return to Varros.

He shrugged. "Perhaps Maxim can come to us one day."

Unlikely, however. His brother had only come to England for his formal betrothal to Princess Anastasia. After that had been broken and Maxim had wed Tansy, there was precious little reason for Maxim to leave the capital city. Particularly since there had recently been unrest with one of their uncle's loyalists. It was safer for the king to remain on his throne with his queen.

Maybe Nando could delay his return to Varros until Eleanora had fallen so hopelessly in love with him that she would never leave when she learned the depths of his depravity.

"Are you ashamed of me?" Eleanora asked quietly.

"God no," he reassured her, wishing he could kick himself in the arse for causing her a moment of uncertainty. "I couldn't be prouder of you, my dear. You are my better in every way."

He meant those words with every speck of the heart he had previously believed he hadn't had.

"Then why do you not wish to go back to Varros?" she asked. "There must be another reason, one you aren't telling me. It makes no sense. An attempt was made on your life here, and yet you remain, with no plans of returning to your home any time soon."

She was far too perceptive and clever, his Eleanora. He was going to have to explain.

He sifted the silken strands of her hair again, considering his words with great care. "My life there...the circles I kept...

they were different. There are people I would not wish for you to meet, stories I would prefer you never hear. I'm not proud of the man I've been."

"Do you suppose I haven't heard the rumors about you?" she asked.

His ears went hot. He hadn't thought she had, although he had been aware that his reputation generally preceded him. Nando had preferred simply not to think of it.

"Which rumors have you heard?" he dared to ask, dreading the answer.

"That you closeted yourself in a brothel for days and had to be removed by your brother the king," she began.

Nando winced. "It wasn't days."

"That you bedded three women at once," she continued. "That you cuckolded an earl, a baron, and a marquess."

"Deus," he muttered. "That is enough. Apparently, I have proven quite the fodder for London scandal broth."

"I'm afraid you have."

He smoothed a stray tendril of hair from her cheek. "Little wonder you scorned me so when you first met me. I am not proud of my reckless ways. But all that is in the past. I am a different man now."

Her brow was furrowed, her look pensive. He could see her warring with herself, and he hated that his past had the power to hurt her, to come between them.

"Princess Anastasia told me you are known for your recklessness," Eleanora added. "She warned me not to marry you because of it."

His spine stiffened, outrage boiling up within him. "The devil she did."

He had thought he was on friendly terms with Stasia. To think that she'd had the nerve to warn Eleanora not to wed him. It was infuriating. Maddening.

But then, how could he blame her?

Eleanora shifted in his lap so she could face him fully. "I didn't listen."

"Why didn't you?" he asked hoarsely, needing to know.

Ye gods, she ought to have run as far and as fast as she could in the opposite direction of him. He was selfishly glad she had not.

"I *wanted* to marry you," she said softly, her words falling over him like a velvet caress. "Her concerns weren't enough to dissuade me."

Disappointment laced through him. What had he expected from her? A declaration of love? Of course not, but he knew why she had wanted to marry him, and it didn't have anything to do with tender emotion.

"Because I'm a prince," he said, unable to keep the bitterness from his voice.

She shook her head. "No, Nando."

"For my looks?" he guessed next, for he was well aware of the effect he had upon the opposite sex.

Women found him very handsome indeed, and it was simply an incontrovertible fact, much like his title.

Eleanora tucked her chin, biting her lip as she shook her head again. "Because you're you, and I like you for who you are, regardless of whether you're a prince."

Her words stunned him. Humbled him.

Shook him.

His hand trembled as he cupped her cheek and kissed her, swift and hard before retreating. "Thank you. No one has ever said that to me before."

Women had wanted him for his power, his wealth, his looks, the pleasure he could give them. But none of them had ever wanted him simply for himself. For Nando, imperfect and flawed, reckless and lost, and now, because of the woman in his arms, found.

"Then I am honored to be the first," she said, cupping his cheek in a fond gesture that had him hardening beneath her.

All she had to do was touch him. Sometimes, it was as simple as her appearance in a room or the faint trace of her scent where she had recently been. Yes, he was thoroughly besotted. Maxim would laugh at him.

Perhaps Nando would take her with him to Varros sooner than he had supposed. And perhaps there was a chance that he *could* earn her love. It was a chance he was willing to take.

"I think that perhaps Benvolio ought to go to bed," he told her.

Eleanora laughed, wriggling her bottom in a way that nearly had him spending in his trousers. "It certainly feels as if he should."

"Minx," he said tenderly, awed by her, and took her lips again.

She kissed him back, and he reveled in the decadent taste of her, the gentle play of her tongue with his. He had never been happier than he was in this salon, Eleanora in his arms, her mouth on his.

And he knew that the future would only be sweeter.

CHAPTER 19

⁂

*I*t had become customary for Bruno to rise early and see that everything was to Nando's liking in his study, where he took his coffee, read *The Times*, and reviewed his correspondence. But this morning, the curtains remained curiously closed, the scent of coffee didn't permeate the air, and his newspaper was nowhere to be found.

Neither was Bruno, for that matter. Nando frowned.

Thinking his manservant's lapse odd, Nando allowed the door to fall closed at his back and ventured deeper into the room. Not even a brace of candles lit. Fortunately, the morning light streamed in through the window coverings, partially brightening the chamber.

That was when he spied Bruno's form, curiously still, in a chair by the hearth.

He didn't think, simply acted, striding forward. "Bruno?"

No answer. Nando quickly found the reason his loyal bodyguard failed to respond. Bruno was slumped over, snoring heavily, a bloody gash on the back of his head. Someone had knocked him insensate.

Sweet God.

There was the brief, prickling sensation on the back of Nando's neck that told him he wasn't alone just before a figure moved forward from the shadows of the darkened room, the double barrels of a flintlock pistol pointed directly at him.

"Don't move," the man ordered, light illuminating his features as recognition hit Nando like a blow.

"Levering," he said with a sinking sensation deep in his gut.

How the hell had the man made it past Tierney's guards? It seemed an impossibility, and yet here he stood, his eyes cold and dead.

"Ah, so you *do* remember the face of the man you cuckolded."

There was no mistaking the rage in the earl's countenance, sharpening his voice. It would seem that the ghosts of Nando's past were intent upon haunting him.

"I recall the face of the man who challenged me to a duel quite well," he said, wondering at the extent of the damage Levering had done to poor Bruno.

And wondering where his bodyguard's pistol was. Bruno's hands were empty. Nando had no weapon other than his fists to defend himself. The challenge facing him was grossly unfair. His mouth went dry as his mind raced to find a solution, some means of saving himself and Bruno.

And Eleanora.

The reminder of his beautiful wife sleeping peacefully upstairs filled him with dread. He had to protect her at all costs. Even if it meant sacrificing himself. He would gladly die for her if he had to. But first, he would do everything in his power to defeat the earl and keep her safe.

Nando pretended nonchalance, knowing that he had to

keep his opponent calm if he wanted to maintain control over the situation.

He smiled, quite as if the earl were an invited guest in his study. "Pray tell me what the devil this grievance you appear to have with me is about."

"Do you truly feign ignorance?" Levering sneered. "This is about my wife, you spineless scoundrel."

Nando clicked his tongue on the roof of his mouth in mock chastisement. "Is it not too early in the day for casting aspersions on the character of your host?"

"You dare to make light of me?" Levering's eyes narrowed as he continued to point the flintlock at Nando. "We shall see which of us has the last laugh."

"That sounds terribly final."

"Death is."

"Then I reckon it would be foolish of me to hope your pistol isn't loaded."

"Loaded with a bullet for you, as it happens."

The determination on the earl's face was chilling. Nando decided to change tactics.

"You mentioned Lady Levering. What has she to do with this? I believed our unfortunate association had been settled."

"She's carrying your bastard," the earl snarled.

The accusation would have alarmed Nando had it not been wholly impossible. Relief washed over him.

"My lord, the last time I bedded your wife was when you unfortunately happened upon us, well over a year ago. If the countess is indeed carrying my child, then she has miraculous capabilities of gestation that surpass her fellow woman. In other words, if your wife is *enceinte*, I regret to inform you that it is impossible for me to be the sire of the infant in question."

But far from reassuring Lord Levering and calming him

as Nando had hoped his revelation would, it only appeared to heighten his rage.

The earl's lip curled. "This amuses you, you witless jack-anapes? You'll not be so pleased when you are on your knees, begging for your life, I'd wager."

Ice trilled down his spine, but Nando refused to show Levering a hint of weakness as he held the man's stare. "There is only one person I will get on my knees for, and it isn't you."

It was Eleanora. Thank God she wasn't here in this room with him now.

Levering laughed bitterly. "You think I won't shoot you? How wrong you are. I've already done it once before, you see."

The earl was a madman, and he had just confirmed Nando's and Tierney's suspicions. He was responsible for the pistol shot that had thankfully gone awry that day. Levering had tried to kill him.

Tried and failed.

Anger chased the fear. Levering was going to pay for what he had done.

"Your aim is atrocious, my lord," he taunted.

"This time, I will find my mark." The earl smirked. "Of that, you may rest assured."

"Are you saying you intend to shoot me here and now, with a house full of servants who will be instantly alerted by the sound of a gunshot?" he asked. "To say nothing of the guards I have stationed about the town house, all of whom are armed as well. How amusing you are, Levering. Either amusing or perhaps you arc…what is the word in English… an idiot?"

As he delivered the stinging assessment, Nando inched toward the fireplace, where the sterling silver fire poker had caught his attention. If he could move nearer to it by distracting the earl sufficiently, there was a possibility he might reach the poker and at least have one means of defending himself.

Unless Levering shot him first, that was.

He shifted ever so slightly.

"Don't move," the earl warned him, voice harsh. "Stay where you are."

Nando forced himself to speak, to offer more diversion and keep Levering off guard. "You say that I'm the father of Lady Levering's child," he continued conversationally, whilst moving another subtle inch. "But what of you? You are her husband, after all."

"I haven't been in that slut's bed in years," the earl snapped. "She has disgraced me, and I have nothing but disgust for her."

Nando slid to the right just a bit. "If you hate your wife, then why do you want to kill me for bedding her?"

"Because someone has to pay for what she's done. I should have forced you to that duel. If I had killed you then, she never would have fallen pregnant. But I needed the funds your brother offered. I allowed myself to be bribed. I was weak and imprudent, just as I was when I married that whore. I'll not be made a fool a second time."

"Actually," Nando offered, "she would have fallen pregnant just the same because as I've already informed you, I am not the man who is fucking your wife."

Another slight step. The poker was almost within reach.

"How dare you speak so callously? Although I suppose that I should not be surprised. You are nothing more than the whoremonger brother of a usurper king."

"See here, Levering. My brother is no usurper." Nando inched closer. "The House of Tayrnes is the only rightful heir to the kingdom. My uncle and his revolutionaries falsely seized power and started the Great War. Perhaps you don't consult *The Times*."

"Silence!" Levering snapped. "Do you think I care about the history of your insignificant kingdom? Your nation is so pathetic that it could be crushed with a boot heel."

One more incremental step. He could grasp the poker in a swift move and then throw it at the earl. His heart hammered painfully against his chest.

For Eleanora, he reminded himself.

For Bruno.

"I merely sought to correct your misapprehensions," he said, keeping his voice smooth with all the control he possessed. "You seem to be suffering from rather a lot of them, my lord. Beginning with your delusion that I have been bedding your wife."

"No more of your lies," Levering roared. "She told me the truth when I confronted her after I learned of the babe. She told me that you are the father, that the two of you are in love, and that she intends to run away with you to Varros."

Nando might have laughed at the absurdity of such a claim, if not for the pistol pointed at his heart. "If Lady Levering made those claims to you, it was only to keep her lover's true identity a secret and protect him from you."

Levering scowled and shook the flintlock wildly. "Cease speaking at once! I'll not be confused by your falsehoods, nor will I be dissuaded from my course."

Nando took the final step as the door to his study swung open, and his heart froze. For there, on the threshold, stood Eleanora. His entire world. The woman who had become dearer to him than his next breath.

"Run," he cried out to her, finally grasping the poker and raising it high.

But she stood there, frozen, stricken. Nando saw it

happening as if from afar, horror seizing his chest. Levering wheeled about, eyes crazed. Eleanora's scream rent the air.

"No!" The ragged cry of pure despair was torn from him as he leapt toward the earl, striking the man's extended arm with the poker as hard as he could.

The pistol fired in the same moment, flying from Levering's hand, and she crumpled to the floor.

Nando rushed for the flintlock, taking it in trembling hands and pointing it at Levering. "Don't you bloody move."

Bruno rose from the chair, pale and bloodied. "Your Royal Highness. What has happened?"

He couldn't find the words to answer. His tongue was as numb as his mind, fear making his heart pound. He had to get to Eleanora. Nando backed toward the place where she had fallen, desperate to assess the damage that had been done, keeping the pistol trained on Levering with every step. He couldn't lose her.

He *wouldn't* lose her. Not now, not ever.

There was a flurry of frightened servants gathering, having been drawn by the cries and the report of the flintlock. "Fetch a doctor at once," he ordered them. "The princess has been wounded."

She was so still, so silent. He saw the blood, red and angry, seeping through her gown, and his stomach gave a violent heave. He sank to his knees at Eleanora's side, and he did something he had not done in many years.

Nando prayed.

$\approx$

THE PAIN in Eleanora's shoulder was excruciating. She could not breathe without agony, each inhalation agonizing. She was mired in the darkness, swirling toward nothingness. Too weak to save herself. And she was cold, so cold, as if she were buffeted by an icy winter's wind, her body trembling uncontrollably.

A voice pierced the emptiness.

"My love, don't leave me."

The voice was familiar, deep, tinged with the hint of an accent.

Nando's voice.

He was here, somewhere. But she couldn't open her eyes. Couldn't raise her arms to reach for him.

"Eleanora, don't you dare die on me. Please." His voice was broken now, the anguish in it so heavy that she longed to reassure him.

But she couldn't speak. Couldn't move. It was as if her body had been weighed down with a thousand stones.

Other voices filtered to her, low and indistinguishable and unknown.

Questions swirled. Who were they? Where was she? What had happened? Why did Nando think she was going to die?

There was a vicious, stabbing pain in her shoulder, and then she succumbed to the blackness surrounding her.

∿

HIS FAULT.

Nando paced the hall outside the room where Eleanora was being tended to by a doctor, sick with worry.

Eleanora had nearly been killed, and he was the only one to blame. If he had not married her, she would not have been in his town house when Levering had stolen within, intent upon murdering him. She never would have been shot. And if he had simply heeded Tierney's warnings and stayed where they both had been safe, she never would have lain on the Aubusson, her life's source seeping into the patterned wool as he frantically held his cravat to her wound to stop the bleeding.

He hated himself.

He would never forgive what he had done. And he knew without a doubt that there was only one way he could do penance for leading her into danger and so recklessly putting her at risk. For nearly costing Eleanora her life.

He'd been an unabashed rake for years, undisciplined and wild, selfish and greedy. Flitting from distraction to distraction without the weight of responsibility, without a care for anything or anyone but himself.

Now, Nando would be selfless for the first time. Because he loved Eleanora enough to recognize he was not worthy of her, loved her enough to realize he needed to put *her* happiness before his own. She had married him because she'd been a woman of few means forced to earn her supper by being a glorified servant, and he had offered her a life of comfort and ease. Whilst he knew that she had found pleasure in his arms, he didn't fool himself that she returned his love. How could she love a scapegrace like him?

Nando knew what he had to do.

He would leave her.

∾

"It is nothing short of a miracle that the bullet did not do more damage," Dr. Crisfield announced as he emerged from the room what seemed an eternity later.

Nando's eyes slid closed, his knees trembling so violently that he almost went tumbling to his arse. The bullet had passed miraculously through, not embedding itself in her body, splintering bone and piercing vital organs as he had feared when he had seen all that blood.

Thank God.

He said a silent prayer of gratitude before opening his eyes and taking a deep breath. "She will live, then?"

The physician nodded. "I was able to stitch her wound and stay the bleeding. She will need to rest and remain abed. Her Royal Highness lost a great deal of blood. I've given her laudanum for the pain and bandaged the wound. As long as infection does not set in, she will recover fully."

The chance of infection was strong, he knew, and the outcome grim. But Nando wouldn't think of that now. Eleanora was alive. The wound had not been as devastating as he had thought. Bruno had taken a terrible knock to the head, but he would recover as well. And Levering, that despicable madman, had been taken away by the watch. Nando didn't give a damn about his own miserable hide, but Eleanora was safe from Levering, and that was all that mattered.

"Thank you, Dr. Crisfield," he said, needing to see her for himself. "May I go to her now?"

The doctor gave him a sympathetic smile. "The laudanum did its job, and she is sleeping, but there is no reason to stay away, Your Royal Highness. You may see your wife now."

Nando was moving before Dr. Crisfield finished speaking. He crossed the threshold to the chamber where he'd carried her limp body earlier in a frenzied rush of fear. It wasn't her bedroom, but it had been the closest and most convenient. She lay quiet and still, her face ashen, looking so small and fragile and unlike her customary vibrant self.

Tears were streaming down his cheeks, but he didn't care. He sank into the chair at her bedside, clasped his hands together, and prayed some more.

CHAPTER 20

$\mathcal{E}$leanora had been trampled by a horse. There was no other explanation, she decided as she came awake, to feel as she did. Her left shoulder ached, her skin felt as if it had been drawn too tight, and there was no way she could move that did not produce a sudden stab of pain. Her eyes fluttered open to find herself in an unfamiliar bed, the light snores of her husband ringing rhythmically through the stillness of the room.

He was slumped in a chair, his long legs stretched before him, crossed at his booted ankles, head lolling to the side. His position looked dreadfully uncomfortable, and for a moment, confusion crowded her mind. She couldn't think of why he was here, asleep in a chair. Or what the cause of her agony was and how she had managed to find herself in this mostly undecorated guest room.

"Nando?" she managed, her voice a rusty rasp, her tone desperately dry.

He jolted awake, stunning blue eyes searing hers with their customary intensity. "My love. What is it?"

It was everything. She tried to speak, but her voice didn't want to oblige this second time.

"I'll fetch you some water," he said, shooting to his feet.

She wanted to protest, for there was some instinct deep within her that said she needed him close. But her raspy words either failed to reach him, or he ignored them. He crossed the room to where a pitcher, cup, and other small bottles sat atop a table. The sound of water filling the cup reached her, and then he turned, striding back, his countenance hewn in granite.

Instead of handing her the cup, he held it to her lips. "Drink."

It was just as well that he performed the action for her, because even her uninjured arm felt as if it had been weighed down by lead. It would seem that her entire body was weak, not just her voice. She took a hesitant sip, the water sluicing down her throat.

Instantly, she wanted more—the whole cup.

But Nando withdrew it before she could drain the entire contents. She made a sound of protest.

"You need to drink slowly," he explained. "I don't want you to make yourself ill. If you vomit your water, you'll pull the stitches and be in terrible pain."

His voice was low, soothing. Vague flashes of memory returned to her, that voice at her side in the darkness that had swirled around her, patient, loving hands stroking her hair, a cool cloth at her brow, words of encouragement. Whatever had happened to her, Nando had been here with her, a steadfast presence.

Stitches, he had said.

"W-what happened?" she managed.

His gaze searched hers, and she couldn't help but note the dark circles marring the skin beneath his eyes. "What do you remember?"

She forced her tired mind to think. "There was a man with a pistol. H-he was going to shoot you. Who was he?"

Nando's jaw tightened as he offered her another small sip of water from the cup. "He was the Earl of Levering. On my previous trip to England, I am ashamed to admit that I dallied with his wife. Levering demanded a duel to satisfy his honor, but my brother Maxim offered him a fortune instead, and Levering accepted. I believed all was forgotten, and when I returned to England, I made certain to avoid crossing paths with the countess."

Eleanora savored her small sip of water, swallowing it, but sensed that there was far more to Nando's story than what he had thus far revealed. "All was not forgotten, however?"

"No," he confirmed, grimmer than she had ever seen him. "The fortune wasn't sufficient, particularly when the countess informed her husband that she was with child and he wasn't the father. That…that I was."

Shock hit her with such force that she jolted, the movement causing pain to streak through her. She gasped sharply, stiffening.

"You must remain as still as you are able," Nando cautioned tenderly. "I am sorry to give you such a start. It's not true, Eleanora. I'm not the father of her child. She's clearly taken another lover, and in an effort to protect him, she told Levering I was the one responsible. He went mad with fury and has been intent upon killing me."

Horror replaced the pain, making her hand tremble as she reached for him. "He was the one who shot at you before?"

Nando took her right hand in his, bringing it to his lips for a reverent kiss. "He was, and so you see, my love, everything that's happened…it's my fault. All of it. It's my fault you were shot and nearly killed, and I'll never forgive myself."

Her heart ached for him. "You cannot blame yourself."

His expression was forbidding. "I can, and I must. It was my conduct that caused the association between Levering and myself. Before I left Tierney's town house, he warned me that there was evidence to suggest Levering was responsible for the attempt on my life. But I was selfish and restless, and I wanted you here to myself. I brought you into danger, Eleanora. Don't you see? I *am* to blame."

"You couldn't have known what Levering was capable of," she argued, wanting to reassure him. "Besides, you saved me, Nando. When he pointed the pistol at me, you attacked him with the fire poker, making him jerk his aim to the side. If you hadn't acted, I would have been shot through the heart instead of the shoulder."

He kissed her knuckles again, smiling sadly. "How like you to believe me chivalrous. I can assure you, your faith is misplaced. You never should have been shot to begin with, and I'll never forgive myself for causing you even a moment of pain."

She was growing weary again. Eleanora didn't like his dour mien or his insistence upon shouldering responsibility for the acts of a madman. But she would argue with him later, when she had more strength. For now, there was only one thing she wanted to know.

"What's happened to Levering?" she asked.

"He's been arrested and taken away to pay for his crimes," Nando said.

Calm crept over her.

"You're safe, then?"

Nando nodded, giving her fingers a squeeze. "And so are you. Levering will never hurt you again."

She managed a faint smile, her eyelids growing heavy. "Good."

And then she fell back into the abyss.

~

ONE WEEK after Eleanora had been wounded, Nando found himself grimly pacing the hall once more as Dr. Crisfield examined her. This time, it was a different hall, for she had finally gained enough strength that Nando had felt comfortable carrying her to her own bedroom. His heart was pounding faster than if he had raced up and down the town house's staircase ten times over.

She was going to live. He knew that. At least, he felt that, given her gradual convalescence. Infection had, thus far, been avoided. Each day, she regained more of her strength. The wound she had endured had been deeper than the graze he had suffered at the hands of Levering. Her recuperation was taking longer, given the nature of her injury.

But she would live. Thank the heavens above, she would *live*.

No thanks to him, and he intended to begin his penance soon. He was going to leave her. In the days that followed her wounding, he had remained at her side, tending to her, scarcely sleeping, helping her to bathe, to eat. When nightmares made her cry out, he slipped into bed with her, tucking her body gently against his, and holding her. Watching her so wan and unlike herself, in so much pain, was akin to a dagger in the heart. And when he cleansed the wound on her shoulder, bandaging it as the physician had taught him, he had told himself each time that he must atone for his sins.

That he was no good for anyone. He was reckless, selfish, greedy, and—worst of all—foolish. He had allowed the woman he loved to be nearly killed. And now, he would give her everything he could to make certain she thrived without the encumbrance of his ne'er-do-well idiocy. The town house would be hers, along with the entirety of his fortune that was his to give.

And an annulment.

It had taken him some time to realize that, much like hasty weddings in England, annulments were nearly impossible. He would obtain one in Varros when he returned. No one would deny Prince Ferdinando of the House of Tayrnes in his own kingdom. There, he could do whatever he pleased.

Not that he was pleased to annul his marriage to Eleanora. The notion made his gut churn. The weeks he had spent as her husband had been the happiest he had ever known. He loved her more than he had imagined possible. And it was because he loved her—truly, selflessly, eternally—that he was going to leave her.

She would be better off without his selfish arse.

The door opened at his back, and he spun about to find Dr. Crisfield, not nearly as grim as he had been one week ago.

"How is she?" he asked, tamping down the thoughts of what he must soon do.

Crisfield smiled—a rarity for such a serious man. "Her wound is healing well. I have every confidence that Her Royal Highness is no longer in danger of contagion and that she will regain full movement of her left arm after the wound is completely healed."

Relief washed over him, quickly followed by dread.

Because Eleanora was well on her way to being whole once again. But Nando would forever be broken without her.

≈

"You are looking well this afternoon," Stasia greeted Eleanora, flanked on either side by Princess Emmaline and Princess Annalise.

Propped comfortably in her bed by a mountain of pillows, clad for the first time since she had been wounded in a true gown, and freshly bathed, Eleanora smiled at the three women who had been paying regular calls upon her during her recuperation. She had come to cherish their friendships greatly.

"Thank you, and the same might be said of all of you as well." She noted that Princess Emmaline was not wearing trousers today, although she had on some previous visits. "A lovely gown, Emmaline."

Emmaline cast a disgusted glance down at her pink muslin. "Dreadfully uncomfortable as well, but I do thank you."

Eleanora had to bite her lip to keep from chuckling at the princess's continued disdain for gowns. "The pink suits you, nonetheless, despite the discomfort. Do have a seat, if you please. I was intending to venture to the drawing room today for tea, but I fear I've been a slug-a-bed, and thus far, I've only managed to dress."

The nature of her injury had rendered proper gowns and undergarments nearly impossible. Today had been the first that she had dared to attempt to don them with her lady's maid's help. Nando had objected each morning, telling her that she needed to allow herself time to heal. However, when he had kissed her good evening the night before, he had told her that he had some calls to make in the morning that would keep him from her side.

Now that she thought upon it, he had been gone for a great many hours. It was afternoon, and she had yet to see him. Her heart gave a pang. He had been such a steadfast presence through her recovery that she had come to take him a bit for granted.

The ladies seated themselves in chairs that had been arranged for the purpose of their visits.

"How is your shoulder?" Stasia asked, concern in her voice.

"The wound is healing nicely."

"It was quite valiant of Nando to intervene as he did," said Princess Annalise, "attacking that vile villain at just the right moment."

There was awe in the princess's voice, and it was matched by Eleanora. Although Nando continued to insist that he was responsible for Levering shooting her, she was simply grateful that he had saved her by ruining the earl's aim with the quick blow from the fire poker. She had no doubt that she would not be here today if he hadn't acted quickly. The memory of Levering's crazed expression, the naked hatred in his eyes, sent a shiver down her spine.

The man had been intent upon murder.

"It was, indeed," she agreed, a fond smile curving her lips as she thought of how he had tended to her, showing her such care. "I'll be forever indebted to him for saving me."

Her ability to withstand his charm had been banished by his attentiveness. Over the last fortnight, he had shown her a side of himself that she had only previously glimpsed. The true Nando, she thought. And he was a man she could love.

A man she was in love with *already*, if she were brutally honest with herself.

"I am relieved to see that the two of you have parted on good terms, then," Stasia said.

For a moment, Eleanora could do nothing but stare at her friend as her words failed to make sense.

"Parted?" she repeated, frowning in confusion. "Forgive me, but I believe I must have misheard you."

Stasia's brow wrinkled, her expression turning strange. "Nando paid a call upon us before he left for Varros this morning. I've never seen him so somber."

Eleanora felt all the blood drain from her face. It was as if the floor had opened suddenly, and she had fallen through the hole.

Varros? Nando had *left* for Varros? This morning? How? It was not possible. He had just been with her last night, kissing her softly, lingeringly. Telling her again how sorry he was for what had happened.

Telling her that he would do everything he could to make amends. That vow suddenly seemed far more ominous than it had the night before.

"Eleanora? You've gone pale." Stasia's fretful voice pulled her from her spinning thoughts. "You did know Nando was leaving for Varros, did you not?"

She could not speak.

He had left her.

Nando had abandoned her, and without a word of why or when he would return, if ever. Stasia's words of warning before her wedding returned with potent, searing force.

Between the two of us, I am not certain he has the capacity to be the sort of husband you deserve.

What she had meant, Eleanora had known then, was that she didn't believe Nando had the capacity to be faithful. That marriage, like most of his vices, would grow tedious. That he would become bored and flit away to something—or *someone* —else.

"Did he not tell you?" Stasia repeated, her tone edged with desperation.

"N-no," she managed, her voice trembling, her gut churning with ominous portent.

All three sisters seemed to gasp in unison.

"I don't understand," Stasia added. "Why would he tell Mr. Tierney and me of his travel intentions and yet not inform his own wife?"

Why, indeed?

Eleanora feared she knew the answer.

Still feeling a combination of numb and ill, she held her friend's pitying gaze. "So that I could not dissuade him, of course."

"Nando detests all manner of conflict." Stasia paused, biting her lip before appearing to collect herself. "Oh, my dear. I am so very sorry."

The naked sympathy on her face was too much. The room had begun to spin, and Eleanora's stomach would no longer be quelled.

She reached for the elegant chamber pot which had been discreetly placed, clean and at hand should she require it, and promptly retched.

~

SCRATCH, scratch, scratch.

The sound brought Eleanora from the depths of her misery at some point after Stasia, Emmaline, and Annalise had taken their leave. An indeterminate span of time had passed since their call and the terrible realization that Nando had abandoned her. She had denied the aid of her lady's maid, refusing to speak to anyone.

Needing, quite desperately, to be alone so that she could weep in peace.

And weep she had.

She had sobbed. Viciously, hideously, and without end. Until her nose had been plugged, her eyes were swollen, her head ached, her wounded shoulder throbbed, and there was seemingly not a drop of tears left for her to shed. She had dampened five handkerchiefs, one of which had been embroidered with Nando's initials in the corner, and that had made her cry harder.

Scratch, scratch, scratch.

Sniffling, she sat up in bed, cocking her head to the side, listening. It was coming from the door joining her bedroom to Nando's. For a moment, her heart leapt. Had he returned?

But no.

For then came the distinctive sound of a meow.

"Benvolio," she murmured, utterly astounded at the prospect.

Had Nando not just abandoned her, but his cat as well?

Still feeling weak, her stomach knotted in threat of another violent upheaval, she rose from her bed, making her way across the room to the closed door. Reaching for the latch, she opened it.

With a trill, Benvolio pranced over the threshold.

He had left the cat behind as well.

She knelt, running her right hand over the lush fur on Benvolio's spine. "He's left the both of us then, hasn't he?"

The cat rubbed his face against Eleanora's ankles in response. Her heart ached anew.

And that was when she saw the letter, neatly folded and bearing her name in Nando's elegant scrawl, awaiting her on the table at his bedside. For a moment, she told herself she wouldn't read it, that she would toss it into the fire instead.

But then her feet were moving of their own accord, and she was almost tripping over an eager and lonely Benvolio, who followed along in her haste to retrieve that lone missive. Perhaps it contained what she wanted most—an answer.

Why? Why had he left her this way, so unexpectedly?

She unfolded the letter and found his reasons, neatly enumerated.

. . .

Dearest Eleanora,

By the time you read this letter, I will have set sail on La Reina, returning to Varros where I belong and where I can no longer cause you harm or bring you danger. You so very sweetly absolved me of my sins where you are concerned, but I have not been so hasty with myself. You are, as ever, generous, kind, and wonderful beyond measure. I can no longer pretend to be worthy of you, given the evil I have brought upon you.

I alone shoulder the blame and responsibility for what has happened. My past depravities are the reason you were nearly killed. I cannot forgive myself for the pain I caused you. All I can do is make certain it never happens again and that you are free to live the life you deserve without me.

The town house is yours. During your convales-cence, I made certain that possession of it and as much of my fortune that I am at liberty to give will belong to you. I will obtain an annulment of our marriage in Varros with ease and haste. Please also watch over Benvolio for me. He has always, quite rightly, loved you more.

Please know that for all my faults, from the moment you first pinned me with a glare, my heart has been, and shall forever remain, incontro-vertibly, only yours.

With eternal love and admiration,
Nando

THE LETTER FELL from her nerveless fingers, floating to the floor, fresh tears burning in her eyes.

Eleanora knew at once what she had to do.

CHAPTER 21

KINGDOM OF VARROS, ONE MONTH LATER

*E*leanora had been hoping a carriage would be awaiting her when she disembarked from *La Reina*. Perhaps even Nando himself. That had been a fanciful notion, particularly when he had failed to answer any of the letters she had sent him over the last month. And it had never seemed more dubious than now, as she and her lady's maid stood in the midst of the bustling Varros docks with a pile of her trunks and a makeshift cage bearing a thoroughly unimpressed Benvolio. The sea journey hadn't been easy on any of them.

At last, they were all on land where they belonged. Even if her body still felt firmly as if it were rocking along on the sea. A wave of dizziness assailed her, and her stomach tightened, bile rising up her throat, as the wind blew and the combined scent of dead fish and horse manure reached her. She fumbled in her reticule, searching for a scented handkerchief.

"Your Royal Highness, are you going to be ill?" her lady's maid asked worriedly.

A young, lively, intrepid thing, Southill had not balked at

Eleanora's request to accompany her on the arduous journey to Varros. And fortunately for Eleanora, her lady's maid had proven far less inclined to suffer seasickness. Although, to be fair, Eleanora wasn't certain how much of her illness had been caused by the sea and how much had been caused by her delicate condition.

"Perhaps," she muttered, unable to manage more words as a second wave of wind sent an even more pungent cloud in her direction.

She held her breath, her fingers not working fast enough to find the blasted handkerchief she kept for just such occasions. Not a foolproof method of keeping her rebellious stomach from embarrassing her, but one that often succeeded. Thank heavens Southill had suggested it, with the kindly observation that it had worked wonders for her own mother whenever she had been expecting. Since Southill was the second eldest of eleven children, her mother had been expecting quite frequently.

"Here you are, Your Royal Highness," Southill said now, offering a fresh square of linen.

Eleanora accepted it and pressed it to her nose with haste, breathing in the calming, floral lavender scent, a marked improvement over the docks' aroma.

"Thank you," she murmured into the handkerchief.

The waves of nausea had yet to completely subside, but now she was more confident that she wasn't going to cast up her accounts all over the pier.

"Do you think His Royal Highness will be sending a carriage for you, then?" Southill asked calmly after a few more moments had passed.

"I fear that he may not have," she admitted.

Eleanora skimmed her gaze over the crowds and realized how ill-prepared she truly was. She had set off on this journey despite the concerns of her friends and even Dr.

Crisfield, who had warned her that traveling newly with child could present some difficulties for her.

The discovery that she was carrying Nando's baby had been unexpected. The doctor had initially feared she had acquired some manner of contagion from her injury. However, after a fortnight of similar symptoms without fever or festering in her healing wound, the doctor had made the stunning pronouncement.

Eleanora had been cautiously happy at the news. And more determined than ever to go to Nando as her letters went unanswered. He was going to be a father. He had claimed in the note he'd left behind that he loved her, and whilst his manner of attempting to protect her had been thoroughly foolhardy, his attempts to give her everything he thought she needed had confirmed that.

But he'd been wrong.

She didn't need a town house or all the wealth he had foisted upon her. She most certainly didn't need—or want— an annulment. All she wanted was *him*. The man she loved. The one who laughed and teased and charmed and flirted, who cuddled her at his side, who rescued stray cats from the street, who had taken care of her when she had been wounded and broken. The man who loved her enough to give her almost everything he had because he thought she would be better off without him.

He had been wrong about that, too.

She wasn't better off without Nando—she was better off at his side. And she had crossed an ocean to prove it to him. But before she could, she was going to have to find a means of transportation.

"Perhaps I should see if we can find a hackney," Southill said at her side.

Benvolio meowed urgently, as if in strong agreement.

Just then, a carriage approached, a dashing young fellow

at the reins with golden hair and blue eyes that reminded her of Nando.

He called out something in his native tongue, which made Eleanora realize anew just how foolish it had been to embark on a madcap journey to Varros without knowing the language or having a true plan in place.

"Do you speak English, sir?" Southill asked on her behalf.

Which was just as well, because another lifting of the breeze had Eleanora's throat going tight. She breathed slowly, shallowly, into the scented linen, trying to think of anything but horse dung and rotting fish.

"Of course I do, milady," the young coachman called, smiling and revealing dimples. "How may I be of service?"

At her side, the ordinarily stalwart Southill was flushing a becoming shade of pink beneath the man's regard.

"Can you take us to the Hotel de Varros?" Southill asked, just a touch breathlessly.

The man grinned. "But of course, madam. I can take you anywhere."

Southill blushed even more.

Holding her handkerchief tightly to her nose, Eleanora moved toward the beckoning confines of the carriage, carrying Benvolio with her.

～

"You look as if you've been shot by a highwayman, thrown off a boat and nearly drowned, and then been dragged behind a carriage."

"That pretty, am I?" Nando winced at the light brightening his apartments at the royal palace and glared up at his brother. "Why are you here, Maxim?"

"Here in my own palace, do you mean?" Maxim's tone

was as severe and harsh as his countenance. "Because I am the king, lest you have forgotten."

His head was throbbing, his mouth was as dry as the sand in a desert, and his stomach was a sickly stew that was threatening to erupt. "I know you're the fucking king. What I meant was, what are you doing in my private apartment?"

"Keeping you alive." Maxim raised an imperious brow as he handed Nando a cup laden with a light-colored liquid. "Drink."

Nando shook his head and felt the room swim around him. "I don't want another drop of anything. Ever."

"But only just last night, you were demanding more whisky be brought to you whenever your glass was empty. You were terribly thirsty."

"Deus."

What he had been was terribly somber. Missing Eleanora. Miserable. Faced with a packet of letters that had arrived in her neat, tidy script—even her handwriting was prim and perfect—he had not been able to read them, for fear of what he would find within.

The missives had all arrived at once, a sure sign that they had been upheld somewhere along their meandering journey before proceeding on to him. He had been terrified that she would tell him she despised him. That she was relieved he had gone. That she never wanted to see him again. That she had found another man to warm her bed.

And so, after a month of self-imposed exile in Varros, which he had spent doting on his nephew to distract from his misery and abstaining from every vice, Nando had succumbed and drowned himself in drink. Anything to postpone the moment when he would read Eleanora's letters.

He had also been despicably stupid, he thought darkly as his stomach churned and his head pounded.

"Do you remember falling off the garden wall?" Maxim asked conversationally, still holding the cup at Nando's nose.

Perhaps that explained the pain in his shoulder and hip, then.

"Everything is a mystery after dinner."

"That is because you drank yourself to oblivion before the fish course," Maxim observed. "Now, drink this bloody elixir. It will help you to feel better."

"I doubt that anything could ever make me feel better, ever again."

"Last night, you seemed to be persuaded that whisky would."

Maxim's tone was sly.

"Shut up," Nando growled, taking the cup and bringing it to his lips.

The liquid tasted vile. He gagged, choking it down.

Maxim presided over him, arms crossed.

"What in the hell are you doing, trying to poison me?" Nando sputtered.

"As tempting as that is, I would fear your ghost would haunt me."

He glared at his brother. "An excellent reason not to murder your sibling. I'm not drinking another sip of this devil's brew."

"Yes, you are. You're going to drink it all. Every. Damned. Drop." Maxim enunciated succinctly, his tone stern.

Nando's stomach gave a violent lurch at the thought of drinking more of the disgusting potion in his hand. "Why should you care if I do?"

"Because there is a woman who has come to see you, and I don't think you would want her to witness you looking as if you've just been dug up from the grave," Maxim said.

"Tell her to go to Hades. There's no woman I want to see. Ever."

There *was* one, but that was impossible. Eleanora was in London where she belonged, living the life she deserved—one without him in it.

"I do believe you'll want to see this one since she is your wife," Maxim told him calmly. "Drink before I force it down your throat."

She is your wife.

Eleanora.

Shock pierced the haze of misery that had settled over him. Eleanora was here? In Varros? She had traveled here alone, and so soon after she had been wounded? What the devil had she been thinking?

"You were right about one thing, brother. I do want to see her. More than I want to take my next breath."

"Then get your arse out of this bed, drink the elixir, and go to her," Maxim said, his tone gentling before he sniffed the air. "Bathe and shave first, however. You smell like a distillery, and you look like a wild dog who's been infested with fleas."

He might have taken umbrage at his brother's words, but Nando was too busy pouring the foul potion down his throat. Eleanora had come to him.

He didn't know what it meant.

All he knew was that he had to see her.

❧

"It is lovely to meet you at last." The queen smiled over her dish of tea.

Eleanora was so nervous that she could not keep her hand from trembling. She had scarcely been settled at the Hotel de Varros—thanks to the hack driver who had slyly left his direction should they need further assistance during their stay—when she had sent a missive to the palace announcing her arrival. It had been met with an instant response and invitation. And although it hadn't come from Nando directly, she had been hopeful that she would see him. She had accepted, willing her stomach to obey and keep from humiliating her.

She had a reticule full of lavender-scented handkerchiefs at the ready, but fortunately, the palace smelled like a summer rose garden on account of all the vases of fresh blooms, and nothing at all like the docks.

"It's my honor to meet you, Your Majesty," she returned.

"You must call me Tansy, please," the queen insisted, seated opposite her in a cozy solar, a tray laden with sweets on the table between them. "We are sisters now."

A brown-haired woman with gray eyes and a regal air, the queen was undeniably lovely. Not nearly as intimidating as her husband, however. King Maxim was tall and stern, with a wall-like chest and black hair with hints of silver flaring at his temples. He was the opposite of Nando in so many ways, the dark to Nando's light.

How she missed her husband.

"I have always wanted a sister," she confided to Tansy, trying to distract herself from thoughts of Nando and how she would be received.

Misgiving returned, swirling, making her question herself, question her actions. What if he had not truly left her because he loved her, but because he had grown tired of her? What if he no longer wanted to be a married man? What if the recklessness he was so known for had overtaken him?

"We shall be fast friends, I have no doubt." The queen took another sip of her tea.

Her easy manner and unfettered kindness had been a pleasant surprise to Eleanora. She hadn't known what to expect, and Eleanora was relieved that the queen had accepted her presence with such grace and ease.

"I must thank you for welcoming me," she said politely. "Particularly since I can only assume my visit must come as a surprise, given Nando's failure to return any of my letters."

"You must forgive us for not giving you a proper welcome. Your letters did not arrive until yesterday. Please know that we are so pleased that you've come to Varros and are more than happy to have you here at the palace with us. Tell me, how did you find the journey?"

Her letters had only arrived yesterday? That knowledge certainly soothed some of her concerns. Nando hadn't ignored the missives she had sent him, then.

"Long and arduous," she admitted, thinking of the some-times storm-tossed journey she had made over the sea, along with the challenge of traveling so far while carrying her first child. "But I am happy to have arrived."

And desperately anxious, too, an ocean of uncertainty rising within her by the moment. Despite learning Nando hadn't received her letters until the day before, she still scarcely knew what to expect from him, or how he would react to the news she brought with her.

"You look overset," Tansy observed gently. "You need not be. Nando will be overjoyed to see you. He has been in misery these last few weeks without you."

She hoped he would be. But she wouldn't be sure until she saw his beloved face. Until she could touch him, speak with him. Box his ears for leaving her as he had.

"I understand the misery," she admitted. "I have been lost without him as well."

Lost did not begin to describe the way she had felt in his absence, as if a gaping hole had been torn in her very existence and there was no conceivable means of mending it.

"Nando is stubborn, just as Maxim is," Tansy said, her tone conciliatory. "I expect he believed he was acting in your best interest by leaving you in London as he did. He was devastated over what had happened to you when he arrived. I have never seen him so disconsolate."

Nando was always quick to smile, to make a jest of everything, especially himself. It wasn't gratifying to hear he had been unhappy and grim, even if it was the same way she had felt without him. Perhaps there was hope for them yet. But she didn't dare to allow her mind to drift any further.

Not until she saw him for herself.

Her heart was already fragile, bruised and battered as it had been by his abrupt departure. She was too afraid to even contemplate what would happen if his mind was unchanged and if he remained unmoved after she had traveled all this way for him.

"I have missed him," she admitted quietly.

"You love him," Tansy said.

Eleanora could not deny it. "I do."

"I believe that he loves you too." The queen settled her dish of tea back upon the table. "Love is stronger than distance and stronger than pain. It is the single strongest bond two people can share. Love tore you apart, and now love will bring you back together again. Trust me, Eleanora. You shall see."

"I hope you are right." Eleanora replaced her own dish of virtually untouched tea on the table as well.

Before they could indulge in further discussion, the heavy footfalls of the king heralded his return to the salon.

"Did you find him?" Tansy asked expectantly, brightening at the sight of her husband.

It was plain for Eleanora to see that the king and queen shared a love match. Their mutual admiration was almost palpable whenever the two were in a room.

She turned to the king, holding her breath as she awaited his answer.

"I did." The king was solemn as he turned his attention to

Eleanora. "You will have to forgive my rogue of a brother. He is presently indisposed. He will come to you as soon as he's able, however."

The news did nothing to reassure her. Indisposed? Did that mean he had moved on to another woman? Or, worse, to multiple women? Her gut curdled as she recalled the rumors she had heard about him in London. Rumors he hadn't denied. Perhaps it had been foolish of her to believe he could fall in love with one woman and remain faithful.

"I see," she managed, rising from her chair. "I think that maybe I should not have come. This was a dreadful mistake."

He had asked her for an annulment. And what had she done? She had boarded a ship and crossed the ocean for him, only to find him *indisposed* when she arrived. But then, she had always known, had she not, that he would break her heart?

"You mustn't go," Tansy said urgently, reaching for Eleanora's hand in a beseeching gesture. "My husband was being politic with his explanation just now, but let there be no confusion. Nando was thoroughly in his cups last night after receiving your letters. I suspect he is suffering the lingering effects of overindulgence this morning."

"Indeed," the king said, inclining his head. "I can assure you that Nando has not been himself since his return to Varros, which is to say I haven't even seen him look twice at a woman, when before…well."

She pressed a hand over her mouth to stifle a hysterical laugh that threatened to bubble forth. She knew what Nando had been like before—a rakehell to the core. The king did not spare her sensibilities.

"Eleanora, are you well?" Tansy asked, concerned.

"Quite," she managed, feeling the room spin.

Her emotions were running wild again, sadness turning to amusement, then back to deep, abiding sorrow. Tears burned her eyes, and she blinked furiously in an effort not to humiliate herself utterly. She hiccupped, then felt her cheeks go hot with mortification.

"My dear." Tansy wore a troubled expression as she linked her arm through Eleanora's. "Come and sit down. I suspect I know what is amiss."

She swallowed hard. "You do?"

"Yes." With a meaningful look at the king, Tansy told her husband. "Leave us for a few moments, my love. There is something I must speak to Eleanora about in private."

"Your servant, spitfire," the king said with a courtly bow before straightening. "I'll tell my brother to make haste before I have him thrown into the dungeons."

Eleanora's eyes went wide, but Tansy waved a hand as the king took his leave. "Don't listen to my husband's bluster. He is only jesting." She guided Eleanora back to her chair. "Sit, if you please."

Feeling suddenly weary, Eleanora did as her hostess ordered, sinking into the chair once more. Her travel had left her exhausted, but it wasn't merely the journey that had left her feeling that way. Tansy seated herself and gave Eleanora a look that was equal parts sympathetic and knowing.

"You're with child, aren't you?" the queen asked.

Eleanora closed her eyes against a rush of emotion, struggling to compose herself before she opened them again. "Yes. But please don't tell Nando. I want him to make his decision based upon his feelings and not out of a sense of duty."

"My dear woman, you have just crossed an ocean for him while you're carrying his child. If he doesn't fall to his knees and kiss your feet, I'll push him out the nearest window."

Eleanora chuckled, thinking she liked the eccentric queen. Yes, she liked her very much indeed.

〜

"How do I look?" Nando asked Maxim nervously.

He had made his ablutions, dressed, and shaved with more haste than he had known he possessed, desperate to see Eleanora. It had only been the desire not to come before her, bedraggled and stinking of his misdeeds of the night before that had him shaving and washing at all. Every atom of his body had been roaring to see her, to the devil with how he appeared.

But this was Eleanora, and she had come to Varros.

For him.

He owed her every respect.

Maxim cast a narrow-eyed look over his form, hands clasped behind his back. "Less like a corpse."

Nando ground his jaw. "That is all you have to say?"

"I'm not a woman. I don't offer flowery platitudes. What would you prefer me to say?"

"Something a bit nicer," he groused. "But never mind that. I don't want to waste another second bickering with you when I could be with the woman I love."

"By all means, let us proceed," Maxim said wryly. "Forgive me, I hadn't realized how much you loved her, given the way you abandoned her."

He turned on his brother, ready to do battle. "I left her *because* I love her. For her own sake."

Maxim smiled. "There is something I've learned about women, brother, and it's that they prefer to be asked their opinion on matters rather than having it decided for them."

Nando's hands had balled into fists at his sides. "What are you saying?"

"That you should have asked her what she wanted before you got on that damned ship. That's what I'm saying." Maxim nodded. "And I'm also saying that she appears to be a good woman who loves you enough to travel an ocean chasing after your stupid arse. If you don't fall at her feet and kiss her slippers, I'll push you out the nearest window."

"No need for threats." Nando scowled at his brother. "We both know you love me too much to toss me out a window."

Maxim held up his hands and mimicked a double-handed shove, his countenance devoid of expression. "Thud."

Nando strode past with a growl. "Tend to your wife, brother. And let me tend to mine."

His brother's irritating chuckles chased him as he fled his private rooms and all but ran to the salon where Eleanora was awaiting him. The familiar distance felt as if it took a lifetime to traverse until, finally, he reached the marbled hall of the first floor. A liveried footman flanked the closed salon door. He offered Nando a bow.

"Your Royal Highness."

Nando brushed past him when he moved to open the portal with a grand flourish. "Thank you, but no need to stand on ceremony."

The man looked startled. "Of-of course, yes, Your Royal Highness."

Another bow that Nando couldn't bother himself to acknowledge, and then he was bursting through the door, racing over the threshold, heart pounding.

She was seated at a table laden with tea and sweets, along with Tansy, but at his graceless entrance, both ladies stood. He had eyes for only one.

"Eleanora." His voice was hoarse with emotion, with need.

He wanted to cross the rest of the chamber and haul her into his arms, but he somehow restrained himself.

"Nando." Tansy's voice, like her smile, was warm and welcoming. "I'll leave you and Eleanora to your talk."

"Thank you, Tansy," he managed.

She went to Eleanora's side and whispered something unintelligible to her before departing from the room.

He was moving before the door to the salon clicked closed at her back, eating up the distance keeping him from the woman he loved. "You're here."

Regardless of how many times Nando gazed upon the seemingly endless glory of the sea, he always found himself in awe, marveling at it anew, captivated by its innate allure. And he experienced that same sensation deep within now as he looked upon her. Starting in his marrow and blossoming outward.

He reeled.

Eleanora was beautiful. More breathtakingly beautiful than she had ever been, even if her skin was a touch paler, her eyes glistening with unshed tears. But everything else, from her lustrous golden hair to her elegant posture, was just as he had remembered every night as he had gone to sleep to memories of her, wondering when their separation would hurt less, if indeed it ever could.

"I'm here," she said quietly.

"How are you?"

He needed to know. He had left when she was still healing, and the silence between them had been torture.

"My wound has healed well enough, if that is what you're asking." She was serious, somber.

"Yes. That is what I was asking."

She gave him a small smile that didn't reach her eyes. "Well enough for travel to you."

Another step, and she was within reach. He wanted to seize her hands. To touch her. But he didn't dare. He didn't know if he had the right. His fingers flexed, useless, at his sides.

"Why?" he asked, needing to know, afraid to allow his

reckless heart to dream that she had come for him, to him. To believe that she could love him, despite what he had done.

She cocked her head, her light-blue gaze searching. "I might ask the same of you. You left me. Why?"

He clenched his jaw against the emotions that threatened to overwhelm. "You were nearly killed because of me."

"I didn't see a flintlock in your hands that day."

"I may as well have been the one to shoot you." He raked a hand through his hair, self-loathing threatening to choke him. "I was the one Levering was after. I dallied with his wife. I made him a cuckold. I was a ne'er-do-well scapegrace without a thought for consequence, and you paid the price for my sins. It was my fault that you were vulnerable that day. Tierney had warned me, but I was too prideful to believe the earl would be bold enough and mad enough to come for me again after the first time. I was wrong."

"You couldn't have known what he would do," Eleanora said softly. "You didn't know. No one has ever championed me or protected me as you have. I have no doubt that if you'd had an inkling of what would unfold, you would have done everything in your power to keep me far from Lord Levering."

"I should have been wiser, stronger. I should have remained at Tierney's until we could formulate a plan. But I was foolish. Reckless, just as Princess Stasia warned you. I left Tierney's protection because I wanted you as my wife. I was selfish and greedy, and look at the cost. *You.* My God, Eleanora, if you had died that day…"

"I didn't." That stubborn chin he loved went up. "I'm still here."

"No thanks to me," he snarled bitterly.

"I have brought something for you," she said, surprising him.

"A gift?"

A small, curious smile played at her berry-pink lips, and he had to tamp down the urge to seize her and take her mouth with his. "Of sorts."

She flitted to the table, retrieving a small, carved wooden box.

Turning back to him, she offered it. "Here you are."

He accepted it, staring at the small box in his hands, then at Eleanora.

"Open the lid," she urged.

His fingers found the smooth underside of the lip carved into the box, and he pulled, the top coming off with ease. Within was a tidy bundle of gray bits. It looked like…

"Ashes?" he asked, more confused than ever.

She nodded. "The annulment documents from Varros and the deed to our town house in London, along with the letter concerning the transfer of your funds in trust to me."

Hope rose within him.

"You burned them."

Another small smile curved her fetching lips. "I burned them."

Nando swallowed hard, the smooth box in his hands scarcely any weight at all, worth almost nothing and yet utterly priceless. "Why did you burn them, minx?"

His pet name for her fell from his lips without thought, naturally.

He didn't correct himself.

"Because I don't wish for an annulment, nor do I want your money. And I certainly don't want to live in the London town house unless you are in it with me."

Her eyes grew wide as she finished her pronouncement, and he could see that she had stunned even herself with her stern words.

He had to take a moment to gather his whirling thoughts.

"Why not?" he asked when he could find his wits and his tongue again.

"Do you not know?" Her brow furrowed, and she took the box from him, replacing it on the table, before she reached for his hands.

He allowed her to take them, threading their fingers together. Sweet God, to touch her again. It was Elysium, pure and simple.

"You'll have to tell me, I'm afraid," he said thickly, more of that hope squeezing his throat, rising inside him so large and so out of control that he was amazed he could fashion words at all.

"I love you, Nando. I have never been happier than as your wife. Levering has been punished as he deserved. There is no more fear of danger, and what happened was not your fault. He was a madman incapable of reason. He wanted to hurt someone, anyone, and he would not stop until he had."

She had said a great deal, but what was sticking with foremost tenacity in his mind were those precious three words she had begun with.

I love you.

Eleanora loved him.

For the second time since entering the room, Nando swayed on his feet.

"You…you love me?" he repeated.

"I do. I love you, and I want nothing more than to be with you, wherever that may be, whether here in Varros or in London. All I want is to be your wife, Nando. To be with you. Not because you're handsome, or because you're a prince, and not for any reason other than you have my heart. You've *always* had my heart, from the moment I first saw you, only I was too scared to admit it to you or to myself, even when you told me you loved me in your letter. I can only hope that it's not too late for us. That you still love me as much as I love you."

She *loved* him.

She wanted to be his wife. She had been shot because of him. She had nearly died because of him, and yet here she stood, his brave and glorious wife, laying her heart before him.

He gathered her to him, holding her tightly. Too tightly, he knew, but he couldn't seem to banish the fear that she would change her mind or that she was nothing but a product of his feverish imagination and that he would awake from a dream to find none of this had been real. He had to cling to these precious seconds.

"I do love you," he murmured, pressing his cheek to her smooth, soft hair. "I love you more than words can convey. I love you more than I even knew was possible. I love you so much that it hurts, and enough to know that you are better off without me."

She leaned her head back at once. "I am better *with* you. Never tell me such nonsense again. And never make my decisions for me. I am perfectly capable of rational thought, you know. I understand your intentions were noble, but if you make me chase you across the world again, I won't be impressed."

He chuckled, for that was his Eleanora, strong and determined and unafraid. And she was not wrong. He should have let her make the choice instead of making it for her. He had believed he was doing the greater good, but in the end, he had only torn them both to bits.

"I promise never to make you chase me again," he assured her. "That is to say, not across the world. If you wish to chase me in our bedroom for sport, however, it could prove vastly diverting."

She laughed, crystalline and melodious, and Deus, how he

loved that sound. Dear God, how he loved the woman. Full stop.

"Excellent. Because should I ever have to chase you again, I cannot promise I won't be tempted to push you out a window for your obtuseness."

Nando laughed too. "Maxim said something oddly similar to me before I joined you here."

"He threatened to push you out a window?" Eleanora asked.

"Yes. I don't suppose he meant it, though."

Her eyes widened. "Tansy said the same thing to me. She said that if you didn't fall to your knees and kiss my feet, she would push you out the nearest window."

"Hmm. Astonishingly bloodthirsty of them. I do believe they're turning into the same person. I'm not certain whether I should be alarmed or impressed."

"It is Machiavellian of them, isn't it?" Eleanora agreed, smiling.

"Do you know what else is Machiavellian?"

"What is?"

"Following me to Varros, telling me you love me, burning the bank and annulment documents and house deed and then bringing them to me in ash, before standing here in this salon, still wearing all your clothes."

Charming color crept into her cheeks. "Nando! I'm not disrobing in the queen's salon."

He was happy. So damned happy. Deliriously, ridiculously, wonderfully happy.

"Then come to my bedroom," he urged. "To *our* bedroom. I'll happily strip you naked there just the same."

She laughed again. "Does this mean you want to remain married to me?"

"God yes, it does." He drew her closer again and bowed

his head to nuzzle her temple. "I only left you to protect you, because I love you enough to let you go."

Her arms were around his waist, a tight, wonderful band he wished he could wear always, for all the world to see.

"And I love you enough to keep you, and to tell you that you're going to be a father."

Everything within him froze. "What did you say?"

He must have misheard. Had she said what he thought she had said? Because, sweet Lord, the thought of Eleanora growing round with his child, of soon having a little girl with her wild golden curls to love or a young lad with her dimpled chin, brought tears to his eyes. He blinked furiously, not wanting them to fall, but it was useless. They slipped down his cheeks, heedless of his masculine pride.

She tipped her head back, smiling shyly up at him. "You're going to be a father, Nando."

Joy seized him. For a moment, he could not speak, so intense was his reaction.

"You're with child?" he managed.

She nodded, biting her lip. "Are you weeping?"

"Not at all," he lied. "There was something in my eye."

Her countenance turned somber. "I know it is unexpected. I didn't intend to tell you so bluntly, and I've only just made the realization. If the news displeases you—"

"Not another word," he interrupted tenderly. He withdrew from her enough so that he could press a hand over her belly, wondering at the life that was growing within her, even if there was no discernible change to her form just yet. "I couldn't be happier, my love. Words can't begin to describe my elation."

Eleanora placed a hand over his, lacing their fingers together. "Promise me that the next time some wrongheaded notion to do what you think is best for me enters your mind, you'll consult me first."

Nando didn't hesitate. "I promise. You're thoroughly stuck with me now, minx."

"I wouldn't have it any other way." Smiling wickedly, she rose on her toes and pressed her mouth to his.

EPILOGUE

KINGDOM OF VARROS, TWO MONTHS LATER

*T*he wonderfully wicked, deliciously sinful, utterly decadent truth was that Princess Eleanora of the House of Tayrnes was presently standing naked in her bedroom whilst her beautiful husband was still disappointingly clothed.

When he had whispered for her to strip off her garments and wait for him nude following the royal banquet that had been held earlier in their honor, she had expected him to come to her equally devoid of clothing. He smiled slowly as he caught sight of her standing across the room, wearing nary a stitch.

He was still wearing his elegant evening finery, his snowy cravat perfectly tied, and he quite took her breath at the magnificent sight he made.

"You're naked just as I told you to be." He sauntered forward, tugging at his coat and shrugging it from his shoulders as he went.

"I thought you would be naked also, my love," she pouted playfully.

He dropped the coat to the floor, prowling nearer with a

leonine grace that made anticipation thrum through her veins. "Presently. There's something I must do first."

She licked her lips, trying not to be too mindful of the changes her condition had caused. Her breasts were larger than before, her belly rounded and protruding now. Fortunately, her altering form only seemed to have made her adoring husband want her more.

"Oh?" She raised a brow, playing the coquette. "And what is it that you must do?"

He reached her then, his hands settling warmly on her waist in a possessive hold she loved. "Turn, and I'll show you."

The notion of baring her bottom to him was both rousing and embarrassing. She remained as she was, breathless, heart pounding, sex throbbing.

"Nando," she protested.

The look he gave her was scorching. "Turn around, love, and place your hands on the wall."

She swallowed hard. "Why should you wish for me to—"

He stayed her further questioning with a swift, hard kiss before raising his head again to regard her with smoldering intensity. "You'll have to trust me."

Trust him?

Of course, she did. With her heart, with her body, with her life.

He kissed a trail of fire along her jaw. "I'm waiting, minx."

He was near enough that her pebbled nipples brushed against his waistcoat in a delicious abrasion as she shifted, and she shivered, wanting, needing, aching. He caught her earlobe in his teeth and tugged, making her go weak in the knees. After the sickness from being with child had faded, a raging desire had taken its place. She was perpetually, desperately ready for him. And now, she thought she might come from just his mouth on her ear.

But she didn't want to succumb so quickly. She wanted to know what sinful pleasures her husband had in store for her. So, Eleanora turned, flattening her palms on the smooth, cool wall coverings, turning to watch him over her shoulder. "Satisfied?"

A wicked grin curved his sensual lips. "Not yet. But presently, I will be."

With that, he dropped to his knees. Liquid heat rushed to her core.

His big hands cupped the cheeks of her derriere, his fingers exerting exquisite pressure. Just enough, not too much. He massaged and caressed. And then his thumbs dipped between her legs, and he parted her folds, baring her to him.

She felt the kiss of the room's air on her most intimate flesh, followed by the moist heat of his breath. And then his tongue was there. On her. In her. Licking up and down her seam, consuming her.

Eleanora cried out, her knees threatening to buckle entirely. His tongue sank deep, seeking, claiming. Giving her such intense pleasure. He lapped at her gently, then with greater insistence as he circled her hip to nestle one of his hands between her legs. He flattened his palm over her mound, the pressure almost unbearable as he drew her more firmly against him so he could devour her cunny from behind. She was caught between his face and his hand, his sinful mouth and tongue rivaling his fingers to send her spiraling into the mindless abyss where pleasure dwelled. He stroked the sensitive bud of her sex and speared her entrance with his tongue.

"Nando," she cried, so near to coming undone.

He increased the pace on her clitoris, swirling his fingers over her in a ruthless, knowing rhythm, even as his tongue plunged in and out of her in a mimicry of lovemaking.

"Good girl. You're so wet for me. So wet and hot, and you taste so fucking good."

She squirmed, her nipples rubbing against the sleek silk damask now, painfully needy, spurred on by his blunt praise and vulgar language. "Nando, please."

His dark chuckle echoed in her core—she knew he liked it when she begged. "I love your cunny. I could lick you all day and night long."

To emphasize his words, he gave her a long, slow swipe of his tongue that seemed to find every part of her. Her forehead hit the wall as she partially collapsed from the sheer pleasure of his teasing.

"Nando," she urged, wriggling.

"Do you want me to tell you how perfect you look? All pink and lovely, dripping with desire." He rubbed her bud to emphasize his words, making her hips jerk.

Her breath was shallow, her heart galloping, her breasts heavy, her nipples tight. The continued ministrations of his fingers and tongue were bringing her dangerously close to release.

"Is it possible…when standing?" she gasped out.

They had never done so before. But she seemed to recall reading about a frantic coupling against a door when she had glanced at *The Book of Love*…

"Very possible," he reassured her, then resumed licking into her in slow, demanding strokes while he strummed her sex.

Of course it would be possible, even if the positioning seemed so odd. And who better to know than the maddening man who had reduced her to this lust-addled state? He was the expert when it came to desire.

"Everything is possible." He kissed her sex, then pinched her throbbing clit and sank his tongue inside her in one fierce motion.

Eleanora exploded.

Or at least, that was how it felt.

Her release was as sudden as it was intense, roiling over her and through her like a force of nature. She collapsed into the wall, crying out, thrusting her hips alternately against his beautiful face and his wicked hand. Trapped in the most glorious way as wave after wave of pleasure rolled through her. Black stars dappled her vision, the intensity of the sensation rendering her helpless to do anything other than close her eyes and surrender.

When at last the bliss ebbed, her heart was pounding, her breath ragged.

Nando lapped at her, as if drinking up every drop of her pleasure, his motions far less measured now, groaning into her sex.

"Such a good girl," he praised again. "Waiting for me naked, coming on my tongue. How shall I reward her?"

He gave her right cheek a playful spank and then sank deep, tonguing her with deliberate strokes that had a second release bolting through her. She came with a moan, collapsing against the wall, shamelessly arching her back to present him with more of her, to get him as deep inside her as she could.

He rose suddenly, one hand finding her hip as the other opened the fall of his trousers. When he sprang free, he glided his cock over her swollen folds, slicking himself in her dew. He kissed her shoulder, his wet mouth flitting over her scarred skin reverently.

"My brave, beautiful princess." The blunt head of his cock pressed against her opening. "I need to fuck you now."

"Yes," she hissed, thrusting her bottom out, trying to get his hard thickness where she wanted it most.

He slammed his hips into her from behind, and his cock surged deep. The angle was exquisite, her already heightened state of need making her muscles grip him eagerly. A spasm went through her.

"God yes," he said, and then he began a steady, determined rhythm.

She arched her back, planting her hands on the wall, and matched his thrusts with pumps of her own hips. Eleanora was nothing but feeling, her body awash in desire, in love. He glided his hand over her hip, his fingers once more finding her clitoris and working in fast, determined flicks that drove her entirely over the edge.

She came with a hoarse cry, clamping down on him hard as wave after wave of bliss overcame her. Nando thrust harder, faster, until he stiffened, sinking deep, emptying himself inside her. The wet flood of his seed made her crumple anew, her cheek pressed to the cool wall coverings, heart racing, breath ragged.

They stayed pinned together that way, Nando's hand on her hip while the other relented, cupping her tenderly. He kissed her temple, a last pulse of his cock tearing another moan from her.

"My beautiful princess. What did I do to deserve you?" he asked with soft reverence, his voice velvety with sated pleasure.

"You loved me," she said simply.

"And I'll never stop," he vowed, kissing the side of her throat as he slowly withdrew from her body. "Come to bed with me now, and I'll keep loving you some more."

She chuckled as he turned her to face him, the circle of his arms around her making her feel protected and loved. "More? I'm not sure I could withstand another moment of pleasure."

He grinned down at her. "You do know I can't resist a challenge, don't you, minx?"

Eleanora smiled back at him. "Of course I do, my love."

Nando's lips found hers, and he quite thoroughly proceeded to prove her wrong.

～

THANK you so very much for reading *How to Tame a Dissolute Prince*! I hope Nando and Eleanora won your heart the same way they did mine. Writing them was a true joy. If you'd like to see what's next from me, read on for an exclusive sneak peek of *Duke with a Reputation* (Wicked Dukes Society Book 1), featuring the Duke of Brandon and Lottie, Lady Grenfell.

Please stay in touch! The only way to be sure you'll know what's next from me is to sign up for my newsletter here: http://eepurl.com/dyJSar. Please join my reader group for early excerpts, cover reveals, and more here: https://www.facebook.com/groups/scarlettscottreaders. And if you're in the mood to chat all things steamy historical romance and read a different book together each month, join my book club, Dukes Do It Hotter right here: https://www.facebook.com/groups/hotdukes because we're having a whole lot of fun!

～

Duke with a Reputation
Wicked Dukes Society
Book One

THE DUKE OF BRANDON is London's most infamous rake. But his world crashes to a decided halt when the sins of his past come back to haunt him in the form of one small she-devil of a child who has green eyes just like his. To make matters worse, his disapproving grandmother has decided he must marry or forfeit his inheritance.

Now, he has no choice but to raise a daughter, find a suitable wife, and keep his harridan grandmother from discovering his sordid secrets as the founder of the Wicked Dukes Society. So when the tempting, fiery-haired Countess of Grenfell propositions him, he offers her something else instead—a marriage of convenience.

Lottie, Countess of Grenfell, is London's most notorious widow. Her doomed, one-sided marriage left her with a broken heart and a determination to never wed again. What she wants is simple—passion, independence, and one night in the Duke of Brandon's bed. Or in his scandalous chair. Perhaps even against a wall. She wouldn't marry him, however, if he were the last man on earth.

Brandon is quickly running out of time and his troublemaking daughter has decided no one else shall do as her step-mama but the maddening countess. He must persuade Lottie to become his duchess with all haste or risk losing everything. As he sets out to seduce her into marriage, he's shocked to realize he's done the one thing he previously believed himself incapable of along the way—he's fallen in love. But Lottie's bruised and battered heart is more guarded than his, and she has vowed to never allow another man to hurt her again.

Prologue

THE SCENE in the Wingfield Hall dining room would have put a Roman Bacchanalia to shame. The Duke of Brandon smirked as he surveyed the tableau before him from his vantage point at the head of the table that had been exquisitely carved at the behest of a long-dead ancestor.

No less than three-dozen bottles of the fine French Bordeaux he had procured on his most recent trip abroad—Chateau Margaux, vintage 1874, truly *une grande année*—decanted and in various states of consumption.

To say nothing of the women in a debauched array of scandalous dishabille. There was a thoroughly sotted brunette with her breasts fully exposed above her bodice like ripe offerings, her nipples rouged to enhance their obscenely glorious display. Then there was the incomparable actress, Mrs. Helena Darby—not to be outdone by a rival—who launched suddenly from her seat, spun about, and flipped up her skirts to expose her full, ivory bottom for anyone who cared to look.

Most of the room, as it happened.

For Helena possessed one of the finest arses Brandon had ever been fortunate enough to see. Or spank. Or…

Well, never mind *that*. Brandon gave his trousers a furtive tug beneath the table at the unfinished thought. Ah, lewd reminiscences. He might fully indulge in another bout of memory-making later, should this evening progress as he intended.

Or perhaps, he would take his pleasure from another of the bevy of beauties in attendance, or two—or even three at once. Helena had never liked to share, which was deadly dull. Even if she had a mouth skilled enough to suck the silver plating off a vicar's spoon. Why limit himself when the possibilities were endless?

Brandon sipped idly at his Bordeaux, a pleasant haze enveloping him that likely had something to do with the latest potion Kingham—King, as his familiars knew him—had insisted he drink. Had it contained opium? Who gave a bloody damn? This night was the culmination of his efforts—a celebration, of sorts. And he intended to savor every moment with every woman he could.

Hair pins had long since been dropped from all the demi-mondaines in attendance, along with the initial pretense of decorum. Tapes and hooks and laces had come undone. Neckties and coats and any hint of formality had been dispensed with at the door to the grand dining hall, where a pile of discarded garments had been discreetly carried away by circumspect servants, who were trained and paid well enough to avert their gaze and hold their tongues.

The vignette before him was as pleasing as it was rousing. Oh yes, indeed. Brandon's coterie of friends, summoned for this inaugural fête of sin, were indulging in every vice he had presented for their delectation. They had come up together at Eton, and they were united by two common goals.

Common Goal the First: their mutual disdain for the wretches who had sired them and their desire to show it at every opportunity, in whatever manner possible, regardless of the ensuing scandal.

Common Goal the Second: their desire to pursue pleasure at any and all costs.

It was the latter, rather than the two former, that currently preoccupied his friends most. Riverdale had a woman on each knee. Camden had his face buried between the bountiful bubbies of a black-haired beauty. Richford was whispering in a fetching redheaded lady's ear. Whitby had his arm around a blonde's bare shoulders whilst his other hand appeared to be in a lovely brunette's lap. King's face was pressed to the ivory throat of an opera singer.

And then there was the *piece de resistance*, a naked wench in repose amongst the feast served *à la française*, covered in an assortment of tarts—the dessert course. No one had taken the cherry tart resting disproportionately on the peak of her left nipple, even if someone had already scooped the gooseberry galette from her cunt; Brandon had his heart quite set upon that cherry tart. He so despised incongruity of any form, and her right nipple bore only the faintest hint of blueberry.

Rising from his chair and swaying on his feet as he reached for the dessert—the bloody Bordeaux had gone to his head as well as King's sweet brew—Brandon snagged the lonely tart and deposited it on his plate. Now that his guests had consumed their feast and the true revelry of the evening had begun, it was time for a small matter of business.

He raised a glass, tapping it with his fork to draw everyone's attention to him.

When glassy-eyed stares settled upon him, the tittering and naughty murmurings dying down, he spoke loudly enough that his voice would carry through the cavernous Wingfield Hall chamber. The majestic maternal ancestral estate was an excellent place to host his revelries, for although it belonged to his grandmother, she had not entered its walls since his grandfather's passing some years before. Instead, she kept to London or paid calls upon friends in the country, giving Brandon the reins since he would one day inherit the massive manor house and grounds as her sole heir. He had given Grandmother's domestics a few days of paid leave, and he had brought his own discreet servants, all paid handsomely for their silence.

"I call to order this first meeting of the Wicked Dukes Society," he said now, his voice echoing through the centuries-old dining room.

It was the silly, bombastic name they had agreed upon after a three-day party at King's country seat, during which they had raided and consumed nearly the entire impressive alcohol stores of Dukes of Kinghams past.

A chorus of enthusiastic agreement sprang up. "Hear, hear!"

Camden's inamorata raised her wine glass with so much sudden force that her Bordeaux splashed all over her silk bodice and bare breasts, leaving Camden with no choice but to lick up the mess.

"We are gathered here this evening," he continued, "united in a common cause—the pursuit of pleasure. What happens within the walls of Wingfield Hall stays within the walls of Wingfield Hall."

King removed his lips from the opera singer's neck long enough to raise his own glass in toast. "We should all speak a vow of secrecy."

Brandon hadn't thought of that, and he was rather put out with himself for the failure. "Excellent idea, old chap. Have you a vow in mind?"

"Camden has always had a head for poetry," King offered. "Cam, what say you?"

Their friend was still drowning in bubbies, but he raised a bleary-eyed stare at his name. "What say I? What are we speaking about?"

"A vow for the Wicked Dukes Society," Brandon intervened. "King thinks we ought to make one, and he nominated you for the sorry task on account of your poetical heart."

Cam issued an indelicate snort. "The only part of my body that is poetical is inside my trousers."

The room burst into guffaws and titters.

"But I seem to distinctly recall the poem you wrote for Lady Flora Seaton," King prodded. "A beautiful sonnet, if I'm not mistaken."

Cam was usually imperturbable, but now his face flamed. Lady Flora was a delicate subject, one which he preferred to avoid. King always knew how to cut a man to his marrow, friend or foe alike, and he was more perceptive than anyone Brandon had ever met.

Cam's eyes narrowed. "Indeed I did. But I find I'm not

nearly as eloquent as Riverdale. Perhaps he ought to write the vows."

"If King thinks we should have one, then King can bloody well write it," Riverdale said, before whispering something into the ear of one of the ladies on his lap and earning a sultry chuckle in response.

"Not terribly sporting of you," King grumbled with a sigh before raising his Bordeaux. "Very well, then. I surrender. You shall have a simple vow from a simple man."

Ha! Brandon couldn't stifle his chortle at his friend's claim. There was nothing simple about the Duke of Kingham. Indeed, King was the most complex person he had ever met.

King raised a brow at him. "Brandon, is there something which amuses you? Perhaps you'd care to share with the rest of the company."

Brandon wiggled his fingers in a dismissive gesture. "Carry on with your simple vow, old chap, before we all grow old and gray."

"Old and gray?" Whitby shuddered dramatically. "I hope I meet my ignominious end well before that day."

"Oh do stubble it, Whit," Richford said congenially as he gave the redhead's breast an indolent fondle. "We all know that you've the devil's own luck. You'll likely be hearty as a stallion at five-and-ninety, quite unlike some of us."

Whitby grinned. "Am I to blame for my own good fortune?"

"Enough," King interrupted in a lighthearted tone. "I've settled upon a vow."

Brandon inclined his head in his friend's direction. "Carry on then, old chap."

King frowned. "We should have a bible to swear upon."

"I haven't got one." Brandon thought for a moment,

frowning. "We'll have to swear upon the Chateau Margaux. Raise your glasses."

All six incipient members of the Wicked Dukes Society raised their glasses.

"Repeat after me," King ordered. "From this moment on, I solemnly devote myself to the pursuit of pleasure and to the utter destruction of my father's legacies."

The friends repeated King's vow, followed by the clinking of glasses and a resounding cry of, "Hear, hear!"

"May he rot in Hades where he belongs," added Riverdale grimly.

In that moment, the Wicked Dukes Society was born, steeped in sin and fine French wine.

Chapter One

BRANDON WAS HAVING A NIGHTMARE.

That was the only explanation for the sight opposite him, he was certain of it. Either that, or he had imbibed one of King's ingenious brews and was now suffering the delusional aftereffects of the dubious elixir.

"Have you nothing to say for yourself, Brandon?"

The sharp, censorious voice, however, was disturbingly real. As was the glacial green-eyed glare so similar to his own. And the massive, billowing silk gown, beneath which hid a crinoline more suited to the fashions of thirty years ago than now.

He blinked, hoping the action would dispel the image before him. Pull him from the throes of sleep. Cast away the demons brought about by one of King's inspired concoctions.

But no.

His grandmother remained.

Hellfire. Perhaps she was real after all.

Brandon cleared his throat. "I do beg your pardon, Grandmother, but I have no notion of what I ought to be saying for myself."

"Have you not heard a word I have just spoken?"

Admittedly, he had been wool-gathering. Hoping he had found himself thrown into some slumberous alternate reality.

"I'm afraid not," he conceded.

Her nostrils flared, and for a fanciful moment, he imagined her breathing fire like a mythical dragon swooping in to scorch him and other unsuspecting mortals in her path.

"I will begin again, Brandon," she said succinctly, as if she feared very much he possessed the mental acuity to comprehend. "Do try to heed me this time."

Her scolding was nothing new; Grandmother had always been harder than granite. Although her dark hair had long since turned snowy and the face that had made her the most-sought-after debutante of her day was now lined, there was nary a hint of infirmity surrounding her. She was a tiny wren of a woman, but sturdy of form.

Now, as ever, she terrified him.

Brandon shifted on his dashed uncomfortable chair, wishing he'd had the forethought to have Grandmother await him somewhere other than the drawing room, a chamber he scarcely used for its Louis Quinze devotion. "Of course. Pray, proceed."

She inclined her head and with a regal air, continued. "As I was saying, a visitor most unexpected and uninvited paid a call upon me yesterday. I am told she was turned away by your domestics. Ordinarily, I would have no desire to concern myself with such matters. Indeed, it is most unseemly. However, the child has your eyes and nose."

Surely he must have misheard.

"The child?" he repeated, feeling as if the world had suddenly turned on its head.

Everything before him was unrecognizable.

"The girl child," Grandmother elaborated, disapproval dripping from her voice.

Brandon was still struggling to understand. Was there wine about? A cursory glance of the drawing room suggested only tea that Grandmother must have requested. He needed something far less tepid.

"Are you attending me, Brandon?" she asked, her voice sharp.

He wrested his gaze from the tea and pinned it back upon his grandmother. "What girl child?"

"The one who was delivered, much to my butler's horror, to my door yesterday afternoon by her mother, just before the woman ran off with her lover."

"Who was the girl's mother?" he managed, his necktie feeling more like a noose by the moment, growing tighter and tighter.

"She said her name was Mrs. Helena Darby-Booth." Grandmother's lip curled as if she had just tasted something spoiled. "A woman of ill repute, to be sure. She was dressed like a harlot, and it is to my everlasting shame that such a sinful creature should have had cause to arrive at my door after having been refused from yours. Have you any notion of the tongues that will gleefully wag? No, I dare say you do not. You are too busy cavorting with your lemans to save a thought for anyone other than yourself. Just like your father. I warned my darling Diana not to wed that scurrilous scoundrel. I didn't care that he was a duke."

His grandmother shook her head, caught in the throes of the past and temporarily distracted from her diatribe. Brandon was in shock. Helena had been his lover off and on over the years until she had abruptly married and left the stage some time ago. Had not that man been called Booth? Brandon searched the dim recesses of his mind for the name and the particulars. He had not seen her since, and nor had he heard from her. What cause had she to call upon his grandmother, bringing a girl child?

One with his eyes and nose?

He swallowed against a rising sea of bile. "The sins of the father, madam. Tell me, if you please, why Mrs. Darby-Booth should have called upon you, bringing a child."

"Because Mrs. Darby-Booth is following her new gentleman friend to America, and according to the letter she left with the girl, the man in question could only afford passage for two." His grandmother's green eyes, assessing and bright, narrowed. "She was required to leave the child behind, and she therefore deemed it better to leave the child in the care of her father's family rather than an orphanage."

No, no, no. He heard the words Grandmother was speaking, but he didn't wish to understand them. Surely this was all a dreadful mistake. Some manner of ploy Helena had concocted. He had always taken care with his mistresses. He used a sheath. Unless…there had been occasions, particularly in times of drunken revelry at Wingfield Hall or in St John's Wood when he may have been too sotted to take care…

Dread seized him, a fist choking his lungs.

"In the care of her…father's family?" he repeated.

"Yes, since the father himself refused to see her. There was a ship leaving, and our Mrs. Darby-Booth only had so much time in which to complete the task of abandoning her bastard child."

His grandmother was forbidding.

Bastard child.

The father.

Eyes and nose like his.

A daughter.

Fucking hell, could it be possible he had a daughter he hadn't known existed? That when Helena had left London, she had been carrying his child?

"How old is she?" he asked hoarsely. "The girl."

"She tells me that she is four years of age."

It was as if Brandon had been dealt a vicious punch directly to the gut. The breath left him. He gasped for a moment, trying to suck in air, to make sense of everything he had just learned. The timing certainly suggested, along with Grandmother's description, that he was indeed the father of the girl who had been deposited at her house yesterday.

Oh God, oh God, oh God.

Surely not.

Surely it was impossible.

Surely he could not be anyone's father.

"You…you spoke with the child." He swallowed hard.

"Of course I spoke with the child." Again, his grandmother's lip curled. "Despite her rude origins, the girl appears polite and well-mannered. But I will warn you, Brandon, that I will not lower myself to playing hostess to your illegitimate children. You must tend to your responsibilities as you see fit. I'll not concern myself with them."

The world was spinning madly about him. How much wine had he consumed last night? Was it the news or was it the despicable after effects of too much indulgence that had him feeling as if he were about to cast up his accounts?

"Her name," he managed. "What is her name?"

Not that it mattered one way or the other. But if he was to be a father, then he might as well know what to call her. Somehow, that seemed of grave importance.

"Her name is Pandora," Grandmother informed him archly. "It seems uniquely appropriate."

Pandora.

He had a daughter. Quite possibly. An illegitimate one.

And she had a name and his eyes and nose.

He patted his nose absently, thinking it perhaps a bit too sharp for a girl. "Where is she now?"

"In the absence of a proper nurse for the child, I've left her under the care of my companion, Miss Heale, at my town house," she informed him icily.

He nodded, wondering what the devil he was meant to do with a child. "I suppose I must have her collected, then."

"Yes, you must," Grandmother said, stern. "I'll not be responsible for her. It is time you bore some duty upon those strapping shoulders of yours."

He stiffened at the judgment in her tone. "I *do* have a great deal of responsibility."

And by that, he meant that he put rather a tremendous amount of effort into being an excellent host. His social gatherings were the stuff of legend. As the founding member of the Wicked Dukes Society, he took pride in his prowess.

As if hearing his thoughts spoken aloud, his grandmother clicked her tongue. "Hosting scandalous routs is not a responsibility, Brandon. When have you seen to any of your estates recently?"

"I correspond with my steward regularly," he defended, even if that was an exaggeration.

In truth, the more recent letters he had received from the man remained stacked and unopened somewhere in the clutter of his study desk. He was far more concerned with Wingfield Hall than the entail.

"How regularly?" she demanded.

"It is none of your concern," he countered. "With all your disdain for the former Duke of Brandon, I wouldn't think you should worry yourself over the present one."

"I do when the present one is my grandson and appears to be intent upon beggaring himself."

He took umbrage at that. "I am hardly beggaring myself."

"You depend upon the vast fortune you will receive from me when I die."

God, she was too damned clever. It wasn't that he anticipated Grandmother's demise. For all that she was as hard-shelled as a tortoise, she was a part of his mother. And Brandon had adored his mother, who had died in childbirth when he had been but a lad of eight.

"I do nothing of the sort," he said, shifting again on his chair.

"Has it ever occurred to you that I need not direct my funds or Wingfield Hall to you, Brandon?"

"No." His answer was swift and honest. "It has not."

Brandon was his grandmother's sole heir, and his mother's side of the family had been hideously wealthy from decades of building a fortune in manufacturing and trade. His father had never allowed his mother to forget her lack of noble forebears, though he'd had no compunction about availing himself of her immense dowry.

"Then perhaps it should." Grandmother's eyes narrowed. "I will not leave my fortune and my family's lands to be pilfered by you as you abandon a string of illegitimate children about London in your wake like your father before you. Wingfield Hall is sacred to me, as you know. I would sooner consign it to Hades than leave it to a profligate to plunder like some sort of modern-day pirate."

Wingfield Hall had become Brandon's most exclusive den of pleasure. Vast and sprawling in the Hertfordshire countryside, it had been the site of the inaugural meeting of the Wicked Dukes Society for its convenience to London and verdant privacy. It had for those same reasons been the host of each meeting thereafter. It was also a desperately lucrative —and intensely secret—business. One he had taken great care to make certain his grandmother would never discover. Losing it had never seemed a possibility.

"You would deny your only flesh and blood his birthright?" he asked with deceptive calm, hoping she would see reason in such folly.

But Grandmother's pointed chin went stubbornly up. "I had hoped it wouldn't come to that, but I will do whatever I must to save Wingfield Hall—and you—from ruin. I would sooner see Cousin Horace have it."

"Ruin?" He might have laughed, were he not still so shattered at the prospect that he had somehow been a father for *four bloody years* without knowing, and had his grandmother not just threatened to give the shining jewel of his estates to a country booby cousin who smelled like sheep.

Grandmother sighed. "I have heard rumors you are a member of some infernal society devoted to iniquity. I needed my hartshorn when Theodosia Dowling told me she had heard it from Lady Agnes Bryson. I never could abide by Lady Agnes—she has hated me for years, ever since I won your grandfather after she had set her cap at him. It goes without saying that I disapprove wholeheartedly of any such scandalous claptrap. I thought better of you, Brandon. *Truly* I did."

She extracted a fan and, despite the relative chill in the air, began fanning herself. Brandon stared at her, everything he had just heard making no more sense than it had when she had first uttered it.

His mind whirled.

Grandmother had heard about the Wicked Dukes Society? But how? Years had passed since that Bordeaux soaked night when he and five of his old Eton chums had first settled upon the notion. He had not supposed word would ever reach anyone, let alone her. After all, it was meant to be a *secret* society. Not that it was much of a society. More than anything, it was a friendship—a brotherly bond that each of them had found absent in their lives previously, whether by lack of blood brothers or lack of blood brothers who weren't arseholes. It was also making them sinfully rich.

"Grandmother, I can assure you that I do not belong to any such society, infernal or otherwise," he said smoothly, "and that Mrs. Dowling and Lady Agnes are indulging in scandal broth. It is idle gossip, nothing more."

"Do not lie to me, Brandon."

He held her gaze. "I would never lie to you, Grandmother."

Unless I have no other option, he added internally.

"I'll not be cozened," she snapped. "Do you think me an imbecile? I've been hearing whispers about you for years, but I have refused to indulge in rumors. Look at where my forbearance has led—to your natural child being delivered to my door."

Blast. This interview was not going well. His head was beginning to ache, and not just because Grandmother had been peppering him with a volley of unpleasant questions and revelations. But also because he was a father, and suddenly, his world had been not just upended, but burned to ash.

He had to concentrate upon what was truly important in this moment. It didn't matter if Grandmother had heard the whispers, or that every man or woman who entered the hallowed walls of Wingfield Hall did so under a vow of strictest silence some had clearly broken. What did matter was the child—Pandora, he reminded himself.

She had a name. Dear God, what was a voluptuary like him going to do with a child? He'd need to hire a nurse. Could he send the girl away somewhere? So many details to sort through, and the lingering effects of the previous evening's merriments still fogged his poor mind. It was too early in the afternoon for such dire news.

"Brandon, are you attending me at all?"

At the shrill tone entering Grandmother's voice, he jolted from his musings.

"Of course, my dear," he reassured her grimly. "It is impossible not to attend you when you are shouting at me."

"I am *not* shouting!"

The echo of her voice in the chamber was a stark rebuttal.

He had never seen his otherwise impassive grandmother exhibit such a frenzy of emotion. She was in fine dudgeon now, twin patches of angry color in her cheeks, eyes sparking with fire.

"I apologize for the child's unexpected arrival," he said. "I'll send someone to fetch her now if you'd prefer it."

"She is a child, not a parcel."

There was no pleasing his grandmother today.

And unfortunately, at that moment, the strains of the final aria from *La sonnambula* pierced the vexed silence that had fallen. Brandon winced, quite having forgotten that the famed soprano, Madame Auclair, had accompanied him home the previous evening. Any hopes he'd harbored of bedding her had died when she had begun to snore on the short carriage ride, the chanteuse having apparently consumed far more champagne than he had realized. He had seen her to a guest chamber.

Grandmother's eyebrows rose. "What is that *sound*?"

Dear God. What was Marie doing? The singing—whilst beautiful—was growing nearer. Where was Shilling, damn it? He relied on his butler to save him from such unfortunate circumstances.

Brandon tugged at his necktie. "Ah, opera, I believe."

"Ah! non credea mirarti," Marie sang.

The horror etched on his grandmother's face would have

been comical had the situation not been so disastrous. "There is an *opera singer* in your house?"

She may as well have said there was a rat in his house, so thorough was her disgust.

"Perhaps," he offered noncommittally just as the drawing room door burst open.

"Sì presto estinto, o fiore."

Marie was wearing one of his dressing gowns, her long, dark hair flowing in waves down her back. Judging by the swaying of her full breasts and her bare feet and ankles, it would appear she was completely nude beneath it. Her voice warbled at the sight that presented her—an august white-haired woman and Brandon fully dressed, a tea service between them—and then her song died entirely.

"Forgive me," she said in heavily accented English. "I didn't realize you had a guest."

Grandmother's tea fell to the floor, the delicate porcelain breaking into shards.

Want more? Get *Duke with a Reputation now*!

DON'T MISS SCARLETT'S OTHER ROMANCES!

Complete Book List
HISTORICAL ROMANCE

Heart's Temptation
A Mad Passion (Book One)
Rebel Love (Book Two)
Reckless Need (Book Three)
Sweet Scandal (Book Four)
Restless Rake (Book Five)
Darling Duke (Book Six)
The Night Before Scandal (Book Seven)

Wicked Husbands
Her Errant Earl (Book One)
Her Lovestruck Lord (Book Two)
Her Reformed Rake (Book Three)
Her Deceptive Duke (Book Four)
Her Missing Marquess (Book Five)
Her Virtuous Viscount (Book Six)

Wicked Dukes Society
Duke with a Reputation (Book One)

League of Dukes
Nobody's Duke (Book One)
Heartless Duke (Book Two)
Dangerous Duke (Book Three)
Shameless Duke (Book Four)
Scandalous Duke (Book Five)
Fearless Duke (Book Six)

Notorious Ladies of London
Lady Ruthless (Book One)
Lady Wallflower (Book Two)
Lady Reckless (Book Three)
Lady Wicked (Book Four)
Lady Lawless (Book Five)
Lady Brazen (Book 6)

Unexpected Lords
The Detective Duke (Book One)
The Playboy Peer (Book Two)
The Millionaire Marquess (Book Three)
The Goodbye Governess (Book Four)

Dukes Most Wanted
Forever Her Duke (Book One)
Forever Her Marquess (Book Two)
Forever Her Rake (Book Three)
Forever Her Earl (Book Four)
Forever Her Viscount (Book Five)
Forever Her Scot (Book Six)

The Wicked Winters

Wicked in Winter (Book One)
Wedded in Winter (Book Two)
Wanton in Winter (Book Three)
Wishes in Winter (Book 3.5)
Willful in Winter (Book Four)
Wagered in Winter (Book Five)
Wild in Winter (Book Six)
Wooed in Winter (Book Seven)
Winter's Wallflower (Book Eight)
Winter's Woman (Book Nine)
Winter's Whispers (Book Ten)
Winter's Waltz (Book Eleven)
Winter's Widow (Book Twelve)
Winter's Warrior (Book Thirteen)
A Merry Wicked Winter (Book Fourteen)

The Sinful Suttons
Sutton's Spinster (Book One)
Sutton's Sins (Book Two)
Sutton's Surrender (Book Three)
Sutton's Seduction (Book Four)
Sutton's Scoundrel (Book Five)
Sutton's Scandal (Book Six)
Sutton's Secrets (Book Seven)

Rogue's Guild
Her Ruthless Duke (Book One)
Her Dangerous Beast (Book Two)
Her Wicked Rogue (Book 3)

Royals and Renegades
How to Love a Dangerous Rogue (Book One)
How to Tame a Dissolute Prince (Book Two)

Sins and Scoundrels
Duke of Depravity
Prince of Persuasion
Marquess of Mayhem
Sarah
Earl of Every Sin
Duke of Debauchery
Viscount of Villainy

Sins and Scoundrels Box Set Collections
Volume 1
Volume 2

The Wicked Winters Box Set Collections
Collection 1
Collection 2
Collection 3
Collection 4

Wicked Husbands Box Set Collections
Volume 1
Volume 2

Notorious Ladies of London Box Set Collections
Volume 1

The Sinful Suttons Box Set Collections
Volume 1

Stand-alone Novella
Lord of Pirates

CONTEMPORARY ROMANCE
Love's Second Chance

Reprieve (Book One)
Perfect Persuasion (Book Two)
Win My Love (Book Three)

Coastal Heat
Loved Up (Book One)

ABOUT THE AUTHOR

USA Today and Amazon bestselling author Scarlett Scott writes steamy Victorian and Regency romance with strong, intelligent heroines and sexy alpha heroes. She lives in Pennsylvania and Maryland with her Canadian husband, their adorable identical twins, a demanding diva of a dog, and one zany cat who showed up one summer and never left.

A self-professed literary junkie and nerd, she loves reading anything, but especially romance novels, poetry, and Middle English verse. Catch up with her on her website https://scarlettscottauthor.com. Hearing from readers never fails to make her day.

Scarlett's complete book list and information about upcoming releases can be found at https://scarlettscottauthor.com.

Connect with Scarlett! You can find her here:
Join Scarlett Scott's reader group on Facebook for early excerpts, giveaways, and a whole lot of fun!
Sign up for her newsletter here
https://www.tiktok.com/@authorscarlettscott

facebook.com/AuthorScarlettScott

x.com/scarscoromance

instagram.com/scarlettscottauthor

bookbub.com/authors/scarlett-scott

amazon.com/Scarlett-Scott/e/B004NW8N2I

pinterest.com/scarlettscott

Printed in Great Britain
by Amazon